"I'M GOING TO MAKE LOVE TO YOU SLOWLY."

Paul's voice was thick with desire as he began to work his magic. A sob of pleasure caught in Robin's throat, and shivers of excitement coursed through her. His mouth was like wet silk as he explored her body, leaving a trail of erotic currents along her neck and shoulders. The sensations he was arousing were so exquisite, she felt as if she was melting beneath his touch. But he had only just begun. . . .

Much later, Robin whispered, "I love you so much, I don't think I could bear it if I ever lost you."

Paul held her tenderly. "I'm not going anywhere, and I'm not letting you out of my sight."

But silently, Robin wondered just where they were going after all. . . .

Books by Judith Duncan

HARLEQUIN SUPERROMANCES
51—TENDER RHAPSODY
77—HOLD BACK THE DAWN
114—REACH THE SPLENDOR

These books may be available at your local bookseller.

For a list of all titles currently available,
send your name and address to:

Harlequin Reader Service
P.O. Box 52040, Phoenix, AZ 85072-2040
Canadian address: P.O. Box 2800, Postal Station A,
                    5170 Yonge St., Willowdale, Ont. M2N 5T5

Judith Duncan

REACH THE SPLENDOR

Harlequin Books

TORONTO • NEW YORK • LONDON
AMSTERDAM • PARIS • SYDNEY • HAMBURG
STOCKHOLM • ATHENS • TOKYO • MILAN

Published May 1984

First printing March 1984

ISBN 0-373-70114-4

Printed in Canada

CHAPTER ONE

DR. ROBIN MITCHELL WAITED IMPATIENTLY in the long cafeteria lineup, chewing anxiously on her bottom lip, her brow creased with a frown. Absently, she tucked a stray curl behind her ear as she glanced at her watch and sighed. She really should skip lunch, but if she didn't eat soon, she would drop from starvation. Damn it, but she wished she wasn't on duty in peds.

Normally, Robin enjoyed the children's ward, and she had been quite willing to fill in for a month to help the overloaded and overworked staff. But the new director of surgery was performing an operation today using a new surgical technique he had developed. As a postgraduate student specializing in surgery, Robin naturally wanted to observe the operation, but there were rounds to do after lunch, and that would take her at least two hours.

Dr. Wilcox had only arrived three weeks ago, and he had already managed to intimidate most of the staff on surgery. The interns and residents humbly bent their heads in awe of his brilliance, to say nothing of his caustic tongue, while the nursing staff was mesmerized by his unquestionable good looks and, when he chose to use it, his charm.

From the stories she had heard, it was apparent that he could cow the most seasoned professional with his sarcasm and his overbearing manner if he even so much as suspected that the individual was not performing to the best of his ability. Third- and fourth-year residents, with considerable medical training behind them, acted like first-year students when they spoke about him, their voices hushed with reverence or quavering with terror.

She ruefully wondered which category she would fall into; she totally expected him to affect her one way or another. She was just as vulnerable as the rest of her colleagues, especially when it came to a physician who had the rather overwhelming reputation Dr. Wilcox had.

Sliding her loaded tray along the stainless-steel rail, Robin glanced into the crowded hospital cafeteria. She grinned and raised her hand in an acknowledging salute when she spotted Bernie Radcliffe frantically waving his arms at her. He went through an elaborate comic pantomime, then emphatically pointed to the empty chair at his table. He grinned broadly when she indicated with a wave that she would join him.

Dr. Bernard Winston Radcliffe III. She smiled to herself, her eyes dancing. He was one of those people whose appearance and personality simply did not mesh with his stuffy aristocratic name. Instead of being the distinguished and haughty gentleman that his name implied, Bernie looked more like a small mischievous gnome who was definitely more inclined to antics than airs.

And Robin adored him—he was the best friend she'd ever had. He was loyal, understanding, empathetic and certainly one of the funniest people she'd ever met.

The two of them had been buddies for a long time. In fact, she had met him on her very first day at university. Never in her whole life had she felt so lost, so alone and so horribly homesick.

Robin had come from a small mining town in the interior of British Columbia, and she had never been away from home for any length of time before. The size and the impersonality of the huge University of Alberta campus in Edmonton left her quaking with fear. She didn't know a single soul, and by noon the first day she was ready to bolt for home.

Then she met Bernie. He had approached her, red faced and stuttering, his voice a nervous squeak when he asked her if she'd go for a coffee with him. Instead of giving him the cool brush-off he later confessed he had expected, she had grasped at his awkward overture like a lifeline.

He was from Vancouver, the offspring of a very wealthy, influential and dominating family. His grandfather and father had a very successful law firm and, without ever consulting Bernie, everyone assumed that he would obediently and without question follow the family tradition.

Consequently there had been one hell of a row when he finally screwed up enough courage to tell them that he had enrolled in medicine. His mother had wept copiously, his grandfather exploded in a towering rage and threatened to disinherit Bernie, while his father treated him like a carrier of the black plague.

When his father finally accepted the hard cold fact that, for once, his son could not be bullied into submission, he grimly declared that Bernie didn't have the fortitude or the stomach to become a doctor. Bernie was doomed, so his father said, to abysmal, resounding failure, and he would be a source of acute embarrassment to the whole family. Not only was he a monumental dud, but he was a cruel, heartless beast. He had, after all, made his mother cry.

Robin's story wasn't quite so dramatic. She had left the security of a close family with all the support and encouragement they could give.

Her father was a physician, and he had been very proud that Robin, his oldest child, had chosen to follow in his footsteps. The biggest problem for her had been a near-fatal case of homesickness. She missed her parents, her four sisters, the dog, the two cats, the mountains and the comfortable familiarity of the community where she had grown up—she missed everything desperately and she was certain she would have died from transplant shock if it hadn't been for Bernie.

And Bernie solemnly stated that he would have eventually caved in to family pressure and taken law if it hadn't been for her.

They became each other's crutch during those first few terrifying weeks of university. By the time the fear and uncertainty faded, Robin and Bernie had become the very best of friends. They were nearly always together; so much so in fact, that their classmates began referring to them as the "odd couple."

Robin grimaced inwardly when she thought about the handle. As much as she hated to admit it, the label did fit.

Short pudgy Bernie with his cherub face and thick glasses—he looked like the kid who never made the baseball team because his mother insisted he take violin lessons on practice nights.

Then there was Robin—tall, sultry and looking like one of those seductive, come-hither models who did the TV commercial for some wickedly expensive perfume.

The long-legged voluptuousness was definitely *not* an asset as far as she was concerned. Other women spent fortunes to attain that ripe sexuality, but Robin did everything within her power to camouflage it. She was bound and determined to overcome what she considered to be a handicap.

Her thick, dark, luxuriant hair was pulled back in an unbecoming ponytail, and when she was on the wards, she always wore a lab coat that was at least two sizes too big.

She almost pulled off the plain Jane image, but the deception would only survive a passing glance. Nothing on earth could disguise the flawless complexion that glowed with a unique golden-tan radiance, or the violet-blue eyes that sparkled with an irrepressible vivacity.

The person behind Robin commented loudly about dreamers in the line, and that jarred her out of her trance. She murmured an apology, then paid the cashier, who was watching her with a pained look. With a sparkle in her eyes, Robin began weaving her way through the congested room.

"Hi, doc," grinned Bernie. "What were you smiling about when you were waiting in line? Or were you just suffering a premature gas pain from the gastronomical disaster they're serving up?"

Robin gave him a slicing look as he moved the napkin holder to make room for her tray. "You have no soul, Radcliffe. I was thinking sweet reminiscent thoughts about our first few weeks of university."

"Ah," he said sonorously, "it wasn't gas pains after all but the onset of senility. The very first symptom is when the aged begin viewing their lives through rose-colored glasses."

Robin grinned as she sat down. "I was not viewing the past through rose-colored glasses, my friend. I remember very well how it was—and that was awful."

"Aw, come on, Mitch. It wasn't *that* bad. It could have been worse. We could have bombed out."

"Now who's senile? It was a horror, and you know it!"

"Yes, ma'am," said Bernie with contrived humility, then promptly helped himself to one of her egg-salad sandwiches.

She smacked his hand and glared at him. "Damn it, why do you always do that to me?"

"I'm just looking after you. You know—calories and cholesterol."

"Watch your own calories and cholesterol and leave mine alone. I'm nearly starved."

Bernie took a bite of the sandwich, then pushed his thick glasses up on his nose as he scrutinized her. "That hairdo of yours is truly hideous."

"Thank you."

He grinned. "You're welcome." He brushed some crumbs off the table, then continued, his voice thoughtful. "That tent of a lab coat adds a nice touch, though. Of course, if you could figure out a way to give yourself varicose veins and a flat chest, it would be the ultimate finishing touch."

"Drop dead, Bernie."

"Do you know," he went on relentlessly, "that there are at least four matrons I know who would hawk their diamond-studded dog collars, to say nothing of their gold-plated coat hangers, if they could come out looking like you."

"Ask me if I care."

"Do you care?" he asked obligingly.

"Do chickens have lips?" she responded tartly. They grinned at each other, then fell into a companionable silence as Robin began to eat her lunch.

She stirred her coffee reflectively. Before they ever graduated from medical school, Robin had decided to specialize in surgery in Calgary. At the time, Bernie was considering going to Toronto to specialize in emergency services. The thought of four years without Bernie around had left her feeling a little lost. She had applied a certain amount of pressure and coaxed him into going to Calgary with her.

She looked at him, her face thoughtful. "Have you ever regretted specializing in surgery, Bernie?"

"Never. I'm glad you talked me into it, especially now that Wilcox is here. The more I find out about him, the more impressed I am. He has one hell of a reputation in his field. I can't figure out how this administration managed to lure someone of his caliber out of Toronto."

"I've heard that he's one of the best."

"In my opinion, he *is* the best," Bernie replied. "Having an opportunity to study under him has to be the most exciting thing that's ever happened to me. His surgeries are something else."

"You're observing his operation this afternoon?" she asked.

"Wouldn't miss it. Are you going to be able to make it?"

"I won't make the beginning, that's for certain. I really want to attend, but I have rounds to do yet."

"I see you're assigned back to surgery next week. Does that mean you're finished with pediatrics?" he inquired.

"Probably," Robin responded. "The only reason I was assigned there was because they had such a heavy case load and Dr. Anderson had a backlog of operations. He's certainly a doll to work for. I've learned so much from him."

"He's supposed to be at the top of the heap when it comes to diagnostics."

"He is."

There was another silence as Robin ate her salad and Bernie idly scanned the crowded room.

"Ah," he said, his tone significant. "The Exalted One deigns to partake with us lowly peasants today." Beneath Bernie's sardonic tone was a certain reverence, and Robin knew to whom he was referring before she spotted Dr. Wilcox at the cash register.

She had had no direct contact with the man, but she had been able to attend two of his lectures and had to admit she had felt a little awestruck herself.

A rueful grin appeared on her face as she watched several staff members directly in front of the doctor diffidently step out of his path as he walked toward a table. What power decreed, she wondered with amusement, that people like Dr. Wilcox were always awarded the right of way? There was a certain bearing about the man that smacked of arrogance, yet no one who had worked with him had ever used that word when describing him.

There seemed to be a general attitude of utmost respect for his brilliance and skill, and shoe-shaking fear of his slicing sarcasm. He was competent, efficient and thorough, and he expected every member of his staff to be the same.

Yet in spite of his extreme clinical professionalism, he somehow managed to develop a very warm personal relationship with his patients. People invariably trusted the man.

Robin's eyes sparkled knowingly as she watched a very pretty nurse flutter her eyelashes at him and turn into a piece of fluffy femininity when Dr. Wilcox spoke to her. If his patients invariably trusted the man, women invariably fell for him.

Bernie had told her that even the most hard-bitten charge nurse would instantly turn into a mellow agreeable female the second he appeared on the ward.

In all honesty, Robin could understand why. No one could deny that the man had magnetic charm and good looks. He was one of those tall, dark and handsome ones who had inscrutable eyes and a rugged chin. There was a look of raw virility stamped on his face that made one think of white-water canoeing and murderous ski runs.

Brilliant, successful, gorgeous—the ultimate man.

"I heard some interesting gossip about our good doctor today," commented Bernie as he smoothly snitched Robin's pudding.

"How come you don't weigh a ton, Radcliffe?"

"High metabolism. Do you want to hear the gossip?"

"No."

"Did you know that Himself graduated from medical school at the top of his class at the ripe old age of twenty-two? And did you know that he has reached the venerable age of thirty-four?" Bernie spooned some of the rather lumpy pudding into his mouth, then continued. "Did you know that he has done postgraduate work with some of the top surgeons in the world? And did you know, as rumor has it, that he doesn't associate socially with *anyone* on staff?"

"You ate my doughnut," accused Robin.

"Doesn't all this fascinating information fire your curiosity? Don't you care?"

"Yes, damn it. I care. You ate half my sandwich, all my pudding, and now you've had the nerve to eat my doughnut!"

Bernie laughed and stood up. "I'll leave you to your coffee then. I'm due back."

"Do you know you are exceptionally bad mannered?"

He shrugged offhandedly, then grinned at her. "That's not true, I was going to thank you for lunch."

"Liar."

"Thank you very much for lunch, Dr. Mitchell. It was delightful."

Amusement was sparkling in her eyes as she answered. "You're very welcome, Dr. Radcliffe."

Glancing at his watch, he turned to go. "I'll give you a call tonight and tell you how Wilcox's surgery goes if you don't make it."

"Do that."

She watched him walk toward the exit, then raised her hand in farewell as he left the room. Sighing, she tucked the offending curl behind her ear again, then took a sip of coffee. Robin hated having to miss Wilcox's operation that afternoon. It was a technique that had never been used in this hospital before and, since it was a rare case, it might not be done again for a long time.

She felt exactly the same as Bernie did—having an opportunity to train under a surgeon of Dr. Wilcox's caliber was a real bonus. It had been quite a coup for the hospital, a major training centre in Alberta, when he accepted the post of chief of surgery.

He might be a stickler to work for and his assessment of junior staff might be brutal, but he was still unquestionably a top man in his field.

There was another facet to his character that was a bonus as well. Not only was he a very skilled surgeon, but he also had a natural ability to teach. His lectures were the most thorough and informative ones she had ever attended, yet he managed, with his keen quick wit, to make them very entertaining.

She wondered if it was true what Bernie had said

about Wilcox's keeping his private life very separate from his professional one. She suspected it was. Realistically, she supposed a man in his position would have to keep an arm's-length relationship with his staff.

Robin looked wistfully at her empty coffee cup, then at the never-ending lineup. She would give her right arm for another cup of coffee, but she didn't have the time to wait in line to get it.

Reluctantly, she gathered up the empty cups and clutter, then stacked them on her tray. As she stood up she had the uncomfortable sensation that someone was staring at her.

Someone was. Dr. Paul Wilcox was seated at a table directly across the room and was studying her intently, his arms folded across his chest, his head tipped to one side.

Robin had the oddest feeling that he knew exactly what had been running through her mind, and with a disconcerted gesture, she pulled her lab coat around her. With as much poise as she could muster, she picked up her tray and carried it to the return window. She felt his eyes on her every step of the way, and there was a peculiar nervousness fluttering in her midriff when she was finally able to flee that scrutinizing stare.

As IT TURNED OUT, Robin was unable to observe even a part of Dr. Wilcox's surgery. There was an emergency in pediatrics, and she was in surgery herself while he was operating.

She had wanted to see his technique very much,

but in one sense she was relieved. That silly incident in the cafeteria had really unnerved her, and that bothered Robin. Usually she was calm and unflappable, and it disturbed her that she had become so unhinged simply because someone was watching her. After silently poking fun at herself for her adolescent behavior, Robin was finally able to dismiss the incident as a simple case of nerves.

She really thought she had put the incident behind her until two days later. Then her case of jitters was magnified tenfold. Not only did she have to contend with her unexplainable agitation, but she also had to contend with the man himself.

The confrontation happened early one morning. She was leaning against the counter of the nursing station waiting for Dr. Anderson, thinking about the time she had spent working with the chief of pediatrics.

She had really benefited from her association with him. He was an older man with years of experience behind him, and he applied a common-sense approach to everything he did. Not only was he extremely good at his job, but he also had a casual, comfortable manner that was almost grandfatherly. The patients and the staff on peds adored him and so did Robin.

"Good morning, Mitch. I finally took your very persistent advice and brought your miracle worker up to see Davy Martin."

He is not my miracle worker, groaned Robin silently as she stiffened her spine and with definite reluctance turned to face Dr. Paul Wilcox.

Her stomach landed somewhere in the vicinity of her ankles when she saw the set look on his face.

For a split second she had an urge to strangle the stout, balding pediatrician who, unaware that he had put her on the spot, was beaming at her. *Why in hell did you have to say that,* she wondered wildly. Her face was hot as she let her eyes slide away from Wilcox's penetrating gaze. Then, taking a slow breath, she tried to ease the sudden paralysis that immobilized her lungs.

She wished she had the nerve to thoroughly explain what had prompted Dr. Anderson's comment, but she knew if she tried she would look like a total idiot. *Brother!*

"Actually," continued Dr. Anderson, "I went to see Paul about Davy, and Paul very kindly offered to have a look at him." He went behind the counter to retrieve the patient's chart then passed it to Dr. Wilcox. "Mitch thinks that with proper surgery there's a chance the leg can be saved."

Dr. Wilcox took the chart and scanned it, then fixed his attention on Robin. "Do you like pediatrics, Dr. Mitchell?"

He's probably wishing I'd stay here, thought Robin. Her voice echoed in her head when she answered, "Yes, I do."

Dr. Anderson interjected. "I'll be honest and admit that I've tried to get Robin to change her specialty, but I haven't succeeded."

"Your loss is surgery's gain, apparently," responded Dr. Wilcox, his voice flat.

Robin gritted her teeth. That was just a little too pat and a little too cute.

"Could you refresh my memory on this case—I'm afraid I was on the fly when you talked to me about it. Not all the facts registered."

Robin leaned against the counter and listened intently as Dr. Anderson reviewed the case. It was rather a tragic one.

Davy was a ten-year-old farm boy who had had his right leg badly mangled in a grain auger two weeks before. After he had been rushed to Calgary, surgery was performed in an attempt to save the leg. For about a week it appeared that the operation was successful, but then complications had arisen. The leg was not healing; in fact, its condition was deteriorating rapidly.

The surgeon who did the initial surgery insisted that the leg would have to be amputated, but Robin was deadly opposed to that treatment.

She had discussed Dr. Wilcox's surgical abilities with Dr. Anderson, and it was during that consultation she had insisted that he be called in. If he was as brilliant as he was reported to be he was probably the only one who could perform a successful operation— she hoped. The thought of amputating that boy's leg made her feel a little sick.

There was a look of intense concentration on Paul Wilcox's face as Dr. Anderson detailed the condition of the leg. "Is there any infection?" he asked finally.

"Very little. We managed to contain that, but I don't think our luck is going to hold out much longer," Dr. Anderson replied.

One of the ward nurses came hurrying along the corridor. "Dr. Anderson, could I speak to you for a moment, please?"

"Certainly."

As Dr. Anderson walked away, Robin felt Paul Wilcox's attention focus on her. "And what do you think, Dr. Mitchell?"

She looked up at him, her eyes filled with concern. "I think there's perhaps a twenty percent chance that the leg can be saved."

"Those aren't very good odds, are they?"

She shook her head slowly and sighed. "No, they aren't, but there is that chance. Davy's only ten, and his whole life revolves around sports. I don't want to be the doctor responsible for taking that away from him, unless I know there is no other way."

There was a definite hint of anger in his voice when he spoke. "I am not a miracle worker, doctor."

Robin looked at him, her gaze direct and serious, knowing full well that she had received a reprimand. "I know that, Dr. Wilcox."

"Well, Mitch, have I got a goody for you."

Robin tore her eyes away from Paul Wilcox's unrelenting stare and managed a lopsided grin as she faced Dr. Anderson. "I don't think I like the way you said that. A goody usually means a very scrappy patient who needs his stomach pumped or one who requires fifty stitches."

Dr. Anderson chuckled as he shook his head. "Nothing as drastic as that. Our little Amanda has managed to poke something up her nose, and she won't let anyone near her."

Amanda was unquestionably the terror of the entire pediatric wing. Everyone dreaded a confrontation with her and avoided one if at all possible.

She *was* a monster, but Robin couldn't help admiring the spunky redhead. The little girl was only six years old, but she had one of those indomitable natures and refused to be intimidated. The child fought everything—needles, baths, temperature checks, naps—but Robin understood that Amanda's rebellious nature was really initiated by fear. She was simply scared to death, and she camouflaged that fear with fight.

"I take it she's all mine."

"All yours. I told the nurse you'd be down shortly to unplug her."

"Thanks," said Robin dryly.

"It had to be you," chuckled Anderson. "You're the only one who can get within fifteen feet of her. I was telling Paul on the way up that you had a knack with kids. Most of the male interns and residents don't know how to cope with the hysterics, so they just ignore them. They methodically try to put the patients back together without settling them down, and then wonder why the kids either bite them or throw up all over them."

While Dr. Anderson was speaking, Robin could feel Dr. Wilcox studying her, and she felt the palms of her hands grow clammy. She suddenly felt like a grade-three student who had been hauled before the principal for the first time.

The feeling was so real that her voice even quavered when she spoke. "Amanda will likely do both. She isn't exactly the mouse of the ward."

The pediatrician laughed as he stroked his chin. "No...not by a long shot. Our Amanda is a scrapper. Mitchell did an appendectomy on her three days ago, and that little wee girl nearly tore the OR apart before we anesthetized her. The only one who can handle her is Mitchell—but then I guess you know what our good doctor's like on the wards.''

Dr. Wilcox's eyes never left Robin as he answered, ''Actually, I don't. You've had her in peds ever since I took over the post.''

Robin stuck her hands in her pockets and looked away self-consciously.

''Hell, I'm sorry. I didn't realize you two hadn't met. My apologies.''

''Well,'' said Robin quickly, wanting to escape from the limelight and a formal introduction, ''I'd better go deal with our little warrior.'' *Bless you, Amanda,* she thought with relief as she walked briskly down the corridor. *I'd rather deal with one of your temper tantrums than deal with one of his.* Robin had the uncomfortable feeling that the ''miracle worker'' comment was going to come back to haunt her—no, she hadn't heard the last of *that*.

A very little girl with carrot-red pigtails and freckles to match was huddled stiffly in the middle of her bed, a mutinous set to her pale, tearstained face, her very raggedy Raggedy Ann doll clutched fiercely in her arms. By the grim look on the nurse's face, Robin guessed that the six-year-old had put up one hell of a battle.

''Good morning, Amanda.''

Narrow-eyed silence.

''How are you feeling this morning?''

The nurse interjected, her voice clipped with impatience. "She was vomiting during the night and with this *latest* ruckus, her temperature has shot up."

When Robin had performed surgery on her the appendix had already ruptured, and the child was fighting a very stubborn infection.

Yet in spite of how miserable she must feel, Amanda never whined or complained. She suffered the nausea and the pain stoically and quietly, providing she wasn't challenged in any way.

Robin walked over to the bed and sat on the edge. "I hear you have something up your nose. Is it something special that you're saving?"

There was the tiniest twitch of amusement around the child's mouth, and Robin grinned at her as she tapped the tip of the very freckled nose. "We can't leave whatever it is in there, honey. You know that."

Amanda glared at her, then gave her a stiff jerky nod. "I don't want them in my room."

Robin glanced over her shoulder. A group of interns had entered the room and were obviously waiting for a doctor to commence his rounds.

She turned back to the little girl. "They're just waiting for another doctor to come. They won't hurt you, pet." Taking the otoscope from her pocket, Robin held it in her hand so the child could see the instrument. "I'm just going to look in your nose. You'll let me do that, won't you?"

Amanda stared at her warily, then reluctantly nodded her head as she grasped the doll tighter. Robin quickly examined her.

Wedged firmly in the left nostril was an object that looked suspiciously like a blue bead. In a low voice,

Robin gave the nurse some instructions, biting back a smile at the disbelieving look on the woman's face as she hurried out of the room.

She glanced down at the fiery redhead. "There's a blue bead in your nose, isn't there?"

With her lips pursed together, Amanda stared up at her defiantly. "Where did you get it, Amanda?" There was a firmness in Robin's voice that told Amanda the doctor expected an answer.

"My mommie's necklace broke last night, and the beads fell on the floor."

The inscrutable look in the child's eyes turned to one of barely suppressed terror, and her mouth began to quiver uncontrollably.

Lifting the child onto her lap, Robin brushed back a wisp of hair that had escaped from one pigtail, then she cuddled the little girl against her. Amanda was rigid and trembling, and the freckles seemed to be painted on the chalk-white face.

Robin's heart contracted with compassion. "I know you're scared, but I'll really try hard to get the bead out without hurting you. If I have to do something that might hurt, I'll tell you, and if you want me to stop, I will, okay?"

"Okay," came the hesitant little whisper against her breast. Robin's arms tightened around the girl and she began to rock her.

"I don't like it here."

"I know you don't, but we have to keep you here until you're better."

"When can I go home?"

Easing the tiny, stiff body away from her, Robin

looked down at the frightened little face, her voice very gentle. "I don't know for certain, but as soon as your temperature is normal you can go home."

She snuggled Amanda firmly against her and made a diversionary move to head off the hysterics she could feel building in the child.

"Do you know that I had a Raggedy Ann doll just like yours when I was a little girl?"

There was a tense silence, then the head tilted back and Amanda, forgetting her panic for the moment, stared up at Robin with round eyes. "Did you really?"

"I really did. And I loved her better than any other doll I ever had." Robin straightened the doll's red wool hair, then smiled at Amanda. "When I had Annie, I knew I was never really alone. I had somebody to love, and things didn't seem quite so scary."

Amanda straightened up and hugged her doll fiercely. "It's okay, Martha. I'll look after you."

Hanging on to her doll for dear life, the child looked up at Robin, her face pinched and white with fear. "Might it hurt lots when you take the bead out?"

Robin's smile was filled with tenderness as she gently stroked the girl's head. "I hope not. I'm going to try something else before I try to take it out."

Just then the nurse bustled in and set a tray of instruments down on the table, then handed Robin two very small plastic pouches. She tore one package open and poured the contents into her hand.

"Do you know what this is, Amanda?"

The child looked at the gray powder in the doctor's

hand, then looked up, a very puzzled expression on her face. "It looks like pepper."

Shifting the little girl onto the bed, Robin stood up. Her stomach did a sickening flip-flop, and she went hot and cold at the same time.

Not only were all the interns watching her with bemused fascination but so was Dr. Wilcox.

He was leaning against the foot of a bed, his arms folded across his chest, and he had the same look on his face as he'd had that day in the cafeteria. *Oh no!* she thought frantically. *What's he doing here? He's supposed to be examining Davy Martin!*

"Is it pepper?" demanded Amanda.

With a feeling of impending damnation, Robin forced her stiff facial muscles into a semblance of a smile. It was too late to do anything but blunder on.

"Yes, it is. Does pepper make you sneeze?"

"Yes."

"We're going to try something that won't be too scary, but you'll have to do exactly as I say, okay?"

"Okay."

"Good girl. I'm going to have you take a big sniff of pepper and maybe, if we're lucky, you'll sneeze the bead out."

The little girl brightened immediately. Sneezing was not at all scary.

Robin gave her a gentle caution. "Now I'm going to have the nurse hold your tummy because your incision will hurt when you sneeze."

For the first time, Amanda smiled and bobbed her head. *Here I am,* fumed Robin silently, *having a kid sniffing pepper while the chief of surgery is watching this insane performance. He probably thinks I'm completely mad.*

Out loud she said, "Let's try it." The nurse lifted Amanda onto her lap, her hands pressed firmly across the child's abdomen. "A big sniff now, Amanda."

Amanda, for once, obediently did as she was told and almost instantly her eyes began to water. For one awful moment, Robin thought that she wasn't going to sneeze, then, "Ah...ah...AH...." Robin quickly clamped the child's mouth shut and firmly pinched the unobstructed nostril.

"CHOO!"

Nothing.

Robin felt like an idiot. *How come this always works for my father,* she thought glumly.

"Ah...ah...ah...CHOO!"

There was a soft "ping" as the bright blue bead flew across the room and struck the metal night table by Dr. Wilcox. He stooped down to pick it up, and Robin fervently hoped that he would leave now that the sideshow was over. But he never moved.

Amanda was smiling broadly at Robin, her eyes red and watery. "It's gone, isn't it?"

"It sure is, but I'll have to check your nose again to make sure you didn't poke something else up there—maybe there's a red bus."

The little girl giggled but sat perfectly still as Robin examined her again. "No bus, Amanda."

There was another giggle, then the girl scrambled off the nurse's lap. She reached up and hesitantly touched the red velvet ribbon with which Robin had tied back her hair.

"I like your pretty red ribbon. Mommy won't let me have red bows."

Anyone who wasn't totally blind could see why. Amanda's hair was the color of red that bordered on orange.

Stripping the ribbon from her hair, Robin smiled down at the little girl. "For someone who was as brave as you were, you certainly can have red bows." She took the scissors the nurse offered her and cut the ribbon in half, uncomfortably aware that Dr. Wilcox was still watching her. *I'm going to get one hell of a lecture over this. He'll have my hide for unethical procedures, especially after the stupid "miracle worker" comment.*

She smiled warmly at Amanda as she tied the scarlet bows around the fat pigtails. The combination was ghastly. The little girl flashed her a brilliant smile as Robin affectionately patted her cheek.

"Did that sneezing make your tummy sore?"

Shaking her head, Amanda tucked the doll under one arm as she squirmed back against the pillows.

Robin tidied the doll's dress, then turned to leave. "You two have a good day, and I'll see you both tomorrow."

"Okay, Dr. Mitchell."

She was nearly at the door when a voice rang out behind her. "Dr. Mitchell."

With a sigh of resignation, Robin turned to face Dr. Wilcox. "Yes, doctor?"

"I'd like you to be in the small lecture hall on the fourth floor—" he glanced at his watch "—in two hours."

He stared at Robin, his face impassive, then turned and walked out of the room, the interns humbly shuffling after him, reminding Robin of a flotilla of tugboats accompanying a supertanker out of port.

CHAPTER TWO

PRACTICING HER "KITCHEN REMEDY" MEDICINE and getting caught at it by one of the top surgeons in Canada seemed to be the solvent that promptly unglued Robin's morning. One crisis after another hit the ward, leaving her feeling a little like a person on a treadmill—she was running like mad but getting nowhere.

It was definitely not her morning to shine. To add insult to injury, a three-year-old did her the honor of depositing his breakfast down the front of her lab coat just before she left the ward. Right then, Robin would have ransomed her mother for a shower and a cigarette. Especially a cigarette.

Why had she decided to quit smoking now, she wondered a little frantically as she waited for the elevator. She was going to die from fright anyway.

Robin's nerves were slithering around in the pit of her stomach like a coiling snake by the time she reached the lecture hall. Pausing briefly, she combed her fingers through her hair in a vain attempt to tame the tumble of curls, then taking a deep and somewhat shaky breath, she resolutely opened the door.

A wave of relief swept through her, leaving her a little giddy. A swarm of interns and residents were milling around, obviously waiting for a lecture to begin. *Boy, do I jump to conclusions,* she thought.

"Mitch!"

Robin scanned the crowd and spotted Bernie motioning to her from across the room. Smiling, she raised her hand in acknowledgment, then made her way along a row of empty seats.

She dropped down into the vacant seat beside him. "Hi! What's this all about?"

"Wilcox is going to be doing an unscheduled operation tomorrow, and he wants to brief us on it." Bernie gave her a peculiar look. "I hope you haven't changed your perfume because if that's what I smell, it's disgusting!"

"Essence of partially digested breakfast—don't you like it?"

Bernie grinned and adjusted his glasses. "I take it you had an interesting morning?"

"So-so." She certainly wasn't going to tell him about her pepper episode now—he'd kill himself laughing, and she'd feel like an idiot all over again.

Just then, Dr. Wilcox entered the room, and there was a scramble while everyone found a seat. He strode toward the lectern at the front of the room, a manila file folder clasped in his hand. Laying the folder on the stand, he looked up, his glance sweeping across the audience.

"I realize that all of you had very short notice about this session this morning, but since the operation I'm about to review with you will be performed tomorrow morning, I'm afraid I had no choice." He folded his arms across his chest, that same look of intense concentration on his face. "The case I'm about to discuss is rather a difficult one. The patient's name is Davy Martin. . . ."

Robin experienced a flash of elation, which was followed immediately by weak-kneed relief. At least he thought there was a chance. With her pulse racing she focused on what the surgeon was saying.

"One of our residents made the diagnosis that there was perhaps a twenty percent chance of saving the limb. After examining the boy I would concur. There has been a substantial amount of tissue degeneration, and that's certainly a critical factor."

For the next hour, Paul Wilcox detailed precisely what he was proposing to do in surgery, why he was using a particular technique and what postoperative complications he was expecting. By the time he was finished every doctor in that room knew exactly what he was going to do.

"Are there any questions?"

"Will Dr. Anderson be assisting you?"

There was a brief pause, then Dr. Wilcox looked directly at Robin, his face sphinxlike. "No, Dr. Mitchell will be assisting me."

Robin, who had been slouched in her seat, sat up abruptly, her mouth hanging open. The man *couldn't* be serious.

"Are there any other questions?"

If Robin could have collected her fractured thoughts in time she probably would have blurted out, "Why me?"

But Dr. Wilcox was speaking before she had time to think. "That's it, then." He gathered up his papers and placed them in the folder. "The operation will be in the OR with the viewing gallery at ten o'clock tomorrow morning."

With that he strode out of the lecture hall leaving a very stunned Robin Mitchell behind.

"Well, well," commented Bernie, his face split with an unholy grin. "Our very own Mitchell must have made quite an impression!"

Robin looked at him with stupefaction. "He never said a word to me after he examined Davy Martin."

"That's the way he operates—no pun intended."

Robin stared blindly at the chair in front of her for a moment while she collected her thoughts. She sighed as she turned to face Bernie. "What's he like in OR?"

"Professional to the nth degree. He dismissed an intern from surgery once because the fellow made an off-color remark about the patient. As far as Wilcox is concerned the patient is to be treated with courtesy and respect, even when he's knocked out cold."

"Well, at least *that's* good news. I loathe the way some of the staff in OR make cute comments about the patient on the table. It really is degrading."

"Well, you won't have any of that going on with Wilcox around I can assure you." Bernie slapped her knee and stood up. "Come on. I'll buy you lunch."

"I think I'll be sick."

He caught her hand and pulled her to her feet. "Don't worry about it, Robin. You'll do just fine."

She gave him a rueful look as they walked down the aisle toward the door. "Why does that man make me feel like a dumb, gawky schoolgirl?"

Bernie laughed. "Why should you be any different? Everybody who comes within ten feet of him turns into a quivering mass of bumbling ineptitude."

Chewing on her bottom lip, Robin stuck her hands in her skirt pockets, a strained look on her face. "Maybe I should go down and talk to him sometime today."

"Not a chance. He has office hours all afternoon."

"Isn't that just dandy!"

"Don't sweat it, Robin. He's easy to work with in OR. He seldom applies pressure during an operation unless someone is doing something really stupid."

She gave him a very skeptical stare as he opened the door for her. He looked like a mischievous myopic elf as he grinned at her. "Would I lie to you, Mitchell?"

"I have no doubt about it." It was a bad choice of words, for suddenly doubts of all shapes and sizes were beating in on her like a flock of unruly birds.

THE RISING SUN was casting long early-morning shadows across the wall of her bedroom when Robin awoke. She rolled over on her back and laced her hands beneath her head as she listened to the breeze rustle through the leaves of the huge old poplar tree that was just outside her window.

With a sigh she turned her head to glance at the clock on the nightstand. Six o'clock. She could either stay in bed for another hour, or she could go to work early and have a half-decent breakfast in the cafeteria. Opting for the cafeteria she rolled out of bed and headed for the shower.

The air outside was crisp and clean and golden, the grass glimmering brilliantly with a heavy dew. Robin paused on the slightly dilapidated veranda that aproned the old brick house.

Taking a deep breath she savored the fragrant bouquet of the spring morning. She loved this time of year. Spring seemed to sneak in the back door, catching winter by surprise. It was as though you awoke one morning to find that overnight the trees had unfurled their delicate green leaves, and the tender new shoots had pushed their heads through the moist sun-kissed soil of the flower gardens.

Tossing her slightly damp hair over her shoulder, she ran lightly down the weather-beaten steps and walked briskly down the cracked sidewalk toward the street.

She was so glad she lived where she did. When she moved to Calgary she had deliberately selected an apartment in an old residential district for a number of reasons.

One very major reason was that she was paying back her student loans, and she couldn't afford the rent of an expensive highrise. Neither did she want to share an apartment. Rooming with someone always fell short of expectations, and besides when she worked shifts sharing would be nothing but a headache.

Her apartment was on the upper floor of the old home, and although it was a tad shabby, it was clean, affordable and convenient. It was only a fifteen-minute walk to the hospital, and Robin loved every step of it. The streets were lined with massive old trees that arched across the street, their outstretched branches nearly touching.

Robin combed her fingers through her hair, then swept it back from her face. It was nearly dry. She felt in her jacket pocket to make certain she had brought a scarf to tie it back.

The memory of Amanda sitting on the bed preening her red bows triggered off a rash of thoughts, and Robin's long-legged stride slowed.

She didn't know why she was experiencing such stage fright over assisting at Davy Martin's operation. Usually she had a fair amount of confidence in her ability, but for some reason that confidence had deserted her.

It was going to be a long, painstaking, delicate operation with no room for error, and to make matters worse she had the gut feeling that Wilcox was deliberately testing her. Normally that wouldn't affect Robin unduly, but for some reason it was nagging at her this time. She wanted to perform to the best of her ability, and instead she was feeling totally unprepared.

Her hair whipped across her face as a car sped by, and she absently brushed it back. She was so preoccupied she didn't realize the car had stopped until she heard it reverse.

A long, sleek Jaguar sports car with a canvas top was backing along the curb lane, its smooth lines gleaming in the sun. Someone looking for directions, she guessed. No one she knew could afford to drive a car like *that*.

"Would you like a ride, Dr. Mitchell?"

She groaned inwardly—obviously Paul Wilcox could. Robin would rather fight off a man-eating alligator than get into that car with him. "Thank you," she said.

He reached across the seat and opened the door for her. Robin felt the now-familiar mute awe settle over her as she slid into the leather seat. Somehow she managed to smile as she groped for something to say. "It's a beautiful morning, isn't it?"

Instead of driving on, he turned to face her, his arm draped across the steering wheel. "I didn't think you'd noticed. You looked like you had the weight of the world on your shoulders."

The not-too-secure smile on her face evaporated and was replaced by a look of disconcertment. Her brain seemed to be suddenly locked in neutral.

His eyes were concealed by sunglasses, but she still felt as though they were drilling straight through her. "You wouldn't happen to be worrying over the Martin case, would you?"

Prevaricating had always been a lost cause for Robin, so she didn't even try. Sighing deeply she looked at him squarely and nodded. "Yes, I am."

"I see." He took a package of cigarettes from the dash and opened it, then offered her one. She looked at it longingly, then wistfully shook her head. "No thanks. I'm trying to quit."

He lit his cigarette with a gold engraved lighter and gave her a wry smile. "Aren't we all?" He tossed the package back on the dash, then removed his sunglasses as he slowly inhaled. With that steady penetrating gaze that she couldn't evade he studied her solemnly. "Now, doctor, why don't you tell me exactly what you're thinking?"

She had been thinking that he had absolutely gorgeous eyes. For the first time in years, Robin blushed, and shrugged self-consciously. "I never once expected you to select me to assist you, and your announcement yesterday left me a little dazed."

"Would you prefer not to do it?" There was a sharpness in his voice that made Robin's stomach shrink with nervousness.

"Oh, *no*! It isn't that." Distractedly, she raked her fingers through her hair. Unable to meet his unwavering stare she looked out the window. "I do want to work with you, Dr. Wilcox, but I feel very much out of my depth."

Leaning back against the door of the car he slowly nodded his head. "I see that the hospital grapevine is as active as ever. I take it that my reputation had preceded me." Suddenly he grinned, the sternness around his mouth giving way to deep laugh lines. "Relax. I'm not going to eat you. I may have chewed off a head or two, but I have yet to devour an entire intern."

Amusement dissolved her tension, and Robin laughed. "But from what I've heard you've left a few walking wounded."

He gave her a slightly cynical smile, then nodded. "That's probably true. I'm afraid I don't have much patience with anyone in the medical profession who isn't deadly serious about their responsibility to the patient."

Robin watched the swirl of smoke from his cigarette drift out the window, then she looked at him, her eyes sober. "It wasn't the thought that you might bite my head off that was worrying me. I've never seen you in surgery before, much less assist, and frankly I don't know what you expect from me."

There was a gleam of humor in his eyes when he answered. "I expect you to be exceptional, of course." He butted his cigarette in the ashtray, then said, "Why don't we head for the hospital, and I'll go over the procedure with you? I'm like every other surgeon in that I have certain quirks when I'm operating. I'll fill you in on my idiosyncrasies."

"That," said Robin with heartfelt relief, "would be just great."

Slipping on his sunglasses he put the car into gear and pulled away. He glanced at her and grinned. "You haven't had breakfast, have you?"

Robin's head snapped around in amazement. "How did you know that?"

His only answer was a husky laugh as he swung onto the avenue that ran past the hospital. "Is the hospital cafeteria okay?"

Robin suddenly felt as if she was breathing in pure oxygen when she realized that he was taking her to breakfast. "The cafeteria will be fine," she answered a little breathlessly. *So this was how Cinderella felt on the way to the ball,* she thought dazedly until her usual realistic self surfaced and snapped, *Don't be a sap, Robin Mitchell!*

Dr. Wilcox parked in his reserved space, set the

hand brake and tossed his sunglasses on the dash. Robin rolled up her window, then slipped out.

"Aren't you afraid someone will swipe this machine of yours?"

The wind ruffled through his dark hair as he walked around the car, a smile on his face. "I doubt it."

She fell into step with him. "Well, I would if I thought I could get away with it."

"Then if it's missing I'll know where to look."

Robin took the scarf out of her pocket and slipped it under her wind-tousled hair. Pausing by the staff door she raised her arms to tie it.

With a shake of his head, Dr. Wilcox pulled the scarf from her grasp, and with a knowing amused gleam in his eyes he wadded it up and stuffed it back in her pocket. Robin felt as though she had a butterfly the size of Kansas unfurling its wings inside her as he held the door open for her.

Robin had to wait for the odd sensation to fade before she dared to speak. "Are Davy's parents still in town?"

"His mother is. His father is coming in this morning. I have an appointment with them at nine."

"Did Dr. Anderson tell you that the father is taking this very badly? He blames himself for the accident, and he's being very hard on himself."

"Yes, he told me." They arrived at the elevator and Dr. Wilcox pushed the Down button. As he turned to face Robin his gaze became serious. "I can't offer them much hope. There's such a slim chance that the leg can be saved, and even if we're successful Davy will probably experience a loss of flexibility in it.''

Concern darkened her eyes as she sighed. "I know, but we have to try.''

"Yes," he said, "we do.''

The cafeteria for once was practically deserted, and in no time they were seated at a corner table. Robin placed the plates loaded with bacon, eggs and toast on the table, then arranged the cutlery.

Dr. Wilcox had turned on his charm and persuaded the waitress behind the steam cabinets to give them a carafe of coffee. He filled their cups as she slid the empty trays onto the next table.

He grinned at her. "Good morning, Dr. Mitchell.''

She smiled into his flashing eyes, her own dancing with amusement. "Good morning, Dr. Wilcox.''

"This smacks of domesticity, doesn't it?''

"Either that or greed. We have enough here to feed an army.''

Robin reached for the salt shaker and seasoned her eggs, then took a bite of toast. Taking a sip of coffee, Dr. Wilcox watched her, a look of pure devilry gleaming in his eyes.

"Would you care for some pepper?''

She choked on the piece of toast, and her eyes were watering liberally by the time she cleared her throat. "That, Dr. Wilcox," she gasped, "was a rotten subject to bring up.''

He was laughing as he handed her a napkin. "You deserve it. I thought I was going to be forced to suspend you for malpractice.''

She wiped her eyes and gave him a slightly warped smile. "Are you going to bite my head off now or wait until I've finished eating?"

"You're safe this time. I thought that was rather a neat trick. One of your 'Old Granny Mitchell' remedies I take it?"

"Old Grandpa Mitchell, as a matter of fact. It's one of my father's favorites."

"He's a doctor?"

As effortlessly as if they had slipped into a pair of old comfortable shoes their conversation assumed a relaxed casual manner. It seemed to be the most natural thing in the world to be sitting there talking to him as though he had been a friend for a very long time.

Sometime later, Robin glanced at her watch, then looked at him, her voice edged with reluctance. "Dr. Wilcox. . . ."

"Could you try Paul on for size?"

Her smile was dazzling as she answered, "I think I could manage it if you could handle. . . ."

"Robin."

That caught her oddly off guard, and she stared at him, her surprise registering in her eyes. He gave her no explanation but gave her instead, a slow smile that did strange things to her spine.

"You were saying?"

His voice jarred her out of her daze, and with a flustered determination she collected her thoughts. "I have rounds to do at eight. . . ."

"Dr. Anderson is having someone else cover for you this morning. I want you to be there when I see

Davy and his parents. I understand that you've met with the parents several times, and it will be reassuring for them to have someone they know present when I see them."

"How's little Davy coping?"

"He's scared but that's to be expected. If I think his parents will give him good moral support without upsetting him, I'll leave orders that they be allowed to stay with him until he's taken into OR."

Robin could have hugged him for that. Not many surgeons would have bent the rules to give a little boy that kind of comfort. He was obviously sensitive to more than the patients' medical needs.

She toyed with her coffee spoon, then finally looked at him, her eyes troubled. "I've had a few sleepless nights over Davy, and I think I owe you an explanation about the 'miracle worker' comment."

Pushing his plate out of the way, Paul Wilcox leaned forward and rested his arms on the table looking at Robin with that unfathomable stare. "I'm listening."

She met that stare with a steady look of her own. "It sounded rather irresponsible coming out of Dr. Anderson's mouth, and that's not how it was intended."

"This has really been bothering you, hasn't it?"

"Yes, it has." With a sigh, she looked at him as she explained. "I asked Dr. Anderson to talk to you—to see what you thought. He said we needed a miracle, and I said you were the closest thing to a miracle worker we had."

He narrowed his eyes slightly as he rocked back in

his chair. "You like everything out in the open, don't you?"

Robin grimaced self-consciously. "I'm not a good poker player if that's what you mean."

His eyes were dancing when he said, "That's not exactly what I meant, but for now it will have to do." He wadded up his paper napkin, threw it on the table and slid his chair back. "Let's go dig up some miracles, shall we?"

By ten o'clock, Robin was feeling very awed and very humble. Whether he liked the phrase or not, she felt as if she was indeed in the presence of a miracle worker.

His consultation with Mr. and Mrs. Martin had given her a very comprehensive insight into the type of man, the type of physician, Paul Wilcox was, and her respect for him soared.

Even though he was pressed for time he never once indicated he was in a hurry but answered each of their questions thoroughly, explicitly and in layman's terms. He was completely honest with them about the operation's having only a remote chance of being a success, yet he somehow managed to convey that essential element of hope.

Robin had seen too many doctors who treated the patient's medical problem as though the condition was divorced from the living, breathing human being. But that was not the case with Paul Wilcox. He was deeply concerned about the whole person, the whole Davy Martin, not just his mangled limb. There was compassion and a sense of caring in every gesture, in every word he spoke, and Davy's parents responded to that caring with unlimited trust. Yes, Robin was going to learn more than surgical techniques from this man.

By the time she went into surgery her stage fright had disappeared, and she was feeling confident and very comfortable with the man. The pressure was off.

The operation went like clockwork. He had so thoroughly briefed her that Robin was able to anticipate his every move, his every thought. He talked his way through the operation, informing those in the gallery what his next move would be, but Robin sensed it was not so much for their benefit as it was for hers.

They were in the OR exactly five hours by the time she had finished the final suturing. She was soaked with perspiration, her back ached, and her legs felt as if they were encased in wet cement. The muscles in her neck and arms were so sore that she could barely lift her arms, but her exhaustion dropped from her like a second skin when Paul murmured just loud enough for her to hear, "Excellent work, Robin."

ARRIVING BACK AT WORK after three days off, Robin received an enthusiastic welcome from the staff on surgery. It really gave her a warm feeling inside to know that they were glad to have her back.

But that welcome didn't make her feel half as warm as did the friendly smile Dr. Wilcox gave her when he appeared on the ward.

"Good morning, Dr. Mitchell."

"Good morning."

He came over to the nursing station where Robin was reviewing the patient's charts and leaned against the counter, his long slim fingers casually interlaced. She wondered how many lives those hands had saved.

"I just came from pediatrics. Davy tells me you were a very frequent visitor over the weekend."

She shrugged self-consciously. "I couldn't stay away. It looks good, doesn't it?"

"There's a marked improvement, but we'll still have to monitor him very closely." There was a subtle caution in his words when he said, "We aren't over the hump with him yet—not by a long shot."

He straightened up and braced his arms on the counter as he scanned the patient reports that were neatly laid out for his inspection.

"I'd like you to accompany me on my rounds this morning."

Aware of the nurse who was seated at the desk in the corner, Robin replied in a very businesslike manner. "Yes, doctor."

He pursed his lips together firmly as though he was trying to smother a grin and glanced at her with amusement.

"I thought you said you weren't a poker player."

Her face was perfectly controlled. "But that doesn't mean I don't know the rules, Dr. Wilcox."

His eyes crinkled as he considered her equivocal comment, then he nodded his head, silently acceding she had scored a point. "Ah yes," he said, "whether we're adept or not we must all know how to play the game, mustn't we?"

She really had to struggle to keep from laughing, and her voice was a little strangled when she answered, "Yes, sir."

"I think," he said very quietly, "that perhaps poker may not be your forte, but fencing certainly is." He gave her an amused look, then straightened. "Nurse, could we start the rounds now?"

The nurse, who had the figure of a Russian discus thrower and the disposition of a lemon, fluffed her hair with a girlish flutter, beaming all the while. "Of course, doctor."

Robin had to work very hard to keep from laughing as the woman actually batted her eyelashes at him. As they walked down the corridor she stole a glance at Dr. Wilcox. Although his face was blank there was an expression of bored exasperation around his mouth that struck her as very funny. A shock wave of laughter threatened to erupt from her, and she ground her teeth together so hard that they actually squeaked.

Paul Wilcox's eyes immediately riveted on her. He took one look at her face, grinned broadly and rolled his eyes heavenward in an expression that clearly said, "God, but isn't this ridiculous!"

The look on his face finished her off. Making an abrupt right wheel, Robin turned into the room that was equipped for viewing X rays and slammed the door behind her.

Presently, the door opened and Paul commented dryly, "I'm glad you're enjoying yourself."

Her shoulders shaking uncontrollably, Robin looked up and raised her hands in a helpless gesture.

"I'm sorry," she gasped as she wiped her eyes with the back of her hand.

He grinned at her. "No, you're not."

Another spasm of laughter shuddered through her, and she sighed weakly. "You're right. I'm not. It's the best laugh I've had in days."

"At my expense."

"Do you know," she teased, "it's just like watching an episode on 'General Hospital'?"

He laughed and came toward her, his stance somehow challenging as he stood before her, his hands on his hips. "Look who's talking?" He reached out and pulled the ribbon from her hair and dropped it in the wastebasket.

Robin felt as if she was caught inside a balloon that had been let loose and was zipping around the room in a wild, careering flight. Somehow she managed to grab onto her senses and neatly sidestep the tricky issue.

Imitating the nurse, she fluffed her hair with the same girlish flutter, then said, "Dr. Wilcox, shall we do the rounds?"

He laughed and ushered her to the door. "By all means, Dr. Mitchell, but I don't want to see even a *hint* of a smile, I'm warning you!"

She grinned, her voice prim and starchy, "Yes, doctor!"

Robin didn't see much of Paul Wilcox for the next two days, but even without his physical presence to give her memory a jog she repeatedly found herself smiling over the episode with the nurse. Even though he found the woman's attentions an embarrassment he saw the humor in the situation, and she liked him for that.

She had a sneaking suspicion that his no-nonsense attitude was a professional cover-up for a very warm, spontaneous person. She couldn't help but think about him. In fact, if the truth was known, she found herself spending rather a lot of time thinking about Paul Wilcox.

Robin gave herself a brisk mental shake—damn it, she was doing it *again*. She was having an awful time concentrating this morning. With a sigh she made herself focus her attention on the X rays she was scanning.

"Dr. Mitchell, do you have a minute?"

Straightening up, Robin turned to face the young nurse who had entered the room. "Sure, Johnson. What is it?"

"Would you have time to check Mrs. Decker's IV? Her hand's beginning to swell."

"Of course. Let's have a look."

Robin liked Mrs. Decker. In fact, the seventy-two-year-old was one of her favorites on the floor. The woman, who had had major surgery a few days before, was one of those people who had never become cantankerous, bullheaded or demanding in old age. She was suffering from extreme pain, but she still managed to maintain a sweetness of disposition and a positive outlook that Robin truly admired.

The tiny, fragile-looking woman was propped up in bed, her wrinkled, weathered skin draped loosely on her thin body, her face faded by an unhealthy pallor, her brown snapping eyes glazed with pain.

"You're having some problems with your intravenous, Elizabeth." Mrs. Decker didn't like being called Mrs. Decker. She said it made her sound like a stuffy old crock.

Laying the book she was reading across her legs, Mrs. Decker made a soft scolding noise at the nurse. "Now, dear, I told you not to bother the doctor."

"That's what I'm here for, and besides you're never any trouble." Robin carefully examined the woman's left hand where the intravenous was inserted. The area was badly bruised and very swollen and obviously very sore.

Taking the woman's right hand, Robin inspected the blue veins that were transparent through the tissue-paper-thin skin. "I can put it in this hand, Elizabeth, but you may not be able to knit."

"It doesn't matter. My knitting was accidentally pulled off the needles, and I'm too lazy to fix it."

Robin patted the woman's gnarled hand and smiled softly. She realized that the real problem was not one of laziness, but instead Mrs. Decker was too exhausted and too weak to make the effort. The nurse brought in a sterile replacement, and quickly and efficiently Robin changed the IV to the other hand then taped it securely. With a nod she dismissed the nurse as she timed the drip. Once she was satisfied that everything was in order, she gathered up the bundle of knitting from the bedside table and sat down.

"Now Dr. Mitchell, what are you doing?"

Robin laughed and gave Elizabeth a conspiratorial wink. "I'm going to use your dropped stitches as an excuse to sit down for a while."

"You don't have to do that, dear," the old lady admonished gently.

"Elizabeth, are you going to make me go back to work?"

Mrs. Decker smiled, her eyes twinkling. "Am I involved in what they call collusion?"

"You certainly are," answered Robin with a grin. She painstakingly untangled the wool, then stretched the unfinished sweater out on her lap and began to pick up the dropped stitches.

"Well, Elizabeth, are you giving lessons to all the staff or just to Dr. Mitchell?"

Robin's head shot up, her eyes wide with an oh, no, look. Paul Wilcox was standing at the end of the bed with a crafty smile on his face. *Damn it, he has me cornered now,* thought Robin, keenly aware that the patient in the other bed was looking on with undisguised interest.

"Oh," sighed Mrs. Decker wearily, her expression that of a helpless aged woman. "I've made such a tangle, and I didn't have the fortitude to straighten it out so I asked Dr. Mitchell to fix it." Robin had to bite her lip to keep a straight face. *You old darling, Elizabeth,* she thought with delight.

"Hmm," said Dr. Wilcox, his tone definitely skeptical. He picked up the book that Mrs. Decker had been reading. The title was *The Birds of Alberta*.

"Are you a bird fancier, Elizabeth?" he casually asked. Robin tried to appear totally engrossed in her task. She had the uncomfortable feeling that she was being cunningly set up.

"Oh, yes. When I was younger I spent nearly every

Sunday tramping through the woods," said Elizabeth, her role as a helpless frail senior suddenly forgotten. "I enjoyed it so much."

"Ornithology is a fine, relaxing hobby," offered the other patient.

"Yes, it certainly is," agreed Paul Wilcox, his eyes flashing as he pointedly fixed his gaze on Robin. "Fascinating, really," he added.

Robin felt her face grow warm, and she promptly dropped three more stitches.

Sitting up, the woman in the next bed turned to face them, anxious to participate in the conversation. "I take it you bird-watch, doctor?"

"When the opportunity presents itself, I certainly do," he answered enthusiastically, his eyes never leaving Robin. *Damn him,* she thought as her face turned pinker.

"There are so many interesting species. They're like people, you know—they have such different personalities," said the other patient.

Paul Wilcox's grin was pure mischief. "That's true. My personal favorite is the robin—particularly cheeky and brazen, the robin."

There wasn't a thing Robin could say that wouldn't give herself away. She had been neatly boxed into a corner, and if she opened her mouth she knew she'd laugh. With a very flushed face she tipped her head, acknowledging that *he* had scored a point.

With a thoroughly indecent look of self-satisfaction in his eyes, he acknowledged her acquiescence, then he turned to Mrs. Decker.

"I hear you were having some swelling from the IV, Elizabeth."

"Oh, it's fine now. Dr. Mitchell changed it."

"Good. I'll be off, then. Don't knit yourself into a corner, Dr. Mitchell, you're due in surgery in an hour."

She heard him whistling as he walked down the corridor. This battle of wits could turn into a very interesting war.

When Robin finally had the knitting restored to order she left Mrs. Decker and returned to the nursing station to review some charts. She found Bernie there, discussing with another resident an operation that was scheduled for the following day.

Bernie grinned broadly when he saw her. "Hello, ugly." The thickness of his lenses magnified the size of his eyes, and Robin always thought it made him look very much like a lovesick owl.

She laughed, then said, "Hello, Bernard." Bernie hated being called Bernard.

He squinted his eyes at her menacingly. "You're asking for it, Mitchell."

"So you keep saying."

The other resident, Mark Lister, who knew them both from med-school days, shook his head and moaned dramatically. "Good grief, don't tell me that I have to put up with the odd couple for the rest of the shift."

Robin was smiling as she made notations on Mrs. Decker's chart. A movement just outside her range of vision caught her eye, and she lifted her head to find Paul Wilcox leaning against the desk, his eyes narrowed as he stared at Bernie.

Her smile sagged into openmouthed disbelief when he snapped impatiently. "When you're quite finished with all your social amenities, Dr. Radcliffe, I hope you can spare me a few moments of your time so I can review this case history with you."

Bernie jerked to attention and did an embarrassed little shuffle as he stammered, "Ah...ah...of course, doctor. Right now, sir."

With a snort of disgust, Dr. Wilcox abruptly turned away and strode rapidly down the corridor. Bernie shrugged his shoulders in bewilderment as he made a face of quaking terror, then hurried after his chief, his lab coat flapping behind him like a white flag of surrender.

CHAPTER THREE

ROBIN STOOD AT THE WINDOW of the doctors' lounge staring at the deluge of rain that was washing against the pane, her spirits as dismal as the weather.

She wearily rubbed the back of her neck and stuck her hands in the pockets of her lab coat. Sighing heavily she tipped her head back and closed her eyes.

The past few days had been a nightmare. In fact, it was the worst shift she had ever endured. The hours had been long and grueling, the usual heavy work load made worse by a rash of critical emergency cases. The human tragedies she had to cope with had depressed her beyond words...a very young man who had attempted suicide with a gun shot to his abdomen; a mother of four who had died from injuries suffered in a car accident caused by a drunken driver; a young woman who had been raped, then viciously assaulted with a knife; a young child who had eventually died from injuries received in a brutal beating....

The senseless waste of life, the brutal violation of human dignity, the outrageous cruelty of human beings toward their fellow man left her feeling sick and filled with despair.

To have that small battered child die beneath her

hands on the operating table because of the in-humane thrashing administered by his own father was the worst experience in her life. To fight a medical battle against sickness and disease was one thing but this was something else altogether. She had never felt so disenchanted, so defeated.

Robin sighed and opened her eyes. She was so tired she could barely see straight. The long hours and the psychological pressure had totally drained her. Added to that was a vague feeling of rejection, which kept gnawing at her.

She folded her arms across her breasts as she rested her shoulder against the window frame. Her brow furrowed in a frown as she stared absently at the rivulets of rain on the glass. Since the episode with Mrs. Decker, Paul Wilcox had pointedly avoided her. At first she thought she was only imagining his aloofness, but after repeated incidents where he had cold-shouldered her she had to face the fact that he was deliberately steering clear of her.

Yet Robin, try as she might, could not figure out why. The only explanation she could come up with was that unwittingly she had crossed his boundaries of familiarity. . . either that or she had only imagined there had been a rapport between them. No matter what the reason was the feeling of rejection bothered her and made her feel very uneasy. Someone she barely knew should not have that effect on her. . . not unless the attraction was much stronger than she wanted to admit.

"Hey, Mitch, let's go for coffee."

Turning to face Bernie, Robin managed a wry grin.

"If you promise me you'll let me have some rest stops along the way."

Bernie laughed as he held the door open for her. "That bad?"

"Yes, that bad!"

He let the heavy door swing shut behind them and glanced at her, his eyes solemn behind his thick glasses. "It's really gotten to you this week, hasn't it?"

Robin shrugged and avoided meeting his concerned gaze. "It really has. I feel totally wrung out. It's the worst shift I've ever put in."

"Yeah," he said sympathetically, "I can understand how you feel. You've put in some damned long hours in surgery, and that pressure and tension really drains a person." His expression was one of understanding as they turned down the corridor that led to the elevators.

"When are your days off?"

"Sunday, Monday and Tuesday. I go back to work Wednesday at midnight."

"Are you going home?"

"No. There's something wrong with my car, and I can't afford to fly."

"Anyone with one shred of pride would never admit ownership of that pile of junk, Robin. One of these days you're going to slam the door too hard, and that rusted-out wreck is going to disintegrate into a pile of iron filings at your feet."

Robin laughed. "It isn't *that* bad."

"It is *that* bad. It's a disgrace!"

On arriving at the bank of elevators, Robin leaned

against the wall as Bernie pushed the button. "Do you want to borrow my car and go? I'm not doing anything special this weekend."

"Thanks, Bernie, but no." She straightened up as the elevator door slid open, then she followed him inside. "I'm just too damned tired to make that five-hour drive."

"Tell you what, why don't we go out for dinner Saturday night? You need something to perk you up. There's a new Greek restaurant that's just opened and it's supposed to be really fantastic."

"I'll see. The way I feel right now I doubt if I'll have the energy to drag myself out."

"I'll make a reservation just in case."

When they finally worked their way through the self-serve lineup in the cafeteria, they entered the dining area to find a number of the surgical staff gathered at one of the large corner tables. Without consulting Robin, Bernie headed toward the group, oblivious to the fact that he was slopping coffee with every step he took.

Robin felt as if she had just stepped out of a second-story window when she realized that the dark head on the other side of the table was attached to Paul Wilcox's body. She wanted to avoid the man at all costs, especially today. If he were to look down his nose at her one more time, she was very apt to burst into tears.

"Geez, you guys. With you two here, who's left on surgery?" asked Mark Lister, who was seated at the table.

"The janitorial staff," retorted Bernie as he pulled

out a chair for Robin, then sat down himself. "We left the cleaning ladies doing our rounds, and old Mike is scrubbing up for surgery." There was a ripple of laughter, and even Robin grinned.

"Say, Mitchell, have you seen the rock Johnson's packing on her hand?" queried Mark.

Robin faced the nurse who was seated beside her and smiled. "Why, Johnson! Have you been keeping secrets from us?"

Alice Johnson blushed and showed Robin her left hand. A very large diamond engagement ring glittered in the fluorescent light. The nurse had always been a special favorite of Robin's, and with unaffected warmth she gave the young woman an enthusiastic hug. "Congratulations! When's the big day?"

"Probably in the fall. Richard started a new job this year so he won't be able to take any holidays until then."

Robin propped her chin on her hand and smiled at the nurse. "You must be really excited."

"Oh, I am!" Responding to Robin's genuine interest, Alice rattled on about wedding plans, her happiness radiating from her. Sensing that someone else was listening to the conversation, Robin glanced up, and a strange sensation flashed through her. Paul Wilcox was staring at Alice with an expression that clearly revealed he definitely did not share Alice's enthusiasm for her upcoming marriage.

It wasn't exactly a look of contempt she saw but more a look of bleak comprehension. . .as though he had some grim insight that the rest of them did not share. It was odd and strangely disconcerting. Very little was known about this man—perhaps he had suffered through a bad marriage and the experience had made a cynic out of him.

With that uneasy thought tucked in the back of her mind, Robin focused her attention on the nurse, a warm look of understanding on her face.

"I'm so happy for you, Alice. But I hope this doesn't mean we're going to lose you."

"Oh, no. Not for a year or two at least. We want to save up enough for a down payment on a house before I even *consider* quitting work."

"Good," interjected Bernie firmly. "It would be a drag without you around."

"Whether you know it or not you're one of the very few who appreciates his sense of humor," explained Robin with a grin. "Of course he doesn't want to see his small, select group dwindle away."

Alice laughed and reached in front of Robin to pat Bernie's hand. "Our numbers may be small, but we make up for it with valor."

As the two of them became involved in a verbal sparring match, Robin leaned back in her chair and quietly studied Paul Wilcox. He sat hunched over the table, intent on what one of the older surgeons was saying to him with that same look of intense concentration on his face she had noticed before. What was he *really* like. . . beneath the exterior of aloof professionalism? She thought she'd had a glimpse of Paul Wilcox the person, but maybe she'd been wrong. Maybe, she thought with wry amusement, she'd been right on her initial assessment. He was simply the ultimate man. . . .

"There's Lisa!"

Jarred from her musings by Alice's exclamation, Robin shifted her attention to the petite blond woman the nurse was waving to. The young woman acknowledged Alice's wave and started wending her way through the scattered tables. Arriving at the table, she smiled shyly as she sat down in one of the vacant chairs across from Robin.

Johnson smiled in welcome and began the introductions. "This is Lisa Gordon everybody. She's replacing Hobson in our postop intensive-care unit."

Lisa Gordon had the most beautiful hair Robin had ever seen. It was a mix of several shades of blond liberally highlighted with a golden red, and it shimmered like satin under the glaring overhead light. Her magnificent hair was truly unusual, but there was something unique about her face, too.

She was a small woman with extremely fine features, but there was an aura of quiet confidence about her that somehow overrode the impression of fragility. The delicately shaped face was dominated by wide blue eyes that were direct and honest, yet innocent and gentle. She was going to like this new nurse, Robin thought with approval. There was nothing artificial about her.

Robin glanced at Bernie and very nearly burst out laughing at the stunned look on his face. He was staring at Lisa like a man in a trance, his eyes glued on her, his mouth hanging open, totally mesmerized by this new nurse.

"You're hyperventilating, Radcliffe," she said quietly.

Bernie swallowed hard and reluctantly tore his attention from Lisa to look at Robin, the stupefied expression still glazing his eyes.

She grinned at him as she snapped her fingers sharply in front of him. "Wake up, Bernie. You look like someone just dropped you on your head."

He stared at her blankly for an instant, then a deep flush colored his face as it finally registered that Robin was watching him, a knowing gleam in her eyes. He gave her a withering look and turned his attention back to Lisa.

Her amusement shriveled inside her like a wizened prune when Robin realized that Paul Wilcox was watching Bernie and her with a look that told her more clearly than words that he would dearly love to bang their heads together. *Not again,* she thought with weary resignation....

"Dr. Mitchell?" Robin turned to find one of the nurses from emergency standing behind her.

"Yes, nurse."

"Dr. Standish sent me to get you. He wants you in the OR immediately. He said to tell you surgery could take several hours."

Robin sighed and pushed her chair back from the table. "Tell him I'll be right there."

Bernie's head snapped around, and he looked at Robin with consternation. "Not another long one, Robin. You've been stuck with every messy case this week." He shoved his chair back and stood up. "I'm going to see if I can fill in for you."

"Dr. Standish specifically asked for Dr. Mitchell," advised the nurse firmly.

With a rueful grin, Robin stood up and patted Bernie on the shoulder. "Well, thanks for trying anyway, Radcliffe."

"Yeah. . . for all the good it did."

She gave him a weak lopsided smile and followed the nurse out of the cafeteria.

They had nearly reached the elevators when a familiar voice snapped out behind her. "Just a moment, Dr. Mitchell."

With an unaccountable feeling of dread settling in her midriff, Robin slowly and reluctantly turned to face Paul Wilcox. "Yes, doctor?"

He ignored her as he directed his attention to the nurse. "Tell Dr. Standish that Dr. Mitchell will be along directly."

With that very obvious and curt dismissal, the nurse hurried away. Robin waited somewhat impatiently, fervently wishing she was somewhere else. He didn't say anything for a moment as he stared at her, his face an unreadable mask.

His voice was brusque when he finally spoke. "Dr. Radcliffe's comment about your work load didn't go unnoticed, Dr. Mitchell. I'd like an explanation, if you don't mind."

From the tone of his voice, Robin knew it didn't matter a damn if she minded or not. . . he expected an explanation and he expected it *now*.

With a tense little motion she glanced at her watch, then looked up at him, frantically wondering how she could diplomatically delay this inquisition until later.

"Yes, I know," he said tersely. "Dr. Standish is waiting for you in surgery."

"Could we possibly postpone this, doctor? It did

sound urgent, and I don't want to keep him waiting.''

He stared at her, his eyes coolly assessing as he considered what she had said. The silence was an ordeal in itself, and Robin didn't realize that she had been holding her breath until he spoke.

''Very well. We'll continue this later. I want to see you in my office immediately after you've finished in OR.''

''But it's three o'clock now,'' she protested a little wildly. ''It could be midnight before....''

''In my office, Mitchell.'' With that abrupt order he turned and strode away, leaving Robin standing dumbfoundedly in the middle of the corridor, staring at his retreating back. Why was he so annoyed this time?

With a defeated little shrug, Robin turned and headed toward the operating theaters, her exhaustion compounded by the feeling of apprehension.

THE CLOCK IN THE SCRUB ROOM indicated half-past ten when Robin finally came through the swinging doors leading from OR. She stripped off her disposable mask and tossed it in the garbage, then tipped her head back and closed her eyes. Massaging the back of her neck, she tried to ease the aching tension that knotted the muscles across her shoulders. She would give her soul if she could go home and fall into bed, but she still had that damned meeting with Wilcox to face.

With a heavy sigh she straightened up and, feeling a weariness that weighed a ton, she left the room.

Her hair was bundled under the surgical cap, and she had on the pale blue pajama-styled OR garb, the pastel color accentuating the dark circles of exhaustion under her eyes.

Her tiredness was tolerable tonight, though. The operation had been a life-saving success, and unless there were postoperative complications the father of three would be fully recovered within two months. He was an extremely lucky man. A fall like the one he had should have killed him.

A weary shiver slithered down her spine as she stepped into the empty elevator and pushed the button. The door whispered shut, and Robin leaned against the paneled wall watching the light flashing along the row of numbers as she was silently carried down to the main level. It was the third night in a row that she had to take a taxi home. She was simply going to have to get her car fixed whether she could afford it or not. This was costing her a fortune.

The elevator halted, and Robin straightened up as the door opened. She stepped out and turned down the deserted hallway that led to the administrative offices. Maybe she would be lucky. Maybe Dr. Wilcox had decided not to wait for her because she was so late. But her hopes died abruptly when she found the door to his outer office open and the lights on. Feeling very much like a kid caught swiping apples, she entered. The feeling intensified when she found the door to his private office ajar, revealing a sliver of soft light. Taking a deep breath, she rapped lightly on the doorframe.

"Come in."

Damn, she thought as she pushed open the door and stepped into the room. Dr. Wilcox was seated at a cluttered desk, the light from his desk lamp casting his face in shadows.

He glanced at his watch, then motioned her to a comfortable-looking sofa that was placed in front of his desk. "Sit down, Mitchell," he directed.

Robin sat down, grateful for the opportunity. He was staring at her with that impenetrable look that did nothing to reassure her.

Shaking his head slightly, he made a notation on a paper in front of him, then without saying a word, he handed it across the desk to her.

There, in very angular concise script, was a total of all her hours; there was also a list of the operations she had been involved with during the past few days, concluding with the surgery she had just finished.

"Is that a complete list?"

Robin looked at him with uncertain speculation, then quickly scanned the document. "Yes, it's complete."

Folding his arms across his chest, he leaned back in his chair and silently studied her. When he finally spoke, his voice was no longer abrupt. "Those hours average out to slightly more than eleven hours a day, and there have been three occasions, like today, when you have practically worked a double shift."

What is he leading up to? Robin wondered. *Why is he making an issue over my hours?*

There was a look of preoccupation on his face as he leaned forward and butted a cigarette that was smoldering in the ashtray.

The familiar smell of the smoke fired Robin's recurring craving for a cigarette, and for a moment she was sorely tempted to ask him for one. She managed to stifle the urge, knowing full well if she had one cigarette now, she would be hooked all over again.

He glanced at her, then lowered his gaze as he toyed with the pen that was lying on the pile of papers in front of him. "I don't like to see residents on my staff taken for granted by the practicing physicians who have admitting privileges in this hospital. They seldom grasp the reality that a resident is subject to demands from a number of doctors and, unfortunately, they seem to suffer from very short memories. Those who have done residency have conveniently forgotten what it was like."

Leaning back in his chair, he hesitated for a moment as he scrutinized her. "Your work load has been brutal this week, Robin. There is no way you can continue to perform efficiently under that intense pressure. I will not have a member of my staff dropping from exhaustion simply because she's a very capable surgeon and heavy demands are made on her. From now on, I want you to let me know if you're being deluged with requests...and *I'll* deal with the matter."

Robin didn't know what to say. She had come to this meeting expecting a lecture, and instead he was offering her the kind of real support that she had never expected to receive from a chief of surgery. Instead of experiencing simple relief, Robin was moved to near tears, and she had to swallow hard against the contraction that tightened her throat.

Her voice was very husky when she was finally able to speak. "Normally, long hours don't affect me, but a number of the cases I've faced during the last few days have been so damned tragic. . . ." Taking a slow breath to ease the ache that was developing in her chest, Robin clasped her hands together tightly in her lap. She was *not* going to cry. . . she wasn't!

Sensing her distress, Paul Wilcox stood up, walked around the desk and sat down beside her. "I'd like you to tell me about them, Robin," he said quietly.

Quickly and covertly, she blinked away the tears that blurred her vision, then looked up at him, her eyes dark with anguish. Robin took a shaky breath and, with a voice choked with emotion, told him the grim details surrounding those cases that had disturbed her so deeply. As she talked, the terrible emotional pressure that had been building in her drained away, leaving only the heavy weight of physical exhaustion.

There was a note of understanding in his voice when he laid his hand on her shoulder and said, "There are many times that all of us wonder why in hell we chose this profession, Robin. But then there are times that it's all so worthwhile. You have to learn to pace yourself so that it balances out."

Robin gave him a weak smile. "Pacing is something horses do."

He laughed and gave her shoulder a pat as he stood up. "You do have a point there. Come on. I'll drive you home."

Glancing at her watch, Robin was stunned to find that it was after eleven o'clock. She stood up quickly, her voice apologetic. "I'm sorry. I didn't realize I'd kept you so long."

He swung his jacket off the back of the chair as he leaned over and switched off the desk lamp. "Don't worry about it. I had a stack of paperwork to clear away tonight anyway."

He followed her out of his office and switched off the lights. Checking the door to make sure it was locked, he draped his sports jacket over his shoulder and turned toward the staff entrance.

Robin's conscience had a silent war with her desire to go with him, but her conscience, as always, won out. "Thank you for the offer of a ride, but I want to go back upstairs and check my patient in recovery before I leave. And I have to change."

Paul Wilcox turned to face her, his mouth pursed in an expression of amused exasperation as he shook his head. Then he grinned. "Very well, but I'm coming with you, just to make sure you get out of the place before sunrise."

Her weariness seemed to fade away to nothing as he caught up to her and walked with her down the corridor.

It was nearly an hour later when they drove up to Robin's residence. She experienced a pang of regret as she reluctantly gathered up her jacket and handbag, then turned to thank him.

He spoke before she had a chance. "I'm changing your schedule for this weekend, Robin. You're to take Saturday off as well."

She stared at him wide-eyed and confused, caught completely off guard by his statement. The soft glow from the streetlight slanted through the windshield, and she saw him smile as he reached for the package of cigarettes lying on the dash. "I would have pulled you off duty on Friday as well, but the case load of scheduled surgery is just too heavy."

"But there was no need...."

"Yes, there was." His lighter flamed in the semi-darkness as he lighted his cigarette and inhaled deeply. "You're dead on your feet, and besides, you've done more than your fair share lately."

She drew in her breath very slowly, then cautioned. "It could be said that that smacks of favoritism."

His laugh was throaty and strangely intimate. "Really?"

The way he said "really" sent a shiver of excitement coursing through her, a shiver that she tried desperately to ignore. Somehow she managed to keep her voice relatively steady as she countered, "Yes, it could." Then she laughed, "But I couldn't care less right now. It's too good to be true."

"You need it, you know."

"Yes, I know I do," she answered quietly. She fidgeted with the shoulder strap of her handbag and she faced him, her voice made a little unsteady by the depth of the gratitude she felt toward him. "Thank you for being so supportive tonight. I've never felt so negative about medicine before and talking it out has really helped to put everything back in perspective."

He reached across the gearshift console and took her hand in his. "It can be damned depressing at times...I've been in that position myself." His grip tightened as he said, "I'm glad I was there to listen."

Every nerve in Robin's body was acutely aware of the warmth of the strong male hand that encompassed hers, and she experienced a vague sense of loss when he finally removed it.

"Have a good night's rest, Robin."

"I will." The very last thing she wanted to do was to break the frail bond between them, but somehow she managed to force herself to slip out of the low-slung car.

She raised her hand in salute as he put the car in gear and pulled away from the curb. The red tail-lights disappeared around the corner, but she continued to stare down the empty, gloom-shrouded street. All of a sudden she felt more lonely than she could ever remember.

THE NEXT TWO DAYS were very unnerving ones for Robin. It wasn't because of her work load, but rather because of one Dr. Paul Wilcox. He was back to the old game of avoiding her, but now she sensed that there was a very personal reason for his aloofness. She would catch him watching her with an odd look on his face, but the moment their eyes met, he would immediately look away. She was perplexed and more than a little preoccupied by his behavior. What was going on in his mind; what was he thinking? Try as she might to eradicate him from her thoughts, he kept straying back into her consciousness.

But by Thursday afternoon, the heavy demands of her job left her very little time to think of anything, except the task at hand. She was in postop, monitoring a critically ill patient of Bernie's and had just finished checking his vital signs when Paul Wilcox, Bernie and a nurse entered the room.

"How's he doing, Mitch?" asked Bernie with a worried frown on his face.

"His condition hasn't deteriorated, except his pulse is more erratic."

Dr. Wilcox took the chart that Robin handed him and quickly scanned the data registered there. He asked Bernie several questions, then pursed his lips as a frown appeared. "I think we'd better have him moved to the intensive-care unit, Dr. Radcliffe. With these symptoms, he could be headed for a cardiac arrest."

Bernie's face was drawn with worry as he turned to the nurse. "Will you see to it right away, nurse?"

"Right away, doctor." She hurried out of the room, and the others slowly followed her. The two men continued to discuss the case but Robin paid little attention to their conversation. She wished she could figure out Paul Wilcox—then maybe she could put him out of her mind for good.

She was jolted back to reality when she realized they had reached the elevators. Robin was going to continue down the corridor, but Bernie directed his attention to her.

With a slightly sheepish grin on his face, he said. "Say, Robin, would you think I was a louse if I broke our dinner date for Saturday night?"

Uncomfortably aware that Paul Wilcox was leaning against the wall with his full attention focused on them, Robin somehow managed to grin at Bernie. "No bigger louse than usual."

She was going to leave it at that until something in Bernie's expression hinted that there was more to it than a canceled dinner engagement. Her eyes were narrowed with amused speculation as she studied him. Then on a hunch, she decided to do a little probing. "Shall I cancel the reservation?"

Bernie's head shot up, and he turned scarlet when he saw the look on Robin's face. "Ah...no. No...don't worry about that."

"Hmmm," said Robin. "I see." Then playing another hunch, she said, "Take her flowers, Bernie. She looks like the type who loves flowers."

Bernie turned even redder, then grinned broadly as he made a menacing gesture at her. "Damn you, Mitchell."

Robin laughed and patted him maternally on the shoulder and turned to walk away as the elevator door opened. "Don't forget the flowers...my guess would be yellow roses." Had Robin looked at Paul Wilcox then, she would have wondered about the odd look that flitted across his face.

Still smiling to herself, Robin continued down the hallway to the nurses' station, where she completed some paperwork, then checked with the lab concerning the results of some tests that were being done on a patient. Hanging up the phone, she glanced at her watch. She had a few moments to spare before she was due in OR. On the spur of the moment, she decided to slip in and have a quick visit with Elizabeth Decker.

Robin was nearly at Elizabeth's room when she was paged over the hospital intercom and asked to call an in-house extension. With a sigh of resignation, she turned and went back to the nursing station. Dialing the specified number, she leaned against the counter as she listened to the hollow ringing in her ear.

"Chief of Surgery," said a female voice.

Oh, no, thought Robin a little frantically. *What have I done this time?*

"Dr. Mitchell here. I was asked to call."

"Oh, yes, Dr. Mitchell. Just a moment please. Dr. Wilcox wants to speak to you."

There was only a brief pause, then a deep masculine voice said, "Hello, Robin. I'm glad I caught you before you went in to OR."

"Is there a problem, Dr. Wilcox?"

"Well, that depends on you. By any chance, could you have dinner with me tomorrow evening?" There was a timbre to his voice that was huskily intimate.

The butterfly was back...twice as strong, twice as big and definitely more unsettling.

She found it extremely difficult to speak. "I'd love to. What time?"

"How would eight o'clock suit you?"

"That would be just fine."

"Great." There was a brief pause, then he said, "I had hoped to see you before I left but I couldn't get away. I would have preferred to ask you directly rather than over the phone."

Closing her eyes, Robin tried to take a deep breath to quell the strange feeling of anticipation that was fluttering inside her. "I understand. It doesn't matter."

He laughed softly and said, "That's good."

Something in his tone of voice made her feel decidedly intoxicated when he continued, "I have office hours all day tomorrow, so I won't see you until tomorrow night."

Robin felt as if her legs had turned to pink play dough. Her voice was definitely breathless when she said, "Until tomorrow evening, then."

"Until tomorrow. . .eight o'clock."

"Eight o'clock." There was a soft click, and Robin dazedly removed the receiver from her ear and stared at it, awestruck. What *was* going on in his mind?

IT WAS FINALLY FRIDAY, and she was just about to go off duty but decided to check on two patients who had undergone surgery early in the day. And that was her big mistake. She was just coming out of the recovery room when a voice boomed out behind her.

"Mitchell! Am I glad you're still here. I want you in OR immediately."

Robin froze in her tracks, then slowly turned to face Dr. Standish. The burly, blustery surgeon was hurtling toward her at a terrific speed, a new resident doing a peculiar hop-skip step beside him in an effort to keep up.

"Dr. Standish, it's five o'clock," Robin protested frantically. "I was supposed to be off duty an hour ago. Besides, I have an important engagement this evening."

"Nonsense! Just nonsense! I need you here. A young lad has just been rushed in. Victim of a hit and run. Think every damn organ in his belly's been ruptured.''

He caught Robin by the arm, his momentum sweeping her down the corridor beside him. ''Need you here, Mitchell. Best damn resident on staff. The boy's in critical condition.''

Robin was geared up to really dig in her heels in protest, but just then she caught sight of the stretcher that two orderlies and another resident were rushing to surgery. There was a very small body on it—the boy couldn't have been much more than six years old.

Her protest died on her lips as the grim memory of the little boy who had died because of the beating magnified in her mind. Maybe this time it wasn't too late. With that thought uppermost in her mind, her bubble of euphoria evaporated, giving way to the grim reality of life and death.

It was a little after nine o'clock when Robin left the operating room, but to her it felt as if a century had passed. She was hot and sweaty and had the energy level of a very old rag doll. The only glimmer of life left in her was a flicker of amusement in her eyes when Dr. Standish nearly dislocated her shoulders and drove her through the scrub room wall when he pounded her back enthusiastically as they came through the swinging doors.

''Fine work, Mitchell. Damn fine work! Cool head. Don't get excited. I like that.''

Somehow a grin managed to work its way through the puttylike muscles of her face as she looked up at him. ''Don't try to pacify me, Dr. Standish. You shanghaied me, and you know it.''

A sound rumbled like thunder in his massive chest as he chuckled. "Damn right I did. Didn't want some scaredy-pants resident who crumbles like dry toast every time I let out a bellow. Like working with you."

As they headed down the corridor, Robin swept the surgical cap off her sweat-dampened hair, then slanted a dry look up at him. "The feeling's mutual...most of the time."

There was another rumble of amusement. "Suppose I did bully you a tad. Was worried about that kid though." He stopped in front of the elevators and stared down at her. "Sorry about your evening, Mitchell. But you did some fine work tonight."

The genuine sincerity in his voice left Robin with a very good feeling, and she instantly forgave him for ruining her evening. "Don't worry about it. It wasn't that important," she lied. "Do you want me to stick around for a while to make sure there's no complications?"

"No. Hell, no. You go home. I'm going down to talk to the boy's parents. I'll check him before I go."

Robin didn't think she had the energy to crawl, let alone walk, but she eventually made it to the foyer leading to the doctors' lounge without falling on her face. Not only was she physically drained, but she was also feeling very much like a teenager who had to miss her first high-school prom because she'd come down with chicken pox. Falling-down-dead-in-your-tracks fatigue and crying-in-the-bathroom disappointment didn't make very good bedfellows, she concluded wryly.

A tiny burst of anger energized her aching muscles, and she slammed open the door to the lounge with considerably more force than was necessary.

"I know how you feel."

Robin's stomach felt like a yo-yo on a string as she turned around. Paul Wilcox was leaning against the mock fireplace, his hands stuck in the pants pockets of his beautifully tailored three-piece tan suit.

She almost expected to see him dissolve before her very eyes as she stared at him in disbelief. Giving herself a mental shake, she collected her wits and started to apologize. "I'm so sorry about tonight. There was an emergency...."

He straightened up and came toward her. "I know. Standish again. I thought something must have waylaid you when you weren't at home."

Robin raised her hands in a gesture of regret. With a smile of understanding, he laid his hand on her shoulder. "Come on, Dr. Mitchell, let's get out of here."

"I have to change first...."

"I'm getting you out of here before Standish comes roaring in with another emergency."

With a dubious look at her OR garb, she shook her head in amusement. "If anyone sees me wandering around in this, they'll think you're out with some looney tune."

He grinned. "I've always had a weakness for looney tunes. Get your things and let's go. You must be damned near starved."

A delightful warmth blossomed inside Robin as

she smiled up at him. So...the dinner date was still on, in spite of the delay.

Upon arriving at her apartment, Robin went into her bedroom and dumped her clothes on her bed, then returned to the living room where Paul was waiting.

"Can I fix you a drink?"

"Sure. What do you have?"

"Not much," she laughed. "Some fairly good Scotch that my father left and some odds and ends from a party I had over a year ago...and some wine."

"The Scotch will be fine...just ice."

He stood in the doorway of her tiny kitchen as she dug out the bottle from the back of the cupboard. "For a resident doctor whose wages barely exceed the poverty line, you have a very impressive liquor stock."

She laughed as she dropped the ice cubes in his drink, then handed it to him. "The chronic problem. Do you buy groceries or pay the rent?" She put the ice back in the fridge and leaned against the cupboard. "Actually the pay wouldn't be so bad if I didn't have student loans to pay back."

"The pay stinks, Robin," he said pointedly.

There was a gleam of devilry in her eyes when she said, "Well, I guess you'll just have to do something about that, won't you Dr. Wilcox?"

"I wish I could, but I'm not quite *that* far up the ladder." He took a sip of his drink and nodded his head in approval. "Your father is a man who knows his Scotch."

"I'll tell him that. Mother loathes the stuff and calls it his rat poison." Little realizing how visible her exhaustion was, Robin rolled her shoulders in an attempt to ease the aching knot of muscles across her back. With a sigh, she pushed herself away from the cupboard. "I'll go change."

Paul didn't move from the doorway, deliberately blocking her. He studied her for a minute, then said softly, "Would you rather we sent out for something? You look like you don't have enough energy to make it down the stairs."

The warmth and concern in his words kindled a response in Robin that she didn't dare define, and she stared up at him, very conscious of the virility, the magnetism that this man possessed.

Her voice was affected by the strange weakness that invaded her, and she whispered, "Are you sure you wouldn't mind?"

"I don't mind at all. In fact, I'd prefer it. Restaurants are not my favorite places." Catching her by the shoulders, he gently propelled her toward her bedroom. "Go have a long, hot shower, and I'll take care of dinner."

"Paul, I . . . ."

"Go have your shower, Robin." He smiled that crooked little smile that did wicked things to her pulse rate, then gave her a gentle push. Robin's knees seemed hinged with rubber bands as she walked past him.

She did as she was told and had that long, hot shower . . . partly because she needed some time to get a grip on herself. She made an almost honest effort to be realistic...she was far too susceptible to the dynamic personality of Paul Wilcox; she was playing with fire, and she would be the one who ended up badly burned; besides, he was her superior, and that was a definite no-no. But the entire exercise was a lost cause. Rationality didn't stand a chance against this light-headed anticipation that was sizzling through her.

Robin hummed softly to herself as she dressed in a pair of white slacks and a simple long-sleeved blouse exactly the same shade of blue as her eyes. Gathering her thick hair into a loose topknot, she allowed the unconfined curls to feather alluringly around her face. After a quick glance in the mirror, Robin returned to the living room. Paul was just coming into the apartment with a large brown bag in his hands.

"You're just in time. Dinner has arrived."

"Was I *that* long?"

"No, they were that fast." He followed her into the kitchen and set the bag on the counter. "Hope you like Chinese food. I've discovered this little restaurant that makes the best I've ever eaten."

"I love it." Robin opened the bag and began to lift out the plastic containers. "Mmm, it smells delicious."

"Here, I'll do that. You get the plates and silverware."

After she had gathered the dinnerware, Robin retrieved a bottle of white wine from the fridge, two wine goblets from the cupboard and a corkscrew from the junk drawer, then set everything on the counter beside Paul.

She groaned when she saw the volume of food he had ordered. "We'll never eat all that."

"Sure we will, but if we don't, you can always have it for breakfast."

Robin laughed as she struggled with the cork in the wine bottle. "I've had stranger things for breakfast."

Clearly amused, he took the bottle from her and neatly extracted the cork. "How come a capable surgeon like you can't even remove a cork from a bottle of wine?"

"Lack of practice," she said, laughing. "You're a very handy person to have around, do you know that?"

"I'm only trying to impress you," he said with a grin as he handed her a plate loaded with steaming food. Paul picked up the bottle of wine, the wineglasses and his plate and turned toward the living room.

"That window seat really gives this room character, Robin. Did you have it put in?"

Robin set her plate down on the coffee table, then sat cross-legged on the floor as he poured the wine. "No, it was here when I moved in. I love it...it's the perfect place to curl up with a good book."

It was, in fact, Robin's very favorite spot in the whole apartment. There was a sizable recess created by a gable that featured casement windows. A very wide, thickly padded base had been built in to fill the entire alcove, creating a cosy nook overlooking a spectacular view of the city. She had purchased several large decorator cushions for it and liked nothing better than to snuggle up in the corner and watch the clouds go drifting by.

"Whenever my sister comes with her kids, they sleep there. They think it's great."

"Do they come often?"

As before, they slipped into an easy conversation that was often punctuated by comfortable silences. In some ways it seemed as though she had known him all her life, yet in other ways, there was something about him that was very new and mysterious. The attraction she felt for Paul Wilcox was becoming more profound minute by minute, and during the entire meal Robin was very aware of the charisma that seemed to radiate from him.

Picking up some kernels of rice that had fallen on the table, Robin sighed with satisfaction and glanced up at Paul. "Would you like a coffee?"

He was sitting in a big easy chair, his long legs stretched out in front of him, his empty plate balanced on the wide arm of the chair. "No thanks. The wine's great."

She stood up and collected her soiled dishes. "Are you sure you don't want any more?"

Laughing, he held up his hands in a gesture of refusal. "I'm afraid you're stuck with Chinese leftovers for breakfast."

Robin grinned at him as she stacked his dishes on top of hers, then carried them all out to the kitchen. She placed them in the sink, quickly cleared away the clutter and returned to the living room.

Paul had taken off his jacket and vest and was

standing by the window seat, staring out at the glittering skyline of the city by night.

Picking up her wine goblet, she crossed the room to stand beside him. "I think I have the best view in the whole city."

He didn't respond. In fact, he seemed to be so engrossed with his thoughts, he didn't even hear her. After a long silence, he turned to face her. "May I ask you a personal question, Robin?" he asked quietly.

Her eyes registered her surprise as she looked up at him. There was only a brief pause before she answered, "You can ask. I won't promise I'll answer."

He stared down at the goblet he held in his hand as he slowly swirled its contents. When he finally looked at her, his face was very solemn. "What exactly is the relationship between you and Dr. Radcliffe?"

Robin's eyes widened as she stared at him in astonishment. Slowly, a faint light of comprehension began to dawn in her mind, and Robin felt hope bud within her. "Are you asking me specifically if there's a romantic involvement?"

Paul drained his glass and set it on a shelf at the end of the window seat, then slowly loosened his tie. His voice was very strained when he spoke. "Yes, that's exactly what I'm asking."

Feeling as though she was poised on the brink of an incredible discovery, Robin tried to still the heady feeling that eddied through her veins. "There's no romantic involvement. Bernie is a very old and special friend."

Exhaling very slowly, Paul Wilcox took the glass

from Robin's nerveless fingers and set it beside his. Then he turned to face her, his intense gaze mesmerizing her, leaving her weak and breathless. A charge of electric tension grew between them, magnetizing them until the anticipation became nearly unbearable.

Very gently, he captured her face in his hands and Robin experienced a surge of galvanizing excitement that pressed the breath from her as he lowered his head. He claimed her lips with a profound tenderness, and his mouth moved thirstily against hers, wakening a depth of emotion that staggered her. The feeling grew and grew, blossoming like a wild exotic flower, leaving her powerless, yet more alive than she had ever been in her whole life.

His hold on her face tightened ever so slightly as with a tremulous sigh, he raised his head and gazed down at her. Robin tried to steady her erratic breathing, but the warmth in his eyes created such a turmoil of emotion in her that it was impossible. A choked sob was wrung from her as he gathered her to him, molding her body tightly against his.

The sensation that a half of her had just become whole swept through her with such intensity that it immobilized her, leaving her dazed and enervated. Cradling her face against his neck, Paul nestled her even closer, and for a long time, they stood silently wrapped in each other's arms, the silence a communication of its own.

Finally, he hooked his knuckles under her chin and gently lifted her face. Taking a deep breath, he smiled down at her, his voice low and husky. "Do you know I've wanted to do that for a very long time?''

Robin was completely captivated by the intimate quality of his voice and she looked up at him, unable to speak. Her breath caught in her throat as she slipped her hand slowly up his neck to the back of his head, her fingers buried in his thick hair. She pressed his head down, and her lips lingered as she kissed the dimple at the corner of his mouth.

Her voice was shaky when she finally murmured, ''I hope you found it . . . satisfactory.''

He laughed softly as he hugged her against him. ''I found it *very* satisfactory,'' he whispered against her hair. Then looping his arms around her hips, he loosened his grip and smiled down at her, a touch of devilment gleaming in his eyes. ''Did you know your friend Bernie came to see me Thursday morning, very concerned about you?''

The dreamy look on Robin's face vanished and was replaced by a frown of bewilderment. ''He did? Whatever for?''

''Well,'' said Paul, his eyes crinkling with wry amusement, ''he thought you were being badly overworked. I had to give him credit for having the courage to face me after the way I've snarled and barked at him lately.'' As he obviously recalled some specific occasion, his smile deepened. ''I felt like bouncing him out of my office, but I managed to keep my cool and hear him out.'' He paused while he brushed back a stray curl that was clinging to Robin's cheek, then continued, his voice soft and sensual. ''I really did believe he had a monopoly on you, and I wasn't very happy about it.''

His unexpected frankness, combined with the caressing tone of his voice left Robin feeling as if she was on a wild amusement ride at the fair.

Her stomach did crazy little flip-flops as she tried to catch her breath. "Sometime," she whispered brokenly, "I'll tell you about Bernie and me."

"Would you mind terribly telling me now?" he asked quietly.

With a touch as light as a feather, she smoothed her fingertips along his lips, then sighed tremulously. "No, I wouldn't mind."

She felt his chest expand beneath her hand as he drew in a deep breath, then kissed her softly on the forehead. "If we're going to talk, I think we'd better put some distance between us. Having you this close is definitely distracting." His lips brushed her temple, then with apparent reluctance, he released her.

Feeling that her legs were going to give way beneath her, Robin sat down abruptly on the edge of the window seat as Paul gathered up the bottle of wine and the goblets. He brought them over to the alcove and set everything on the wide window ledge. Robin slid over and curled up in the corner as Paul stretched out beside her, his back propped against a pile of pillows.

He filled their glasses, then handed her one. "I feel like I've had too much of this already," he said, then took a sip before placing his glass on the ledge.

"But you only had one...."

There was a low throaty laugh as he gave her a long eloquent look. "Don't be obtuse, Robin."

Robin felt as though the room was going into a

lazy spin as he slipped his arm around her and drew her against him, his lips moist and tangy from the wine. A deep aching need within her responded to his pliant, arousing kiss, and she was keenly aware of the masculine body beside her. She felt as if she was surfacing from a bottomless amber pool of golden emotions when he finally lifted his head.

His breathing was ragged when he murmured, "That's the very intoxicating stuff I was referring to." Robin closed her eyes as he gently traced her features with his fingertips, entranced by the feel of his touch against her skin. Spanning her chin with his hand, he held her head immobile as he kissed her again. Her lips parted, her mouth yielding immediately to the pressure of his.

He groaned softly as he pulled away. "You're supposed to be talking to me, not tormenting me."

With trembling hands, Robin set her glass on the windowsill, then looked at him, her eyes dark and misty. Her voice quavered treacherously as she said, "You want me to tell you about Bernie and me."

"I want you," he said pointedly, "to tell me about Dr. Radcliffe."

There was something about the way he said that that made Robin laugh, and she looked up at him, her eyes dancing. "Dr. Radcliffe is really Bernard Winston Radcliffe III in disguise," she began in her very best narrator's voice, "and this is his story."

Paul chuckled, then listened attentively as she told him about her very first meeting with Bernie and the friendship that had developed over the years.

By the time she finished, Paul had smoked several

cigarettes, and between them they had finished the bottle of wine. She was lying with her head nestled on Paul's shoulder, her arm resting on his broad chest, enveloped in his secure embrace.

His breath feathered warmly against her forehead when he laughed softly. "I think I owe Bernard Winston Radcliffe III an apology. I've been giving him one hell of a rough time, you know."

She shifted her head slightly and grinned up at him. "You've been giving everyone a rough time, including me," she pointed out dryly.

He laughed again, then cuddled her closer as he began to stroke her back. "Then I'll have to change my tactics, won't I?"

With a soft smile lingering on her lips, Robin closed her eyes, the warmth of his embrace seeping through her like a drug. Through the open window, a cool evening breeze fanned across them, carrying with it the soft sweet fragrance of spring.

CONSCIOUSNESS SLOWLY PENETRATED Robin's slumber, and she stirred drowsily, aware of a warmth that wrapped her in a deep feeling of contentment.

Sighing softly, she stirred again and the warmth seemed to enfold her more securely. She nearly succumbed to the invitation of sleep, but a steady distant rhythm penetrated her mind, intruding on her soft drifting state.

Recognizing the slow throb as a heartbeat, she momentarily felt oddly disoriented, then she remembered and came sharply awake. It was morning—and she was cradled firmly in Paul Wilcox's arms, her head nestled comfortably under his chin. The feeling of confusion was quickly followed by stunned surprise, the progeny of the two turning into old-fashioned dismay. How could she have actually fallen asleep on him? How could she have been so...?

"I would give everything I own to know exactly what you're thinking right now, Robin Mitchell," Paul commented, his voice laced with laughter.

Robin's response was instantaneous. Jerking her head back she looked up at him with wide eyes. "How long have you been awake?" she asked, her voice husky with sleep.

There was a smile working its way around his mouth when he responded. "About a half an hour, I suppose." Tapping the end of her nose with his forefinger, he laughed softly. "Don't look so horrified. By the expression on your face, you'd think you had just awakened with some drunken derelict in your bed."

His hair was tousled and his jaw was dark with a growth of beard, but by no stretch of the imagination could he be classed in that category. He was just too attractive. Smiling, she asked pointedly, "Just for the sake of clarification, how much wine *did* you have to drink last night?"

"Not enough to turn me into a derelict, but enough to say to hell with propriety."

Robin laughed again, then rested her head on his shoulder and idly rasped her thumbnail across his stubbled chin. "I didn't mean to fall asleep on you last night, you know."

"I know. I could have left if I'd wanted to."

She slipped her arm around his chest, and it was only when he drew the afghan up over her shoulders that she realized they were snuggled under the knitted blanket that had been lying in the corner of the window seat the night before.

"Did you cover us up?"

"No," he responded with dry amusement, "it was some old wino who staggered through here in the dead of night."

She grinned and jabbed him lightly in the ribs. "Don't be difficult." He laughed, then kissed her on the forehead as he nestled her closer.

"Would you like some breakfast?" she asked.

"Not if you're going to feed me the rest of the Chinese food."

"Then how does bacon and eggs sound?"

"Tolerable."

She started to ease away from him but his hold on her tightened. "There's no rush, Robin," he said softly as he brushed back her disheveled hair.

Robin was more than willing to remain where she was. The weight of his arms around her back, the lingering scent of his after-shave, the warmth of his body hypnotized her with a tranquil feeling of well-being. Closing her eyes, she shut her mind to all else as she savored the serene intimacy and the unblemished contentment of the moment.

It was quite some time later when Paul shifted slightly and looked at his watch, then sighed. "As much as I hate to, I'm going to have to go. I have a surgery at nine."

"What time is it now?"

"Quarter to eight."

Lifting her face, she kissed the smooth skin of his neck, then reluctantly eased out of his arms and propped herself on one elbow. "I'll fix you something to eat before you go."

With a provocative touch, he smoothed his hand slowly along her shoulder and up her neck until his thumb hooked under her jaw. "I'd better go. I'll have to go home and have a shower and change," he murmured, his eyes reflecting his unwillingness to leave.

His sensuous mouth was so very tempting, so enticingly near that Robin longed to lean over and kiss him, but she took a shaky breath instead. "There are some disposable razors in the drawer of the bathroom vanity, and there's a new toothbrush in the medicine cabinet. I'll have breakfast ready by the time you've had a shower."

His long fingers caressed the sensitive hollow behind her ear, and the tranquility gave way to a breathtaking silence. His gaze was fixed upon her, and Robin felt as if he was absorbing her with his dark seductive eyes. Her heartbeat quickened, and his unwavering stare intensified as he felt her pulse accelerate beneath his sensitive fingers. There was a spellbinding intimacy building between them, drawing them together with a powerful force. Robin wanted desperately to submit to it, but now was not the time.

She took another deep breath, then whispered shakily. "It would save you time—unless you're going to suddenly assume the role of a very proper gentleman."

His eyes crinkled disarmingly as he smiled that slow, disturbing smile. "With your ruined reputation already on my head? I don't think so."

Her laugh was husky as she caught his chin and gave his head a gentle shake. "My reputation may be in tatters, but I'm not going to ruin yours—and it will be ruined if the punctual Dr. Wilcox is late for surgery."

He chuckled, then ruffled her hair playfully and kissed her soundly. His eyes sparkled as he caught her around the waist and lifted her off the window seat as he stood up.

Robin found herself smiling as she prepared breakfast. The revelation that Paul had assumed there was something more than friendship between her and Bernie had certainly explained his odd behavior during the past few days. She said a silent little prayer of thanks that Paul Wilcox was the type of person who confronted a situation. If it hadn't been for his directness, a silly misconception might have ruined everything. That thought was more than a little disconcerting.

Her feeling of well-being didn't last very long, however. As she puttered away in the kitchen, Robin started thinking about her breach of convention the night before, and the more she thought about it, the more uncomfortable she became. How, exactly, did Paul interpret the incident?

By the time Paul entered the kitchen, Robin was so convinced he would have the wrong impression that she had difficulty in meeting his gaze. Though she tried, she could not think of the words with which to tactfully explain.

Leaning against the fridge, he silently studied her for a moment, then he straightened up and came toward her. His grip on her shoulders was firm as he turned her around and gently raised her face.

"Don't make an issue out of something that isn't one, Robin," he said quietly. "You were dead on your feet—falling asleep is no big crime." His voice softened as he massaged her shoulders with strong fingers, his touch turning her to butter. "I was flattered to think you trusted me enough to do that." His mouth lingered briefly as he kissed her, then he laughed softly as he turned her toward the stove. "I'll forgive you for falling asleep, but there's no way I'll forgive you if you burn my breakfast."

The meal was one of those quiet homey interludes that made Robin think of her mother and father and the warm secure relationship they shared. She tried to dismiss that dangerous line of thought from her mind, but it kept hovering in the background like an illusive melody.

Robin had just sat down after refilling their coffee mugs when Paul covered one of her hands with his. "I've made another commitment for today, but I'd like very much to spend tomorrow with you, if you're free."

"I'd like nothing better," she answered, her voice treacherously low-pitched. That look in his eyes seemed to hypnotize her whole body, even her vocal cords, she thought with a touch of bemusement.

He smiled at her, his thumbs inscribing tormenting little circles in the palm of her hand. "There's some truly beautiful country southwest of the city that we could explore. We could pack a picnic lunch and spend the day.''

"I'd love it."

"I'm very glad to hear that," he said as he smiled at her with that disturbing smile that left Robin feeling decidedly weak.

CHAPTER FOUR

THE NEWLY BUDDED LEAVES of the huge old cotton-
wood tree rustled in the breeze as Robin sat gazing out
at the pastoral scene before her, her back propped
against the rough trunk.

Springtime had transformed the usually bleak and
barren foothills, bringing them to life with verdant
lushness. The treeless hummocks of the rolling range-
land humped off to the eastern horizon like a herd of
green prehistoric creatures, while to the west, the Liv-
ingston Gap folded open, revealing the breathtaking
splendor of the mountainous wilderness. Virgin
forests of towering spruce and pine nestled against
the rugged magnificence of the snowcapped Rocky
Mountains, their craggy peaks shadowed with purple
and gray.

The silver sparkling ribbon of the Old Man River
wound its way through the rough terrain, brilliances
of sunshine rollicking gaily along its crystal clear
waters as it tumbled along its flat rocky bed.

The gentle wind ruffled through Robin's hair, carrying with it the earthy fragrance of sun-warmed soil,
the scent of spring grasses and the freshness of clean
mountain air. And overhead, a lone golden eagle
wheeled and soared on the warm air currents of the

bright blue, cloudless sky, its graceful flight magnifying the silence, the solitude, the serenity.

Sighing with contentment, she gazed down at the man who was stretched out on the blanket, his dark head cradled on her lap, his breathing deep and even. His long lashes fanned against his cheeks, his sensuous mouth parted in sleep.

With infinite tenderness, she brushed back a lock of hair that had fallen across his forehead, then rested her hand lightly against the back of his head.

Robin had certainly had her share of male companions over the years, but there had never been another man who had affected her as Paul had. In fact, her feelings for him were deepening at an alarming rate. Absently, she slowly combed her fingers through his thick hair, her face pensive. He had unlocked extraordinary feelings of awareness, and the impact of those feelings had shaken her to the very core. And it went much deeper than simple sexual attraction—much deeper.

Sighing restively, Paul stirred against her, and Robin gently stroked his head. He quieted beneath her soothing touch, and she smiled down at him, her gaze soft with tenderness.

Taking a deep breath to ease the heady anticipation that stirred in her, Robin tipped her head back against the trunk of the tree. The breeze feathered her hair across her face and she brushed it back, then shifted her position slightly, careful not to disturb him. She crossed her ankles, then lightly rested her left hand on his broad chest. As she felt his steady heartbeat beneath her palm, the recollection of awakening in his arms flashed into her mind and she smiled in amusement. At least this time, *he'd* been the one to fall asleep.

"A penny for your thoughts."

"You can have them for nothing," she said, laughing as she glanced down at him. "I was just thinking that falling asleep must be an occupational hazard."

He laughed as he covered her hand with his. "It seems to be." Lacing his fingers through hers, he inhaled slowly. "It feels so damned good to be able to relax and forget about work for a while."

"You have so much responsibility, Paul. I don't know how you cope with the pressure."

"There are times when I question my sanity." He stared lazily off into space for a moment, then he looked up at her. "Dr. Radcliffe assisted me in surgery yesterday morning. He's a fine surgeon." Paul suddenly chuckled, his eyes dancing.

"What's so funny?" Robin asked.

"When we came out of OR, I complimented Bernie on the excellent job he had done. I don't think he would have been more flabbergasted if I'd held a gun to his head."

Robin laughed. She could plainly picture the look of openmouthed shock on his face. "Poor Bernie. He's been so conditioned to you growling at him lately that he's probably totally confused by your change of attitude."

"You think Bernie was confused," he said pointedly, as his hold on her hand tightened. "I was going in circles."

Laughing softly, Robin stroked his hair, then

nestled his head against her. "Serves you right for making assumptions."

A reminiscent grin appeared on his face as he glanced up at her. "I thought I had everything sorted out until that day in the cafeteria. He was so taken by that new nurse, and you seemed to think it was so funny. But it didn't really dawn on me that I might have come to the wrong conclusion until he canceled that dinner date."

"Just out of curiosity, how did you arrive at that conclusion in the first place?"

There was evidence of a wry smile tugging at the corners of his mouth when Paul slanted a slightly sardonic look up at her. "Haven't you ever tuned in to the hospital gossip mill?"

Rolling her eyes heavenward in an expression of distaste, Robin snorted. "Frankly, I pay very little attention to the rumors that are circulated. How facts can end up being so distorted is unbelievable."

Paul laughed. "Well, the facts about you and Bernie were certainly distorted."

There was a wicked sparkle in her eyes when she grinned down at him. "Well, if it's any consolation, our new chief of surgery has all the gossips buffaloed. No one has been able to ferret out one iota of personal information about him, and it's driving them all crazy."

"Good," he said with blunt satisfaction. "I learned a long time ago how to play their game."

Something about how he said it, the touch of resentment in his voice, recalled the incident over Alice Johnson's engagement to Robin's mind. On more than one occasion, she found herself mulling over the possible reasons for his reaction that day. As she reflected on it again now, she was unconscious of the fact that her expression had become very thoughtful. She couldn't help but wonder what had happened in Paul's past to. . . .

"What is it, Robin?" he asked quietly, propping himself up on one elbow.

Her gaze was unwavering and solemn as she stared at him for a moment, then she said, "Would you mind if I asked you a personal question?"

"Like what?"

A small frown appeared as she glanced away, uncertain about the wisdom of prying into his personal life, especially when he made such a point of protecting it.

"Robin?"

She inhaled slowly, then met his questioning gaze. "Were you married at one time?"

He sat up and draped his arms across his flexed knees as he watched her with penetrating eyes. "No. Why do you ask?"

Robin would have preferred to drop the subject, but there was something about the set look on his face that told her he was *not* prepared to dismiss her question.

A flutter of nervousness stirred in her stomach. "That day in the cafeteria—when Johnson told us she was engaged. There was something in your expression, something hostile, that made me wonder."

He gazed off across the rolling hills, then sighed, his voice tinged with cynicism when he spoke. "I didn't realize it showed."

"It showed."

He gave her a warped smile. "Apparently." Abruptly he stood up, then reached down and grasped her hand and pulled her to her feet. "Let's walk."

They walked along the rocky edge of the river for quite a distance before he finally broke the silence. "I wasn't very old when I began to realize that marriage was a destructive, hellish existence, Robin. And the older I grew, the more convinced I became."

She glanced up at him and experienced a sinking sensation when she saw how troubled his expression had become. "It isn't always like that, Paul," she countered softly.

He stopped and turned to face her, his eyes darkened with distress. "But it is. Of all the married couples I know, I can't name one who has a solid happy marriage. Not one."

His opinion of marriage so diametrically opposed hers that Robin wanted to disagree with him, but a strong gut feeling told her that now was not the time to press her point.

Her eyes were intent on his as she very seriously considered what he'd said. "Perhaps your viewing of these particular marriages as someone outside the relationship doesn't really give you an accurate insight."

The wind rippled through his dark hair as he bent his head in sober reflection. Very slowly, Paul began walking again, his arm still around her. "I wish that were true, but it isn't. Something changes in a relationship after marriage. I've seen it happen over and over again. Maybe they start taking each other too much for granted. Maybe they stop respecting each other's space. All that I *do* know is after a few years, if it even takes that long, everything starts collapsing. And you end up with two people who once cared deeply about each other turning on one another like two vicious animals. Marriage becomes an ugly, twisted trap, and it sickens me.''

Robin thought about her parents and the contented life they'd shared for so long. They'd certainly had their share of disagreements, and there had been some rough spots in their marriage, but they always worked things through. With her arm still around his waist, she leaned against him slightly as she began to absently kick at the loose pebbles on the rocky ground. She seriously examined his point of view. Was Paul not seeing the ongoing growth that she saw? Or was he only seeing the negative side?

She glanced up at him, her eyes earnest. ''But marriages do survive, Paul. They aren't all hopeless failures.''

''Yes, they do survive, but for all the wrong reasons. The most common being that there are kids involved and the adults stay together, as miserable as they are—and that's the most destructive reason of all. Even if there isn't a divorce, I know what a bad marriage does to a child.'' There was an edge of bitterness in his voice that Robin found very disquieting. She longed to argue with him, but there was something about the intractable look on his face that deterred her.

Instead, she took a different tack. ''Have you ever thought about a family of your own?''

"And risk exposing helpless kids to eventual emotional abuse? No way!" He spoke with such quiet adamancy that there was no questioning his sincerity. That same inflexibility was in his voice when he continued, "I could never handle that kind of destructive breakdown in a relationship, Robin. I'll never marry. Never."

He said it with such unwavering conviction that she realized he had given the matter considerable thought. He meant what he said; there was no question in her mind. She stopped and gazed up at him, her eyes solemn. Her hair was whipping across her face, and he brushed it back with a lingering gentleness that made Robin ache inside. As she gazed into his troubled eyes, the ache intensified. This complex sensitive man had been badly scarred, and she was suddenly filled with an anger that shocked her.

Her fingers were trembling as she reached up and tenderly caressed his cheek. With a ragged sigh, he drew her against him, and she again slipped her arm around his waist. With his arm firmly around her shoulders, they continued to stroll along the river.

After they walked a fair distance in silence, she sensed that his intentness was becoming less acute, and she tried to gently reason with him. "Sometimes people get married for the wrong reasons, and there's no solid foundation for a lasting relationship, no matter what."

"I know. It makes me shudder to think of the number of guys I know that jumped into marriage simply because the girl had a terrific body, and it was the only way to get her into bed."

Robin shot him a scornful look that spoke volumes. "Well, if that's the only criterion they used for selecting a wife, they richly deserved everything they got!"

Paul laughed and hugged her against him. Still smiling broadly, he stopped and draped his arms across her shoulders. There was a truly devilish sparkle in his eyes as he said, "After that comment, I suppose you'll slap my face if I say that you have a terrific body?"

Robin could feel a hot flush stain her cheeks as she slanted a disdainful look up at him. "I should wash your mouth out with soap. . . ."

"Somehow, you didn't impress me," he said with the same wicked sparkle in his eyes, "as the type of woman who'd blush."

"I didn't used to be," she retorted sharply.

For some reason Robin's answer delighted him and they stood smiling at each other, the spring sun beaming down on them, caressing their faces with its warmth.

Finally he loosened his hold on her and grinned down at her. "Do you want to turn back?"

She shook her head. "Let's see what's around the bend in the river."

Reaching a steep rocky bank that had been carved away by an ancient river channel, they scrambled up it and surveyed the scene before them. They were standing on a craggy peninsula of land that thrust out into the sparkling waters like a pointed finger. Just below them, a sun-dappled sandy cove nestled against the bank that was crowded with poplar and spruce. Above the green of the towering trees, the snow-crowned mountains provided the picturesque background for a scene so magnificent, so beautiful that it took Robin's breath away.

She stood quietly absorbing the perfection of it for a moment, then she murmured absently, "This would be a great spot for trout fishing."

Her words jolted Paul out of his reverie, and he looked at her with a mixture of skepticism and amazement. "Don't tell me I've uncovered a woman who doesn't turn up her nose at fishing!"

Robin laughed. "Not this one. I love it."

"Saints be praised," he said in a tone of voice that bespoke a miracle.

"It's my father who should be praised, if you want the truth. Mom hated it. She loved to go along with dad, but there was no way he could ever get a fishing pole in her hand. Dad liked company, so from the time I could walk, he hauled me along with him."

Paul was grinning broadly as he grabbed her hand and dragged her along as he started striding back in the direction from which they'd come. Robin tripped over an exposed root and staggered along haphazardly until she managed to regain her balance.

"Are you trying to kill me?" she demanded as she scrambled beside him.

"You and I," he said with resolution, "are going fishing."

"But I don't have a license...."

"Well, I do—and we're going fishing."

"If the game warden catches me fishing without a license, he'll impound your gear...."

"Don't make excuses, Robin Mitchell, or I'll think you've been stringing me a line."

"Was that supposed to be a pun of sorts?" she gasped breathlessly as he towed her down the embankment at a breakneck speed.

"You can read it anyway you like. You and I are going fishing." She had to give him credit. He *did* catch her before she fell headlong down the remainder of the rocky slope.

"You *are* trying to kill me," she accused, her breathing labored. "It must be well over a mile back to where we parked—then all the way back here—I'll be dead for sure."

"We'll drive," he said indulgently as he pulled her along. "Come on."

By the time they arrived back at the tree where they'd left the blanket, Robin's face was flushed with exertion. She was about to flop down and catch her breath but Paul, anticipating her intentions, snatched up the blanket. "Oh, no you don't." He aimed her toward the path. "If I let you stop now, I'll never get you moving again."

"You're as bad as my father," she moaned as she reluctantly followed him. "Show him a good fishing hole, and he turns into a raving lunatic."

He was grinning as he helped her up the steep incline to the road. "Quit crabbing, woman." Paul more or less dumped her inside the cab of his four-wheel-drive truck.

When he picked her up that morning, Robin had expected to find the Jag parked outside, but instead there was the Bronco. Apparently it was a fairly recent acquisition for him. He had become acquainted with some of the vast tracts of wilderness area west of Calgary and had fallen in love with the country. And a Jaguar was not the vehicle for that kind of rough driving.

She gave him a dubious grimace as he started up the vehicle and aimed it down the steep incline. "You really believe in endangering life and limb, don't you?"

"Would you rather walk?" he asked bluntly.

"No, I don't want to walk. But I don't want to die, either."

"Hang on then," he directed without a single shred of compassion. With a dash of recklessness, they lurched and careered down the precipitous bank to the rocky high-water line of the river. By the time they reached the clearing just above the sandy cove, Robin was certain that every tooth in her head had been jarred loose.

"You're insane," she muttered as she climbed out of the truck.

Paul made quick work of hauling his gear out and laying it on the blanket. As he assembled his rod and reel, Robin sorted through his tackle box.

"This is a mess. Everything's tangled together."

"I don't doubt it. I imagine it was tossed around a fair bit when I moved. Can you find a decent lure?"

"Depends on what you want. Are you going after trout, or are you going after grayling?"

"Grayling? In Alberta?" he asked in a tone of voice that questioned her sanity.

She made a face at him, then grinned. "Well, they

aren't really grayling, but everyone in this part of the country calls them that. They're really Rocky Mountain whitefish.''

"Never heard of them. Are they any good?''

"They make great eating. They're bottom feeders, so you'll need either live bait or wet flies.''

"Let's see if they're biting. There should be some flies in that bottom compartment.''

Robin found the lures and handed him one. She watched him as he attached it and a small lead weight to his line. Her father would give his soul for Paul's top quality gear—the reel alone was worth a small fortune.

He flashed her a smile. "All right. Let's see what happens." Stepping out on a slab of rock, he studied the currents, then with an easy fluid motion, he sent the line arching out over the water in a long sweeping cast. It was beautiful.

"Not bad," said Robin.

She could see the dimple at the corner of his mouth twitching as he slowly reeled in his line. "Does that mean I'll pass?''

Nodding her head in approval, she laughed. "Yes, you'll pass." She sprawled out on the warm sand, her arms braced slightly behind her to support her weight.

For several moments she watched him, then finally she said, "I think you're going to have to cast farther upstream. I think there's probably a hole right in line with that big tree on the opposite bank.''

"Robin," he said with exaggerated patience, "there are two hundred big trees on the opposite bank. Could you be a little more specific?''

She grinned as she scrambled up. Dusting her hands off on her jeans, she walked over to him.

There was a challenging look on his face as he handed her the rod. "Okay, smarty. Do your stuff."

Robin tested the flex of the rod, then smiled up at him. "What will you do if I pitch it all in the river?"

"I will," he said with certainty, "pitch you in after it."

"Thanks." With an expert snap of her wrist, Robin sent the lure zinging out across the water. She could barely suppress a look of smug satisfaction as the bait plopped exactly where she wanted it to. "*That* big tree," she said as she handed him the fishing rod.

There was a gleam of admiration in his eyes and a tone of reverence in his voice when he said, "Well, I'll be damned!"

Between them, they landed four fish in half an hour and then argued briefly over who would clean them.

Finally Robin said, "This is really silly, you know. Two highly trained surgeons fighting over who's going to clean four little fish."

Paul laughed as he rammed the handle of the fishing knife into her hand. "My feelings exactly. You do it."

Robin narrowed her eyes at him menacingly, but her withering look misfired into laughter. "If I clean them, you have to cook them."

"You're on."

By the time she had them cleaned and washed, Paul had a fire pit built and a small bonfire going. He produced a blackened and battered frying pan from the back of the Bronco, and in no time at all, the fillets were sizzling in butter over the open fire. Robin had packed an ample picnic lunch, and with appetites whetted by fresh air and exercise, they devoured a good portion of it.

After they finished eating, they loaded the picnic hamper and the cooler back in the truck. Picking up the fishing rod, Robin headed to the water's edge to try her luck again. But she didn't even get a nibble.

Paul sat watching her with his back propped against a fallen tree as he smoked his cigarette. "You've lost your touch, Mitchell," he observed after several casts.

"I wish we had some marshmallows."

"I suppose no picnic is complete for you without roasted marshmallows."

"Not to eat—for bait."

"I think you've had too much sun," he said, his tone significant.

She stuck out her tongue at him, then cast again. "No. It really works. You hook a little chunk of marshmallow on your lure. Fish aren't very bright, you know. They think it's a maggot."

Flicking his cigarette into the water, Paul stood up and came toward her, a grimace of distaste on his face. "I will *never* eat marshmallows again."

She laughed as she began reeling in her line. "Don't make it sound like such a sacrifice."

Draping his arm across her shoulders, he grinned down at her. "Do you want to walk farther upstream?"

The lure broke from the water and Robin tightened the line, then set the lock on the reel. "Not really. I'm basically lazy. I'd rather lie in the sun and let all those calories I ate at lunch turn into fat."

Paul laughed, and she felt the same eddy of pure pleasure she always experienced when he did. His laugh was such a delight to hear—deep and throaty, with a rich musical quality to it. It made her feel warm all over.

They walked back to where the blanket was spread out on the sand. It wasn't until Robin went to lay the fishing rod down that she realized the little barbed hook was snagged in Paul's shirt.

She couldn't suppress her amusement as she worked the barb free. "Well, at least I didn't come away completely empty-handed. I did manage to hook you."

Paul was watching her with dark intense eyes. "Yes, Robin," he murmured huskily, "you certainly did."

That look stunned her, almost stopping her heartbeat. Everything seemed to be suspended, then her pulse began to hammer with anticipation as Paul took the fishing rod from her hand and dropped it on the sand. He framed her face with his hands, his fingers thrust into her wind-blown hair. She swayed toward him, drawn to him by his compelling gaze.

The breathless, intoxicated feeling came flooding back as she rested her hands on his chest when he finally possessed her mouth with a moist kiss. The strength drained out of her, leaving her helpless as the kiss became more provocative. His mouth moved searchingly against hers, drawing forth a swell of emotions that were as heady as warm wine.

Slipping her arms around his neck, she moved against him, and he enfolded her in a powerful embrace. The heat and the strength of his body seemed to encase her like a protective cocoon. His hold on her never slackened as he pulled her down on the blanket. She moaned softly against his mouth as he stretched out beside her, then pressed her hips tightly against his. The feel of his body molded so closely against hers fired a warmth in her that pulsated through her veins like liquid fire. In her mind, she was conscious of only him as she clasped his head in her hands and returned the ardor of his kiss.

With infinite care, he eased her onto her back as he smoothed his hand up her torso. Whispering her name, he trailed his heated kiss down her neck, sending shivers of pleasure through her body. Then very gently, he cupped her breast in his hand.

The contact was electric, jolting her with a raw current of desire that sent her senses reeling. For endless moments, she was lost to all else but his galvanizing touch as he explored her trembling body. Slowly, so slowly, he was kindling a need in her, a need as old as Eden.

She felt his hands on the buttons of her blouse, and she was filled with an untamed excitement as he brushed back the fabric. He seemed to be bewitched by her as he slowly stroked her naked skin with tormenting lightness.

A sob was wrested from her and she involuntarily arched against him, her body agonizingly sensitive as he caressed the swell of her breast.

With a hoarse whisper, he drew her beneath him, their bodies fusing together like two pieces of hot wax. A throbbing ache pulsed through her as he moved his body against hers, carrying her to heights of desire that she had never known before. With a muffled groan, he claimed her mouth in a scorching kiss that fanned the fire consuming them. Soon, there would be no turning back. No turning back....

Somehow that thought pierced through her consciousness, and Robin fought to gain control. She hung onto him as she twisted her head away, her breath coming in tortured gasps.

Slowly, sanity returned and she managed to whisper brokenly, "No...Paul...no."

She could feel his body stiffen against hers, then abruptly he released her and rolled away. A sickening cold feeling swept through her as she watched him get to his feet and walk away.

Robin rolled onto her stomach and buried her face in her arms as she tried to deaden the unsatisfied ache that knotted her insides. It took a long time before she could find the strength to push herself into a sitting position, and even then she was still trembling so badly that she could barely do up her buttons. Why had she let it go so far? God, what had she done....

"It seems that I misread the signals." There was no mistaking the icy edge of anger in his voice, and she nearly cried out as he caught her chin and roughly jerked her head up. Her anguish was compounded when she saw the look on his face. Crouching down, he stared at her for a moment, his face like granite. "Don't make a big deal out of it," he said, his voice harsh and inflexible. As he continued to watch her, his hold on her slackened, and his eyes narrowed slightly.

She had to say something, to give an explanation—she owed him that, at least, but she didn't trust herself to speak.

Swallowing painfully she managed to whisper. "I'm sorry...I didn't mean...." But there was no way she could continue. The lump in her throat would not permit her to speak. She tried to look away, but his hold prevented it.

"Robin?" His voice had an odd strangled quality to it, and she looked at him, her eyes distressed.

His hands were unsteady as he held her face. "Talk to me, Robin." There was something about his entreaty that made her hurt inside, and she knew she would weep if she unclenched her teeth. A frown appeared on his face as he stared at her, and Robin had the eerie feeling that he could read her mind with that piercing look. And maybe he could—for comprehension slowly dawned on his face.

His voice was very quiet and very gentle when he voiced his conclusion. "You never have, have you, Robin?"

Mutely, she shook her head. For a second, he continued to stare at her, then he swore softly as he gathered her against him. "God, Robin...I'm sorry...I just assumed...."

She took a breath that bordered on a sob as she rested her head weakly on his shoulder. Stretching out on the sand, he braced his back against the weathered trunk of an uprooted tree, then he nestled her body across his. He rubbed her back with slow soothing strokes as he cradled her in a protective embrace. Bit by bit, the charged tension seeped out of her, and she looked up at him, her eyes dark and troubled as he gently caressed her face.

"Don't look like that," he said softly. "It isn't the end of the world, Robin."

"I'm so sorry...."

His smile deepened and his eyes were lit with humor. "Well, I'm not," he said with firm conviction.

Her expression was unsure as she gazed up at him, but his obvious amusement finally drew a weak smile from her. Sighing tremulously, Robin slipped her arms around his waist as he drew up his knees.

"Paul, I feel so...."

He laid his fingers across her lips. "Don't, Robin. I don't want you apologizing for anything." He eased her away slightly so that he could see her face. His voice was rich with a sincerity that made Robin feel like crying. "I never once considered that in this age of sexual emancipation there would be a woman who still valued old-fashioned morals." He nestled her face against the curve of his neck as she felt him take a deep breath. "There was something special about you right from the beginning. A warmth radiated from you, and I was fascinated by it." His lips brushed against her temple as he murmured, "Now I find out there's something more special than ever."

His breath seemed to catch as he whispered her name with a hoarse fervor. Crushing her against him, he buried his face in her hair as a tremor shuddered through him. Robin clenched her eyes shut against the sting of tears as she clung to him with all the strength she possessed.

A surge of magnificent energy welded them together with a devastating force. It went beyond the physical need—far beyond to an ethereal union of mind to mind, soul to soul. It spread within them to reach the splendor of a magical oneness.

THE DAY HAD BEEN GLORIOUS. There were no other words to describe it. Robin experienced a sharp pang of nostalgia that nearly choked her as Paul parked in front of the house. She didn't want it to end—but it was ending. The sun was slipping behind the mountains, its final rays setting the clouds on fire.

She turned to face Paul. Reaching out to smooth her wind-tangled hair, he allowed his hand to rest on her cheek. He just sat there looking at her for the longest time, his face unreadable in the failing light.

"What's the matter, Robin?"

The throaty intimacy of his voice, the warm caress of his touch made Robin feel like warm honey inside, and she had trouble speaking. "It was such a perfect day. I wish it wasn't over."

With a soft smile, Paul leaned over and kissed her, his lips moist and gentle against hers. With a deep sigh, he reluctantly pulled away. "Nothing's over, Robin. Today was just the beginning for us."

His words, spoken with a quiet conviction, filled her with a hypnotizing headiness, and she touched his face with trembling fingers.

Drawing a ragged breath, he closed his eyes as he

pressed her palm against his mouth, sending a shiver of hot and cold pulsing through her.

"I think," he said with a low, husky laugh, "that we'd better get the hell out of here."

Somehow, Robin's saner self managed to take charge of her swimming senses, and she smiled tremulously at him. "I think you're right." She took a deep breath, and when she continued, her voice was just as husky as his. "But I have this problem. All of a sudden, I feel like I'm made out of putty."

Paul laughed and tousled her hair. "I also think," he said decisively, "that we both need very cold showers."

Robin couldn't have agreed with him more. She was still feeling definitely light-headed when she entered her apartment, and the warmth of his arm around her shoulders didn't help the situation, either. Kicking the door shut behind them, Paul pulled her against him, and gave her a deep, scorching kiss that dissolved every bone in her body. She could hardly move by the time he finally released her.

"I am," he said with a tone of firm determination, "going down to the truck and bring up the picnic hamper. You," he continued with a resoluteness that made her laugh, "are going to the kitchen to put on the coffee."

"Yes, sir," she answered smartly.

Paul laughed as he gave her a little shake. "You are going to drive me to distraction, Robin Mitchell!" With that, he turned and left the apartment, and Robin staggered into the kitchen on legs that felt like rubber.

After they had eaten the light meal Robin had prepared for them, Paul led her through the living room to the window seat, where they stretched out. With a satisfied sigh, he nestled her firmly against him, then rested his head on the top of hers. Tucking her knee between his, she slipped her arm around his chest and snuggled against him. Contentment seemed to drape around them like a cozy blanket, and Robin closed her eyes, silently relishing every second of their shared serenity.

A long time had passed when Paul finally spoke. "Can I ask you another personal question?"

She smiled drowsily as she tipped her head back and looked up at him. "If I can ask you one in return."

The laugh lines around his eyes crinkled disarmingly as he smiled at her. "Sounds fair." His face became very serious as he gazed down at her. "How come you never got caught up in the sexual merry-go-round?"

She sat up beside him, her own expression thoughtful as she contemplated his question. "My parents have very specific values. They firmly believe that moral standards are really important—that they give you a sense of self-respect, a sense of worth, a sense of security." There was a pensive air about her as she took his hand in hers and began to absently trace idle patterns on the back of it. "Right from the time we were very little girls, they nurtured those principles in us. They never harped at us about it or threatened us with what would happen. They simply used every opportunity they could to reinforce that kind of behavior."

"There must have been times when you were tempted to stray, though."

"Sure there were. There's always that element of curiosity about sex, but we'd been brought up with the moral view that sexual intimacy was the most profound loving you could ever share. That really made each of us stop and think—that and the fact that none of us wanted to disappoint mom and dad."

"Was there ever anyone special?"

There was a muscle twitching in his jaw, as though he had his teeth clenched together, and Robin sensed that the answer to his question was very important to him.

Her own expression became very solemn as she met his gaze with open honesty. "There was somebody once, but it didn't work out."

His hand tightened around hers, "What happened?"

"I started dating him during my last year of premed. He was a graduate engineer back for his master's degree. When he finished university that spring, he landed a fantastic job with an oil company." Robin's expression became very thoughtful as she recalled that upheaval in her life, and Paul studied her face with unwavering concentration.

She sighed, then continued her story. "He never did understand why becoming a doctor was so important to me. He wanted me to quit and get married. The more he pressured me about quitting, the more I rebelled against his possessive attitude. Eventually, the relationship just collapsed."

"Were you badly hurt?" The tone of his voice was quiet but taut.

Shaking her head, she smiled ruefully. "By the time the last battle had been fought, I was so sick of the situation that I felt nothing but relief."

Very gently, he cupped her chin in the palm of his hand and lifted her face. "No regrets?"

The look she gave him was unquestionably candid. "No. No regrets."

With a sigh that sounded like one of relief, Paul drew her down, then nestled her head on his shoulder. "Good. It serves him right," he said with such a wealth of satisfaction that it made Robin laugh.

"And what about you, Paul Wilcox?"

There was a self-mocking dryness in his voice as his arms tightened around her. "I don't think you really want to know. During my university days, my behavior could best be described as scandalous."

"Anyone special?"

"No, no one special—not until now." He smiled softly. "And you, Robin Mitchell," he said with intensity, "are the most important thing that's ever happened to me."

"Oh, Paul," Robin whispered shakily, but he never gave her a chance to continue.

Her lips parted as he covered her mouth in a deep searching kiss that ignited sunbursts of anticipation in her, obliterating reality. She melted against him as the fever of an aching hunger licked through her veins like wildfire. And it was fire to fire. . . .

The harsh buzz of the doorbell sounded, and Robin froze, the fire suddenly doused by ice-water alarm.

"Robin...."

"It's Bernie," she whispered as she weakly rested her forehead against his. "He has a key for the downstairs door...."

Paul groaned, then with a throaty laugh, he raised her into a sitting position. "It seems you were saved by the bell, so to speak."

They could hear Bernie running up the stairs, and Robin stared at Paul, her eyes wide with dismay. She was really shaken, and it showed. "I can't let him in...not with you here...."

Taking her face in his hands, Paul said quietly, "Do you trust him?"

"With my life," she said simply.

"Then that's good enough for me." He kissed her soundly, then grinned. "You'd better open the door before he knocks it down."

Bernie was in such a state that he never noticed that Robin was in a bit of a state herself. "Robin—God, I've been trying to phone you all day. Where in hell have you been? I've been going nuts. I have to talk to you before I come right out of my tree. I-iieee...." His voice trailed away to a dumbfounded squeak, and his eyes widened until they looked like saucers behind his thick glasses. A thunderstruck paralysis rooted him to the spot as he stared openmouthed at Paul Wilcox. Like a man in a trance, he turned to stare dumbly at Robin. His mouth worked, but no sound came out, then all the air rushed out of his lungs as though someone had just punched him in the stomach.

He looked as if he had suffered the shock of his life as he stammered, "Hell, I'm sorry...I didn't know...I'll call you later...." His face turned scarlet, and he looked as if he would like nothing better than for the floor to open up and swallow him. He muttered something else, then turned to go.

Robin blocked his path, her face animated with humor as she gave him a hug. "You aren't going anywhere, Bernie Radcliffe. You're going to come in and have a coffee with us...." She peered at him closely and added, "Or something stronger. Then you're going to tell me what has you in such a panic."

Bernie stared at her for several seconds with the stupefied look of a stuffed owl, then he swallowed. "I think I forgot."

Paul laughed as he came toward him. "And here I always thought you had a cool head in a crisis, Radcliffe."

Bernie shook his head as if to clear it, then his face relaxed into a broad grin. "Crisis I can handle. It's this feeling that I've just been struck by lightning that leaves me a little stunned." He gave Robin a hopeful look. "You did say something about something stronger than coffee, didn't you?"

"I did. Follow me."

By the time Robin had fixed each of the men a drink, Bernie had completely recovered his equilibrium, and he sat hunched at the end of the table, his eyes riveted on her.

As she sat down at the table, he rocked on the back legs of his chair, an unholy gleam in his eyes. "Can I ask you something?" he stated.

Paul and Robin exchanged amused glances, then she gave him a blank look. "No."

"How long has this been going on?" he asked, blatantly ignoring her response.

"Drop dead, Bernard."

The sparkle in his eyes intensified. "I very nearly did."

Both Robin and Paul laughed, and Bernie grinned. Then he pursed his lips together as he squinted at some unknown spot on the ceiling. He was obviously sorting out something in his mind, and he kept bobbing his head as if satisfied with his deductions.

Robin knew that look. Bernie was doing his wise-man-of-the-mountain routine. She smiled. Paul, however, managed to remain poker-faced, except for the telltale twitching of the little dimple at the corner of his mouth.

"Do you know, Dr. Mitchell," said Bernie in a theatrical, sermonizing tone of voice, "that the grapevine at the hospital has us involved in a very steamy affair?"

She grimaced with amused distaste. "Not with each other, I hope."

With a broad grin splitting his face, Bernie let the chair slam down on all four legs. "Disgusting thought, isn't it? It would be like having a relationship with myself." He pushed his glasses farther up his nose and stared intently at Robin for a moment. Then, as though he was musing out loud, he muttered, "I don't suppose that nasty little rumor has anything to do with the unexplainable ire I seem to arouse in our chief of surgery?"

Struggle as she might, Robin could not keep a straight face, nor could she keep a hot blush from coloring her cheeks.

"Seems that you developed a rather bad sunburn all of a sudden," said Bernie with a touch of malice.

Robin flashed Paul a look of helplessness, but he only grinned in response.

"Hmmm," said Bernie with a sagacious nod. "I see."

With a voice nearly strangled by suppressed laughter and unchecked embarrassment, Robin made an attempt to change the topic. "I thought you had a big crisis to talk about when you came thundering in."

With a dispirited sigh, Bernie hunched his shoulders as he rested his arms on the table. "I do. It seems that someone else heard the rumor this afternoon, and she just recommended in no uncertain terms that I should go drown myself. She wouldn't even give me a chance to explain—just tore into me for being such a contemptible bastard for sneaking around behind your back." Bernie gave Robin a weak excuse for a grin. "Ironic, isn't it? She accused me of sneaking around behind *your* back, when in fact you've been sneaking around behind mine."

Robin laughed, then her expression softened into one of genuine concern. "I'll talk to her, Bernie. One way or another, we'll straighten out this whole mess."

He gave her a hangdog look, but Robin knew Bernie too well to be misled. She could detect the sparkle of pure mischief in his eyes. "It isn't fair, you know.

Because of an insane rumor—because of *you*, Mitchell, I've been getting nothing but a hard time.''

Laughter erupted from Paul, and he acceded with a nod. "All right, Radcliffe—I admit it. I owe you an apology."

"You sure as hell do," said Bernie with heartfelt agreement.

Paul and Robin smiled at each other, and Bernie rocked back in his chair, his hands laced across his chest. "I'll be damned," he said. "The gossip scoop of the year, and I have to—"

"Sit on it, Bernard," Robin commanded bluntly.

"Sit on it," he relented with a woeful look of disappointment, then he twisted his face into a menacing leer. "Who knows, Robin. Maybe there's hope for you yet."

Not much hope, Robin thought dismally. *I'm falling very hard and very fast for a man who thinks marriage is a trap.*

CHAPTER FIVE

CLOSING HER EYES, Robin stretched out in the steaming tub and let the delicious liquid warmth seep through her. Her thoughts rambled at will, and the recollection of her infamous dinner party the night before focused in her mind. She smiled to herself as she silently cursed Bernie.

In an attempt to solve his dilemma, Robin had gone over to the hospital Monday afternoon and persuaded Lisa Gordon to go for coffee with her. Lisa had been very withdrawn and very pale until Robin explained that there wasn't one shred of truth in the rumor about Bernie and herself. The nurse had stared at Robin for a moment before a stricken look swept across her face. She had, apparently, been quite cutting with poor Bernie.

To try to straighten out the whole mess, Robin had invited the younger woman to dinner that evening, deliberately neglecting to tell her that Bernie was also receiving an invitation. After contemplating the situation further, she called Paul and asked him as well. She told him that she would certainly understand if he elected not to attend.

Robin had definite misgivings about the wisdom of his coming at all—she really wanted him there, but she realized that exposing their association to anyone other than Bernie meant running a risk, and she did not want Paul to be the target of any gossip.

If it ever leaked out that they were seeing each other, it would be circulated on every ward, in every OR, in every staff room. And she guessed that Paul had less tolerance for the gossipmongering than she did.

As it turned out, her anxiety had been for nothing. After half an hour in the presence of Lisa Gordon, Robin intuitively knew that the girl was a highly principled person who would never stoop to any kind of sensationalism.

When Bernie and Paul arrived, it was very apparent that the young nurse had been caught completely off guard. On one hand, there was the young doctor to whom she had administered a blistering tongue-lashing, and on the other, there was the imposing presence of the chief of surgery.

Bernie was in rare form, however, and before too long he had them all in near hysterics. Her carefully prepared dinner had rapidly turned into a three-ring circus as he proceeded to foul everything up with his impersonation of a slightly intoxicated Swedish chef. And Robin, helpless against his wild antics, ended up laughing until she had tears in her eyes. In spite of the slightly mutilated food, the evening had turned into a roaring success.

With a smile still hovering around her mouth, Robin began to absently soap herself. Her world seemed to take on a whole new dimension since Paul had become a part of it. Everything had a new tang to it, a new zest, and she was happier than she'd ever been.

With a contented sigh, she relaxed against the sloped end of the big old tub and considered what she'd wear that evening. Paul was going to try to get away from his office right at four, and they were planning on driving to Banff for dinner.

The jangle of the phone interrupted her musings, and with a muttered oath, she scrambled out of the tub. Snatching up a towel, she dashed into the bedroom, leaving a trail of soggy footprints on the carpet.

Catching it on the second ring, she gasped, "Hello."

It was Paul, and he sounded absolutely furious. "We're going to have to change our plans for tonight, Robin." She experienced a twinge of alarm. There was an unnerving harshness in his voice as he continued, "My parents just arrived in town unexpectedly and I have to sign some papers my father brought. I told them I had plans, but they insisted I bring you along."

"That's fine...."

"Damn it," he snapped, "it's not fine."

The small twinge of alarm grew into a very large knot of uneasiness, and Robin sank down on the bed, completely confused by his anger.

"I'll pick you up around eight," he snapped.

"Paul, is there something wrong...?"

"Yes, damn it, there's something wrong. But you wouldn't understand." There was a slicing edge to his voice that unnerved her when he said, "I have to go. I have a patient waiting."

With that, there was a loud click in her ear, and the line went dead. Slowly, Robin replaced the receiver, then sat staring at nothing for the longest time. He was furious and she didn't even know why, but she was left with a nagging uneasiness that for some unknown reason he was annoyed with her.

And it was a feeling she just couldn't shake. In an attempt to override her growing apprehension, Robin deliberately kept herself very busy. She set about doing a number of tedious tasks that she'd put off for ages, went for groceries, and took her car to the garage. But keeping busy didn't really ease her feelings of uncertainty. They just became more and more acute.

It was about seven o'clock when her doorbell rang, and thinking it was the paperboy collecting his monthly fee, Robin grabbed a ten-dollar bill off her dresser and ran down the stairs.

But it wasn't the small sandy-haired boy with a *Calgary Herald* carrier bag draped around his body who was standing at her door; it was one chief of surgery who looked almost as miserable as she felt.

"Can I come in?" he asked quietly.

Her voice had little strength when she answered, "Of course you can come in."

The strained silence that hung between them was so thick it was nearly tangible as they tramped up the squeaky stairs.

The door had barely clicked shut behind them when he caught her around the waist and twisted her around. Raising her head, he winced slightly as he studied her solemn face. His face was drawn, and there was a look of abject regret in his eyes.

"I'm sorry, Robin," he said huskily. "I behaved like a bastard this morning."

"It doesn't matter...."

"It *does* matter." With a dispirited sigh, he gathered her against him, his arms enveloping her in a fierce embrace. "I lashed out at you for no reason at all."

She swallowed hard against the sudden lump in her throat, then whispered, "But there was a reason. You were really upset about something."

Burying his hand in her hair, he nestled her head firmly against his shoulder. "But it had nothing to do with you."

She looked up at him, her eyes beseeching. "Can't you tell me?"

He didn't say anything for a moment, then he released his hold, and taking a deep breath, he gently cupped her face in his hands. There was an unfamiliar tautness around his mouth, and his dark eyes registered an inner conflict.

"After the way I snapped at you this morning, are you sure you want to go out for dinner tonight?"

Her expression was slightly puzzled as she gazed up at him, her eyes intently searching his for an explanation. "Yes, I'll go."

His touch on her face became caressing, then he closed his eyes as he exhaled slowly. When he finally looked at her, the rigidity of his jaw had softened. "It won't be a pleasant evening, and I hate to drag you through such a miserable ordeal. But I guess I'm being bloody selfish because I really want you there with me.''

Sensing that he desperately didn't want to talk about what was troubling him so deeply, but knowing that she was going to find out, Robin smiled at him, her eyes lustrous with tenderness. ''I'd rather spend a rotten evening with you than spend a pleasant one with somebody else.''

''Ah, Robin, Robin,'' he whispered raggedly as he crushed her against him. ''You are so damned forgiving.''

Robin's uneasiness continued to mount. All the way to the hotel where his parents were staying, Paul remained grimly silent. Only once had his expression altered, and that was when Robin appeared in the living room after she had changed. She had on a white slubbed silk suit that was stunning, and his expression changed to one of open appreciation. The remainder of the time, his face was fixed with such disciplined harshness that it made Robin's throat ache.

As they walked through the concrete bunkerlike structure of the underground parkade, Paul held her hand in a tight grip that communicated a deep feeling of dread. But he said nothing. As they approached the rendezvous with his parents, his face became more and more stony, and his hold on her hand tightened. It was obviously going to be a wretched ordeal for him, and Robin couldn't help but wonder why.

It didn't take her long to find out, however. The Wilcoxes were seated at a corner table in the lounge waiting for them. Mrs. Wilcox, who was an extremely beautiful woman, was in her early fifties, Robin guessed. She was perfectly groomed and expensively dressed, but there was a look of such bitter dissatisfaction stamped on her face that it made her appear very brittle.

Paul's father was probably somewhat older than his wife. He wasn't exactly handsome, but he had that same virility that his son possessed, except he had a touch of ruthlessness and a hint of contempt that left Robin feeling cold and uncomfortable.

The introductions had been made, and Paul and Robin had barely sat down before the interaction between his father and mother answered all of Robin's questions—and answered them more effectively than any verbal explanation. They very obviously hated each other, and they didn't give a damn who knew it.

They gave no consideration to the fact that Robin was a stranger to them, or that they were placing Paul in an extremely awkward position. With a vindictiveness that horrified Robin, they set out to humiliate, verbally annihilate and psychologically mutilate each other. As they brutally attacked, each parent made childish attempts to force Paul into taking sides. It was appalling. It was also very revealing.

Paul downed two double Scotches in a matter of minutes, and as the evening ground relentlessly on, he started lighting one cigarette from the butt of another. Robin frantically hoped that the terrible tension would ease when they were ushered into the dining room for dinner, but it didn't. In fact, it worsened.

Under the cover of the table, she unobtrusively

slipped her hand into Paul's. As he laced his fingers through hers in an iron grip, he looked at her with eyes so dark and tormented they were almost black. Right then, she could have happily strangled both of his parents for making his life such a hell.

The only time during the entire miserable evening that there was any change in him was when he returned to the table after purchasing another package of cigarettes. Robin simply couldn't stand the pressure any longer. Knowing full well that she was tossing her high-minded intentions of quitting smoking out the window, she extracted a cigarette from the package. Paul shot her a censuring look, and for a second, she expected him to slap her hand and take it away from her. Then, shaking his head slightly, he gave her an irresistible, lopsided smile as he lit it for her. The sparkle in his eyes intensified as he watched her inhale slowly, a look of pure ecstasy appearing on her face as she thoroughly savored her first cigarette in weeks.

"I hope it makes you sick," he said.

"Ah. . . ambrosia," she breathed with sincere pleasure.

He grinned, and for a moment they enjoyed an intimate exchange of shared amusement.

But that was shattered by Mrs. Wilcox when she snapped sarcastically, "Did your *father* tell you he bought *another* boat?"

And once again, they were caught in the ugly cross fire of a battle between two people bent on destroying each other.

By the time they arrived back at her apartment,

Robin felt totally drained from the nerve-racking ordeal.

Setting the hand brake on the car, Paul sighed heavily and wearily tipped his head back against the headrest and closed his eyes. Compassion surged within her with strangling force. She would sell her soul if she could only erase the lifetime of hurt and emotional abuse that had been inflicted upon him.

Finally, after a long while, Paul caught her hand and pressed it against his lips. He turned his head to look at her. "So now you know," he said in a low voice that was laced with disgust.

"Yes, now I know," she answered softly as she tightened her grasp on his hand. There was a brief silence before she gently asked, "Was it always like that?"

"Always. At least ever since I can remember."

"Why didn't they ever get a divorce?"

Paul snorted sarcastically, "And have their only son come from a broken home?"

Robin shifted in the bucket seat so that she faced him, then she reached out and caressed his rigid face. "But there had to be more to it than that."

"Yes, I guess there was," he acceded with a sigh. "I think each of them was so afraid that the other might find happiness if they split up—and their hate goes so deep that neither of them could bear even the thought of the other being happy."

"That's one damned destructive rationale to use for maintaining a marriage."

"The whole situation is sick. They're the reason I left Toronto. If I had been offered a job in Vancouver, I would have taken it, simply because it was another thousand miles farther away from them and their constant bickering.''

The night breeze ruffled through his hair as he once again leaned his head against the headrest. He pressed Robin's hand against his chest as he gazed blindly into the distance. For a long time they remained silent, bathed in the haloed glow from the streetlights, the quiet marred only by the far-off hum of distant traffic.

With a reluctant sigh, Paul straightened up and released his hold on her. "Come on. I'll see you in."

Without speaking, they walked up to the veranda, and taking the key from her hand Paul unlocked the front door. It wasn't until he handed the key back to her that Robin realized he intended to leave.

She turned to face him. "Come up for a drink, Paul," she implored softly.

"No, I'd better not."

"But why?"

With his hands rammed into his pants pockets, he stood staring at her for a moment, then he stepped into the foyer and closed the door behind him. Taking her in his arms, he gathered her tightly against him, his breath warm against her cheek as he murmured hoarsely, "Because it isn't wise."

She was keenly aware of the hardness of his body as he possessed her mouth with a moist, heated kiss that sent a familiar charge of electric anticipation searing through her, igniting a response in her that was fevered. Her heartbeat increased its tempo, pumping a hot weakness through her body that drained her of all strength. His mouth moved against hers ravenously, and she melted against him, holding nothing from him.

As if pushed beyond the realm of rationality, he clamped her hips against his, then began to slowly move against her in a rhythm that aroused her to a fiery need. Desire—an increasing, scalding desire—boiled through her, setting in motion a passion that she didn't know she possessed as her body responded to his. Primitive emotions consumed them, and they were aware of nothing but the raw hunger that was demanding fulfillment.

Then with a tormented groan, Paul tore his mouth from hers and buried his face in her hair. Her breath was coming in ragged sobs, and Robin was trembling so badly that she would have collapsed if he had released her, but his hold on her didn't slacken as he struggled for control.

"Robin. Oh, Robin," he murmured tremulously against her ear, "that's why I don't dare come up tonight. You are so damned warm and giving, and I simply wouldn't be able to resist you."

Robin stroked his dark head as tears of heart-wrenching emotion slipped out from beneath her lashes. His hands roamed over her back in strong soothing caresses as they held each other until the aching, driving need abated.

With gentle hands, Robin lifted his head and gazed up at him, her eyes swimming with tears. Her voice broke as she whispered, "I love you, Paul. God, how I love you."

His dark eyes searched the depths of hers, then he

inhaled sharply. With a low groan, he crushed her against him in an embrace that was nearly savage. His voice was shaking with emotion when he finally whispered, "I thought this evening would be the worst one I've ever endured, and now you've given me a night I'll remember for the rest of my life."

Robin couldn't respond. Everything she felt for him was suddenly magnified tenfold, and such an emotional storm was raging within her that she was helpless against it. But amid the inner turmoil, there came a central glorious surge, and as that surge swept up, it became a magnificent fountain of pure, soaring joy.

Her eyes were glowing with a radiant happiness as she gazed up at him through glistening tears. No longer were his eyes dark with misery, but instead they were smoldering with a barely suppressed flame that seemed to radiate from him like the heat from a fire. He burrowed his fingers in her hair as he took her face in his hands, his voice low with a deep sincerity. "There aren't enough words to describe how you make me feel. You fill me up, Robin—you make me whole." The look in his eyes softened to warm velvet as he continued, "I didn't think anything like this would ever happen to me." With immeasurable tenderness, he molded her against him as he nestled her head against his shoulder. "I want you, Robin. But above all else, I want to protect you." Slowly stroking her hair, he whispered, his voice as soft as a caress, "That's why I won't come up. I don't dare. Not tonight."

"Paul, please. . . ."

"Listen to me, Robin," he said gently as he continued to fondle her hair. "My need for you goes far beyond the physical thing. Life is so damned sweet right now, and I don't want to spoil it by some rash act. On Friday night, I could have easily left, but I never knew that kind of contentment before in my life. Just being able to hold you while you slept was the most incredible experience for me." His lips brushed against her temple, then he tipped her head back and gazed down at her. "We're going to savor every beautiful moment. It's so special—so damned special." Then with a tremulous sigh, he kissed her, his sensual mouth moving moistly against hers in a poignantly sweet kiss—a kiss that spoke of tenderness and passion; of wanting, but not taking; a kiss that spoke of a deep longing.

With a reluctant sigh, he loosened his hold on her and gently brushed her hair back from her face, his eyes reflecting a deep tenderness.

He kissed her softly, his mouth lingering only a moment against hers, then with another sigh, he held her against his side as he turned toward the stairs. "Come on, love," he murmured huskily, "I'd better get you tucked safely away behind a locked door."

Slowly they climbed the dimly lit stairs, his arm clasped tightly around her shoulders, her arms resting on his slim hips. Once they reached the landing outside her door, Paul turned her to face him, his arms looped around her waist as he gave her a gentle, fleeting kiss. Robin melted against him, her fingers softly caressing his rugged jaw as his mouth moved lightly against hers.

He whispered against her lips, "You do make it so hard for me to leave." He drew away slightly and smiled down at her as he slowly smoothed back a tendril of hair that was clinging to her cheek. "You'd better find your keys before I change my mind."

Robin couldn't marshal her swimming senses enough to think straight and she looked at him helplessly. "My keys?"

His smile broadened as he said patiently, "Yes, your keys." He felt her jacket pocket, then slipped his hand in and retrieved them. With one arm still around her, he unlocked the door, opened it, then pressed them into her hand.

"You can keep those," she whispered, her voice still very unsteady. "I have another set."

His expression changed and became very intense as he stared at her, his eyes smoldering. Slowly he slipped the keys into his own pocket. "Do you have any idea what a temptation those are going to be?"

Wordlessly, she stared up at him, unaware that her eyes revealed how much she longed to have him stay with her.

His eyes darkened, his gaze never wavered from hers, and the pulse in his neck began to throb as he smoothed his hand along her cheek until his fingers were thrust into her thick hair. There was a flutter of expectation in Robin as she moistened her lips, and she pressed against him as his lips sought hers. His gentle kiss turned into a fever of excitement as he provocatively probed her moist mouth with his tongue, and a hot weakness invaded her body as his kiss became more demanding as his own passion ignited. With a low groan, he took a ragged breath as he pressed his face against the curve of her neck.

She could feel his heart pounding wildly beneath her palm as he lifted his head. With his strength supporting her, he drew her inside the apartment and closed the door, all his good intentions forgotten.

The room was lit only by the streetlight in front of the house, and without speaking he guided her over to the window seat. Slipping out of her shoes, Robin moved over on the padded seat as Paul removed his jacket. He whispered her name as he stretched out beside her and gathered her against him in a crushing embrace. She tried to move, but he held her firm, and finally the realization he was holding back penetrated her senses.

"Just let me hold you," he whispered against her hair. She yielded to him, and they hung on to each other until their scalding passion began to ebb.

After a long while Robin stirred, and touching his face she whispered, "I didn't want it to end this way, Paul."

He cradled her head against his shoulder. "It's not the end of the world, Robin." His voice was gentle when he murmured, "I just don't want to pressure you into a decision."

"But you weren't pressuring me."

There was a quiet pensiveness about him as he slowly stroked her hair. "I'm not some hot-blooded adolescent who doesn't consider the consequences, Robin. You mean far too much to me for me to do anything that might ever hurt you."

There was just a touch of wry humor in her voice when she said, "Well, you're not an adolescent, but I'll debate the hot-blooded issue."

Paul's laugh was throaty as he hugged her hard. "Perhaps that was the wrong choice of words." He fell silent for a moment as he absently planted small kisses in her hair. The amusement in his voice was replaced with seriousness when he finally spoke. "I meant it when I said I don't want to pressure you, Robin. If we ever make love, I want it to be a clear-headed, conscious decision for you, not one that you've made during an unguarded moment." His arms tightened around her as he murmured against her temple, "I want you to be sure it's what you really want. Because if we ever do, I'll never be able to let you go—it's going to mean a very deep commitment for both of us—one that could lead to major changes in our lives."

His words were more than a little disturbing. For the first time, Robin realized that she had subconsciously not wanted to be accountable for that decision—she had simply wanted it to happen. But that wasn't the complete reason for her troubled thoughtfulness. There was yet another realization. Paul couldn't be really certain of her, or the depth of her feelings, until he knew she had really made up her mind.

But knowing how deeply he cared for her filled her with an effervescent happiness that bubbled through her like champagne, but that was headier than any wine. And that effervescent happiness bubbled through her long after Paul left.

BUT WHEN ROBIN AWOKE early the next morning, the champagne had lost its sparkle, and she was faced with some cold realities that were sobering. She lay in bed, her hands laced behind her head, staring at the grotesque light fixture on the ceiling.

The evening spent with his parents had been a very disturbing revelation. She had often wondered what, or who, had turned Paul so adamantly against marriage. Now she knew. And the discovery was certainly not a pleasant one. The Wilcoxes' attacks on each other made her think of two deadly snakes coiled to strike—ugly, threateningly lethal and unpredictable.

And Paul. Deep, sensitive, compassionate Paul had to survive in that environment, an environment where the only emotions were demoralizing self-pity and consuming, twisted hate. No wonder he had so bitterly stated that he would never marry.

And where, exactly, did that leave her? She had grown up in a house that had been a real home. It was usually cluttered and untidy, often totally disorganized, but always, always comfortable and relaxed. Her parents' relationship had been filled to the brim with affection and humor, and the five girls had grown up in an atmosphere of caring and sharing, an atmosphere of security and love. And it was the kind of life that Robin had always wanted for herself.

Marriage? Definitely. Children? Most certainly. She wanted a home—a home with newspaper scattered by the reclining chair; kids who left a trail of clutter and laughter behind them; shedding cats that clawed the furniture when no one was watching; a dog who left his nose-prints all over the front-room window. The thought that she might never have that, that it might not eventually become a reality, left her feeling very empty.

The childhood dream of someday being a bride in a fabulous satin-and-lace gown with a sweeping veil was no longer important, but the dream of marriage, with all its ups and downs, was. She wanted to have someone sitting across the dinner table with whom she could share a look of suppressed amusement when a very small daughter said she was going to run away to grandma's, because grandma loved her enough not to make her eat cooked carrots.

She wanted to have someone who, upon realizing he had forgotten their wedding anniversary, would go out in the dead of night, in the pouring rain, and pick a bouquet of bedraggled daisies from her own flower garden. She wanted to have someone for whom she could knit a sweater that was miles too big, but he'd wear it until it was out of shape and full of holes simply because she had taken the time to make it for him. She wanted someone with whom to share that kind of life, but the someone she wanted, beyond all reason, was Paul Wilcox.

With a heavy sigh, Robin rolled over on her stomach and looked at the clock on her bedside table. It was only six o'clock, and here she was, wide awake. She might as well get up; she knew she'd never go back to sleep while her mind was chewing away at such disconcerting thoughts.

The taste of stale cigarette smoke in her mouth made her grimace as she swung out of bed. That was one bridge she'd certainly blasted out from beneath her. She knew that before the day was over, she'd end up marching down to the corner store to buy herself a package.

Going into the bathroom, she brushed her teeth vigorously, mumbling to herself about her lack of self-discipline the entire time. She was just about to step into the shower when her phone rang, and she sprinted across the bedroom to answer it.

"Hello."

"Good morning." The dearly familiar voice, throaty and provocative, kindled a very pleasant warmth that rapidly spread through her whole body.

"Well, good morning," she responded in a husky voice that seemed lower than usual.

"What would I have to do to persuade you to come for breakfast with me?"

Robin had trouble breathing as she answered, "That depends whether it's a lumpy porridge breakfast or bacon and eggs."

She could tell Paul was grinning when he answered, "I think I could manage the bacon-and-eggs variety."

"You're on."

"I'll pick you up in fifteen minutes."

She laughed. "If you do, I'll still be wearing a bath towel."

"Fifteen minutes, Robin," he warned softly, his seductive laugh turning her to jelly. "Bath towels are very enticing, my love."

In spite of the short notice, Robin was sitting on the sagging worn steps of the veranda when the sleek Jaguar pulled up in front of the house. Paul eyed her appraisingly, a scandalous grin on his face as she walked toward him. She had on a deep red tube top with matching slacks and a white linen smock-styled jacket.

"You look sensational, but I must admit I was hoping for the bath towel."

"What do you want a towel for?" she said, deliberately misinterpreting his meaning.

He gave her an eloquent look as she slipped into the car. "For a bright girl, you can be amazingly obtuse."

"Speaking of obtuse—where do you think you're going to get a decent breakfast at this hour of the morning? It's too damned early."

"Well, Robin Redbreast," he murmured softly, his tone intimate, "isn't the early bird supposed to get the worm?"

Robin flashed him a sidelong glance as she tried valiantly to keep from blushing. "You can eat worms if you like, but I'm having something less revolting."

With laughter sparkling in his eyes, he leaned over and kissed her. "You, Robin Mitchell, are definitely addictive."

As on that very first time he gave her a ride, Robin was swept up in the fascinating spell of his eyes. The dark brown irises were flecked with bits of gold and green, and the thick dark lashes seemed to accentuate the intensity of them. They really were gorgeous.

Gently stroking her bottom lip with his thumb, Paul softly asked, "What are you thinking, I wonder?"

In a voice that had little strength, she finally told

him. "Do you know that you have absolutely gorgeous eyes?"

He slipped his hand across her face until his fingers were thrust deep in her hair, his touch sending little shivers of excitement down her neck. His gaze kindled as he read her eyes, and the expression on his face changed abruptly. As though drawn against his will, he drew her head toward him and kissed her again, his mouth searching hers with a warmth that ignited a flame within her.

She could sense his reluctance when he finally eased away. "You're too damned hard to resist," he whispered. Then a smile lightened his eyes. "Do you know you taste delicious?"

With a mischievous twinkle in her eyes, she feathered her fingers across his mouth. "Do *you* know that the milkman is watching us?"

Paul grinned. "Is he really?"

"Yes, he certainly is. He's sitting in his milk truck across the street with his eyes hanging out of his head."

"I hope he ruptures his retinas," said Paul with a touch of good-natured vindictiveness. He released her and settled back in his seat. "Doesn't he know that this isn't a spectator sport?"

Robin laughed. "Probably not. But it *certainly* is participatory!"

Paul gave her a bold and lusty look. "You're living dangerously, Robin Mitchell."

"It's the company I keep."

"I think," he said through clenched teeth, "that we'd better get the hell out of here."

"Aren't you going to wave to the nice milkman?"

"God," he said with feeling as he slipped his sunglasses on. Putting the car in gear, he tramped on the accelerator, sending the powerful automobile lurching away from the curb. He flashed Robin a piratical grin, then turned and raised his hand in a royal salute to the milkman.

Robin was still grinning when she spotted Paul's cigarettes lying on the dash. She reached for them, but he intercepted her hand and snatched up the package.

"Oh, no you don't, woman! I'm not contributing to your habit today."

Robin neatly wrenched them out of his hand as she made a face at him. "Quit acting like my father."

"I have no intention," he said with a meaningful inflection in his voice, "of ever acting like your father."

With him safely installed behind the steering wheel of a moving vehicle, Robin couldn't resist baiting him just a little. "It seems to me that you've managed a fair imitation so far."

Casting her a quick glance, Paul laughed as he accepted the lighted cigarette she handed him. "That could change damned fast, so don't push your luck!" He shot Robin a look of amused rebuke as she lit a second cigarette and inhaled deeply. "You're going to regret that, you know."

"Probably," she answered mildly.

He grinned. "You could at least have the decency to look a little repentant."

"I'll repent tomorrow."

There was a brief lull in the conversation, then Paul said, "I wish like hell that I dared pull you off midnights this week. Our time together is going to be so limited."

She flashed an impish smile at him. "If you *really* feel that way, you could come over every night and cook me dinner."

"Could I now?" he responded with definite interest.

"Yes, you could."

"And when, exactly, are you going to sleep?"

"I usually go straight to bed when I get home, then I don't get up until four or five in the afternoon. If I'm really wiped out, I'll try to grab another couple of hours later in the evening."

He grinned at her, his eyes glimmering with humor. "In that case, you've just acquired a cook, Dr. Mitchell."

"Just what I've always wanted," she said with a delighted laugh. "Do you do dishes, as well?"

"I told you before not to push your luck," he answered dryly.

"You can't blame me for trying."

Paul checked for oncoming traffic before he changed lanes, then grinned at her. "I don't suppose you'd trade your day of lazing around for my three colostomies?"

Shaking her hair back as the wind caught it, Robin laughed. "Not a chance. Not unless I can throw in my upcoming battle with the mechanic at the garage."

"Why, may I ask, are you expecting a fight with a mechanic?"

"In a fit of frustration, I took my car in yesterday. He's going to give me his usual spiel about what a wreck it is and how much work it needs. And then the fight will be on." Her expression was rueful. "He says if it were a horse, he'd shoot it and put it out of its misery."

There was laughter in Paul's eyes when he said, "A humane mechanic—he must be one of a kind. Where does he work?"

She told him, then grinned. "Maybe I could work a trade with him. I'll give him one of your colostomies in exchange for the repair bill."

Paul laughed. "You've been hanging around with Bernie Radcliffe far too long. You've developed a twisted sense of humor."

ROBIN ALWAYS HAD TROUBLE switching her hours around in preparation for her first midnight duty, and today was no different. She lay on her bed in the darkened room trying to empty her mind, but thoughts of Paul and his parents were ineradicable. The Wilcoxes had, with their vicious bitterness and verbal venom, poisoned Paul for life. And Robin was sure there was nothing she could do or say that would change his mind. He would have to experience the warmth and security of a stable relationship before he could perhaps believe there was another side.

And that's where Robin's values interfered. Could she turn her back on him and the intense feelings he aroused in her? Could she turn her back on the morals with which she had been raised? Her intuition gave her a grim warning that no matter what, she was going to be hurt, and hurt badly—because with a man like Paul Wilcox, it was all or nothing.

After two hours of tossing and turning, Robin finally faced an inalterable fact—that if she was forced to make the choice, the choice would be Paul Wilcox, no matter what. She loved him; it was as simple and as complex as that.

It was late afternoon when she finally awakened, but by the time Paul arrived, she had had a quick shower and had dinner started. He had changed from the clothes he'd been wearing that morning into jeans, a plaid shirt and very expensive leather boots. He looked terrific.

Catching her up in a powerful embrace, he kissed her soundly, then smilingly acknowledged the aroma of grilling steaks. "What's the matter? Didn't you trust me?"

"Oh, I trusted you. But I thought I'd take pity on you this once."

His smile broadened. "I spoil very easily, you know."

Robin made a face at him. "That sounds serious—do I have to keep you refrigerated?"

"That's *not* what I meant." He laughed as he hugged her hard.

With their bodies pressed together, Robin closed her eyes as a feeling of intense protective love surged within her, wringing her heart with such force that it was almost frightening. In a few short days, Paul Wilcox had become more important to her than she ever imagined, and she knew she'd do everything humanly possible to make him happy.

His face was still alive with laughter when he eased his hold and looked down at her. Masking the profound emotions that were nearly overwhelming her, Robin managed to smile into his gold-flecked eyes. "If I'm going to spoil you, I'd better be quick about it," she said with a light laugh, "or those steaks will be burned beyond recognition."

What followed was a commonplace scenario that was probably unfolding in thousands of homes in Calgary right then, but for Robin it was very special—having the man she loved seated across the dinner table from her—this was her dream. This, more than anything else in the world, was what she wanted.

It was while they were eating that Paul told her he had started Davy Martin on a regular therapy program.

"How's he doing?" she asked with keen interest.

"It's hard to say. He's really determined, and the patient's state of mind can make the difference." Paul helped himself to more salad, then continued. "He was asking about you. I told him you were on days off."

"I'll stop in to see him tomorrow morning."

"He'd like that." There was a wicked look in his eyes when he said, "He has this tremendous crush on you, you know."

She grinned at him. "I have a crush on him, too. I think he's an absolute doll."

The gleam in Paul's eyes intensified as he offhandedly commented, "I can't say the mechanic at the garage is too fond of you, though."

Robin choked on a bite of food as her head shot up and she stared at him in astonishment. "You went to the garage?" she wheezed.

"I did. And I heard the whole horror story about you and your car."

"Damn him," seethed Robin, referring to the mechanic. "He's so bullheaded!"

"I think," said Paul with a dry look, "that he's not nearly as bullheaded as you are. That car wasn't fit to be on the road." There was a brief pause, then he calmly added, "So I sold it to an auto wrecker."

"You what?" gasped Robin with a look that was a mixture of horror and disbelief. "You *what*?"

"I sold it to an auto wrecker." He folded his arms across his chest and had the nerve to grin at her. "Right now, that hunk of junk should be a neatly compacted cube of scrap metal."

"You can't *do* that. That's *my* car! Damn it, I'll sue that garage. . . ."

"I thought you'd react that way, so I simply forged a bill of sale. As far as the mechanic knows, you sold that thing to me." His grin was so smug it was sinful. "Now what are you going to do, Dr. Mitchell?"

Robin was absolutely speechless. She sat staring at Paul as though someone had just clobbered her on the back of the head with a very large board.

His face grew serious as he said quietly, "Robin, the brakes were shot, the steering was defective, and the transmission was about to fall apart. It simply wasn't safe—and it wasn't worth fixing."

"But I need a car. . . ."

"I know you do."

"I can't afford to buy a new one...."

"I know that, too." He rested his arms on the table and watched her with a penetrating stare. "I can only drive one vehicle at a time. I'd let you use the Jag, but everyone at the hospital knows it's mine. But I've never taken the Bronco to work, so no one will be any wiser."

"But, Paul, I can't do that," she argued, as her mind finally slipped into gear. "It just isn't right."

"I'm not having you careering around town in an undependable jalopy, especially at night. You could be stranded at any time. And you damned well aren't walking, nor are you taking the bus. It's just too risky," he said with a firmness that smacked of bossiness. "Besides, I'd worry like hell, so—you're going to use the Bronco."

"I can't *do* that...."

There was a mulish look on his face, and his eyes were glittering dangerously as he snapped, "If you don't take that damned vehicle, I'm going to bloody well drive you back and forth to work. I will not have you wander around at weird hours of the night by yourself!"

If anyone else had dared to dictate to Robin what she could or couldn't do, she would have exploded like a bomb. But even though she was annoyed, his obvious concern touched her very deeply, completely disarming her vexation, and she sat staring at him, unable to respond.

His face softened dramatically as he came around the table and pulled her into his arms. "I just don't want anything to happen to you, Robin," he explained softly, "so please, just use the damned thing."

Swallowing hard against the sudden ache in her throat, she pressed her face against the soft fabric of his shirt, then spoke, her voice husky, "I'm not your responsibility, you know."

"Yes, you are," he responded firmly. He tilted her head back so he could see her face, his eyes serious. "I want very much to be able to look after you, Robin," he said quietly. "If this wasn't something completely new to you—if this thing between us hadn't happened so fast—I would simply bundle you up and take you home with me for good." His hand was gentle as he softly caressed her cheek, his eyes compelling her to understand. "But it *is* new and it *has* happened fast. I don't want to pressure you. I want to give you all the time you need to think things through. Just remember, I'm waiting for you whenever you're ready." His expression relaxed and he smiled at her, the warm sparkle in his eyes beguiling her. "So in the meantime, humor me, love. And allow me some peace of mind knowing at least you have a dependable vehicle."

She gazed up at him for a moment, her expression solemn and thoughtful, then she smiled tremulously. "Do you always get your own way?"

The laugh lines around his eyes crinkled as his smile deepened. "Usually." His hand slipped to her neck, his fingers caressing her sensitive nape, his tone coaxing. "Will you use it?"

She sighed in capitulation. "Yes, I'll use it."

"Good," he said with such a wealth of satisfaction that it made her laugh.

"You *are* spoiled."

"I told you I was." He gave her a swift kiss, then said, "Let's do the dishes, and I'll take you for a drive."

She gave him a melodramatic look of horror. "You mean you'll actually put *those* hands in dishwater?"

"I'll dry," he said with remorseless candor.

Their drive eventually took them to Fish Creek Park. The park, which bordered the southern edge of the city, encompassed hundreds of acres of land and had been designated a natural urban park by the provincial government. It was a beautiful location, especially the western boundary that terminated at the Sarcee Indian Reserve.

The picturesque valley was heavily treed with towering spruce and pine that were intermingled with poplar. Hand in hand, they strolled along the red cinder path that rambled along the shallow gurgling creek and through dense copses of trees. Sunlight dappled through the boughs, sending little splashes of brightness dancing along the path. The smell of spruce was tangily fragrant, stirred to life by the soft spring breeze, while off in the brush birds twittered their mating songs.

Sprawling out on the grassy bank of the creek, they relaxed as they watched the sunbeams pinwheel along the surface of the clear water, both of them silently absorbing the tranquillity. Eventually, they ambled on until they came to an arched wooden bridge that spanned the creek.

Here the valley had broadened out into a small

grassy meadow lightly bushed with stunted willow and wild rose bushes. Beaver dams across the creek had created a series of ponds, and two dark-haired boys with fishing rods were standing on the muddy bank. Leaning against the high rail of the bridge, Robin and Paul watched them cast for a while, then she shot him a knowing look.

"Itchy fingers?"

He narrowed his eyes at her, then grinned. "I wonder if I could persuade them to let me try my hand."

Just then, a loud dispute broke out between the two boys, and Robin laughed. "Now *that* sounds familiar."

The arguing voices increased in volume, and Robin looked down at the pair, then shook her head, her eyes flashing with amusement. "Kids! Do they ever learn?"

One boy was securely stuck, and the older boy, obviously his brother, was complaining loudly and bitterly as he tried to extract the rubber-booted feet that were being slowly sucked deeper into the mud.

Paul watched the goings-on for a moment, then chuckled. "I think I'd better haul him out before he disappears completely."

"You do that, Sir Galahad," said Robin with a smile. The warm breeze caressed her face as she watched him lope down the curved structure of the bridge and along the bank. Robin rested her elbow on the rail and propped her chin on her hand. Paul tossed the rotted stump of a fallen tree down beside the boy, then walked out on it. He took the fishing rod from the lad's hands, tossed it onto the bank and grasped him under the arms and hauled him out, leaving the rubber boots firmly implanted in the mud.

This should be interesting, she thought with delight as Paul carried the youngster back to solid ground. Extracting those boots from that bog would be no easy task, especially when Paul had to maintain his balance on a wobbly log.

He very nearly did lose his balance, but he somehow managed to retrieve both boots without pitching in. Knocking off the globs of mud that were clinging to them, Paul helped the boy get his footwear back on, wiped his hands on his jeans and picked up the fishing rod. Robin's grin broadened as the two boys and Paul walked farther along the bank to one of the beaver dams. Paul crouched down, apparently untangling the line on the reel, and as two dark heads bent over his, Robin's expression became very sober. It was the first time she'd ever seen him with children outside a clinical environment, and his easy, unaffected manner with the two boys was a new facet of his personality that she hadn't really considered before. It wasn't because he disliked children that he swore he'd never have any of his own; it was simply because he'd had such a miserable, unhappy childhood himself that he was turned off. It was sad, so very sad that he had taken that stance; he would make such a wonderful father. . . .

She dismissed that disturbing reflection and let all the love she felt for him fill the emptiness that her thoughts had created.

Laughter bubbled in her as Paul stood up, and

with an expert cast sent the lure flashing out across the water. He did seem to get his own way with inordinate ease. That damned charm—it worked on everybody.

After a few moments, Paul left the two boys contentedly fishing and started walking back toward the bridge, a broad grin on his face.

Robin went to meet him, her lips pursed in the same expression her mother adopted when she really wanted to laugh, but was trying not to. "Now that you've had your fix, are you feeling better?"

He draped his arm around her shoulders and laughed. "I think I hear sour grapes talking!"

She made a face at him as she slipped her arm around his waist. He glanced at his watch, and Robin spoke before he had a chance to comment. "Don't you dare make a proclamation that it's time to take me home and put me to bed. I'm not going to turn into a pumpkin."

His arm tightened around her shoulder as he relented with a soft chuckle. "All right. Just this once."

They walked on, and Robin reached out to break off a small branch of a spruce tree that was overhanging the path.

They were crossing a little patch of open land when he said, "I've been asked to a barbecue Sunday, and the invitation includes a guest." He glanced down at her, his eyes squinted against the glare of the setting sun. "I know you have your last midnight shift that night, but if you think you could manage it, I'd really like you to come with me."

She tightened her arm around his waist as she smiled up at him. "I should be able to manage it. If we weren't too late getting home, I could always grab an hour or two of sleep." She probed his ribs with her fingers and grinned when she discovered he was ticklish. "I'm on to you, Paul Wilcox. I know you're just asking me out so you won't have to make me dinner that night."

He captured her tormenting hand in his, then laughed. "If you want the real reason for me asking you to come, it's so I'll have a legitimate excuse to arrive late and leave early."

"You're devious." She took a deep smell of the slip of spruce she held in her hand, then said, "It sounds like you don't want to go very badly."

"I don't. It will be as boring as hell, but I'm obligated to go. Keith and I started pre-med together, and we became fairly good friends. He switched to computer sciences during his third year, but we still spent a lot of time together." Paul drew her off the trail to allow a cyclist to pass, then continued. "He and his family moved out here about six or seven months ago, and they've just moved into a new house. This bash on Sunday is a housewarming."

She glanced up at him, her eyes quizzical. "If you're such good friends, how come you don't want to go?"

Paul's voice was infused with disgust when he answered, "He and his wife are nearly as bad as my parents."

Oh, isn't that just dandy, thought Robin grimly. But she kept her voice deliberately light when she said, "Then we'll just arrive late and leave early."

Paul's arm tightened around her shoulders as he smiled down at her. Then he paused, and his eyes became dark and very intense as he gazed at her. When he finally spoke, his voice was low and charged with emotion. "I hope you know how very much I love you, Robin."

Those words, spoken with such intensity, touched her as nothing ever had, and Robin's eyes were glistening with tears when she whispered, "I know."

THE MONOTONOUS RHYTHM of the windshield wipers magnified the strained silence that hung in the air like an unfriendly fog.

Robin sat in the bucket seat of the car, her arms wrapped tightly around herself as she fixed her gaze on the ceaseless and futile motion of the wipers. Every raindrop swept away was instantly replaced by another. They, too, were fighting a losing battle, she thought dismally.

With a weary sigh, she rested her head against the headrest and closed her eyes. The housewarming at the Dennisons' had been such a nerve-racking ordeal from beginning to end.

It had been one of those days when nothing seemed to go right. To start with, Paul had been late picking her up. He had been called in for an emergency surgery, and because of the inexperience of one of the interns, the operation had not gone well. Consequently, Paul had been in a bad mood when he arrived, and that seemed to set the tone for the rest of the day.

To make matters worse, the Dennison home was in

a development of exclusive acreages located in an isolated area about forty miles southwest of the city. Paul had been broodingly introspective during the drive, and he had inadvertently missed a turn. By the time he had discovered his mistake, they had gone several miles out of their way. They were very late arriving, and their hostess, Nicola Dennison, had not been pleased. She hadn't said anything, but the tight-lipped look of exasperation with which she greeted them certainly expressed her annoyance.

Robin instantly felt she was an interloper. She had never cared for large social gatherings to begin with, but she was more uncomfortable than usual. The other guests were quite a hodge-podge. Some were business colleagues of Keith Dennison's, some were members of the exclusive country club to which the Dennisons belonged, others were members of Nicola's bridge club, and a few were neighbors. But no one mixed. They all remained protectively huddled in their secure little cliques as if they were threatened by the presence of a stranger.

Maybe the situation wouldn't have been so bad if it hadn't rained, forcing everyone to remain indoors, but Robin doubted that. Each group seemed wary of the others, creating a strained atmosphere. Everyone was talking too loud, drinking too much, and soon she was fervently wishing she had stayed home and caught up on her laundry.

And Paul's moody withdrawal didn't help the situation, either. She knew that he was still inwardly seething about what had happened at the hospital, but she suspected that his bad temper was being further rankled by the loud, offensive behavior of Keith Dennison. Their host was very drunk, very scurrilous, and some of his comments, especially those directed toward his wife, were downright rude. If Nicola hadn't made a point of telling them she had postponed dinner to accommodate their late arrival, Robin would have suggested that they leave. She had the uncomfortable feeling that the situation was turning into a ticking time bomb.

Unfortunately, she had been right. And to add to Robin's growing edginess, the nasty little scene had started over her.

The guests had served themselves from the sumptuous buffet and were seated around the living room. One of the waiters from the catering staff was serving wine, and when he approached Robin with a selection, she declined. For some unknown reason, her abstinence seemed to annoy one of the ladies from Nicola's bridge club, and the woman made a very cute but very catty comment about Robin's not drinking because she had to watch her figure.

For the sake of politeness, Robin had let it pass. Paul, however, did not. With the same glacial look of disdain that he used to intimidate the staff, he snapped, "Robin happens to be a very competent surgeon, and she has to go on duty later this evening. It's because of a deep sense of responsibility, rather than some foolish vanity, that she's not drinking."

An embarrassed hush fell upon those who heard his cold, quiet rebuttal, and the woman's body seemed to slowly deflate beneath Paul's withering stare. He had slammed his plate down on the coffee table and stared out the cathedral window, his face like granite. In an attempt to play down the incident, Robin forced herself to continue eating, but everything tasted like paste, and she could barely swallow for the nervous knot in her throat. Eventually, pockets of conversation dispelled the taut silence, but the voices were now subdued by the tentacles of tension that had snaked through the room. . . .

Robin opened her eyes and stared out the foggy window at the dreariness of the wet, sullen sky and the rain-drenched landscape. They should have left right then. Or better still, they should never have even attended. But then, she thought with grim amusement, hindsight was full of wisdom. If she had been able to foresee what was going to happen, Paul wouldn't have been able to drag her within a hundred miles of the wretched housewarming.

She had certainly been keenly aware that the Dennisons had been sniping at each other, but she never once expected it to go beyond that—not with a houseful of guests. When Keith had made a mumbling attempt to apologize to Robin because of the bitchy comment made by Nicola's friend, she had tried to smooth it over, but he was so drunk that nothing seemed to register. He had staggered out to the kitchen where Nicola was serving dessert, and a hysterical mudslinging battle erupted.

But it was the last burst of fury that had made Robin's whole body shrink with horror. Never would she forget the cold shock of revulsion that had swept through her when Keith yelled, "You snobbish bitch! If you hadn't deliberately gotten pregnant, I sure as hell wouldn't have married you, I can bloody well tell you that!'' It had been so ugly, so exposing—and so awkward. Of course, everyone pretended not to hear, but every shrill word had been crystal clear. Robin could feel the hot flush of embarrassment rising in her just thinking about it. It had been awful.

With a shiver of distaste, Robin drew the folds of her shawl around her. It had been enough to turn anyone against marriage....

"Are you cold?"

"No, I'm fine." Casting a quick glance at Paul, she experienced a sinking sensation in the pit of her belly when she saw the unyielding set to his jaw. He was furious, and she didn't have a clue what she could say or do that would defuse his anger. And it certainly wasn't the type of incident one could simply ignore....

"I'm sorry I asked you to come," he said tautly, his voice edged with disgust.

With her fingers laced tightly together, she asked quietly, "Are you sorry you asked me to go, or are you sorry that it was such a lousy experience?"

Her question obviously jolted him, for he gave her a startled look of consternation. Checking the rearview mirror, he pulled onto the gravel shoulder of the road and braked. He stared out the windshield for a moment, then he dragged his hand across his face in a exhausted gesture before he looked at her, his eyes darkly somber. "I'm sorry, Robin," he said, his voice very low. Reaching out, he grasped her hand in his, his tight grip telegraphing his heartfelt regret. "If there's anything I hate, it's an ugly scene. It leaves a vile taste in my mouth, and I feel like a heel for dragging you into such a mess."

The rain pattered against the canvas top of the car with a gently echoing tattoo as Robin stared at him with very troubled eyes. With a dispirited sigh, she returned the pressure of his handclasp, longing to erase the disquieting negative thoughts that she was certain were churning through his mind.

Listening to the Dennisons screaming, malicious battle must have been like a very disturbing rerun of a nightmare for him, dragging up grim recollections of the hundreds of similar scenes he had suffered through with his parents. It had been bad enough for her; it must have been much worse for him.

She tightened her grasp on his hand. "Do you want to talk about it, or do you just want to drop it?" she asked quietly.

Paul looked at her, his voice imbued with weary resignation. "There isn't much to talk about. It's just another bad marriage."

"Was it true what he said about her being pregnant?"

Paul sighed as he slouched down in the bucket seat. "Yeah, it's true. They'd lived together for nearly three years before they were married. They both seemed to be really happy with that arrangement. Once they got married, though, everything started to change.

"Was the pregnancy deliberate?"

"He said it was. She said it wasn't." Paul looked at Robin and shrugged. "That's irrelevant—they were both to blame. Once the baby came, she quit work, so they were struggling to make ends meet on top of everything else—and Keith was still in university. They just couldn't handle the extra responsibility and pressure, and the relationship turned into a nightmare.''

She had to agree. It was a nightmare. And with this ugly incident acutely fresh in their minds, what could she say to change his tainted outlook? She could give him the old standby that both partners in a relationship had to make an effort, and there had to be give and take on both sides. He would agree with her, but it wouldn't change his opinion one bit. He had been too affected by situations that had gone sour, and he'd never seen a case in which two people cared enough, or were mature enough, to work the problem through. It was tragic. So tragic.

She looked at him intently, her expression guarded. ''Do you think it would have been any different if they hadn't had the baby—if they hadn't married?''

Releasing her hand, Paul fished a package of cigarettes out of his jacket pocket, then offered her one. There was a reflective frown on his face as he lit her cigarette first, then his own. Inhaling deeply, he faced her, his expression grave. ''Yes, I do. As soon as they were married, they both tried to change the other. It was almost as though they were challenging each other for control.'' He drew in sharply on his cigarette, then added, ''Let's face it. The reason marriages used to last years ago was because the roles were clearly defined. But times have changed and those roles aren't defined anymore. When Nicola and Keith were living together, they had no preconceived ideas about who did what—they made their own rules. But once they were married, they tried their damnedest to make the other fit into the mold of what they thought a husband or wife should be—and it just didn't work.''

There was an element of truth in what Paul had said that Robin couldn't argue with. The roles *were* changing. In her mother's generation, few women had careers. They stayed home and raised their families, looked after the home and catered to their husbands. But she still didn't agree with him that all marriages were doomed to failure.

She wanted to argue with him, convince him that he was wrong, but debating the issue was pointless. No words would ever change his mind. And she knew that. She realized she had nurtured a secret hope that something would happen to change Paul's mind, but now she finally had to face the hard, cold fact that nothing ever would. She stared blindly at the glowing ash of her half-smoked cigarette.

She was left feeling very cold and hollow. He had been very frank with her, but she had an ominous premonition that she dared not be frank with him—especially after what had happened today. Robin somehow sensed that if she were to really level with him about what she wanted out of life—a home, a family—he would walk away. And she loved him far too much to take that risk. Never again, she vowed silently, would she ever try to reason with him. He had to learn to trust her before all else, and then, maybe someday....

"Robin, look at me."

Simulating a calmness she didn't feel, she looked at him. His expressive eyes were so solemn, and there was an intensity radiating from him as with immeasurable gentleness, he cupped her face in his hand. "Don't let this thing with the Dennisons get to you. It's never going to be that way for us." His voice was quiet with sincerity as he murmured huskily, "You're the most important thing in my life, and I don't want anything to ever change that."

As she gazed at him, she realized that this was her last chance to be open with him, but she could not make herself say the words. Even though they had never actually discussed it, she knew what he wanted; he wanted to live with her, to love her, to look after her, but he definitely did not want marriage. He was too afraid to take the chance that it might be different for them. By remaining silent, she was forfeiting her own values, but that was a small price to pay. She couldn't bear to lose this man.

Choking back the aching need to cry, she leaned across the car and kissed him softly on the mouth. His hands were warm against her skin as he touched her face, his lips soft and pliant against hers.

On a tremulous sigh, he murmured softly, "Let's go home."

CHAPTER SIX

THERE WAS A VERY DEFINITE CHANGE in their relationship after that bleak, rainy night, and Robin knew she was the cause of it.

On the drive home after the Dennisons' housewarming, Paul had assumed that the ugly incident between Nicola and Keith was the reason she was so introspective, but the real reason she was so quiet was that she had finally realized she was faced with a major decision in her life. They had gone to her apartment and that, she realized later, had been a big mistake.

Feeling oddly desolate, she had desperately needed the warmth and security of physical contact. Paul had sensed she needed some comforting, but what started out as a tender, protective embrace rapidly escalated into a very torrid session that nearly left Robin with no decision to make.

Ever since then, Paul seemed to be holding back, as though he was avoiding any intimate contact with her. So much so, in fact, that he was deliberately engineering situations so that they could spend very little time alone. He was withdrawn and tense, his bearing that of a wild caged panther—restless, edgy—as though he was forcefully restraining a nervous animal energy.

And Robin was feeling much the same way herself. She was locked in a peculiar limbo with so many doubts and unanswered questions chasing around in her mind. It wasn't just because of her moral standards; there was more to it than that. She had always wanted a family. Robin simply couldn't imagine growing old without children of her own. Yet neither could she imagine having anyone else's child but Paul's. There were so many conflicting feelings, and they were tearing her in two.

The more introspective she became, the more Paul seemed to withdraw, leaving her more uncertain than before. She had reached the point where she had nearly convinced herself that he was experiencing very grave reservations about their relationship. And Robin, who was feeling more vulnerable than she ever had in her life, would probably have continued to think that way if it hadn't been for her birthday.

It was a rotten day right from the beginning. To start with, she woke up in an absolutely foul humor. To make matters worse, she was covering a late shift in Emergency that week, and that meant her chances of seeing Paul were practically nonexistent, especially when she wouldn't likely get off work until after midnight. Bernie was the only one who knew it was her birthday, and she was more than happy to leave it that way. He had taken Lisa to Vancouver to meet his parents, and Robin didn't expect them back until late the following day. She was relieved that there would be no acknowledgment of a day she'd just as soon forget.

Somehow she managed to get through most of the

emergency caseload without biting somebody's head off, but she was well aware of the "what's bugging her" looks that were flying from one staff member to another. She was sure she would feel a whole lot better if she could just punch someone.

It was nearly eight o'clock, and Robin had just finished dealing with a hard-to-manage drunk who had sliced his hand open on a broken wine bottle. The fuse on her temper had grown dangerously short, and she decided she'd better do everyone a favor and go for a very belated supper. She was striding down the corridor, her jaw set with vexation, when a nursing assistant approached her.

"Dr. Mitchell, you're wanted on the phone."

Robin shot her a withering look as she stomped by. The aide stared at her in amazement. There was so much animosity radiating from the usually even-tempered Dr. Mitchell that even her hair seemed to crackle.

She went to the desk and picked up the phone. It was Paul. And he sounded so tired. "Robin, is there any chance that you could get away for a few minutes?"

Robin glanced at the nurse behind the desk who was busily filling out an admitting form, but who obviously had one ear tuned to the conversation. "Yes, I can."

"Could you meet me in my office?"

"Of course, doctor."

There was a brief silence, then he said, "I take it this call is being monitored?"

"That's right."

He swore and Robin nearly smiled. "I'll be right there," she said. Hanging up the phone, she looked squarely at the nurse. "I'll be in Dr. Wilcox's office if you need me."

Paul was standing at the window, his arm braced against the window frame, his other hand resting on his hip, that same aura of tightly reined animal energy emanating from him.

She closed the door behind her. "Hi," she said softly.

He turned to face her, his smile lacking its usual sparkle. He was exhausted; she could tell by the lines etched around his mouth and eyes.

"I shouldn't even speak to you, you know," he said gruffly, but there was a glimmer of amusement in his eyes.

Her frown was puzzled. "Why?"

He didn't respond but simply stared at her for a moment. Then he stooped and picked up a gaily wrapped parcel from the floor. "It *is* your birthday, isn't it?" he asked pointedly.

She grimaced sheepishly, then sighed in resignation. "Yes, it is—but I was hoping this one would slide by undetected."

He smiled warmly as he came toward her, his body moving with athletic grace. Thrusting his hand into her hair, he cradled the back of her head as he kissed her, his moist, warm mouth moving tantalizingly against hers. Robin swayed toward him, longing to feel his arms around her and his body molded against hers, but he released her abruptly and stepped back. There was a tense inscrutable look on his face as he handed her the gift.

His voice was husky. "Happy birthday, love."

She took the gift, her eyes intently searching his solemn face, then she sat down on the sofa and unwrapped it. Nothing could have ever prepared her for the heart-wrenching surge of emotion she experienced when she lifted the lid. Inside was the most beautiful Raggedy Ann doll she had ever seen. A piece of paper was tucked in the pocket of the doll's dress, and Robin's fingers trembled as she unfolded it.

Her name is Annie, and she's the granddaughter of another Annie that I'm sure you'll remember. I hope you love her just as much.

With all my love, P.

Robin's eyes were so blurred with tears she could barely see, but a glimmer of silver around the doll's neck glittered beneath the lights, and Robin tenderly fingered the chain. Her control very nearly shattered when she recognized the bright blue bead that was suspended on it. He had kept it. For some unexplainable, sentimental reason, he had kept it.

With suppressed sobs choking her, she raised her head and met his gaze. The muscles in his face were so taut that he looked as if he were carved from stone, but there was nothing inhuman about the look in his dark eyes. They were smoldering and tormented by a denied hunger, and it was only then that she fully understood why he had been so remote the past few days. He had been pushed to the extreme limit of his control; he simply didn't trust himself any longer.

She wanted so desperately to fling herself into his arms, but somehow she managed to restrain the nearly overwhelming urge. With her body visibly trembling and her voice so choked with emotion she could barely speak, she whispered, "She's so beautiful, Paul—and so special." She couldn't go on. She was so shaken by her feelings that she knew she would break down into uncontrollable weeping if she opened her mouth. She could only sit there, gazing up at him through her tears, her heart in her eyes.

He made a movement toward her, then checked himself sharply. When he finally looked at her, she felt the heat from the fire in his eyes. Her own unbridled feelings responded to that look, and Robin's pulse began to race with untamed desire.

Just then the phone rang, and for one unnerving moment, Robin thought he was going to drive his hand through the wall. He remained motionless for a moment. His tone was glacial when he answered the phone.

There was such a storm of emotions in her that Robin could barely breathe, and she sat there transfixed, knowing that neither one of them could endure this sexual tension much longer.

Paul slammed the receiver down, then wearily rubbed his hand across his eyes. "That was Emergency. The ambulance has just arrived with the patient you were expecting from Lethbridge."

Robin's face was ashen and her hands were trembling as she tenderly gathered up her gift and stood up. "I have to go, Paul," she whispered, her tremulous voice weighted with deep regret. "It's a critical case."

He came to her then. Gathering her against him in a gentle embrace, he kissed her softly. "I know." He stroked her head, then released her, his own face haggard. His voice was low and hoarse. "We have to talk, Robin."

"I know we do."

"It will have to be tomorrow after you're off work," he murmured, his words clipped. "My first surgery is at six in the morning, and I probably won't be out of OR until very late in the afternoon." There was such frustration in his voice that he seemed almost angry. But this time, Robin understood.

Wiping the tears away with the back of her hand, she smiled at him gently. "Then we'll wait until tomorrow." Her voice was barely audible when she whispered, "I love you, Paul."

A grimace of anguish flitted across his face when he groaned, "God, Robin...." With his hands clenched, Paul stared at her like a starving man, then with his face fixed into an enigmatic mask, he turned away. "You'd better go."

ROBIN AWOKE THE NEXT MORNING, feeling slightly light-headed from the lack of sleep. She was so tired that she was really relieved she didn't start work until that afternoon. Yet on the other hand, she felt more relaxed than she had in days.

For somewhere between midnight and four in the morning, she had finally come to terms with herself. There was no denying that the problem of different values was still there, but she had seen it from a different perspective last night. It had really hurt her to see the anguish Paul was going through, and she could not inflict that kind of torment on him any longer.

Yes, she still wanted a family, and yes, she was still strongly committed to her beliefs about marriage, but she knew she had to give him time. Once Paul realized that it simply wasn't in her nature to turn into a frustrated woman like Nicola Dennison or his mother, he would begin to develop a different outlook. Robin was certain of that, but she was also certain that he had to learn to trust her first.

Once he was truly confident of her, once he realized that she was the type of person who made a lifetime commitment, his attitude about having a family would also change. All he needed was time. And Robin was still young enough that she *did* have time to play the waiting game.

It had taken some very intense self-analysis, but she had finally made her decision. Right or wrong, there would be no turning back. She would go to him; he needed her and wanted her with him. And that above all else was where she wanted to be. The tension-riddled waiting was over.

But as the morning progressed she became more and more preoccupied, and eventually she found herself restlessly pacing back and forth. She paused in front of the window seat and stared down at Raggedy Ann.

Her frown disappeared, and her expression was softened by a tender smile as she picked up the doll.

Stretching out on the window seat, she propped her back against the pile of cushions as she slowly fondled the red wool hair. There was nothing in the world he could have given her that would have touched her more deeply or meant as much. He had heard her that day; he had really *listened* to what she'd said to Amanda. And the blue bead—it wrung her heart to think he had kept it.

The familiar ache slowly grew in her as Robin thought about him. Folding her arms around the doll, she rested her chin on the woolly head as she stared soberly out the window.

She never wanted to give him any reason to doubt her feelings. Never. The past few days had been a tremendous strain for both of them, and Robin knew there would be very little conversation once they were alone. Their emotions were just too explosive and too close to the surface for them to suppress much longer.

She wanted him to know that her decision had been made before she saw him later that night. It was essential—but how? He was in surgery all day, and besides, the thought of trying to sneak a few minutes alone with him at the hospital left her a little cold.

She creased her brow with a thoughtful frown and absently looked at the button eyes and embroidered face of the doll. A slow smile appeared as an idea germinated in her mind.

By seven o'clock that night, Robin was beginning to feel slightly foolish. By seven-thirty, her stomach was in a knot, and she had that very hollow sensation that was caused by uneasiness. Why didn't she think things out before she reacted on an impulse? What had Paul thought when he walked into his apartment and found Annie with that note pinned on her dress, sitting on his sofa?

By eight o'clock, the feeling of embarrassment had been overtaken by a feeling of despair, and Robin finally faced the fact that he wasn't going to call. With a quiet desperation, Robin became very grimly conscious of how slowly time was passing.

With a weary gesture, she rubbed the back of her neck, then once again attempted to drag her attention back to the contents of the file spread out on the desk before her. For the third time, she reread the patient's case history, and for the third time, nothing registered. Not one word.. . .

"What's the matter, Mitch? You look like hell."

Robin's head shot up. Bernie was leaning against the counter of the Emergency-ward station, peering at her through his glasses.

"What are you doing here? I thought you were still on days off."

"I am—I was," he amended with a grin. "But I just got a phone call from guess who, asking me if I would cover the rest of your shift for you." His eyes narrowed as he studied her more closely. "Are you sick?"

Robin felt suddenly weightless as she stared at Bernie with the oddest look. "No, I'm not sick."

"Hmmm," said Bernie. He pushed his glasses up on his nose, then continued to stare at her with a speculative frown as he said, "I'm to give you a message. Annie—who in hell is Annie?" he asked with a look of bewilderment.

Robin felt as if there were fireworks exploding inside her as she grinned. "Never mind. What about her?"

Bernie was looking at her with an expression that clearly said he was very suspicious. "I'm to tell you that he received Annie's message, and that she's more than welcome to use the spare bedroom for as long as she wants. I'm also to tell you he would have let you know sooner but he didn't get home until well after seven."

Robin had an awful time keeping her voice steady when she asked, "Are you going to finish my shift?"

"Yep." He inspected his fingernails, then pursed his lips as he studied her. "You're up to something, aren't you?"

"I don't know what you're talking about."

There was a gleam in his eyes. "The hell you don't." He tipped his head to one side as the grin broadened. "Yes, Robin Mitchell, you are definitely up to something—but I wonder what?"

Robin didn't really care what Bernie was wondering. By the time she went to her apartment to gather a few things, then drove to Paul's, her mind was in such a turmoil that she wasn't even sure if *she* was thinking straight.

In that short time she had been caught up in a whirlwind of emotions—from soaring happiness to weak-kneed nervousness to galvanizing excitement. But as she rode up in the elevator, they all fused together into one basic emotion, and that was the kind of anticipation that had her heart pounding so wildly that it felt as if it was going to hammer right through her ribs. Her hands were shaking as she tried to select his apartment key from among the others in the case that he had given her when she started driving the Bronco.

Closing her eyes, she rested her head against the doorjamb as she tried to smother the heady excitement that was racing through her. Just the thought of Paul making love to her left her feeling faint.

Taking a very shaky breath, she unlocked the door, quietly opened it and slipped inside. From the shadows of the entryway, she could see Paul sprawled on the sofa in the living room, his arm draped across his eyes, one bare leg drawn up. He was dressed in tennis shorts and a sports shirt he hadn't bothered to button, and even in the dusk of evening she could see he was very much on edge. There was something oddly vulnerable about him as he lay there alone in the twilight, his body tensed.

Sensing her presence, he shifted his arm slightly and stared at her. His dark solemn eyes were smoldering with an intensity that bewitched her, and drew her to him like a moth to a flame. As she moved toward him, his eyes never left hers, mesmerizing her with their black magic. A compelling energy radiated between Paul and Robin, and the feeling of breathless anticipation churned in her abdomen as she rested her hand on his broad chest and bent down to kiss him. Her hair tumbled around her face and Paul thrust his fingers into her dark curls as she covered his mouth with hers. Her lips were soft and inviting as he tasted the sweet moistness of her mouth, his gentle caress intoxicating her, filling her with a vital warmth.

His kiss had been tender and restrained, but Paul's breathing was very ragged as he whispered against her lips, "God, I thought you'd never get here." His arm weighed her down, but as much as Robin wanted to yield to him, she knew if she experienced the arousing pleasure of his body against hers, she would be lost to the onslaught of stampeding emotions. And Paul would hate himself later for taking her that way.

For him, and him alone, she resisted. She cupped his rugged, taut face in her hands as she kissed him once more, then with a whispered explanation, she slipped out of his arms.

Closing his eyes, he clenched his teeth together as she straightened up. For a moment she nearly weakened when she saw the tormented expression on his face, then with her body braced against her desperate longing to stay, she left him. Picking up her suitcase in the hallway, she turned toward the master bedroom.

She found him on the balcony, just as she knew she would. He was leaning against the rail, his hip thrust against the marble facing as he gazed out over the city. He inhaled deeply on his cigarette, then crushed it on the top of the rail before he flicked the butt over the edge.

The blaze of color from the setting sun silhouetted his broad shoulders and chest against the vibrant oranges and pinks of the fiery sky and cast his handsome face with a patina of bronze. He stood there unmoving, his body like a statue, his gaze fixed on some distance point. Yet there was that aura of animal power surrounding him, as though he was tensed and waiting, ready to spring.

Her breath caught as Robin absorbed the masculine beauty of him. God, how she loved him.

As she stepped through the patio doors leading from the bedroom, the light evening breeze caught at the gauzy fabric of her negligee, and it billowed around her like white froth. The soft light from inside framed her in a silver glow as the wind whispered around her, first revealing then cloaking the full curves of her body with the shifting, shimmering fabric.

For a very long time, Paul just stared at her, seemingly entranced by the vision before him. His eyes devoured every inch of her as he slowly came toward her, his heated gaze kindling a warm spiraling sensation in her abdomen that rapidly spread through her whole body.

When he was very close, he reached out and slowly caressed her naked shoulder, his warm, lingering touch sending shivers of pleasure through her as he smoothed his hand up her slender neck. Tipping her head back, Robin closed her eyes, her breasts rising and falling with strained breathing as she lost herself to the sexual tension that was building up between them. With the gentlest of caresses, he ran his hand beneath the heavy fall of her hair and slipped his fingers up the back of her neck sending little needles of excitement quivering through her.

Robin felt the strength drain out of her as he continued to caress her, his touch like silk against her skin. With every nerve in her vibrating, crying out for more, she swayed toward him.

Whispering her name, he swept her up in his arms and cradled her against him in a powerful embrace, the muscles across his shoulders flexing as he carried her into the bedroom. With his eyes never leaving her face, he gently eased his hold on her until she was standing before him. The gold flecks in his brown eyes were like tiny flames as he gazed at her, his ardent look penetrating her very soul. With trembling fingers, she reached up and stroked his full, sensitive mouth.

Taking her face in both of his hands, he kissed her, his mouth moving thirstily against hers, sending shock waves of heat coursing through her. As his mouth sought the moist warmth of hers, Robin trailed her hands down his flat torso to the waistband of his shorts, and she felt the muscles in his belly tighten beneath her touch when her fingers fumbled with the clasp.

He sucked in his breath sharply as he caught her wrist and tried to pull her hand away. "Robin...not yet, love," he whispered.

With gentle firmness she loosened his grip, then brushed his hand away. With her lips feathering across his in a light tormenting kiss, she undid the clasp at his waist, then slipped her hands down his slim hips until the fabric fell away. A tremor shot through him as she slowly smoothed her hands up his midriff and chest to push his shirt from his shoulders.

His body remained very rigid for a moment, then another shudder rippled through him, snapping the final thread of his control, and his arms enfolded her in a viselike hold. His mouth slanted across hers, and Robin felt as if she was melting from the heat of that ravenous kiss. His light stubble of beard rasped against her cheek as he dragged his mouth away from hers to leave a scorching trail of impassioned kisses down her neck, igniting a response in Robin that was unbelievable. The only things she was conscious of were his arousal as he welded his body against her, and the searing desire that was pumping through her veins.

His arms were like bands of steel as he crushed her more tightly against him and claimed her lips once again. Her mouth slackened beneath his, famished for the sustenance that only he could give her, and she clung to him as he continued to fuel the fever that left her senseless and shaking.

Tearing his mouth away, he groaned softly, "God, I want you so badly."

Through the turmoil of her mind, Robin knew he was desperately trying to brake his wild, escalating need, but she didn't want him to hold back—not when the throbbing ache in her was impelling her on. This time there would be liberation; this time there would be no turning back.

With a low moan, she pulled his head down. The hot liquid thrust of her tongue against his was like a jolt of electricity through him, annihilating what little resistance he had left. His hand supported her head as Paul ground his mouth against hers, lifting her to a realm of consuming passion that carried her beyond reality. The tortured cravings of his male body finally overpowered his reason, and he began to move against her with a slowness that drove her wild.

Their need became an obsession, a stormy, erotic obsession that was propelling them deeper and deeper into a passion from which there was only one escape. And the filmy fabric of her negligee was the only barrier.

With his arm molding her hips against his, Paul undid the tie at the back of her neck with the other hand, and with unsteady strokes, he eased the chiffon down her body until it slithered to the floor. His arms tightened around her convulsively, his mouth drawing on hers for the fuel to fire his desire to a white-hot heat. His maleness seemed to encompass her as he lowered her on the bed, his hold savagely possessive, yet poignantly tender.

Easing his sweat-dampened body away from hers, he exposed her nakedness to his hungry view. Paul looked down at her, his eyes blazing. He stroked her full breasts with intimate caresses that paralyzed her, and the gnawing emptiness in her grew and grew until she could stand it no longer.

She reached her limit, and he knew it. With her writhing body clutched in his arms, he pulled her beneath him, and after what seemed like a tempestuous eternity, he finally claimed her.

With his arms molding her soft body against his, he surged against her, bringing her to the very edge of splendor.

With a strangled sob, Robin stiffened beneath him, her hips thrust against his as golden, hot waves of immobilizing relief ripped through her with the power and force of a tidal wave. Her stormy response sent a violent tremor slamming through him, and Paul moved his body against hers as his release came, the weight of his body crushing her beneath him as he held her as though he would never let her go.

The evening sky darkened into night as Paul soothed her with gentle caresses, his words of love filled with tenderness. As the torpor of spent passion ebbed, Robin was filled with a satiated serenity that wrapped her in mellow contentment.

Propping his weight on his elbows, Paul cradled her face with his hands. With a deep sigh of unblemished happiness, Robin gazed up at him, her violet eyes glowing with a soft luster.

He smoothed back a damp tendril of hair that was clinging to her cheek, then smiled, his eyes glimmering with a bewitching warmth. "You," he said with provocative huskiness, "are quite a woman, Robin Mitchell."

Feathering her fingers through his tousled hair, she softly smiled at him as she trailed her fingers down his neck. "I only followed where you led me," she whispered as a pink tinge crept into her cheeks.

There was a look of intimate tenderness in Paul's eyes as he slowly caressed her flushed cheek with his thumb. He covered her mouth with his in a tantalizing kiss that made her feel as if she was floating. A whisper of a sigh escaped from him when he finally raised his head. "You've given me a sense of completeness that I've never known before," he said gently. "And I thought I would never find that." He gave her another soft, fleeting kiss that was as sweet as honey. When he raised his head, there was a glow in his eyes that nearly masked a sparkle of amusement. The tiny dimple at the corner of his mouth appeared and his eyes crinkled, and she knew he was going to flash one of those irresistible grins.

"Now if you can only cook."

"Go to hell," she said with a laugh.

With a throaty chuckle, he eased himself off her, then rolled onto his back, pulling her against him. He stuffed another pillow behind his shoulders before snuggling her head on his shoulder. Reaching out, he gathered his lighter, cigarettes and an ashtray from the bedside table. Paul nestled the ashtray on his nude abdomen, then lit two cigarettes and handed her one.

The cool spring breeze eddied in through the patio door and whispered across Robin's naked shoulders. Grasping the tangled sheet, Paul yanked it free and tucked it around her.

"Do you tell bedtime stories, too?" she teased lightly.

"Just polishing up my bedside manner," he said, his voice full of humor. Robin grinned lazily. As they smoked their cigarettes, Paul stroked her back, his touch inducing a dreamy languor.

After a long, easy silence, she gave him a droll look. "Poor old Bernie is likely going crazy trying to figure out what was going on tonight."

In a slightly cynical tone, Paul replied, "If old Bernie is half as bright as I think he is, he certainly has everything figured out by now."

Knowing Bernie the way she did, Robin didn't

doubt it. Paul butted his cigarette, then held the ash-tray steady as Robin did the same. He set everything back on the night table and snuggled her firmly against him.

She looked up at him when he laughed softly. "I loved Annie's note. I couldn't believe my eyes when I walked in here tonight and found her sitting on my sofa."

Robin grimaced, and she could feel a flush of embarrassment stain her cheeks when she recalled how truly idiotic she had felt over that note. Paul was watching her with a puzzled look, obviously waiting for an explanation for her very apparent chagrin.

With a disconcerted little shrug, she grimaced again. "By eight o'clock, I was certain that was the most juvenile, stupid thing I had ever done."

He lifted her face, forcing her to meet his eyes. "It wasn't juvenile or stupid, Robin. Nothing could have pleased me more, believe me."

Her voice was low and slightly unsteady when she said, "I wanted you to know that I was coming to stay before I saw you."

"I'm glad you did. It meant so much." He stroked her hair, then pressed her head against him as he kissed her softly on the forehead. "I knew you need-ed some time, but I was going quietly insane waiting."

"I didn't mean to make it difficult for you," she whispered.

His voice was filled with gentle understanding. "I know you didn't, Robin." His arms tightened around her as he said, "When emotions run this deep, they're so overpowering that you can't think rationally. And I knew I had to give you time." His voice became very husky as he whispered, "I wanted the first time to be special, with candlelight and roses, but when you walked in here tonight, I just couldn't wait any longer."

The regret in his voice touched her profoundly, and compassion for him swelled within her. She slipped her arms around him and held him very close. "It was special, Paul—very special, and nothing could have made it better."

"But I was so damned afraid it wouldn't be for you," he said, as he massaged her shoulders.

Robin closed her eyes and quietly savored both the feel of his warm strong body against hers and the concern he had expressed for her. Finally she tipped her head back, an impish sparkle in her eyes as she gave him a very significant look. "Paul, my love, I am informed enough to know that one usually doesn't play first violin in a symphony until one has practiced a little."

For a split second, there was a very blank look on his face, then he threw his head back and laughed. "Well," he said, with an outrageously bold grin, "I didn't think you'd need much practice, but I did want your...debut to have the proper backdrop."

She could feel herself blushing again when she asked softly, "And this isn't the proper setting?"

Her breathing became erratic as he forced her onto her back, then gazed down at her with a hypnotizing warmth that sent a shiver of excitement along every nerve in her body.

His smile was filled with mesmerizing charm as he murmured provocatively, "This is most definitely the proper setting, but I had planned it to be different."

"How different?" she breathed.

"I was going to whisk you off to Banff for a romantic weekend...wine, roses, candlelit dinners...but my good intentions were shot to hell the minute you touched me."

Robin fought down the beautiful butterflies in her stomach and somehow managed a husky laugh. "It sounds lovely, but I'm afraid you would've had to go by yourself. I work this weekend."

There was a look of self-satisfaction on his face as he said, "I'm not changing the arrangements, nor will I be going alone. One very beautiful bird is coming with me." His eyes crinkled disarmingly as he explained. "You see, I took it upon myself to alter the schedules. Because of the shuffle, it just so happens you have this weekend off."

"You didn't!" Her eyes widened in alarm.

"I did." He grinned.

"Paul Wilcox, how can you possibly justify a shift change like that?"

"Very easily. The reason for the change—" he paused, a scheming glint appearing in his eyes "—is because I have two very long and very complicated operations early in the week, and I want you and Bernie to assist."

"I'm sure," she said, her tone disbelieving.

"It's true," he said with boyish innocence.

She didn't know whether to believe him or not,

and she stared at him, a doubtful look on her face. "Really?"

He laughed. "Really." Slipping his hand beneath her head, he trailed his lips across hers with seductive softness as he whispered against her mouth, "But the most important reason is that I wanted some uninterrupted time alone with you." His kiss awakened a heady anticipation that started her pulse racing—and once again, he kindled the fire that would eventually engulf them in flames of passion.

THEIR WEEKEND TOGETHER WAS PERFECT: beautiful weather, breathtaking scenery and nights that were filled with incredible tenderness and blazing passion.

It was such a special interlude, but there was more to it than just the romantic setting. There was time—time to talk, to laugh, to discover each other. And there was time to relish the glorious sense of freedom. They could do what they liked and go where they wanted without fear of exposing themselves to the gossip mill at the hospital. Granted they deliberately stayed away from the major tourist attractions and chose secluded areas of the park for their rambles, but that was the only caution they took. It was wonderful having that freedom to be young and in love, especially for Robin.

She discovered the one thing that filled her with the deepest sense of contentment was his physical closeness. Perhaps she was hopelessly old-fashioned, but his obvious protectiveness made her feel very feminine and more than a little pampered.

He had a thousand ways of telling her, without

saying a word, how much she meant to him. Touching, subtle ways—the way he'd gently tuck back a loose tendril of hair when the wind whipped it across her face, then let his hand linger on her neck; the way he seemed to shield her with his size and strength when they went hiking on mountain trails; the way he'd look down at her with that irresistible, intimate smile as he'd take her hand in his.

Even during the night, Robin would awaken to find herself cradled securely in his arms, and she would drift back to sleep, safe and content in the warm sanctuary of his embrace. Each gesture made her feel so cherished, and Robin responded to him like a flower to sunshine. With every passing moment, her love for him became more profound and more binding. Every second counted. And Robin savored every one.

It wasn't until they arrived back at Paul's apartment that the euphoria faded, and the sober facts of the real world finally surfaced. She was in the kitchen making coffee when it finally hit her that she was going to be living with Paul Wilcox—in *his* apartment.

And that fact threw her into an unexpected quandary. A host of perturbing questions peculiar to the situation were suddenly staring her in the face, leaving her feeling very much like a gauche and gawky kid. What, exactly, was her role, and what did he expect of her? Did she treat him like a roommate, or did she treat him like a husband? Did she simply assume the responsibility of running a home...*his* home? Were they to share expenses? What about something as simple as using the phone? Did she just assume it was her privilege, or did she ask first? She was going to have to cope with *that* issue fairly quickly. Without fail, Robin always phoned home sometime on Sunday, and here she was, standing in *his* kitchen, watching *his* coffeepot brewing, wondering a little wildly what she should do about using *his* telephone. . . .

"Do you want something to eat, Robin?"

His perfectly ordinary question, asked in a perfectly ordinary tone of voice, startled her. With a voice oddly distant, she stammered, "Oh. . .ah, no thanks." Then taking the bit between her teeth, she took a deep breath and asked, "May I use your phone?"

Paul gave her an odd, penetrating look, then waved his hand toward the telephone sitting on the cupboard. "There's one there, or you can use the extension in the bedroom if you prefer." Taking an orange from the bowl of fruit on the table, he began to peel it as he watched her dial. Robin dialed the O for operator assistance, then the area code and her parents' number. She was staring blankly at her indistinct reflection on the fridge door when the operator came on the line.

"What special service did you wish, please?"

"Would you please bill this call to my home number. . . ." Paul's arm shot out, and she gave him a startled, bewildered look as he clamped his hand over the disconnect button on the phone. With a look of strained patience, he took the receiver from Robin's hand and replaced it on the cradle.

"What in hell are you doing?" he asked, his voice brusque.

"I was phoning home. . . ."

"I gathered that. But what's this crap about billing it to your home number?" He was staring at her with an unwavering look that was sparked with annoyance, and Robin was totally unnerved by it. How did she explain without looking like an idiot?

"Robin?"

She looked up at him, then gave a self-conscious little shrug.

"And what in hell is that supposed to mean?" he asked, his voice dangerously low. Bracing his arms against the cupboard on either side of her, he effectively trapped her as he continued to stare at her.

She swallowed and looked up at him with an expression of uncertainty, her eyes troubled. "I'm new at this game, Paul, and I don't know the rules."

For one awful moment, he just stared at her with a determined set to his jaw, then his expression relaxed as he straightened up and drew her into his arms. "There aren't any rules, love," he murmured, his breath warm against her temple as his arms tightened around her. "This is going to be *our* home at least until we can find something that suits us better." With a husky laugh, he lifted her face so he could look at her. "You can paint the walls orange and green if it will make you happy. I don't really give a damn, just as long as you're here."

With his hand buried in her hair, he gave her one of those soft lingering kisses that sapped her strength, then he raised his head, his voice suddenly unsteady. "Now you'd better make that phone call before we get sidetracked."

Robin took a deep breath to steady her erratic heartbeat before she direct-dialed her parents' number. With her legs braced in front of her, she leaned against the cupboard, then glanced at her watch as she waited for the call to be completed.

With a knowing grin on his face, Paul shook his head, and sighing in exasperation, he unclasped the timepiece from her wrist and stuck it in his shirt pocket.

Robin made a face at him and smiled just as her father's voice came on the line.

"Hello."

"Hi, dad. How are you?" Her father hesitated, and Robin pursed her lips in amusement. Neither her mother nor father could distinguish her voice from that of her sister Dana. And as always, she identified herself. "It's Bimmy, dad."

Jerking his head around, Paul stared at her. There was a disbelieving expression on his face while he mouthed "Bimmy?" and Robin could almost see huge question marks spilling from his mouth. She nearly laughed out loud, and she had to look away as he kept silently repeating it.

If she watched his performance, she wouldn't hear one word her father said, and she did enjoy the news from home. Robin had no idea how long she talked, but it was long enough to have a good chat with both her mother and father, and long enough to drink the coffee and smoke the cigarette Paul had passed her.

With a sigh of satisfaction, she hung up the phone. It was so good to hear their voices. . . .

"Bimmy?" demanded Paul. "How in hell did you get tagged with Bimmy?"

Robin laughed as she pushed herself away from the counter. "When my sisters were little, they couldn't say Robin and somewhere along the line, I got stuck with Bimmy."

Draping his arms across her shoulders, he gazed down at her with a preoccupied frown on his face. "Bimmy," he said softly, as though he was a connoisseur tasting a very unusual wine. Then he grinned at her, his eyes gleaming roguishly. "I don't know why, but for some strange reason, it suits you."

She gave him a withering look as she looped her arms around his waist. "How can you say that? It makes me sound like such a baby."

"Some baby," he murmured with a low throaty laugh that made her senses tingle. Her breath caught as he lowered his head, his mouth covering hers in a searching kiss, and Robin melted against him, savoring the tangy taste of orange on his lips. His hands roamed across her back, molding her closer as the kiss became more tantalizing, more exciting, more provocative as the heat of his body invaded hers.

The chime of the doorbell echoed in the silent apartment, and the only indication that he had heard it was that the muscles across his shoulders tensed. It sounded again, and with a groan of frustration, Paul finally raised his head. "Damn it anyway," he seethed. "Can't they leave us alone for five minutes...?"

Pressing her fingers against his mouth, Robin glanced up at him, her eyes sparkling with barely suppressed amusement. "Think of your blood pressure," she said solemnly, "and just answer the door."

Paul's eyes narrowed threateningly, and he grinned as he reluctantly released her. "Doctors with mundane values are a pain," he muttered as he walked away from her.

Robin swept her hair back with unsteady hands as she murmured to herself, "You *do* pack a punch, Paul Wilcox!"

As soon as her knees quit behaving as if they were molded of jelly, she wandered into the living room and curled up on the sofa. She heard the door close, and there was just a moment of silence before Paul burst into laughter. He was still chuckling as he entered the room. She looked at him quizzically as he handed her the telegram he held in his hand.

"This," he said with a grin, "was delivered late Friday afternoon."

She cast him another puzzled look as she unfolded the paper.

TO DOCTORS MITCHELL AND WILCOX:
APPRECIATE RESCHEDULING EFFORT STOP
HOPE YOUR WEEKEND SEMINAR WAS A SUCCESS STOP LOOKING FORWARD TO FUTURE ASSOCIATION STOP
          DOCTOR BERNARD WINSTON RADCLIFFE III

Robin had to read it twice before it made any sense, then she felt herself turning scarlet as she glanced up at Paul. He was watching her with such a wicked gleam in his eyes that she turned even redder.

"Damn him," muttered Robin, "I'll strangle him."

Plucking the telegram from her hand, Paul tossed it on the coffee table and pulled her down on top of him as he sprawled on the sofa. "Invite him to dinner instead," he said, laughing. "Strangulations are so low class."

Propping her arms on his broad chest, she squinted as she glared at him, trying her level best not to laugh. "And what's that supposed to mean? Are you implying that my cooking would kill him?"

Paul adopted an innocent expression and Robin, smiling mischievously, dug her fingers into his ribs. His reaction was instantaneous. With a yell of indignant laughter, he twisted beneath her as he caught her hands and held them.

"*Real* men aren't supposed to be ticklish," she said primly.

"Real men can be anything they want," he retorted with a grin. His expression changed to one of infinite tenderness as he gazed up at her and murmured wonderingly, "Oh, Robin, how did I ever exist without you?"

The laughter in Robin was suddenly dissolved by heady expectancy as she gazed down at him, spellbound by his dark eyes. She was drawn toward him, and as she covered his mouth with hers, her love for him filled her with a glorious excitement. His arms came around her in an all-encompassing embrace and his lips parted, his mouth moving hungrily against hers, stirring the embers of desire that were smoldering within her.

CHAPTER SEVEN

TWO WEEKS HAD GONE BY since Robin had moved in with Paul, and her happiness seemed to deepen with each passing day. This was her first stretch of time off since that initial weekend with him, and she was thoroughly enjoying a chance to putter around the apartment.

She had gone downstairs to get the mail, and upon returning, placed Paul's on the little table in the hall, then opened the single letter addressed to Dr. R.E. Mitchell. Her attention was still focused on the document as she absently closed the door behind her and leaned against the wall.

Robin's bewildered expression changed to one of annoyance as she reread the two pages. Obviously somebody somewhere had made a blunder, and she couldn't understand how it could have possibly happened. With an abrupt shake of her head, she flipped over the paper and once again checked the date and her account number. What was going on? She knew very well that she still owed several thousand dollars of student loans, yet this letter plainly stated that they had been paid in full.

With exasperation, she strode into the kitchen and picked up the phone. Knowing how the wheels of bureaucracy ground out red tape, she assumed it would probably take her the rest of the afternoon to straighten the whole mess out. Damn it, anyway! She had no patience with foul-ups; besides, she had other things she should be doing.

After a half a dozen phone calls, Robin was no further ahead than when she started. As far as anyone she spoke to was concerned, the loan had been repaid. How, or by whom, no one knew, but the account had been mysteriously cleared. Robin grinned wryly—maybe she had suddenly acquired a fairy godmother.

With a snort of frustration, Robin checked the casserole in the oven before she started preparing the vegetables for the salad. Of course there had to be an error, but how was she ever going to get it resolved if everyone kept insisting that there wasn't one? She shook her head again in disgust. Maybe Paul would know whom she could contact to sort it out. Suddenly the invisible tape recording in her mind rewound to the little voice saying, *maybe Paul would know...* *maybe Paul...* . Robin froze, her hand gripping the handle of the paring knife she held. *Maybe Paul!*

Dropping a stalk of celery in the sinkful of cold water, Robin wiped her hands on her jeans. She lit a cigarette and stared rigidly at the basket of cherry tomatoes that were sitting by the sink. Of course it was Paul. It had to be he.

With a groan of irritation, she strode into the living room to the balcony where she soundly kicked the cedar tub full of red geraniums. What was he trying to do to her? she fumed inwardly. He refused to take anything for rent; he wouldn't let her pay for phone bills, for groceries, for gas for the car—nothing. Now he'd paid off her student loans to boot. Fury was building in her like steam in a kettle. He was so stubborn! He simply refused to see her point of view, and he would not listen to reason. But this time he'd gone *too* far!

When Paul arrived home from work, Robin met him at the door, her hands on her hips and fire in her eyes. For a moment, that old weakness undermined her fury as she stood there glaring at him.

He looked as though he had just stepped out of a stylish advertisement for an exclusive menswear shop. He had his light tan suit jacket slung casually over his shoulder, his tie was undone, and his white shirt was unbuttoned. The wind had ruffled his dark hair, leaving it appealingly tousled, and his tinted sunglasses added just the right touch of mystery to the most attractive picture. He was a study of a man totally indifferent to his good looks.

But Robin tried to ignore it all as she thrust her chin out with determination.

"Lord, but it's hot out there," he said as he closed the door.

It's going to get damned hot in here, too, she thought, her head of steam building dangerously.

He laid his coat on the hall table, then took off his glasses and tossed them on top of his jacket. He gave her a penetrating look before he said, "Is something wrong?"

How nice of him to notice, she thought peevishly. She had her ammunition all lined up to really let him have it, but she recognized the drawn lines of exhaustion carved around his mouth. All right, she'd give him one concession.

"Dinner's going to be ready in about twenty minutes, so you'll have time for a shower," she snapped as she turned to stomp into the kitchen.

His arm shot out and he grasped her wrist, stopping her dead in her tracks.

"Would you mind telling me what's wrong?" His voice had that ominous ring to it that said he was in no mood for playing games.

She faced him squarely, seething with suppressed anger. "I don't suppose you know one damned thing about the mystery of my loan repayment?"

He stared at her with that look that could quell a riot, then he turned and picked up his jacket and sunglasses. "I think I'll have a shower after all," he said, with invisible icicles dripping from his voice.

With her teeth clenched, her fists clenched, in fact, with her whole body clenched, Robin glared at his retreating back. Damn him, he didn't think he could walk away from the issue that easily!

She vented some of her frustration by slamming around in the kitchen as she finished preparing dinner, but she was still riled. This was a very large bone of contention between them, and they were going to have to bury it one way or another, and if she had her way it would be tonight.

But when Paul appeared at the dinner table dressed in white shorts and a T-shirt, he had his sphinx face on, and Robin knew with one glance at the rigid set of his jaw that she wouldn't get a single word out of him. So they ate in silence—a cold and heavy silence that seemed to grow heavier with each passing moment...until Robin couldn't stand it a minute longer.

Her voice had lost most of its angry edge when she said, "We're going to have to talk about this, Paul."

He glanced at her with a frigid stare that drilled right through her, then he shoved his chair away from the table and stood up. "We aren't going to discuss it," he said flatly, his voice as unyielding as steel, "because I refuse to fight over it."

With that he turned and walked away. Robin sat staring at his empty chair as if she really couldn't believe her eyes, then she bolted after him. She found him sitting on the edge of the bed, his shoulders hunched forward as he tied the laces of his running shoes.

"Paul, damn it...."

"Shut up, Robin," he snapped as he straightened up. Her stomach dropped when she saw the look on his face. She'd seen *that* one before—it was the same expression he'd had the night she'd met his parents.

"Paul, just listen to me for a minute—"

"I'm going for a run," he cut in abruptly as he stood up and tucked his T-shirt into the waist of his shorts. With that, he brushed past her, and Robin felt his cold remark squelch the remainder of her vexation, leaving a hollow uneasiness in its stead. The uneasiness grew as the sound of the door's slamming reverberated through her. And she didn't like the feeling.

Robin sat on the edge of the bed for quite a while,

trying to sort through her own mixture of feelings. The more she thought about the whole incident, the more she realized that she had handled it very badly, especially with the kind of family background Paul had. Her own parents, on occasion, openly and very loudly disagreed with each other, but they had been so secure within their marriage that they vented their grievances in what her mother laughingly referred to as "swiftly moving tempests in a teapot." And that's exactly what they'd been—hot, and often very loud, rows that would blow over quickly, leaving the usual calm in their wakes.

They would confront an issue, deal with it, then forget about it—and their children would simply dismiss it as a mild temporary upheaval in their very normal lives, knowing full well that their mother and father would eventually cool off, and likely as not laugh about their outburst an hour later.

But Paul had never seen a quarrel end that way. In fact, Robin thought grimly, he'd never seen a quarrel end. It just went on year after year after year. Because of how she'd been raised, Robin was not threatened by a disagreement, while Paul on the other hand would not argue with her because of the turbulent upbringing he'd had. She could only assume, but it seemed that he viewed any quarrel as the vehicle that could carry them down the same path of destruction his parents had taken.

By the time Robin had tidied up the clutter from their dinner, she was feeling sick at heart for the mistake she'd made in approaching the problem the way she had. She still believed she had every right to be annoyed by his doing what he had done without once discussing it with her, but she'd been at fault for confronting the issue the way she had. She would give anything if she could only turn back time, but she couldn't—she could only watch it inch slowly forward.

An hour passed, then two, and still there was no sign of him. And the longer he was gone, the more concerned she became. With her stomach tied in knots, Robin began pacing the floor, her thoughts becoming more tainted by niggling uncertainties. She kept telling herself she was overreacting, but those disturbing little anxieties kept piercing through her barricade of rationality.

Just how serious was this? Was it serious enough for Paul to decide that the "live-in" arrangement was a bad idea? Was it serious enough for him to call it quits? She'd tell herself she was being damned silly, that Paul wasn't that shallow, then the cycle would start all over again.

Two and a half hours had passed and Robin had smoked a dozen cigarettes, the knot in her stomach growing bigger by the minute. Where was he?

When he finally did enter the apartment, Robin could feel herself go weak with relief. At least he was home.

She looked up as he came through the entryway. He was soaked with sweat, his face was flushed from exertion, and he looked about ready to drop. Without even so much as glancing at her, he stripped off his shirt as he turned down the hallway, and Robin's uneasiness settled inside her like a lump of glue when she saw the grim set of his mouth. There was no anger left in her—just an awful feeling of inadequacy that kept pricking at her guilt. If only she had thought things through before she shot off her mouth.

The sound of the shower was a little comforting, but not much. Lighting yet another cigarette, she sprawled in his big easy chair and closed her eyes. *Please come out here and talk to me,* she pleaded silently. *Don't just shut me out.*

But he didn't. The time stretched into an edgy waiting game, but there wasn't a sound from their bedroom, and the silence was deafening. After waiting what seemed like a lifetime, Robin crushed out her cigarette, and with her serpent of uncertainty twisting and coiling inside her, she headed toward the bedroom.

Paul was lying on the bed, sprawled on his stomach, his face obscured by the crook of his arm. Drops of water from his shower were still beaded across his shoulders and back. He never moved...never made the smallest indication that he was aware of her presence.

Robin gazed at him, her eyes suddenly blurred by tears. Would she ever really understand this complex man? She would lay down her life for him, but she didn't know how to heal the psychological wounds he carried.

With such a swell of emotion she could hardly speak, she whispered, "I'm sorry, Paul. It wasn't you I was attacking but the problem." She swallowed hard as she brushed her tears away with trembling fingers. "I know you don't understand why I was angry, but it's because I feel like a parasite. You carry all the load...at work as well as here. It isn't that I'm so independent that I resent it...."

Her voice broke treacherously, and she forced a ragged breath past the tightness that was strangling her. "I just want to contribute something toward a sharing relationship." She couldn't say anything more. With tears blurring her eyes, she turned and left, closing the bedroom door softly behind her.

There was a kind of pain building in her she'd never experienced before—regret for having acted so impulsively, regret for having unwittingly displeased him, but most of all, the deep regret for his silent withdrawal from her. Suddenly she was overcome with an overpowering need to escape, yet she felt trapped.

No matter where she went, all her feelings of despair would come with her. She felt frightened, confused and so terribly alone.

With a heavy heart, she wandered out onto the balcony and leaned against the rail. She was filled with a different kind of sorrow, a sorrow of uncertainty. This was not a marriage—a marriage like her mother and father had—but an indefinite arrangement, and an ominous foreboding grew within her. It was not going to be forever. That thought terrified her, and there was no way she could hold back the tears any longer; with her hand pressed against her mouth, her desolation poured out.

Strong arms encircled her and pulled her back into a secure embrace. "Don't cry like that, Robin," Paul whispered against her hair. As he turned her toward him, she clasped her arms around him and pressed her face against the smooth skin of his neck as she tried to choke back her sobs. He held her for a long time, his arms enveloping her with an unbreakable hold that silently communicated his own regret.

He released her and, grasping her hand tightly in his, he drew her across the balcony to the patio doors that led to the bedroom. His hand was like an iron vise around hers as he stretched out on the bed, then, pulling her down beside him, he gathered her up in his arms.

"I'm so sorry, love," he whispered, his voice very husky. "I didn't mean to hurt you like that."

Her own voice quavered when she said, "I was so wrong—"

"No, you weren't," he interjected firmly. His voice softened as he continued. "No, you weren't. I was nettled because I couldn't see what the big deal was... it's only money. But when you spoke about building a sharing relationship, I realized we were seeing things very differently."

She shifted her head and searched the depths of his troubled eyes. "In what way?"

There was a guarded expression in those eyes as he gazed down at her, and Robin sensed he was carefully searching for words. "Money means very little to me, Robin," he said. "There's very old money in my family, and I've always had more than I needed. It's an easy thing for me to give away." He gently pushed her hair back from her face, his expression sober and reflective.

"I hated having to watch you survive on such a skimpy paycheck before you came here, and I just assumed it would be different." Pensively, he continued to caress her hair. His voice was unsteady when he finally spoke. "I never considered how you felt; I never thought about it. I just know. . . ." There was an odd catch in his voice, and Robin saw him swallow with difficulty before he continued. "I just know how damned wonderful it feels for me to be able to look after you—to provide for you."

It caused a tight pain in Robin's chest when she realized how hard he was battling to suppress the deep feelings that were burning inside him—feelings he mustn't reveal because he'd been raised in a society that decreed men must never permit themselves the liberty of revealing their emotions.

With infinite tenderness she softly kissed his eyes, then pleaded, her voice trembling with emotion, "Don't shut me out, Paul. Don't be afraid to let me see your vulnerabilities." She softly caressed his face as she gazed at him with solemn eyes. "There are bound to be times when we disagree, love. But that doesn't mean we have to hurt each other. If we're open about what we feel, it can only bring us closer together."

His eyes were intense and grave as he said, "This is all so new to me, Robin. It's going to take me a while to learn." His arms tightened around her fiercely, as though she was a vital part of him—such a vital part that he didn't dare let go.

"You don't know what it means to me just having you here," he whispered gruffly. "Before I left for the hospital this morning, I stood by the bed for the longest time just watching you sleep. You'd kicked the covers off and looked so damned beautiful lying with your hair spilling across the pillow." He shuddered against her, as though he was fighting for breath. "God, Robin—knowing that you trust me, that you love me, is all I ever want from you."

The pain in his voice as he uttered those heartfelt words was like setting a torch to tinder for her. With a storm breaking in her, she twisted her head until her mouth found his with a wild and hungry kiss that ignited their passion.

And the passion carried them through the tempest to the absolute, the perfect, the supreme fulfillment.

THE NEXT MORNING Robin awoke very early, her body still satiated from their uninhibited lovemaking the night before. As always, she had fallen asleep with her head cradled on his shoulder, her knee tucked between his, his arms wrapped securely around her.

With a deep sigh of satisfaction, she began to slowly stroke his shoulder and neck, not even really aware that she was doing it. She loved the feel of his skin, the smell of him, how the light film of sweat fused their bodies together.

"By any small chance, are you trying to seduce me?" he murmured drowsily.

She laughed softly. "Of course."

He ran his hand slowly up her naked back. "You could make the alarm clock an unnecessary evil, you know."

There was an effervescent amusement in her voice when she asked, "Speaking of alarm clocks, when is yours set to go off?"

He shifted his head to check the clock radio on the bedside table. "In ten minutes, unfortunately."

"Damn! I was hoping for a half an hour."

Paul laughed and gave her a hearty hug. "That's what I like—a woman who's reluctant to get out of bed."

"Don't let it go to your head," she warned. "I told you I was lazy."

"Liar."

For a few more moments, she savored his closeness, then reluctantly she extricated herself from his embrace. The sheet slipped from her as she swept her hair back and Paul grinned lazily, his warm gaze vibrating with virility as he thoroughly studied her. "You do make it damned hard to get up in the morning."

"And you have an overactive imagination."

"I don't have to *imagine* anything," he said with a provocative huskiness. There was pure mischief gleaming in his eyes as he reached up and slowly caressed her breast.

Robin experienced the familiar breathless flutter as his touch aroused an electric response in her, and her eyes darkened. "Paul...."

He caught the back of her neck and pulled her head down. His kiss was moist and tantalizing, luring her into his intoxicating spell.

With a murmur of regret, he released his hold on her as he spanned her chin with his hand. "If I didn't have two surgeries scheduled this morning, I would book off. . .with a little persuasion.''

She grinned as she looked down at him in disbelief. ''I'll bet a month's pay that you've never missed a day in your life.''

He laced his hands behind his head as he eyed her brazenly and smiled. ''I've never had a good reason before.'' He idly trailed his fingers across her naked midriff with tormenting slowness as the gleam in his eyes intensified. ''But you, Robin Mitchell, are the most tempting reason of all.''

''If that's true,'' she said with a throaty laugh, ''maybe I could tempt you into coming home early tonight.''

There was a bold glint of aroused interest in his eyes as he gave her that slow disarming smile that had her heart doing erratic skips and hops. ''I think,'' he drawled softly, ''that certainly could be arranged.''

After Paul left, Robin became very thoughtful, and for quite some time she lay in bed, her hands laced behind her head as she stared at the ceiling. When she considered it, finding out about Paul's personal wealth didn't really come as a big surprise. His extensive wardrobe alone must have cost a fortune, but on the other hand, he took meticulous care of everything he owned.

Robin stretched and grinned ruefully. And now he wanted to take meticulous care of her. She really couldn't condemn him for that. Not really. If she had bags of money, she would treat it in the same matter-of-fact way he did. Her grandmother's extreme frugality drove her nuts—and her cautious spending must affect him the same way. Her grin deepened. Going on a spending spree with his money would certainly be a fantasy come true, except she knew her pride would choke her first. But she could spend her own...the sheer extravagance of blowing one full month's pay in one fell swoop was just too tempting. And besides, nothing would please Paul more.

She started her morning out by stopping at a sporting-goods shop that specialized in fishing gear, where she bought Paul an outrageously expensive fly rod and a tackle box that was the ultimate in tackle boxes. Then with excitement bubbling through her, she headed for an area in Calgary that was renowned for its exclusive boutiques. She'd never experienced such a giddy sense of financial recklessness in her life, and she enjoyed every minute of it.

She found, however, that some old habits die hard, and her practicality balked at excesses, so on the way home she stopped at one of the discount department stores to pick up some mundane odds and ends she needed.

With her purchases packed in a plastic bag, she was walking through the womenswear department on her way to the parking lot when a beautiful shade of crimson caught her eye. She pulled the dress from among the others on the rack, then grinned wryly. The color *was* gorgeous, but the style of the dress was something else.

It was made out of that slinky fabric that would cling to every curve—what there was of it to cling anywhere. It had a neckline that went down forever and the skimpy shirt boasted a very long slit up one side. Robin grimaced. She'd look like a first-class trollop in *that* dress! With a flick of indifference, she let the dress fall back among the others, then turned and walked away. Halfway down the aisle, Robin paused, a speculative gleam growing in her eyes as she unconsciously chewed on one nail. Then with a suppressed grin tugging at her mouth, she turned and walked back to the rack. She studied the dress again. It was probably a shade too small, but that would only add to the effect. She rolled her eyes in an expression that clearly said she thought she had taken leave of her senses, then she gathered the dress up and marched back to the cashier.

The phone was ringing as Robin staggered into the apartment, her arms loaded with parcels. She unceremoniously dropped everything on the floor and dashed into the kitchen to answer it. She glanced at the clock on the back of the stove as she picked up the receiver. Four o'clock already! She didn't realize it was so late!

It was Paul, and he sounded very irritated. There was a budget meeting scheduled, and he probably wouldn't be home until seven. She was not to worry about dinner—he'd grab something at the cafeteria. Robin managed to sound dutifully sympathetic, but for once she was delighted he was going to be late. She needed time.

It was just before seven when Robin finished dressing. She stood before the full-length mirror and critically studied her appearance. The outfit was indecent enough to make one blush! The dress simply could not be any sexier. Robin had added to the suggestive effect by sweeping her hair to one side and fastening it with an ornate comb. Gaudy black-and-red dangly earrings a misguided aunt had given her, more makeup than usual and some strappy high-heeled sandals completed the ensemble. It was dynamite.

For .years she'd done everything she could to disguise her voluptuous figure; now she was doing everything possible to flaunt it! If she could only keep from laughing.

She was just coming down the hallway when she heard Paul's key in the lock, and with her hips undulating, she sauntered into the entryway. The stunned look on his face nearly snapped her composure, but somehow she managed to keep a straight face as she deliberately thrust her hip out, revealing a long shapely leg.

Showing rather a lot of cleavage, she slithered her arm up the wall and with her very best come-hither voice, she breathed, "Hi, gorgeous. I'm Eleanor." Eleanor was Robin's middle name and she hated it, but Paul insisted it had always been a favorite of his. After tonight, he would probably be more keen on it than ever, she thought dryly.

The look on his face was something to behold, and like a man in a trance Paul stared at her. Then he shook his head as if to clear it before he very thoroughly studied her from head to toe. A broad grin creased his face, and a roguish gleam grew in his eyes as he continued to let his gaze slide over her. His voice had a low and meaningful quality when he said, "Well, hello, Eleanor."

She swayed over to him, slowly and sensuously slipping her hands up his torso and along his broad shoulders before letting them rest at his neck. Making rather a big production out of it, she languidly undid his tie. "Let's make you a little more comfortable, shall we?" she murmured, her voice silken.

The heated look in Paul's eyes increased as he tossed his jacket toward the hall table, his gaze never leaving her as he looped his arms around her. "That sounds like a good idea," he murmured. With bold familiarity, he slowly stroked her hips, the satiny fabric slipping smoothly over her naked skin. She gave him a sultry look, her eyelashes drooping seductively. "Is there anything more I can do for you, handsome?" she breathed.

"Oh, I'm sure I'll think of something. . .eventually," he said. With his knuckles brushing against her skin, he let his hand trail down the revealing front of her dress to her naked midriff, his electrifying touch sending a shiver of excitement coursing through her. "I think," he drawled softly, "this is going to be a very interesting encounter, Eleanor."

For some reason the way he stressed "Eleanor" finished it for Robin. She simply could not hold back her amusement one minute longer, and she backed away from him, her shoulders shaking with a fit of silent laughter. Paul's eyes narrowed, and there was a menacing glint in them as he pulled his shirt loose and began to undo the buttons, a villainous grin on his face as he sauntered toward her.

"Bit off more than you can chew, didn't you, Eleanor?"

With a helpless shrug, Robin continued to back away from him, unable to speak.

"That's not how you play the game, Eleanor," he said as he stripped off his shirt and dropped it on the floor as he continued to stalk her.

"Paul," she managed to gasp, "I didn't mean... for you to...take it so seriously." She dodged behind the sofa and took a deep breath in an attempt to gain control of her merriment.

"That's too bad," he said. His eyes were flashing dangerously, and he was smiling that smile that made him look so piratical. "I'm deadly serious about it. You started it; now you're going to finish it."

Keeping the sofa between them, she wiped away the tears of laughter that were suspended on her lashes, then took a deep breath to quell another fit of giggles. "Look," she said, trying to distract his single-minded pursuit, "I brought you a present—a new fly rod and the tackle box you wanted."

"Lovely," he said. Totally ignoring the gift she indicated, he circled behind the sofa, his eyes riveted on her.

She continued to move away from him. "I thought you'd be pleased," she said, struggling to inject a hurt tone into her voice.

"I'll be pleased tomorrow," he said as he undid the buckle of his belt. "What I'm interested in right now is the package that's so temptingly wrapped in red satin."

Robin's eyes were dancing with keen anticipation as she kicked off her shoes. He was slowly out-maneuvering her; it was time to get serious about this game of cat and mouse. Moving to the far end of the sofa, she waited, poised for his next move. With the confidence of a hunter who knows he has his prey trapped, he came toward her, his eyes flashing. As his arm snaked out to grab her, Robin dodged away. With the grace of a practiced athlete, he vaulted over the sofa. Like lightning, Robin swerved and made her escape behind the leather chair, then sprinted toward the dining area. With laughter leaving her breathless, she managed to put the table between them, her chest heaving.

Paul shot her a very heated look of lusty approval. "Just watching you breathe in that dress is a fantastic experience," he said, grinning.

"Paul," implored Robin, her voice breaking with breathlessness and amusement. "I only bought it as a joke."

"Some joke," he said with feeling. Edging around the end of the table, he watched her like a hawk ready to strike.

Robin was beginning to feel truly trapped, and she eyed him warily as he came steadily toward her.

If she could get around the table before he cornered her, she had an open path to the hall. If she could make it that far, she could get to the bedroom and lock herself in—and she could get out of this ridiculous getup. As if the devil himself were after her, she wheeled and ran. But Paul had anticipated her move, and she hadn't gone twenty feet when he brought her down with a very neat tackle. Before she could get her wind and recover, he hoisted her across his shoulders and packed her into the bedroom. With laughter robbing her of her strength, she couldn't even struggle as he dumped her on the bed, then sprawled on top of her, pinning her securely with his body.

"Now, Eleanor," he said, his expression one of immense satisfaction, "you're going to pay dearly for your 'joke.'" Grasping her face firmly, he lowered his head. The kiss was meant to be all part of the game, but when his mouth possessed hers with a torrid ruthlessness, it was no longer a game. Robin felt as if she'd been struck by a thunderbolt of desire that unleashed a hot tide within her. Her response was scorching, and Paul shuddered. He fought for breath like a drowning man, his arms locked around her in an unbreakable hold as he groaned, "God... babe." Then he sought the moistness of her yielding mouth with a stormy urgency.

Robin awoke the next morning just as Paul was putting on his tie. Brushing back her tousled hair, she rolled over on her hip and propped herself up on one elbow.

"Good morning," she said, her voice husky with sleep.

Turning to face her, Paul smiled, his eyes alight with warmth and amusement. "Good morning." As he sauntered toward the bed, he let his gaze slide slowly over her body with a thoroughness that left her feeling very intoxicated. There was an unholy gleam dancing in his brown eyes as he bent over and gave her a very provocative kiss, his hand sliding sensuously up her leg to her thigh. He exhaled sharply then groaned, his voice laced with laughter.

"If you keep this up, I could become a habitual truant."

She laughed softly and caressed his cheek. He kissed her again, then swore under his breath as he straightened up. With his shoulders set resolutely, he walked over to the valet and picked up his jacket. There was an aura of sexual excitement radiating from him as he gazed at her with hooded eyes, then he shook his head.

"Do look me up again, Eleanor," he said, grinning lazily. "It's been great." With one last lingering look, he left the room, and Robin smiled. The dress had been worth every penny. . . and then some.

THAT NIGHT, ROBIN MET PAUL at the door, her happiness shining in her eyes. Paul smiled and hugged her hard. "You're incredible, do you know that?"

"So are you." She pressed his head down and kissed him warmly. He shifted his hold on her, his hand cradling the back of her head as his lips parted against hers, his tongue lightly caressing her bottom lip.

It was only after he eased away and buried his face in the tumble of her hair that Robin felt the exhausted sag to his body. Her violet eyes were soft with compassion as she touched his face and gently lifted his head. "You've had a rough day, haven't you?"

He sighed wearily as he rested his forehead against hers. "It's been a bitch, to put it bluntly."

Quietly she asked, "Do you want dinner now or do you want to wait?"

"If you don't have anything started, I'd rather wait."

Slipping her arm around his waist she steered him down the hall to the bedroom, then took his jacket from him. After hanging it on the valet, she folded back the covers of the bed and rearranged the pillows. A full day in surgery was brutal, and she knew exactly how damned drained he felt. He didn't want to talk, he didn't want to eat, he didn't want to shower; he just wanted to collapse in bed and die.

Stripping down to his briefs, he sprawled on the bed on his stomach. "Do you want a rubdown, or do you just want to be left alone?" she asked softly.

As tired as he was, there was a gleam in his eyes as he rolled over on his side and gave her a mischievous grin. "I don't think I can handle Ingrid the Swedish masseuse right now." Raising up on one arm, he reached out and caught her wrist and pulled her down beside him. "But I don't want to be left alone either."

Robin stretched out beside him. She slipped her arm around his shoulders and eased his head against her breast.

Paul sighed with heartfelt satisfaction as he draped one leg across hers and tucked his arm around her. "God, but this feels good."

With idle movements, Robin slowly stroked his thick hair, relishing the feel of its silky texture. She felt him smile, and she shifted her head to look at him. "What's so funny?"

"Eleanor," he said succinctly. The laugh lines around his eyes deepened as he slowly grinned, his gold-flecked eyes dancing. "I felt like someone yanked the rug out from under me when you came around the corner in that getup."

Robin laughed as she pressed his head against her. "You *did* look a little stunned."

"Stunned! You nearly blew my mind!" He chuckled softly then slowly stroked her arm. "Where on earth did you find that dress?"

She told him.

"Well, don't you ever throw it out," he directed. "It was terrific."

She kept her voice perfectly solemn when she said, "If you like it so much, I'll wear it the next time we go out for dinner."

"Not on your life, woman. I won't let you out of the house in *that* dress!"

Robin slipped her hand down the back of his head and began to massage his neck muscles.

"Mmm, that feels good," he murmured. There was a brief silence before he asked, "You have Saturday off, don't you?"

"Yes. I don't go back to work until Sunday."

"Let's go fishing on Saturday. I want to try out my new fly rod."

Robin nearly laughed, but she managed to restrain herself and instead, she adopted a miffed tone. "I didn't think you were very impressed with it last night."

Paul snorted, then slowly caressed her thigh and hip, his touch firm and very intimate. "I had more important things on my mind," he said pointedly, his voice laced with amusement.

Trying very hard to keep her tone serious, Robin said, "You could always practice casting off the balcony. You know, you might snag one of Eleanor's...colleagues."

Paul laughed. "No chance! It has to be Eleanor or no one."

For some silly, feminine reason, his answer pleased her to no end. With her cheek resting against the lustrous softness of his hair, Robin began to gently knead the taut muscles in his broad shoulders, and he groaned with gratification. "You *do* know where I ache."

"Only because I've ached there myself."

There was another comfortable silence, and Robin thought he had drifted off to sleep, but when he spoke, she realized he'd been deep in thought. "Robin, let's start looking for another place to live. I loathe apartments, and I don't think you're too keen on them, either."

He shifted his head to look up at her, and Robin gave him a rueful smile. "No, I don't like apartments, but I hate looking for a place even more."

Raising himself on one elbow, Paul looked at her, a strange, penetrating expression in his eyes. "Then you won't mind if I handle it?"

"Not one bit," she said with certainty.

"You're sure?"

She frowned slightly as she smoothed the palm of her hand along his jaw. "No, I won't mind," she answered, a little baffled by his seriousness. He dropped a soft fleeting kiss on her parted lips, then he rolled onto his back. He gathered her against him in a possessive embrace, and buried his hand in her hair. "I could hold you like this forever," he whispered, his lips brushing lightly against her forehead. "It feels so right, and so damned good." He closed his eyes, and Robin felt his weariness claim him, and very soon, his body relaxed against hers as he drifted off to sleep.

CLOSING HER EYES, Robin leaned against the leather headrest of the sports car, relishing the feel of the cool breeze whipping through her hair, the clean freshness against her skin dispelling her weariness. It had been one of those hot, beautiful June weekends that seem to breed carelessness, and the hospital had been flooded with a host of accidents. She had spent her entire shift in Emergency. On top of the heavy caseload, the air conditioner had quit, leaving the ward unbearably hot and stuffy.

When she arrived home shortly after five, she had been delighted to find that Paul had the cooler loaded with a picnic lunch. After he had given her time to change into a pair of shorts and a cool top, they headed off. She hadn't even asked him where they were going—she didn't care as long as they could find a quiet little spot that wasn't packed with a crowd of Sunday picnickers.

Sighing deeply, she turned her head and looked at him. Even in a pair of blue-jean cutoffs and a favorite faded yellow T-shirt, he'd still stand out in any crowd. He had that air about him—that magnetic appeal that was so dynamic, so overwhelming and so attractive.

With his left elbow propped on the leather padding along the top of the door, he rested his hand against the upright chrome frame for the vent window. His other hand lightly grasped the wheel as he maneuvered the high-powered car through the traffic.

The wind ruffled through his hair as he turned to check for oncoming traffic before he swung into a merging lane. Even though his eyes were obscured by sunglasses, Robin could tell they were narrowed. She frowned slightly. He had been unusually quiet for the past three days, and she wondered what it was that was troubling him. He was definitely brooding about something, and she hated seeing him like that—so isolated.

The traffic light changed from green to amber as Paul pulled into the intersection and turned down one of the old residential streets that was densely lined with huge trees. This district was Robin's favorite. Beautiful old homes with vast sweeping yards nestled along the Elbow River in a rustic serenity that she found absolutely charming. It was a tranquil pastoral setting in the middle of a booming metropolis, and Robin thought it must be an ideal location in which to live. The best of both worlds.

Without making any explanation, Paul pulled over to the curb and parked the car. A look of puzzlement registered on Robin's face as he climbed out, came around to the passenger side and wordlessly opened her door for her.

Casting him a questioning look, she took the hand he offered her and stepped out of the Jag. There was something about the taut look on his face and the charged silence that suddenly hung between them that made her feel strangely uneasy. Mutely she fell into step with him, his hand gripping hers, and she gave him another bewildered frown as he opened a wrought-iron gate set in a five-foot stone wall. What on earth was going on, anyway?

The squat two-story brick house was wonderfully quaint, and Robin instantly fell in love with it. The house seemed to snuggle into its setting like a friendly matron settling into a cozy rocking chair, sunlight winking from its gable windows, the flag walk silently inviting you up to the front door, which was nestled appealingly among some shrubbery. *The only thing that's missing,* she thought bemusedly, *is a big brass door knocker.*

Once again she looked at Paul, but he remained silent, his face expressionless. A light of comprehension began to dawn in her eyes when he took a strange set of keys from the back pocket of his shorts. Avoiding her gaze, he released her hand, then unlocked the oaken front door. Feeling somewhat uncertain, she followed him inside.

The house was vacant, but even so, the charm was not diminished by the echoing emptiness.

She was standing in a large foyer, and her breath caught as her gaze was immediately drawn to the curved staircase to the second floor, its steps thickly carpeted in an odd shade of blue. The wide handrail was of dark-grained oak, supported by sturdy spindles set in bold brass fittings.

It was magnificent. With a childlike awe settling upon her she followed Paul into the living room, and

she gazed around the room, her eyes wide with wonder. It was absolutely enchanting. A huge fieldstone
fireplace with a long, broad slate hearth dominated
one end wall, the space on either side of it filled with
built-in bookshelves. The outer wall had two sets of
French doors opening onto a private atrium that was
completely glassed in, allowing sunshine to spill
across the slate floor.

All the woodwork around the doors and windows
was of oak, and whoever had installed it had been a
master craftsman. The walls were painted the same
blue as the carpet, only a shade lighter, the off-white
drapes adding the needed touch of lightness. As she
stood transfixed in the middle of that room, Robin
could feel the warmth and coziness seep into her
bones.

She turned to face Paul and experienced a little
start of alarm when she realized how intently he had
been watching her face.

Her voice was hushed with reverence when she
said, "Are we going to rent *this*?"

He gave her an intense look for a moment, then he
walked over to the fireplace. Bracing one arm against
the mantel, he stared at the brass fire irons that were
standing on a pedestal at the end of the hearth, his
expression enigmatic.

"It isn't for rent," he said. There was a charged silence before he added, "It's for sale."

That knocked the wind out of Robin, and feeling
rather disoriented she walked over to the fireplace
and sat down abruptly on the hearth. Staring numbly
at the splash of sunshine that angled in through the

casement windows at the other end of the room, Robin took several breaths to quell the butterflies of uncertainty that were breaking loose. "You're planning on buying this?" she managed to stammer.

Sitting down beside her, he hunched forward, his elbows resting on his thighs, his hands hanging loosely between his knees. There was a pregnant pause before he answered. "I've put a deposit on it, subject to your approval."

There was a ring of determination in his voice that made her feel very cautious, and suddenly there was an indefinable tension between them. Now she knew what had been bothering him the past three days. He had been up to something, and she had the nagging feeling that she wasn't going to like whatever it was. Her fingers curled around the edge of the hearth, her whole body fortified for bad news.

"Paul, if you want to purchase this house, it's your decision. Even I know that property along the Elbow is damned expensive, and if you want to make that kind of capital investment, that's your business."

He glanced at her as he laced his fingers together. There was an edge of anger in his voice when he said, "If we were married, would you still feel that way?"

That little bombshell really took the starch out of Robin, and she stared at him in stupefaction. What was he driving at? He certainly wasn't leading up to a proposal, so what *was* he leading up to? She didn't like the tone of his voice, and the set to his chin made her very suspicious. Trying very hard to maintain her cool, she put together a reasonable response. "I honestly don't know," she finally answered. "Besides, that's a hypothetical question, and you know it."

He straightened up and studied her, his piercing gaze drilling straight through her. "Do you like the house and location?"

"Yes—of course. Who wouldn't?"

"Then do you agree that we should buy it?"

Feeling very much as if she was undergoing an inquisition, Robin stood up and walked away from him, her body stiff with wariness. "It isn't 'we,' Paul. It's your money. You spend it however you see fit."

There was a quietness in his voice that sent a chill down her spine when he said, "If we buy, it will be *our* house."

She froze, then turned slowly to face him, her attention riveted on him. "What, exactly, does that mean?"

He stood up, and turned his back on her. "That means," he said flatly, "that the deed will be registered in both of our names."

Robin could feel the blood drain from her face as she stood staring at him in disbelief. She swallowed, then swallowed again before she countered, "You know damned well there's no possible way I could arrange for that kind of financing yet...."

That tone of unbendable stubbornness was in his voice as he cut her off. "I've told you before, and I'm telling you again—money is not the issue."

He's doing it to me again, she thought with a mixture of alarm and anger. Aloud she said curtly, "Just what is the issue, Paul?"

He turned to face her, his eyes unfathomable, his face like granite. "You know the issue—and it isn't money."

"I don't, damn it! You simply don't make a gift of—what? What's this house worth—half a million? You don't make a gift of a quarter of a million dollars to... to your roommate! That's insane!"

The menacing look on his face was forged by fury as he came toward her, his eyes flashing fire. "You are a damned sight more than a roommate, Robin, and you bloody well know it. Your values are all screwed up. If we were married, you'd think nothing of me buying this house. If those were the circumstances, and if you were honest, you'd have to admit you'd be ecstatic. But because we aren't, you seem to think that you must deny yourself the privilege of a life-style I can provide for you. Damn it, why do you have to dig your heels in? Why can't you just accept the things I want to do for you with a bit of grace? What difference does it make if there's a marriage certificate or not?"

She very nearly snapped, "One hell of a lot!" but she clamped her teeth together and bit back that retort. With her vision suddenly blurred by angry tears, Robin stomped out of the living room through the perfectly charming dining room into the equally attractive kitchen. Her fingers fumbled with the dead bolt on the back door, then she yanked it open and stepped out, slamming it hard behind her.

Damn him! Damn him anyway! Why hadn't he just bought the house and left her out of it? Her owning half a house, especially half a house like *this* one was so preposterous it was unbelievable. What was he trying to do to her, anyway? She strode across the yard, then flung herself down on the lush carpet of green grass beneath a huge old willow tree, her jaw thrust out.

Why couldn't he see her point of view? Why was he so bullheaded about ramming his rotten money down her throat? A tiny inner voice penetrated through her wrath with sardonic logic, "And why can't you see his point of view, Robin Mitchell—or are you choking on your pride?"

Drawing up her knees, she locked her arms around them and rested her forehead on them. She didn't move; she just sat there like a slab of rock until her temper cooled down, and she could think straight.

After a very long time, she finally raised her head and took a deep breath. She had to think this through. Was she choking on her pride? Was she overreacting? Maybe she was. Some of what Paul had said had a very distinctive ring of truth to it that made her squirm a little. If they were married, she would have had a different reaction about buying the house. And why? Because a marriage certificate made it right, and the absence of one made it wrong? Or was it because subconsciously she still had the old-fashioned idea that it was a man's role to provide a home for his wife, but since she wasn't his wife, she must maintain her independence at all costs? How unreasonable was she being? Was her attitude twisted by a conflict between her own deeply ingrained values and the standards of today's society? Or was it even more basic than that—she didn't enjoy feeling like his mistress?

Robin lost track of time as she sat there sifting through her thoughts, rejecting some and retaining others. No matter how much she mulled it over in her mind, she was no closer to an answer—she was left sitting on the fence.

A group of noisy teenagers who were floating down the shallow river on an assortment of tire tubes distracted her, their laughter drifting up to her like discordant, yet not unpleasant, music. A river at your back door—it would be heaven. With a contemplative squint, she let her gaze sweep slowly across the backyard.

Even it was perfect. Like a bolt of green velvet, the expanse of lawn sloped down to the rocky edge of the river, its vastness punctuated by clumps of mature trees.

The property lines on either side were defined by stone walls. Along one side, there was a hedge of lilac and honeysuckle, their deep purple and bright pink blossoms adding bursts of color against their dense green foliage. Just off to the east, a stand of clump birch and some blue spruce sheltered a little weather-beaten gazebo that had clematis climbing over it. It was all so right. . . .

A shadow fell across her, and Robin tensed as she looked up, Paul was watching her with a stony expression, but she sensed the tight lines around his sensitive mouth were not etched there by anger. Instead, they were probably the result of his brooding, which made her feel sad—and a little guilty.

"We have to talk this out, Robin," he said, his voice subdued.

She sighed heavily. "I know we do."

He sat down beside her, leaning back against the massive trunk of the willow. He pulled out a broad-leaf weed that was staunchly fighting for survival in the thick grass and began to methodically shred the leaves from the stem of the plant.

Sighing heavily, he tossed the stem away and with thoughtful, dark eyes, he looked at her. "Will you listen to what I have to say?" he asked quietly.

She held his gaze for a minute, glanced away and nodded. Paul held out his hand, and Robin recognized the action for what it was—an offer of a truce. Without hesitation, she slipped her hand into his, her fingers curling tightly around his.

His own grip was firm when he finally began to speak. "I'm not certain if I can explain my feelings adequately, Robin. I've never trusted anyone enough to really open up, so this isn't going to be easy for me. I just know that I have to be honest with you."

He bent his head as he soberly reflected on some thought, before turning to look at her squarely. "I told you once that my money doesn't mean a damn to me, and I really meant it. But after thinking about it, I realize there's a contradiction in what I said. It doesn't mean a damn to me, but all of a sudden I discovered that I like what my money can buy for you."

A taut frown creased his forehead as he carefully considered his next words. "When I first saw this house three days ago, I knew the minute I walked in the door that you'd love it. Your presence, your personality seemed to be there in every room. And I felt pretty damned good knowing that I could buy it for you.''

He bowed his head as he slowly caressed the back of her hand with his thumb, and Robin saw him swallow with difficulty. His voice was very strained when he spoke. ''You give me things money simply cannot buy. Without even considering what a wealth of happiness you bring into my life, you give your love, your trust, your understanding. I've never experienced that kind of emotional security before, and you'll never know how much I value that.''

His grip on her hand became painfully tight, and a constricting ache grew in Robin's throat as she sensed his desperate need to make her understand. She could feel him struggling with his intense feelings when he said, ''You give of yourself—without fail. And because of that—because of your giving and caring—I know a kind of inner peace that I honestly didn't believe existed.''

He looked at her, his eyes revealing the anguish his profound emotions were causing him and Robin could no longer hold back the tears that were threatening. With a choked whisper, Paul pulled her into his arms and cradled her against his chest as he held her tightly. ''Do you know what it means to me to have someone who doesn't expect me to be superhuman—someone who supports me every step of the way, who accepts me as I am?''

His arms tightened convulsively around her, and Robin buried her tear-dampened face in the curve of his neck. Slipping her arms around his chest, she clung to him with every ounce of strength she possessed as he whispered against her hair, "I didn't believe that two people could ever share the kind of intimate compatibility you and I do. . . and you've made me so damned happy." Now that Paul was finally sharing his innermost feelings, it seemed impossible for him to stop.

"I hate it when you aren't around, and I can't wait to get home when I know you're there. I've never wanted to protect anyone before, and that need to protect is a very real part of the male ego. . . yet you allow me my weaknesses without ever once condemning me for having them."

His voice quavered as he caressed her back. "I never once saw anything like that between my parents, and I can't quite believe that it's happening to me. You've given me all that, yet you won't let me give what I can. The cost of this house is irrelevant. What is important, at least to me, is will you be happy here?"

Struggling into an upright position, Robin gently took his drawn face in her hands and gazed at him through the blur of her unshed tears. With her need to reassure him so profound, she whispered brokenly, "But Paul, you give so much of yourself without even realizing it—"

"But I've learned all that from you," he interjected hoarsely. "You've trusted me, and through that I'm learning to trust in return. You've taught me so much about genuine caring." His voice trembled as he whispered, "So much."

Rising on her knees, Robin wrapped her arms

around his shoulders and hugged him fiercely against her, an agony of emotions swelling within her as she cradled his head against her breast. But mixed in with the agony was a poignant sense of joy. At least she had given him a measure of happiness and contentment, and that was what counted most of all. Her face wet with tears, she pressed her cheek against the softness of his hair, her voice full of emotion. "Will you at least let me buy a brass door knocker for the front door?"

She felt him take a deep breath, then he crushed her against him in a viselike hold before he managed to whisper, "As long as it's one of those dreadfully British ones with the lion's head on it."

Blinking back her tears, she murmured huskily against his hair, "We'll go shopping for it together."

In response he lifted her to her feet with a powerful surge of strength, and with his arm clamped around her, he led her back into the house. After locking the door behind them, he guided her into the dining room, where he swept her against him in a nearly savage embrace.

There was a raw passion in him as he claimed her mouth in an urgent, scorching kiss that had her melting against him. His hands on her back telegraphed his need, his unleashed longing, as he molded her more closely against him until they were welded together with a searing insistence. With her own deep emotions so close to the surface, Robin's keen desire was intensified by his. It was like a blast from an inferno—white-hot and savage, and it was consuming them both in its fire. His every touch, his every caress scorched her aroused body, firing a passion that was as beautiful as it was devastating, and Robin's senses reeled beneath its violent force....

WHEN ROBIN FINALLY DRIFTED back to earth she lay nestled beside him, her head cradled on his shoulder as his strong hands stroked her back.

With a massive effort, she raised her head and gazed down at him. Warmth glowed in his dark eyes as he touched her jaw, then kissed her, his mouth moving gently against hers, his tenderness calming her spinning world. With a tremulous sigh, he again cradled her head against him as he held her protectively.

Suddenly the reality of their situation penetrated Robin's benumbed mind and her head snapped up in alarm.

"Paul, what are we *doing*...what if the real-estate agent shows up with some other prospective customers?"

Paul grinned at her. "You're too late. He wandered through with a group about twenty minutes ago."

"Paul...!"

He was laughing when he kissed her again. "Don't worry, love. The doors are all locked, chained and bolted; the curtains are drawn, and I assure you, we're quite alone."

She let out her breath in a rush of relief, then with mischief gleaming in her eyes, she looked at him solemnly, her voice crisply prim and proper as she asked, "And how would you rate the dining room, sir? Is it to your liking?"

Paul broke into unrestrained laughter, and he hugged her so hard she could barely breathe. When he could finally respond, there was a wealth of satisfaction in his voice as he said, "I'd rate the dining room as excellent, as a matter of fact." Then very deliberately, he dropped the pitch of his voice seductively when he continued, "And I can't wait for you to show me the rest of the house, room...by room...by room...by—"

"If the distance we've come so far is any indication," she broke in, "that could take quite a while."

"So it could." His expression changed, and he gazed up at her with a smile that spoke volumes. "I love you, Robin Mitchell."

She tipped her head to one side as she slowly traced his thick eyebrows with her fingertips. "If you love me, how come you always get your own way?"

"I'm more persuasive."

She flushed a little as she laughed. "You certainly are." She kissed him softly, then looked down at him, her face radiant as she whispered, "I do love the house, Paul. Thank you for such a charming and generous gift."

He let his hand rest on her shoulder as they exchanged a loving look. He smoothed his finger across her bottom lip as he murmured huskily. "You've already thanked me for it, Robin...a thousand times more than it's worth." He kissed her again, his lips soft and tantalizing. "I don't think I can ever get enough of you." He nestled her against him and held her for a long time, neither of them wanting to dispel the intimate serenity that encompassed them.

When Robin finally did get the promised tour of the house, she loved it even more. It was a house that had character and charm, a house built for a family with room for kids to grow—but she snapped the lid down on that disturbing thought and instead concentrated on soaking up the happiness that seemed to drench the place. Each room had something special, something that made it unique, some fascinating nook or cranny that made it feel like home. Home. Hers and Paul's.

In the shade of the willow tree they ate the picnic lunch Paul had prepared. While Robin packed up the remains, Paul spread the blanket in the middle of the yard, then glanced at her. "We can take possession of the house the first of July. How does that strike you?"

She shot him a tart look that was full of humor. "You mean you're asking me?"

He laughed. "Yes, I'm asking."

"Well, since *we* own it, we might as well live in it."

He flashed her a broad grin, "Grudging compliance—I like that." Stripping off his shirt, he stretched out in the sunshine, his hands tucked beneath his head.

Robin lay on her stomach beside him, propping her head on her hand. "I hope you like cutting grass."

He turned his head to look at her, laughter sparkling in his eyes. "If I don't, I'll hire a gardener."

She laughed, then grimaced. "You'd better hire a housekeeper while you're at it, or we'll spend all our time with either a lawnmower or a vacuum in our hands."

His response was deliberately offhand. "I already have."

Her head jerked up and she stared at him. "Have what?" she asked sharply.

"Hired a housekeeper."

Her tone was a mixture of disbelief, exasperation and unwilling amusement. "Paul, honestly...."

He ignored her. "She comes on Tuesdays and Thursdays. Her name is Mrs. Butterfield, and she's a doll. You'll love her."

Robin let out a long groan of frustration. "You're doing it to me again."

"Yep," he said with a broad grin. "I am."

"You're impossible," she said, her voice still tinged with exasperation.

"Not impossible," he corrected. "Practical. Your hours are too damned hectic as it is without giving you two acres of house to look after." He was still smiling at her, his eyes flashing a challenge. "Are you going to fight me over this, too?"

"No," she relented with a hopeless sigh. "What's the use? You maneuver me into submission every time." She leaned over and gave him a light kiss. "You're impossible, you're stubborn, and you're bossy, but I love you anyway."

He laced his fingers through hers, and with his other hand he reached up and brushed back a curl of hair that was clinging to her neck. His gaze was warm and tender, but there was a wealth of humor in it, too. "That's what I like about you, Robin. You cut through the garbage and get right to the heart of the matter.''

She smiled down at him with genuine amusement. ''I wonder what other little surprises you're going to spring on me?''

''You'll have to wait and see, won't you?'' he said teasingly. He lay smiling at her but apparently recalled something and his expression became more serious. ''Do you like antiques?''

She gave him a look of mild rebuke as she shook her head. ''You mean you need to ask?''

He grinned. ''No.''

Robin laughed, then gave his hand an abrupt shake as she narrowed her eyes threateningly. ''You drive me crazy. Now what's this about antiques?''

''I inherited all my grandmother's estate, and there must be a whole warehouse full of furniture stored in Toronto. If you like, I'll have it shipped out.''

She smiled at him. ''I'd like that.''

His eyes darkened, and he caressed her face with that gentle touch that was so distinctly his. His voice was husky when he murmured, ''Happy?''

The old attraction was there, drawing them together, and her voice was unsteady as she whispered, ''More than I can say.'' And it was true. For the first time, she let herself consider that the future for her and Paul might hold something more than indefiniteness. Maybe this was the real beginning. Maybe.

CHAPTER EIGHT

THEIR DAYS WERE WOVEN TOGETHER in a tapestry of contentment, love, laughter, tranquillity. But every now and again, Robin would have an unsettling feeling that her time with Paul was measured, but she always pushed it to the back of her mind. She kept telling herself that he just needed time.

And time marched on. The blue sky and yellow sunshine days of summer gave way to the gray rain-chilled and golden-leaved days of fall. And each day, he became more vital to her existence. But it wasn't just the love they shared. It was work, too. They were both dedicated to their profession, and Robin respected his skill and knowledge with a near reverence. Paul spent hours with her, instructing her on different procedures and techniques, and because of his thoroughness, her own skill and knowledge were growing steadily.

Bernie tormented her relentlessly about the benefits of being the teacher's pet, insisting that they had obviously succeeded in cloning Paul's brain, and she had been the recipient of the first successful cerebral transplant.

October's vibrant brilliance gave way to November's bleakness, and she had little time to think about anything other than work. A virulent epidemic of a new strain of influenza was sweeping the province, and not only was it overloading every hospital in the city, but it was also cutting a swath through the staff, as well. The virus was vicious when it struck—the combination of extremely high fevers and acute nausea often left the victim severely dehydrated. To add to the severity of the illness, a stubborn case of pneumonia always accompanied it.

Since it had been the cause of three deaths in the city, the medical community was regarding it with great seriousness. Because it was so rampant and so contagious, all elective surgery had been postponed. Only emergency operations were being performed, and those were carried out under the most rigidly enforced restrictions. The cutback hadn't decreased the work load on surgery, however. Surgical staff were slotted into positions in other wards where the hospital was critically short of help. Robin and Paul were both putting in twelve-hour shifts, he in the medical ward, she in pediatrics.

Robin's heart ached for the little ones. They were so desperately ill, so weak, so scared, and the hospital was so short of staff that there simply weren't enough people to dispense some comfort along with the medical treatment. She hated seeing those children, those babies, suffer, and it really upset her that she could do so little for them.

The stress, the worry, the long hours were beginning to take their toll, and she was exhausted. There were countless times she stayed even later, just so she could hold some scalding hot, vomiting, coughing and very frightened child. Paul would watch her, his eyes dark with concern, but he never once admonished her about her grueling hours.

In time the virus cases became fewer and fewer, and the work load was almost back to normal at the hospital, but Robin still felt rotten. She was so exhausted all the time. She had five days off coming up, and she dragged herself through each day with that thought in mind. All she had to do was make it through Friday, and she'd have five heavenly days. She was going to crawl into bed and not get out until she *had* to go back to work.

As it turned out, the Wednesday-morning surgery was longer than expected, and they had only enough time to grab a quick bite to eat before they went back into OR.

That afternoon the operating room seemed hotter than usual, the heat draining Robin of energy as perspiration soaked her back and trickled between her breasts. Her back was aching and the muscles across her shoulders and in her legs were throbbing painfully, but she'd drop dead before she'd let Paul see how tired she was. Two more days and she could sleep for five....

She turned to the nurse, who mopped her brow with a swab gauze. She glanced across the operating table at Paul and felt a surge of respect for the surgeon he was. Not only was he brilliant at his work, but he had the stamina of an ox.

"We're getting a little seepage from that artery, Mitchell—you'd better clamp it." Robin felt a brief twist of queasiness when his long fingers probed the incision, the thin membrance of his rubber gloves turning red with blood. She was more exhausted than she thought—Robin hadn't felt sick in OR since her first operation.

"How's the blood pressure, Mac?"

"It's 100 over 40—a little low but the pulse is hanging in there," was the offhand response.

As tired as she was, Robin couldn't help but grin. She liked working with Dick MacDonald. The first time she had been in OR with him, she had had her doubts about the capability of the man. He was un-shaven, and he looked as if he'd barely recovered from a four-day binge, but it didn't take her long to discover he was the best anesthesiologist around. In a crisis, Mac would do a flip-flop of roles so fast it would make your head spin—fast, alert and definitely on the ball.

"Say, Wilcox, I've been meaning to ask you. What in hell has happened to you lately? When you first came on staff, you lived at this goddamned hospital. Now we're lucky if you put in sixteen hours a day."

Paul laughed. "I've taken up a hobby."

"What's that?"

"Bird-watching." Robin nearly laughed out loud. He hadn't hit her with that one since the time he'd trapped her in Elizabeth Decker's room.

She had to bite her lip to keep control when Mac snorted, "Bird-watching! You've got to be kidding! Bird-watching?"

"Bird-watching," confirmed Paul, and Robin could see him grinning behind his mask.

"Hell, man, what kind of a hobby is *that*?"

"You'd be surprised."

Robin clenched her teeth together to hold back the bubble of amusement that was threatening to break loose.

Paul deftly made another incision as Mac stared at him, a knowing gleam in his eyes. "Gorgeous two-legged birds, no doubt."

Robin couldn't resist. "I don't ever recall seeing a four-legged bird, doctor."

Paul shot her a look of amused approval as Mac laughed. "You stay out of this, Mitchell. How the hell can I ever corner this guy if you keep helping him escape?"

Robin swabbed around the incision and tossed the soiled gauze into an enamel receptacle. "I just made an observation," she said.

"You're grinning behind that damned mask, lady. I can see it in your eyes. Now really, can you believe that this guy's an ornithologist?"

"I never said I was an ornithologist—I said I like watching birds. There's a difference."

"In a pig's eye!"

Her amusement refused to be stifled any longer, and Robin laughed. "If this poor woman knew that you were discussing pigs' eyes while we were removing her gall bladder, she'd go into acute shock."

"I'd like to get you on that table, Mitch," threatened Mac with a grin. "I'd fix you."

"I don't have gallstones, Dr. MacDonald."

"Maybe not, but you sure in hell have your share of gall."

Paul removed the gravel-impacted organ and

dropped it in the pan, then grinned at Mac. "Okay, that's it! You two can quit your verbal sparring. Close up, Mitchell."

Dr. MacDonald made an adjustment to his controls, then sat watching Robin suture. "I know I shouldn't tell you this, but you do have class when it comes to closing them up, Mitch. You do a fine bit of needlework."

Robin turned her face for the nurse to wipe her forehead. "Thank you."

"Where did you learn to sew like that, anyway?" he teased.

Her response was dry. "I embroider tea towels in my spare time."

"You can embroider on me anytime."

"That sounds like a great idea," she grinned. "May I have your permission to blanket-stitch your lips together?" She heard Paul chuckling as he left the operating theatre.

It felt as if her body weighed a ton when Robin finally walked out of the OR. She wearily pulled off her mask, then stripped off her cap. She closed her eyes as she stretched her shoulders back in an attempt to ease the aching stiffness in her muscles. With a deep sigh, she straightened and reluctantly opened her eyes.

Paul was leaning against the scrub sink, his arms folded across his chest, his eyes unwavering as he watched her with a worried look.

Just then, Mac came out of the surgery and made quick work of tossing his mask, hat and gown in the proper chute. "If I didn't have to work tomorrow, I would go home and promptly anesthetize myself with four stiff drinks. God, but I'm beat.''

''It's been one hell of a day,'' Paul agreed. He glanced at Mac, then at Robin, his gaze lingering on her. His voice was quiet and touched with concern when he said, ''Let's go grab a coffee.''

Robin took off her gown and glanced at the wall clock above the door. ''You two go ahead. I have rounds to do yet.''

Mac caught her arm and propelled her toward the door. ''You,'' he said firmly, ''are coming down for refueling before you go anywhere.'' He grinned at her as he held the door open. ''Besides, I deserve the opportunity to get even.''

The minute Robin walked into the cafeteria and the smell of fried onions hit her she was nearly sick, and with the surge of nausea came a hot flush and acute dizziness. She could feel perspiration dampen her body, and without thinking she reached out and caught Paul's arm to steady herself when the room began to swim. His eyes riveted on her, and a look of alarm flashed across his face. She'd gone deathly pale, and her face was beaded with sweat.

She heard Dr. MacDonald say something but his voice was oddly muffled, as though her hearing was impaired. With his arm securely around her, Paul guided her out of the room and down the corridor to a little-used waiting room. He sat her down on the battered sofa and pressed her head between her knees.

''Do you want me to get a stretcher for her?'' asked Mac.

The dizziness began to clear, and Robin slowly lifted her head. She took a deep breath, then whispered, "No, please don't."

Paul stared at her, his face drawn as he wiped the perspiration from her forehead with the palm of his hand. He turned to Dick MacDonald and said, "I'm going to take her home, Dick. The keys to my car are on my desk. Would you mind getting them for me and sending someone down to the parking lot with them?"

"Sure thing." Mac looked at Robin and gave her a lopsided grin. "My wife always said my jokes made her sick." His grin broadened, "But I had no idea how bad they really were until now."

Robin managed a smile at his good-natured teasing. He turned to go. "I'll run the keys down to the parking lot myself. I'll be there in a jiffy." With that he left, closing the door behind him.

As soon as he was gone, Paul sat down beside her and nestled her throbbing head against his shoulder, his arms supporting her drooping body. "Why didn't you tell me you weren't feeling well, Robin?" he queried gently. "I knew you were exhausted, but I had no idea you were ill."

She closed her eyes. "It didn't hit me until we walked into the cafeteria."

"We should stop by emergency and get a throat swab for a culture."

"Just take me home, Paul," she pleaded weakly. "I've had enough of this hospital for today."

He brushed her damp hair back off her forehead and kissed her softly. "I'll take you home."

By the time Paul got her home and into bed, Robin was feeling a little like a fraud. She had a splitting headache and she felt like her muscles were mush, but the nausea and dizziness were gone.

Paul had had a quick shower and changed his clothes, and Robin lay in bed, watching him button up his shirt. "Did it ever enter your head that I might be malingering?"

He tucked his shirt in his slacks and did up the zipper. Lacing his leather belt through the belt loops, he grinned at her. "No one, not even you, can sweat on command." He came over to the bed and sat down, gently stroking her bare shoulder. "Are you certain you're going to be okay?"

"I'll be fine."

He bent down and gave her a soft kiss, then drew the covers up. "I'll try to get home early."

"Don't worry, Paul. Really. I'll be fine."

With a worried frown, he took her hand in his. "I hate like hell leaving you alone." He glanced at his watch and stood up. "I'm taking a cab back to the hospital so I can bring the Bronco home. Where will I find your keys?"

"Lisa can get my things for you. The keys are in the side pocket of my handbag."

"Side pocket," he confirmed. He bent down and dropped another soft kiss on her mouth. "You phone me if you want me, okay?"

Robin's eyes were as soft as blue velvet when she gazed up at him. "I'll always want you," she whispered huskily.

Her answer pleased him, and his eyes were sparkling as he smiled down at her. "That's nice to know." He turned toward the door. "Why is it so damned hard for me to get out of here when you're in bed?" he groaned.

Robin was asleep before he was out the front door. And she slept for five straight hours without moving a muscle. She was drifting at the edge of consciousness when a sound brought her fully awake. The bedroom was in total darkness, except for the rectangle of light that spilled in from the open bedroom door.

"Paul?"

The dim glow from the bedside light hurt her eyes, and she squinted at him drowsily as he sat down on the edge of the bed. "Hi. I was beginning to think you'd sleep right through until morning."

"What time is it?"

"A little after eight." He laid his hand on her forehead as he asked, "How are you feeling?"

"Dopey—and thirsty."

"Would you like something to eat?" he asked.

"No, just some juice."

"What kind do you want—apple or tomato?"

"I'll come down," she said as she struggled into a sitting position.

He had that obstinate expression on his face as he arranged the pillows behind her and firmly pushed her back against them. "No you aren't. Trips to the bathroom, and that's it, kiddo."

"I can get up. . . ."

"You," he said forcefully, "are staying in bed."

She stared at him for a minute, silently wondering if she could get away with challenging him. As though he was reading her mind, he shook his head, his jaw jutting out stubbornly. "Bed, Robin."

She grinned at him. "Is that a proposition?"

He tried to maintain a stern look but he ended up grinning at her. "Maybe."

After he came back upstairs, he did relent on letting her have a quick shower. Robin felt a little shocked at how weak she was. She had practically no strength left, and every muscle in her body ached. But she did feel better. After toweling her hair dry, she wrapped a towel around her like a sarong and went back into the bedroom.

Paul had changed into his dark brown velour robe, and he was stretched out on the bed reading the newspaper. She crawled into bed beside him.

"Do you know this is the first time in days that we've been in bed at a decent hour?" he said, tossing the newspaper on the floor.

Closing her eyes, Robin smiled as she slowly trailed her fingers along his naked thigh. "That depends on what your definition of going to bed is."

His voice carried a husky warning. "Robin...."

She opened her eyes and made a face. Actually, she didn't feel that bad when she was lying down—if only she didn't feel so achy.

"Want a back rub?" he asked.

"You're reading my mind again," she said accusingly.

"I know." He sat up and pulled the towel from around her. "Roll over, Eleanor."

"Yes, doctor."

She loved it when he gave her a massage. If there

was one definition of bliss, this had to be it, she thought, as his strong hands started working up one leg. More than once she'd fallen asleep as he kneaded her aching muscles.

She rested her head on her arms and closed her eyes as he slowly worked up her legs to the small of her back. She gave a groan of pleasure as he massaged the aching muscles in her shoulders. "You have no idea how good that feels."

"Oh, yes I do," he said as he thoroughly worked across her back. Robin smiled. For all the times she'd rubbed his back, she had never once put him to sleep—in fact, just the opposite. And he was having the same effect on her now. He was straddling her legs, and as he shifted his weight, Robin twisted beneath him. There was a sparkle of impishness in her eyes as she slowly untied the belt of his robe.

He gave her a warning look. "Don't go into the kitchen if you can't stand the heat."

"All work and no play makes Jack a dull boy," she countered.

He stared down at her through squinted eyes, then very slowly he smiled, a wicked gleam flashing in his dark eyes. He shrugged off the robe and tossed it on the floor.

"So," he said suggestively, as he lowered his body against hers, "We have a cook in the kitchen who's going to smarten up Jack."

Robin laughed as she looped her arms around his neck. "You could put it that way if you like."

"I like," he said, then brushed his lips against hers, his tongue softly caressing her bottom lip.

"Mmm, I definitely like," he murmured as he slid his arms around her, molding their naked bodies together.

BY LATE FRIDAY MORNING, Robin knew that this was no mild virus she was fighting. She had slept little the night before, and her condition continuously worsened. She feigned sleep when Paul got up, partly because she felt too weak to talk, and partly because she didn't want him worrying about her all day. By noon, she couldn't keep anything down, her temperature was climbing, she was developing congestion in her lungs, and she had a headache such as she'd never had before. By the time Paul arrived home that evening she was really ill.

With a grim set to his mouth, he thoroughly examined her, his expression becoming more grave by the minute. "I'm going to hospitalize you," he said as he took the stethoscope from his ears. "I want some lab work done on you *now*."

She swallowed painfully and whispered, "We both know what it is."

He wiped the perspiration from her face and neck with a cool, damp cloth, and Robin longed to smooth away the chiseled lines around his mouth, but she simply didn't have enough strength to raise her hand.

"That's why you're going into the hospital," he said firmly.

Tears of exhaustion blurred her eyes as she swallowed again. Her throat felt absolutely raw, and speaking was such a painful effort, but she forced herself to do it. "I'll do anything you say, but just don't put me in the hospital," she begged.

"Robin, this damned virus is dangerous."

"Please, Paul. Just give it another day."

He finally gave in, but she knew he did it with very serious misgivings. She really didn't think she could get much worse.

But she was wrong. She didn't know how many times that night Paul had to strip the bed because she was soaked with sweat. By early morning, spasms of retching gripped her, and when traces of blood appeared, that was it. She was vaguely aware that Paul made some phone calls but by then she didn't really care. All she wanted to do was die. She was so exhausted she couldn't even respond when Bernie and Lisa arrived.

With Lisa's help, Paul managed to get a modest nightie on her, but the soft cotton was damp the minute it touched her body.

Bernie entered the bedroom just as Paul was sponging her face. "The ambulance is here."

"Send them up," came Paul's terse command.

"Paul," she whispered.

His expression softened as he bent over her. "What is it, love?"

"Can you admit me? I don't want anyone else touching me."

He cupped her hot face in his hands and kissed her with immeasurable tenderness. "Do you think I'd let another doctor within ten feet of you?" he admonished softly. His hands were so cool against her skin as he brushed back her hair that Robin's eyes drifted shut beneath his gentle ministrations.

She thought she was going to start retching again as they moved her onto the stretcher, but she was so weak her body didn't respond to the involuntary urge.

"I'm going in the ambulance with her," stated Paul. "You can meet us at the hospital."

"I think you'd better let Bernie go with her, Paul." It was Lisa's voice, quiet and firm.

"No, I'm going—"

"Use your head, Paul," interjected Bernie quietly. "If you show up at the hospital with her in the ambulance, she'll be hounded to death by every nosy snoop there." Bernie's voice was sympathetic when he added, "It's only ten minutes to the hospital from here, and nothing's going to happen to her between now and then."

Robin didn't open her eyes as she whispered, "It's all right, Paul."

The ambulance ride was a blur for Robin, except the swaying of the vehicle started her retching all over again. But she was aware that Bernie held her, his arms firm and reassuring.

Paul was waiting for them in the ambulance bay, the collar of his leather bomber jacket turned up against the autumn chill. When the electronic doors rumbled shut, a cool refreshing breeze feathered across Robin's face and it felt like a touch of heaven. She was so hot, but she knew that the violent convulsions and shivering would follow the scalding sweat she was in now.

There were no delays at admittance. With Paul and Bernie in control of the stretcher, they rushed her right through to an elevator. Normally, Robin would have been sent to the medical ward, but Paul was booking her in on surgery. On that ward he was in control, without having to worry about infringing on anyone else's territory. As they wheeled Robin down the corridor toward a private room, Paul snapped out commands to his staff, who had obviously been notified of Robin's condition and her arrival.

Positioning the stretcher next to the bed, Paul folded back the blanket that was wrapped around her, then shifted her over. Robin started to shiver violently, and she clenched her teeth together as she tried to will her rigid muscles to relax, but she couldn't. Her mind seemed to be disconnected from bodily control. She just didn't have any energy left, and she closed her eyes, severing her awareness of what was going on around her.

FOR THE NEXT EIGHTEEN HOURS, Robin drifted in and out of consciousness that seemed to be drug-induced. But even in that dazed comatose state, she sensed that Paul was always with her.

It was night when she finally came fully awake. For a moment, she was completely disoriented, then she realized she was propped up in a hospital bed. With a determined effort she turned her head to look at Paul, who was slouched in a chair by her bed, his face haggard and unshaven, his eyes sunken with worry and exhaustion. Even in the soft night light, she could see the tension in him. She longed to reach out and touch him, but her arm would not respond to the weak mental command.

Robin swallowed painfully. Her chest hurt terribly and so did her head, but she could tell that her temperature was down. Her mouth was so dry that she had to swallow several times before she could speak.

Her voice was a barely audible whisper. "Paul."

His head pivoted abruptly, his attitude suddenly alert. She swallowed again, then whispered, "Could I have a drink?"

Slipping his arm around her shoulders, he supported her slightly as he offered a glass of ice water with a flexible straw in it.

As he opened his mouth to speak, she managed a feeble smile. "I know. I can only have a little."

His smile didn't reach his eyes, and he watched her intently as she took a sip. The cool liquid against her parched, sore throat was so soothing. Without releasing his hold on her, he set the glass back on the table and leaned over to kiss her softly on the forehead. "How are you feeling?"

"Better," she whispered hoarsely. Vaguely aware of the IV tube taped to her hand, she reached up and combed her fingers through his untidy hair. "Don't look so worried. I'll be fine in a few days."

He took an unsteady breath and buried his face against her damp neck, and Robin slipped her arms around his shoulders as he held her in a restrained embrace that was immeasurably tender. "You scared the hell out of me for a few hours. Your temperature kept climbing...."

His voice faltered, and Robin gently stroked his head as she murmured, "You'd never get rid of me that easily, Dr. Wilcox."

When he raised his head, there was a glimmer of

genuine amusement in his eyes. "I'm bloody well relieved to hear that."

He gave her a soft lingering kiss, then with reluctance he eased her back against the pillows and slowly withdrew his arms. "Now, my very fair lady, you're going to sleep."

She smoothed her hand along his cheek, her glazed eyes filled with concern. "*You* go home and get some sleep. You look exhausted."

"I'm not leaving this room, Robin," he stated flatly.

"I wish you wouldn't. . . ."

"I'm staying right here." His tone softened as he squeezed her hand. "I'll get far more rest here than I would at home, believe me." He tucked her hand under the sheet and smiled at her. "Besides, I have to make sure you don't talk in your sleep."

Robin smiled back, and he gave her hand another squeeze. He hitched the chair closer to the bed before he sat down and slipped his hand under the sheet to grasp hers. Slouching down in the chair he rested his head against the padded back as he closed his eyes.

For a long time, she lay there, just looking at him, then finally she, too, closed her eyes, her fingers twined with his.

By Monday morning the worst of it was over, and finally Paul relented to Robin's insistent pleas. After canceling his morning lectures, he used one of the rooms assigned to doctors on call and slept for most of the morning.

As her strength returned little by little, Dr. Robin Mitchell discovered she did *not* like being a patient. It seemed as if she was living in a fishbowl, and she came to resent the constant invasion of her privacy.

She silently endured it, but she didn't like it. There was always somebody hovering around her bed: nurses bustled in and out with everything from temperature checks to bedpans, the physiotherapist came in with annoying frequency to give her therapy for her congested lungs, a technician from the lab took blood samples—it was a never-ending stream. If it wasn't one thing, it was another, and Robin hated it all.

Then there was Paul. He looked so tired, and she seldom had a moment alone with him. The strain from the weekend had certainly left its mark on him, and that worried Robin. She wished Paul would quit stewing about her—she was feeling much better.

"You must really rate with someone, Dr. Mitchell," said the ward aide Tuesday morning as she carried a huge plastic-wrapped bouquet of flowers into the room. Placing the flowers on the swivel table that had been pushed to the foot of Robin's bed, the aide carefully stripped off the protective cellophane and chatted brightly as she added water to the arrangement.

But Robin hadn't heard a word the girl said. The bold familiar handwriting on the card made her feel suddenly very homesick, and the words made her feel doubly so. "Annie and I are missing you like hell," it read. "All my love, P."

Robin read the card twice and glanced at the ward aide. "Would you mind getting a few things out of my suitcase for me? I'd really like to freshen up a bit—I feel like such a wreck."

She looked like one, too. No color in her face, dark circles under her eyes, and her hair looked as if it was home to a flock of birds.

The aide was delighted to help. The entire exercise used up what little strength Robin had, but by the time she had put on a fresh nightie, a little makeup, and the aide had spent several minutes fussing with her hair, Robin definitely looked much better. She had the aide roll up her bed, and she was determined to look alert when Paul Wilcox made his rounds.

But her determination was eroded by weariness, and she had drifted into a light slumber by the time he arrived. The sound of the nurse drawing the curtain around the bed awakened her, and she opened her eyes to find Paul watching her with the oddest expression on his face.

She smiled. "Good morning, doctor."

"Good morning. You're looking much better today, Mitchell."

Get rid of that damned nurse, she thought silently. There was an immediate telltale quirk around Paul's mouth as he stared at her, and she felt a flush color her cheeks as she said, "I am feeling much better."

His mouth twitched again as he said, "You can go, nurse. And would you close the door behind you? I have a few cases that I need to discuss with Dr. Mitchell."

"Certainly, doctor."

Paul shot Robin a knowing, amused look, then studied her chart, his face fixed with concentration. He didn't look up until the door hissed shut behind the departing nurse.

Robin smiled at him as he came around the bed. "Thank you for the flowers, Paul. They're so beautiful."

With his hand resting possessively on her shoulder, he bent down and gave her a kiss. "I'm glad you like them." Sitting down on the edge of the bed, he slid his hand up her neck until his fingers were buried in her hair, his thumb softly caressing her ear as he murmured, "That house is damned empty without you."

"You could take me home," she offered hopefully.

He laughed. "Not a chance!" He dropped another fleeting kiss on her mouth, and slipped his arm around her to ease her forward. Unclipping his stethoscope from around his neck, he clamped it in his ears. "Let's have a listen."

He pressed the cold metal disc against her back, and with mischief gleaming in her eyes, Robin held her breath.

"Breathe, Robin," he commanded with a throaty laugh.

"I was."

"It won't work—now breathe."

He listened to her back, then pressed the device against her chest, his touch most certainly intimate and completely unprofessional. After he removed the stethoscope, he stuck it in the pocket of his lab coat, and stared at her. "You certainly won't be leaving here for a while."

She made a little grimace. "I hate it here."

"I know you do." With a soft sigh, he gathered her against him and nestled her head against his neck.

"And I hate having you here, but you are going to need more therapy." His hold on her slackened as he started to lay her back down. Robin's arms tightened around his neck, and her voice was husky when she whispered, "Just hold me a little while. Please."

She felt him shudder slightly as his arms tightened around her and he pressed his cheek against hers. "God, but I've missed you," he murmured against her ear. "You have no idea how relieved I felt when I walked in here just now and saw how much better you looked."

She stroked his head, her fingers weaving through his dark hair. "Please don't worry about me, love. I hate seeing you so tired."

With the curtain around the bed protecting them from the eyes of an unexpected intruder, they continued to hold each other, both of them needing the comfort of physical contact. They didn't talk; they just savored the quiet, intimate interlude. Finally, with a murmur of reluctance, Paul gently moved her against the pillows. Giving her a warped smile, he chided, "Don't you ever scare me like that again."

Her eyes were luminous as she smiled softly. "I won't."

He cradled her face in his hands as he tenderly caressed her mouth with one thumb. "I phoned your parents yesterday—I thought I'd better let them know you were in the hospital."

Robin's eyes widened in surprise. After discovering that the odd battle didn't mean a never-ending war, Paul had stopped walking away from disputes. One of the worst fights they'd had had been over

Robin's parents. He couldn't understand why she refused to invite them for a visit after they had moved into the house, or why she was so reluctant to tell them that she and Paul were living together. In fact, the spat had created quite a strain between them, with his stance being that she couldn't protect them forever from the facts, and with hers being that he didn't understand.

It wasn't until the senior Mitchells spent a weekend in Calgary, staying in a hotel, that Paul had an opportunity to spend some time with them. It was only then that he had gained any insight into Robin's point of view. From then on, he had been insistent about her making visits home, and he had agreed to go home with her at Christmas. Nevertheless, the issue of her parents was one that Paul always skirted with caution.

A wry grin appeared on his face when he saw the stunned look on her face. "Don't look at me like that, Robin. You know damned well I like your mother and father—I just don't agree with you about hiding the facts from them, that's all."

"I know, but—"

He kissed her, his lips moving softly against hers as he murmured, "Let's not get into that now, love. I told you before that I wouldn't bring it up again—that it had to be your decision." He straightened up, a look of self-reproach in his eyes as he continued, "I should have phoned them earlier, but I'm afraid I wasn't thinking too clearly this weekend."

Her eyes soft with understanding, Robin caressed his cheek. "What did they say?"

"They wanted to know if they should come."

"No, I don't want them here."

"Robin, I give you my word I won't say anything to them about us."

She shook her head, her gaze locked to his with an open honesty. "It has nothing to do with that. I don't have the energy for company, Paul. Would you mind phoning them again and tell them I send my love, but that I'm just too damned tired to talk to anyone."

"If that's what you really want." His eyes darkened as he leaned over and kissed her again, his mouth lingering against her in a sweet, poignant kiss that left her breathless. There was that old sparkle of amusement in his eyes when he finally lifted his head. "I'd better get off this bed before I end up in it."

She slipped her hand into his. "Do you have to go?"

"Not for a while. I have a lecture in—" without releasing her hand he glanced at his watch "—half an hour." With a thoughtful look on his face, he abstractedly smoothed down the curled corners of the adhesive tape that anchored the IV needle in the back of her hand, then looked at her. "Robin, are you really sure you don't want them to come?"

She squeezed his hand. "No—I just want to go home. I don't want anyone else around me but you."

He couldn't resist the unspoken appeal in her eyes, and he slipped his arms around her and held her protectively, his own emotions tightly leashed. His voice was unsteady when he whispered, "I'll take you home the minute I dare to, love. And I'll hold you for as long as you want." Robin closed her eyes and lost herself in the warmth and security of his enveloping strength.

She vowed that she wouldn't keep pestering Paul about discharging her, but that only lasted until Thursday when he did his morning rounds.

As soon as he finished examining her, she jumped at him. "When can I go home?"

He totally ignored her question as he made a notation on her chart, and Robin suddenly felt a surge of irritation with the young nurse who was doing rounds with him. The redhead kept staring at Paul the way a fat kid gazes at cotton candy, and it annoyed Robin to no end.

When she looked back at Paul, he had his arms folded across his chest, his lips pursed to repress a grin, and there was a scandalous gleam in his eyes.

"You were saying, Dr. Mitchell?" he asked, his voice perfectly steady.

"I was asking when I could go home."

His voice was impersonal. "Are you needed at home?"

So, he wanted to play games, did he! She looked him straight in the eye as she said, "I have this dog that's creating some problems." She shot a pointed look at the nurse, who was still gazing at Paul hungrily. "He's apt to start straying, and I put a fair amount of time into training him—I'd hate to have him wander off."

"Hmmm," he said as he stroked his chin. "I take it that this dog is a purebred?"

Robin nearly choked on that one, and she really

had to fight to keep a straight face. "Yes, he is—quite a handsome specimen." She batted her eyes at him as she tossed a zinger his way. "He's working on his points for best of a breed. But that's under women judges, and they're particularily partial to his type."

She scored with that one, and she could see him fighting to keep from laughing. The redheaded nurse had a confused look on her face, and Robin could almost see her mentally replaying the conversation with, "He said, she said, he said," in an attempt to figure out where they'd lost her. Paul opened his mouth to say something, then shut it abruptly. Robin smiled sweetly. "Do you think I might be discharged soon?"

He gave her his most inscrutable look and said, "Perhaps."

Right then Robin could have strangled him, especially when he turned and walked out of the room with the redhead drifting beside him with that cotton-candy look still in her eyes.

Robin nearly went crazy that day. Her room had turned into a drop-in center for people going on duty, going off duty and for those on coffee break. And she was beginning to feel very guilty.

She genuinely liked the people she worked with, and she wouldn't hurt any one of them, but she heartily wished they would go away. Usually a visitor would only stay a few minutes, but when there was a score of people popping in and out, she was beginning to feel as if her room was the arrival area of an international airport.

Through her entire stay, Bernie's approach was completely different. He'd tear into her room, slap a glass of juice in her hand, insist that she drink it, check her IV, make her laugh and tear out. His frequent visits were a breath of fresh air; unfortunately, the other visits were like an oppressive fog. She wanted to sleep, and she couldn't. She wanted to be left alone, and she wasn't. And she wanted to have time with Paul, and that was out. She was beginning to feel rebellious, and she didn't like that feeling, either. She simply wanted to go home.

When Paul came by early in the evening, Dr. Standish was with Robin, and as tired and as cranky as she felt, she was deeply touched that, without fail, the burly surgeon took time from his grueling schedule to visit her daily. But she was more touched than ever when she discovered that he was, in fact, an understanding ally.

He and Paul were discussing a patient's recovery when he waved at Robin. "When are you letting her out of here?" he barked in his booming voice.

Paul responded that she was still suffering from an acute case of pneumonia, and until her lungs cleared, he was keeping her in.

With his arms folded across his chest, Dr. Standish rocked back in his chair and blatantly propped his feet on the end of Robin's bed. He looked at Paul. "Ever been a patient?"

Paul leaned against the wall and stared at the older doctor, his expression ambiguous. "No. Why?"

"I was—two years ago. Had a kidney stone removed. The staff fussed and fumed over me like old mother hens. Nearly went crazy.'' Standish waved his hand at Robin and grinned knowingly when he saw the look of relief on her face. "Makes you feel like hell. All you want to do is sleep, and they're bound and determined you won't be neglected—being one of the flock, so to speak. Ends up they damned near kill you with kindness.''

"Are you saying I should discharge her?'' Paul's voice was tinged with incredulity.

"If she was a regular patient, I'd say no damned way. But having been in Mitch's position myself, I know what it's like. As long as she has someone to look after her when she goes home...." He shot Robin a penetrating stare. "Do you have someone who can look after you properly?''

Smothering the urge to glance at Paul, Robin grinned. "There's someone who could follow basic medical instructions.'' Paul narrowed his eyes at her with a menacing glare, and Robin nearly laughed.

Dr. Standish dropped his feet off the bed, his chair slamming down on the floor as he did so. He reached out and patted Robin's hand reassuringly, but there was a stern warning in his voice when he spoke. "You're going to have to do exactly what Paul tells you, Mitch, no matter when he lets you out, or you'll be back in here, sure as hell. This damned flu is a nasty one. Don't want complications. But I know you need some peace and quiet now more than anything else. All this fussing can get to you after a while.''

Dr. Standish was grinning broadly as he shook his head in recollection. "Yep, killing you with kindness," he reiterated. "While I was cooped up in here, it leaked out that I enjoyed a good Western novel now and then. By the time I got out of here, I had over seventy trundled in by the staff. Still reading through that damned boxful of books."

His grin softened into a reminiscent smile as he shook his head and sighed. "It was their way of showing that they cared, God bless them, but all that attention was so wearing." With that he slapped his knees and stood up.

He faced Paul, his voice sincere. "Hope you don't think I'm poking my nose in, Paul. If Mitch was an off-the-street patient, there's no way I'd let her out. Especially after I saw the X ray of her lungs." He clapped his associate on the shoulder in a fatherly gesture. "Just wanted you to know that there's another side of the coin."

Paul grinned at Dr. Standish. "There's no offense taken, George—except for the smug look on Mitchell's face right now."

The older surgeon winked at Robin. "No harm in her looking smug. Still think she's the best damned resident around."

Robin's eyes were shining with gratitude and affection. "You're no slouch yourself, Dr. Standish. And thank you for coming. I really do appreciate it."

"Horsefeathers!" he snorted.

After Dr. Standish had left, Paul went to the window and stood staring out, his arm braced against the wall.

"Can I go home?" she asked tentatively.

He turned to face her, and with a deep sigh he relented. "I've some misgivings about it, but yes, you can go home."

"Take me now," she begged, her face vibrant.

A provocative grin slowly creased Paul's face as he studied her, his eyes scanning her scantily clothed body. "If there was a lock on the damned door, I most certainly would," he laughed huskily.

Robin flushed as she grinned at him. "That's not what I meant, and you know it."

"Well, I meant it," he said with feeling as he came toward her, his dark eyes flashing dangerously. Just then, a nurse bustled into the room, and with a barely suppressed groan of frustration, Paul headed toward the door, swearing under his breath as he did so.

CHAPTER NINE

PAUL KEPT HIS PROMISE. By noon Friday, Robin was at home in her own bed. Mrs. Butterfield, who had become indispensable to them since they'd moved into the house, was almost too attentive.

As soon as Robin had finished her light lunch, the housekeeper took her tray, closed the drapes, and with a broad smile, warned her charge that she'd better sleep or Dr. Wilcox would skin them both alive.

Just being in the familiar surroundings of their bedroom was like a powerful sedative for her, and Robin slept—a deep, unbroken sleep. In fact, she didn't awaken until Paul arrived home later that evening.

He totally ignored her and didn't submit to her very obvious feminine maneuverings but instead gave her a brutally thorough session of therapy that jarred every bone in her body and left her coughing violently.

It wasn't until after dinner that he finally relented. He had a quick shower, donned his robe, and with weariness etched into his face, he stretched out on the bed beside her. Sighing with satisfaction, he gathered her into his arms and nestled her firmly against him. "It does feel so good to hold you again, Robin. I missed you like hell."

A warm feeling of immeasurable contentment encompassed her as she pressed her face against his neck, savoring the smell of soap that lingered on his skin. "I was so homesick," she whispered. "I felt like a part of me was missing."

With infinite tenderness, he stroked her hair, his gentle caresses drugging her. Almost immediately her eyes drifted shut, a soft smile hovering around her mouth as she lost herself in the warmth and security of his strong arms.

She didn't know what time it was when she awoke, but the room was dark and she sensed that it was very early in the morning. Paul's regular breathing told her he was asleep, but even in his unconscious state, his hold on her was still secure.

Repositioning her head on his shoulder, she slipped her hand beneath the soft fabric of his loosened robe, quietly relishing the feel of his warm skin beneath her palm. With whisper lightness, she moved her hand along the muscled contours of his body, absorbing the feel of him with a lingering touch.

His hard, broad chest, the flat tautness of his belly, the rigidity of his well-developed thighs—his body was still such a marvel to her. Athletic, strong, imbued with such animal grace—like a living, breathing David. A man. A man who was all things: gentle, forceful, loving, passionate—a man whom she loved beyond all reason. And the feel of him filled her with a beautiful glow as she continued to caress his virile form.

He stirred, his breath warm against her forehead as he sighed and slowly dragged his hand across her buttocks and up her back. Not yet fully awake, he began to stroke her body with languid movements, his touch kindling a response in her that was heady and sweet. They lay in the darkness, touching, exploring, savoring the warmth and texture, the curves and planes of each other.

For a moment Paul's body tensed before he relaxed beneath her gentle touch. One arm tightened around her as he whispered huskily, "I don't think this is part of the prescribed treatment, love."

She shifted her head, her moist, parted lips brushing against his as she slowly drew her hand along the inside of his thigh. His breath caught as Robin began to lightly stroke him, her mouth covering his in a deep, liquid kiss that was meant to tempt, to tantalize, to arouse.

Cradling the back of her head in his hand, he pressed her mouth more firmly against his as the kiss intensified, awakening sensations neither of them had the will to deny. With his arms holding her protectively, he eased her onto her back, then with his mouth moving slowly, enticingly against hers, he undid the buttons of her housecoat and brushed the fabric back.

She could feel his heart pounding against her breasts as he gathered her beneath him. A sob of pleasure caught in her throat and shivers of excitement coursed through her as with tormenting slowness, he traced the outline of her ear with his tongue.

"I'm going to make love to you so slowly," he whispered, his voice thick with desire. "I need to discover you all over again. I want you to let me savor every inch of you.''

Closing her eyes, Robin felt as if she was drowning in the whirlpool of sensual excitement his words aroused in her. He was asking her to surrender herself to sensation, knowing that he would drive her wild with an agonizing desire.

If she touched him, it would shatter his control, and above all else he wanted to give her his fullest measure of pleasure. And by giving her that, he would heighten his own pleasure with a searing eruption that would wring his body dry when he finally joined with her.

Clenching her hands to keep from touching him, she whispered brokenly, ''Love me. I need you to love me.''

He inhaled raggedly, then with provocative tenderness, he kissed her, his tongue probing her mouth with a sensual thoroughness that sent her blood pulsing hotly through her veins, turning her bones to water. And slowly, so slowly he began to work his magic.

His mouth was like wet silk against her sensitized skin as he explored her body, leaving a trail of erotic currents along her neck and shoulders. The sensations he was arousing in her were so exquisite that she felt as if she was melting beneath his touch, allowing him to mold her heated flesh with his gentle hands.

But he had only just begun. He would draw her further and further into a dimension of passion until they were lost in a spiraling universe. He knew her body; he knew where to torment her with the moist caresses of his tongue; he knew what to do to inflame her senses to a fever pitch. And Robin battled to suppress her longing to touch him, to give him the kind of searing pleasure he was giving her, to experience the fulfillment of his arousal; instead she surrendered to him totally as she clenched her teeth against the pulsating ache that was swelling inside her.

She could deny him nothing, and once again his lips moved against hers as his tongue sought the sweet recesses of her mouth. Unable to repress the urge to respond any longer, she moved her tongue against his, and she felt him shudder as she probed the depths of his hot mouth.

He eased himself on top of her, his hips pressed between her thighs. With a low groan, he tore his mouth away from hers as he shifted his body farther down. Cupping her breasts in his hands with infinite care, he began to explore their fullness with his searching, tormenting tongue. He drew a taut nipple into his mouth, and a groan was wrung from her as his movements escalated the agonizing hunger growing within her.

Robin knew he would continue his onslaught until she could stand it no longer, and only then would he succumb to his own burgeoning need for release—a need he was fighting to control as he continued to awaken every vibrating nerve in her inflamed body. It was for her—all for her.

Sensation slammed into torrid sensation as his mouth captured her other breast, and Robin moved beneath him, her hips arching against his naked chest. With his hands still cupped around her breasts, his thumbs stroking the taut nipples, he moved farther down, his mouth scorching her as he gently explored the softness of her flat stomach and thighs.

Robin tried to brace herself for the explosion of raw desire that ripped through her body as he moved lower still, but her response was involuntary, out of her control. A film of perspiration covered her skin as she twisted beneath him, but his hands imprisoned her hips, holding her fast.

The heavy throbbing in her loins became more intense, driving her to the very brink of a wrenching climax. With a tortured sob, she caught his head and jerked it away. With one powerful, fluid movement he entered her, his body meeting the frantic rhythm of hers as they strained together. With one mighty rendering force the dam of hot, rich passion exploded with a shattering brilliance, and Robin hung on to him, unable to breathe, unable to move, engulfed by a pleasure so intense it was stunning.

Paul buried his face in the tumble of her hair, his body heaving as he fought to fill his laboring lungs. It took a long time for rationality to return and when it did, Robin was astounded to find that she was trembling violently.

Pressing her face against his neck, Paul whispered, "Robin? What's wrong?"

She was filled with such turmoil that she couldn't answer him.

He shifted slightly as he reached out and turned on the bedside light. Framing her face with his hands he gazed down at her, his dark eyes still smoldering with the heat of spent passion. "What is it, love?" he asked, his voice soft with concern.

She gazed up at him, her eyes glowing with the intensity of her feelings for him. "I love you so much," she whispered, her mouth trembling. "I don't think I could bear it if I ever lost you."

His expression softened, then he closed his eyes and ever so gently kissed her. When he lifted his head, he smiled, his eyes filled with warmth. "I'm not going anywhere, and I'm not letting you out of my sight, so quit worrying." There was a teasing tone to his voice as he continued, "I'm too big to misplace, and I have no intention of straying, even if you think I am a dog." That made her laugh delightedly. "I was relieved to hear that I'd scored a few points, though."

Robin gave him a rueful look. "I didn't like the way that nurse was reacting to you. She was staring at you like a starving man eyes a T-bone steak."

"I didn't notice. I was engrossed with the very alluring neckline of your nightie."

"Like hell!"

He laughed and gave her head a gentle shake. "Why would any man in his right mind consider cold porridge when there was a very hot and tasty dish sitting under his nose?"

"Out of curiosity," she retorted.

He laughed again as he slowly trailed his fingers across her lips. "I never did like porridge—and never will."

Robin drew in a deep breath, and both of them heard the nasty rattle in her chest. Without giving her a chance to respond, Paul kissed her soundly, then moved away from her. "Sounds like you need another session of therapy, and that's exactly what you're going to get!"

He stood up, pulled his robe around him, then re-tied the belt. "What's with you, Paul Wilcox?" she inquired. "First you make love to me, then you want to thump me."

"Don't get cute, Mitchell. If you start sassing me, I'll stick you back in the hospital."

"You wouldn't dare!"

He stared at her, his eyes flashing a warning, then he relented. "You're right. I wouldn't."

Being home was like a newly discovered antibiotic for Robin. Hour by hour she could feel herself becoming stronger. She was getting the sound sleep she so desperately needed, and Paul was relentless about her therapy and medical care.

After the previous weeks of long hours, a heavy work load and her illness, they both needed some time alone, so she was delighted when she found out that Paul had booked Monday off. And they enjoyed every single minute of it. Just the opportunity to lie in bed and talk was a heaven-sent reprieve. The extended weekend might have been initially arranged for her benefit, but Paul needed that time just as much as she did.

The house was so quiet and empty after he left for work Tuesday morning that Robin found herself wandering aimlessly from room to room until Mrs. Butterfield arrived. After whipping through her cleaning chores with whirlwind efficiency, the house-

keeper insisted on preparing something for their dinner.

After Mrs. Butterfield had departed for the day,
the solitude was even more oppressive, and in an attempt to break her state of boredom, she finally
decided to give herself a facial while she had a leisure-
ly soak in the tub.

Humming softly to herself, she went into the bathroom and opened the drawer of the vanity to retrieve
the tube of masque. Suddenly, she felt as though she
couldn't breathe, and the strength drained out of her
with a sickening rush, leaving her in a cold sweat.

"My God! No!" she groaned in a stricken voice.
But the sudden weakness had nothing to do with her
illness. With trembling fingers, she picked up the flat
dial dispenser that held her birth control pills and
stared at it in horror. How long had it been since
she'd taken them? Six days in the hospital and
three...no...four days at home.

Her stomach was churning as she stumbled into the
bedroom and collapsed on the edge of the bed. She
buried her face in her hands and tried to make herself
think. But there was no way she could marshal her
frantic thoughts. Her body was shaking and clammy
with sweat as she stared blindly at the wall. She
couldn't think straight; she couldn't sort out the
dates in her mind. Clasping the dispenser tightly in
her hand, she raced downstairs, her desperation giving her strength.

Her heart was pounding wildly as she flew into
Paul's study and grabbed the calendar from his desk.
She counted the empty slots in the dispenser, then

checked the calendar. With rising panic, she checked again. No! It couldn't be! Her knees gave way beneath her and she collapsed in his chair. It just couldn't be! How could she, a doctor, be so stupid? She had to *think*, not panic! And she had to think rationally.

She and Paul had made love many times since she'd come home, and that was certainly a high risk time for her. But on the other hand, she had been very ill, and that could have thrown her cycle off. It was a game of Russian roulette and there were only two possible outcomes. She was either pregnant or she wasn't. And she couldn't hazard a guess what her odds were. Probable? Possible? Unlikely?

And what would Paul's reaction be if she told him there was a possibility that she was? She had no idea, but the longer Robin thought about it, the less she wanted to find out. Besides, it would solve nothing if she confided in him; in fact, it could create a whole new set of problems—problems that could put a tremendous strain on them both.

He would never walk out on her, leaving her to cope with this catastrophe alone; he would, however, feel obliged to marry her. And above all else, Robin did not want him to be pressured by a sense of responsibility into making that choice. The ugly scene that had occurred at the Dennisons' focused in her mind, and she would never forget the bitterness in Keith's voice when he had yelled that he wouldn't have married Nicola if she hadn't been pregnant. Robin shivered just thinking about it. She would avoid cornering Paul like that, no matter what. If he ever decided he wanted to marry her, it would have to be *his* conscious decision—not because he was forced into it.

If she thought for one minute that he'd be willing to let things ride until they knew for certain, she'd consider telling him, but Paul would see it as his duty, and she'd have effectively pushed him into the situation he wanted least. She knew all too well what his feelings were about marriage, let alone having a family of his own. He'd had such a miserable childhood that he was completely blinded to the positive side of parenthood. Besides, she had promised herself when she made her decision to live with him that she would give him time.

And there was that chance she wasn't pregnant... a chance.

Her heart filled with dread, Robin finally made her very difficult decision. She wouldn't say anything to Paul. It was, after all, her problem—a problem she alone would have to deal with.

She looked at the calendar again. If nothing happened in the meantime, she wouldn't be able to have an accurate pregnancy test done until the middle of December. She would know one way or another before she and Paul went home for Christmas. Until then, she had to play the waiting game without giving Paul cause to be suspicious.

But that nagging feeling of foreboding filled her with sickening apprehension. Yes, there was a chance she wasn't pregnant. But she had to face the fact that there was an equally good chance she was. Then what? What would she do then?

THE FOLLOWING DAYS were contradictions of highs and lows for Robin. There was a noticeable change in Paul since she had been so sick. It wasn't that he had ever treated their relationship casually before, but now he seemed to be more committed.

Often in casual conversation he would comment about their future—long-term plans such as developing their own clinic in four or five years or the possibility of buying vacation property on the west coast that they would eventually use as a retirement home. He had never done that before.

When he had purchased the house, it had given Robin a sense of security. A house meant roots for her. Now it was as though those roots had finally grown strong enough to support the idea of a future for him as well. She really began to believe that he expected to spend the rest of his life with her, and she was happier than she'd ever been.

Then there were the times when she was alone when her newfound happiness would shatter like crystal beneath the onslaught of fear. At those times, her future with Paul was a giant question mark, and her doubts were punctuated by barely controlled panic. Sometimes she'd awaken at night with bleak thoughts rolling in like an ominous tide to torment her. The only way she could block out the despair was to concentrate on the warmth and strength of Paul's arms around her.

The single time she ever really lost control was the day she received the phone call from her father saying her sister Cecile had given birth to a beautiful baby girl. That hit her very hard. Fortunately, the call had come when she was home alone, so by the time Paul arrived much later, she had carefully collected herself. She would *not* panic. . . not yet.

Nor did it help that she felt so listless. She hadn't recovered her sparkle since she'd been in the hospital, and she didn't know if it was simply the aftermath of her illness or the burden of apprehension. She'd catch Paul watching her, his eyes dark with concern, and she would experience an alarm she was quick to disguise.

She reached the point at which she didn't dare let her guard down for a moment or the oppressive weight of worry would overwhelm her. And the strain was beginning to show.

But she didn't realize how much until late one evening. She and Paul had finished dinner and were relaxing in front of the crackling fire in the family room. Robin was curled up in one of the big easy chairs, her gaze fixed on the dancing flames, unaware that Paul had let the newspaper he'd been reading slip to the floor, his attention welded on her.

"What's the matter, Robin?" came his softly spoken query. "You haven't been yourself in weeks."

Her stomach lurched, and she felt herself grow pale. It took every ounce of control she had to force herself to meet his unwavering scrutiny and to keep her voice even when she responded. "I'm just tired."

"Are you sure that's the real problem or is there something else bothering you?"

Her insides folded into a hard knot, making it very

difficult for her to breathe, but somehow she managed to keep her eyes from sliding away from his. "You obviously think something else is bothering me."

"Yes, I do."

Fear seized her in its invisible clutches when she made her stiff lips form the words, "Like what?"

He stared at her for a moment, then he lit a cigarette and inhaled deeply. "It has crossed my mind that you're regretting asking me to go to Kimberley with you for Christmas."

That was the last thing she had expected and Robin straightened abruptly, a look of disbelief on her face. "Why would I regret asking you to come home with me?"

Slowly, he rolled the ash from his cigarette into the ashtray on the table by his chair. "Because it's going to create one hell of an awkward situation with your family, especially since they don't know we've been living together for several months." There was the same strained tone in his voice that she'd heard in her own only a moment before, and it hurt her to hear it. With consternation apparent in her violet eyes, she rose and went to him. Slipping her arms around his neck, she curled up on his lap and nestled her head against his shoulder.

As he wrapped his arms around her, she swallowed in an attempt to ease the tight contraction in her throat. "I don't know how they'll react, and I truly do hope they'll understand, but I plan on telling them the truth, Paul. I want it out in the open."

His arms tightened securely around her as he

pressed his cheek against hers. "Are you doing that because you really want to or are you doing it because you feel you owe it to me?"

Robin was silent for a moment as she considered his question, then she lifted her head and gazed at him, her sincerity lending unquestionable conviction to her words. "It's not just for you—it's for me, too. I don't want to continue this game of deceit any longer. I hate not being honest with them. They may not approve, but they'll never disown me because of it. I know that."

Her eyes filled with tears as she gently took his face in her hands. "I want to be able to live my life with you openly, instead of avoiding the issue because I'm afraid of hurting them. If I don't level with them simply because of what their reaction might be, I may be unwittingly closing the door on their acceptance of the situation. Mom and dad must be wondering why I come home so seldom now."

She didn't wipe away the tears that were slipping down her cheeks. "I'm not going to pretend with them any longer that you're just a casual acquaintance. You're too important to me, Paul—and they have to know that."

Paul stared at her for a second before he gathered her against him in a powerful embrace. "I don't want you to alienate them because of me, Robin. I know how much they all mean to you."

"If that happens," she whispered, returning his embrace, "it won't be because of *you*. It will be because of *us*." She pressed her lips against the soft skin of his neck, then murmured brokenly, "It terrifies me just imagining what my life would be like without you.''

As Paul covered her mouth with an intense, searching kiss, her tormenting, unspoken fears fueled a desperation in her, and she responded to him with a blistering passion that obliterated the anguish, the doubts, the grim uncertainty that plagued her. There was that chance, that one slim chance that this nightmare would soon be over.

THE DAY ROBIN HAD THE LAB WORK DONE was an agony of waiting. She had told the technician that she needed the test done unofficially, as a favor. Her story was that she suspected a possible pregnancy in a patient who was due for surgery, but supposedly the woman's physician had dismissed the possibility as totally ridiculous. Robin wanted to be sure she was right before she pressed the issue.

The technologist had rolled her eyes heavenward and made some very unflattering comments about doctors who weren't thorough in having adequate lab analysis done before they plowed into a case.

She told Dr. Mitchell she'd make it a priority, and she'd get word to Robin as fast as she could.

With a calmness that belied her inner turmoil, Robin thanked the woman and walked away on legs that felt as if they'd collapse beneath her. Apprehension left her mouth dry and her stomach churning as she suffered through the morning, each second seeming like an hour as she waited for the results. Yet when the sealed envelope was delivered to her by a nursing assistant, she didn't feel anything—at least not until she opened it and realized she was holding her own lab report in her hand. With all the discipline she could muster, she walked down the corridor to the doctors' lounge.

Her hands were shaking so badly she could barely unfold the green requisition form. There was no notation on the form itself, so she turned the paper over to read the note scrawled on the back. "You score full points for good medical practice, Dr. Mitchell," it read. "The lady is definitely pregnant."

Robin crushed the note in her hand as a tortured groan of denial was wrung from her. *No! God, no!* Panic ripped through her with the force of a lightning bolt. Through sheer carelessness on her part, she was carrying Paul's child inside her. What was she going to do now?

Panic was clawing at her insides like a wild demon trying to break free, and Robin knew she had to get out of the hospital before she came apart. With frantic haste, she grabbed her belongings out of her locker and fled from the lounge. Somehow she managed to control herself long enough to tell the charge nurse she wasn't feeling well and that she was going home.

The charge nurse stared at her with undisguised consternation. Dr. Mitchell was as white as a sheet, and she was shaking like a leaf.

Robin could never remember afterward how she had managed to escape from the building or how she had ever driven home. But once within the safety of their bedroom, Robin flung herself on the bed and let all the frightening pressure that was cresting inside her break from her in tortured sobbing. She was experiencing such emotional upheaval she felt as if she was being torn apart.

In time, the panic subsided, leaving Robin totally drained.

Her face was masklike as she climbed listlessly off the bed and went downstairs to the family room. Extracting a cigarette from the package that was lying on the coffee table, she lit it, then went to stand before the patio door that overlooked the backyard.

Huge snowflakes were drifting down from a dreary leaden sky, frosting the trees and shrubs with thick velvet jackets of white. Blindly she stared out at the hushed beauty before her, her thoughts channeled in a tormenting groove.

Now what? What did she do now? She could tell Paul, but was there any solution in that? He didn't want to bring children into the harsh reality of today's society—he'd said it more than once. Yet under the circumstances, he'd feel obligated to marry her, and if that happened, she'd be trapping him by the oldest trick in the book. And what kind of marriage would that be?

An abortion? Paul wouldn't even consider that as an alternative, and besides Robin wasn't sure if she could bring herself to destroy the life of a child that she wanted with all her heart. This baby had been conceived by a passionate, enveloping love that was very special, and knowing a part of Paul was growing inside her made that creation even more special, more wanted.

What other choices did she have? Only one, and it

was devastating. She could leave him...but just the thought of walking away from Paul, from the man she loved, filled her with an unbearable pain. Could she do that to him? And could she survive without him? She doubted it.

She inhaled the smoke from her cigarette, then folded her arms across her breasts. If only.... She closed her eyes in a grimace of despair. No, she wouldn't climb on that merry-go-round of "if only." She was pregnant, and nothing, absolutely nothing, would change that fact. She had to face the problem squarely, without dodging behind the luxury of wishful thinking.

There were only three options before her. She could tell Paul; she could have an abortion; she could walk out of his life. Of those three, what could she *not* do? One grim reality stood out among the others. She could not tell Paul.

She loved him far too much to do that to him. Besides, it would break her in time to live with the knowledge that he had married her because he felt he had to...and that in turn would destroy them both. She couldn't live with that guilt. Never.

So that left her with only two options: an abortion, or walking out of this life. That was it. Those were her choices.

And could she really bring herself to leave him, knowing how desperately that would hurt him? Could she inflict that kind of pain on him? Could she do it?

An abortion. It would be the hardest thing she would ever have to do and that aching emptiness would haunt her forever, but it would be her private anguish, not his. And he'd never know. She could arrange to have it done out of the province, in a major center such as Vancouver.

If she went to Vancouver, she could use a trip to visit her grandmother as a perfect camouflage. Paul was to attend a week-long medical convention in Houston early in January, and she could have it done then, without his ever finding out . . . as long as she was very careful not to arouse his suspicions beforehand.

As soon as they returned from Kimberley after Christmas, she could follow through with her plans—''grisly plans'' a little voice in her head kept repeating, but Robin blocked it out, and tried to ignore the awful ache in her heart. This was going to be her silent agony to bear, and it would be hers for the rest of her life.

With tears slipping down her face, she finally acknowledged the grief, the heartbreak that was hers alone. Her child that would never be. Never could she hold her sleeping baby in her arms, marveling over thick eyelashes that fanned out over pink cherub cheeks; never could she know the maternal thrill of watching chubby legs master the intricacies of those first precious steps; never would she know the delight of having a sturdy five-year-old present her with a battered bouquet of dandelions that he'd picked in the back alley with hands that were sticky and stained with the milky sap.

It would never be, and by destroying the miracle of life that was growing within her, she would be forever destroying a vital part of herself.

Once Robin had made up her mind to have the abortion, the next few days were a nerve-racking ordeal for her. She managed to erect a facade of quiet determination that was her only salvation, especially when she'd catch Paul watching her intently with that dark analytical stare of his, his expression solemn and unfathomable.

On several occasions, he tried to penetrate her shell, but she dodged his questions with such evasive answers that he finally quit trying to find out what was troubling her.

The only time she could ease her despair was at night when she could lose herself in their lovemaking. It didn't seem possible, but there was a new depth, a new richness to it that lifted them both to an incredible plateau of pleasure. Before, Robin had been eager to reach that peak of rapturous climax, but now she wanted to avoid her private hell, and as long as he was making love to her she could forget—at least for a little while.

Now each kiss, each caress was prolonged to its fullest, and it might be hours before their slowly kindled desire would be consummated in a wild blaze of passion that was indescribable. And afterward Robin would sleep, safe and secure in his insulating embrace, undisturbed by tormenting thoughts.

The day they left for Kimberley was one of those bright, crisp winter days that had always exhilarated Robin. There seemed to be a revitalizing tang in the air that swept away her inner pain. For the first time in weeks, her eyes were alive with a vivacious sparkle, and there was a lightness in her that she hadn't experienced for a very long time. It was as though some onerous restraint had been removed, and she could finally take a full, deep breath.

It was the strangest feeling, but as soon as they reached the highway and Calgary was behind them, her private anguish seemed to diminish with each passing mile. It was as though she was leaving her tormented self behind, and the few days that stretched before her were a temporary reprieve from the hell created by her very painful decision. The sudden change in her mood was very apparent, and Paul responded with equally apparent relief.

As they sped along in the Bronco, she sat next to him, her thigh pressed against his, her hand resting lightly on his leg. She said something that made him laugh, and with his eyes flashing behind his tinted sunglasses, he slipped his arm around her and hugged her hard. He dropped a quick kiss on her forehead, then nestled her firmly against him, her head resting on his shoulder. Robin could feel the tension and weariness drain from him. It seemed as if her well-being was his source of energy, and it was only then that she realized it had been a very long time since she showed that kind of lighthearted spontaneity. She vowed then and there that she would make this time with Paul as happy and as carefree as she possibly could.

BUT IN REALITY, her carefree attitude was very short-lived. In fact, it lasted only until after dinner that first evening home.

Robin and her two younger sisters were cleaning

up after the evening meal, and Alana, who was in her last year of high school, was trying to coax everyone into going skiing that evening.

"Come on, Bim. You used to live on the ski hill. Why don't you want to go?"

Setting a stack of pots and pans into the sink full of soapy water, Robin flipped soap suds at her sister. "Don't be a pest, Alana. I want to stay home and visit with mom and dad tonight."

Jennifer came into the kitchen carrying the last of the dishes from the dining room and started loading them into the dishwasher. "Well, *I'm* going. I promised myself I would go skiing as soon as I got home. This semester of university has been a killer, and I really had to keep my nose to the grindstone."

Robin tweaked her sister's nose and laughed. "It doesn't look to me like you had it pressed *too* hard against any grindstone—and I can't quite believe that you didn't have *some* fun." Jennifer turned pink and made a face at her.

Paul walked into the kitchen and placed his empty coffee cup in the top rack of the dishwasher, then leaned against the cupboard beside Robin. "Have they browbeaten you into submission yet?"

There was still laughter in her eyes as Robin looked up at him. "After all I ate tonight, I couldn't even make it down the bunny hill without killing myself."

"Oh, come on, Bim! Who do you think you're kidding?" snorted Jennifer in disgust. "You've been skiing black-diamond runs since you were twelve."

Picking up the tea towel that was draped over

Robin's shoulder, Paul began to dry the pots she had already washed. "Your big sister is getting lazy in her old age," he said dryly, a wicked gleam growing in his eyes. "She thinks going to bed is the best form of recreation now."

A telltale flush began to creep up her cheeks as she shot him a loaded look. He gave her a lazy, provocative smile as he let his gaze sweep down her body with meaningful thoroughness that left Robin more than a little breathless.

To cover up her flustered response, she retorted, "Well, hotshot, why don't you go with these two monsters?"

Alana was bubbling over with enthusiasm. "You've just got to come, Paul. It's a fantastic hill, especially at night. Besides, there aren't many slopes that have longer lighted runs than ours."

His eyes moved from Alana to Robin. "Are you sure you wouldn't mind if I went?"

She smiled and shook her head. "No, I don't mind—as long as you don't let these two bad apples lead you astray."

"Hey, lay off the insinuations," said Jennifer with a mock look of indignation. "We aren't *that* bad!"

Robin raised her eyebrows in an expression completely discrediting her sister's protest. "Jennifer Mitchell, how can you stand there with an angelic look on your face and say something like that— especially after the stunt you pulled on Cecile?"

Jennifer tossed her hair and looked at Alana, an impish grin on her face. "We weren't that bad, were we?"

"You were both outrageous, and you know it," Robin said.

Paul leaned back against the sink and folded his arms across his chest, his eyes flashing with amused interest. "I think maybe I ought to hear this story."

The two youngest Mitchell girls exchanged conspiratorial glances as Robin looked on, her expression one of an amused adult dealing with two slightly naughty children.

Alana grimaced and shrugged in childlike embarrassment. "Well, our Cecile has a bit of a temper."

"And these two just love to get her going," added Robin, her voice animated with suppressed humor.

Jennifer laughed. "But you have to admit, it was funny."

Paul let out a groan of frustration. "Are you going to tell me what this is all about?"

"Well. . ." Alana stalled as she tried valiantly not to laugh.

"Out with it."

"Well, Cecile used to give us all a hard time whenever we brought guys home," Jennifer explained, her eyes dancing. "So when she brought Eric home for the first time Alana and I thought it was about time we got even. Sooo. . .we flirted with him just a little."

Robin rolled her eyes heavenward. "A *little*?" Her voice sounded incredulous.

"Well, maybe more than a little," conceded Alana with a twinkle. "Anyway, Cecile blew her cork, and poor Eric looked like he'd been hit by a truck when she exploded—he'd never seen her mad before."

Robin stared at them with narrowed, knowing eyes. "And if I know these two—which I do—I think they were probably planning a similar stunt for my benefit." She reached out and tapped Jennifer firmly under the chin. "But I'm older and wiser than Cecile was, and I know their devious minds."

Paul was grinning broadly, his eyes gleaming with delight. Just then, Edwin Mitchell ambled into the kitchen, his pipe cradled in his hand. He had on an ancient and somewhat bedraggled navy blue cardigan sweater that had certainly seen better days. "Are those two giving you a bad time?" he asked, indicating Jennifer and Alana with the stem of his pipe.

"I think I can handle them," said Paul, the grin still plastered on his face.

Edwin gave his two youngest daughters a skeptical look, then sighed with feigned hopelessness. "I told their mother some years ago that we'd probably be wise to drown the pack of them."

Alana laughed and patted her father on the cheek. "And we know you don't mean one word of it." She gazed at her father with obvious affection, then stuck her finger in a hole in his sweater. "Dad, when are you going to retire this awful sweater? It really is a mess. Why don't you get mom to knit you a new one?"

Her father smoothed his hands over the knitted garment as he gazed down at it. "Because I like this one," he responded with a touch of stubbornness.

Robin fondly studied her father, a discerning look in her eyes. The sweater was a wreck, but no one would ever be able to pry it away from him. Her mother had knitted it for him years before, and it had become as much a part of him as was his pipe. Suddenly, a peculiar ache tightened in Robin's chest and the sparkle in her eyes died, replaced by a haunted look of desolation. Without letting anyone see her face, she turned and busied herself at the sink. And only through determination was she able to maintain a facade of lightheartedness until Paul and the girls left for the ski hill.

Her mood was reflective as she finished tidying up the kitchen. Squirting a daub of hand lotion in her palm, Robin leaned against the cupboard and slowly smoothed the scented cream into her hands, her eyes bleakly solemn. Maybe the thing with her father had hit her the way it had because she was really dreading talking to her parents. But she couldn't put it off.

Dana and Cecile were arriving the following day with their children, and once the entire family was gathered together, her chances of talking to her parents alone would be nonexistent.

With a sigh of resignation, she straightened up and walked out of the kitchen, turning off the light as she left the room.

Her parents were sitting in the living room, her mother seated in her favorite chair, knitting mitts for one of her grandchildren. Her father was stretched out in his recliner, his pipe clenched between his teeth as he read the newspaper. Robin stood in the doorway silently watching them, a strange hollowness inside her. Thirty years of marriage behind them, five grown daughters and three grandchildren, yet they remained so close. Their devotion to each other had never wavered through all those years, through the good times or bad. The commitment that bound them together was so solid, so strong, so invincible—and so enviable.

Dorothy Mitchell glanced up, her expression becoming suddenly concerned when she saw the look on her eldest daughter's face. "Is something wrong, darling?"

With a feeling of dread knotting her insides, she walked over to her mother. Sitting down on the floor by her easy chair, Robin crossed her legs, keenly aware that her father had lowered his paper and was studying her solemnly.

"What is it, Bim?" he asked quietly.

Leaning forward, Robin rested her arms on her legs, her face drawn. She picked up a piece of white lint from the carpet and began to roll it between her fingers, her eyes fixed intently on her hands. It took a moment before she could screw up enough courage to speak. "I have something to tell you, and I'm afraid you're going to be very disappointed in me."

His pipe in his hand, Edwin looked at her bent head. "I doubt that, my dear." He said it with such unwavering conviction that it made Robin feel like crying. There was a note of reassurance in his voice when he said, "Now, why don't you just tell your mother and me what's troubling you."

Taking a deep breath, Robin looked up at him, her voice unsteady. "For the past six months, Paul and I have been living together."

There was a brief lull, then Dorothy Mitchell leaned forward and stroked her daughter's glossy hair in an age-old maternal gesture. "We already knew that."

Robin's head shot up and she stared at her mother, her eyes wide with surprise. "How did you know?"

There was a rustle of paper as Edwin haphazardly dropped the paper on the floor. "We suspected there had been a major change in your life some time before we went to Calgary, but once we met Paul, we knew what was going on."

"But nothing was ever said...."

With a soft chuckle, Edwin tipped his head in agreement. "Nothing was *said*, but neither of us is blind. It was as plain as the nose on your face that Paul idolized you—besides, my dear, you were always very readable."

The big tabby cat curled up in Robin's lap and she began to absently stroke it, her face very pensive. So they had known all along.

Dorothy Mitchell laid her knitting down and gazed at her daughter's profile. "What's troubling you, Bim?"

Robin sighed, her face solemn. "It's a long story, mom."

Edwin struck a match, the fragrant aroma of his blended tobacco permeating the room as he puffed on his pipe. "We're good listeners, you know," he said quietly.

So in a subdued, strained voice, she told them everything—she omitted nothing, except that she was pregnant. No one was ever going to find out about that. By the time she had finished relating the whole story, the cat had slipped off her lap, and Edwin's pipe had grown cold.

The room was cocooned in one of those peculiar silences that seem to magnify every sound. When Edwin cleared his throat, Robin looked up sharply, her stomach tense when she saw her mother wipe her eyes.

Edwin's voice was slightly gruff when he spoke. "If we'd had any doubts about what kind of a man Paul was, or how he felt about you, your mother and I would have been very concerned. But once we met him and saw for ourselves how much he thought of you, we felt it was best if we didn't pry."

Her mother patted her shoulder reassuringly. "I don't think you have any idea how worried he was when you were sick, Bim. His attitude revealed far more than just concern." She paused, obviously considering something. When she spoke again, her voice was tinged with anger. "To think a child had to grow up in that kind of environment just incenses me. No wonder he has such a negative outlook on family life."

Feeling a sudden surge of anger herself, Robin said, "His parents are so damned hateful to each other, mom. One evening with them was nearly more than I could tolerate."

"I'm sure it must have been." Her mother's tone softened as she smoothed her daughter's tousled hair. "I know the decision you made came after considerable thought, love. And I also know it wasn't an easy one for you to make."

Edwin nodded in agreement, his voice very

solemn. "You have to live your life the best way you see fit, my dear. And no matter what, your mother and I will always be here for you. Always."

Robin's heart swelled as she rose and went to her father. Wrapping her arms around his neck, she hugged him lightly. "I do love you two so much," she whispered brokenly.

He chuckled a little gruffly as he patted her back firmly. "You mean you've finally forgiven me for the time I wouldn't let you keep the eight kittens you found at the old Rutherford place?"

Robin's laugh was a little shaky as she kissed his cheek, then straightened up. "Yes, dad, I finally have."

His eyes were twinkling. "I always hoped you would."

They were still sitting in the living room when the others came back from skiing. Paul entered the room, his dark hair windblown, his face pink from the cold. He had on a white turtleneck sweater that hugged his broad shoulders and tapered waist, accentuating his powerful build. He looked magnificent.

Edwin hauled himself out of his chair and said congenially, "How would a shot of my rat poison strike you?"

"It would strike me just fine," said Paul, as he made a move to sit down in an upholstered chair by the window. There was a loud, urgent chorus of "Don't sit in that chair!" and he straightened sharply, the strangest look on his face.

Robin burst out laughing. She indicated the chair with a wave of her hand, "That chair collapses on a whim," she explained, her voice shaking with laughter. "Mom only keeps it because the cats always sleep on it."

"Dorothy," said Edwin with a fair amount of annoyance, "why don't you throw that damned thing out?"

"Because the cats sleep there," his wife reiterated calmly as she continued knitting. "As long as they have that chair, they aren't shedding all over the rest of the furniture."

"Should have drowned them, too," he mumbled as he headed toward the kitchen.

Paul went over to Robin and stuck his cold hands down her neck. Hunching her shoulders against his icy touch, she let out a groan of protest. Paul laughed. "That's for scaring me half to death. I thought that chair was a priceless antique."

Dorothy Mitchell retorted dryly, "The only antiques in this house are Edwin and I. The kids completely destroyed the rest."

Robin rose then and sat down on the sofa beside Paul. "Did you have a good time?"

He draped his arm around her shoulder, the smell of cold air and snow still clinging to him. "It was great."

She gave him an amused glance. "I hope that you realize that father is digging out his very best Scotch on your behalf."

"That I am," said Edwin as he entered the room with the two drinks in his hand. "The best there is." He handed Paul one then sat down in his chair. "I hear you and Bim have quite the house in Calgary," he said casually.

Paul's expression sobered instantly, and there was a guarded tenseness about him as he met Edwin Mitchell's steady gaze. "Yes, sir, we do," he said quietly, his voice taut.

"A river at your back door—that would be a touch of heaven for an old fisherman like me," Edwin mused as he reflectively tamped his pipe. "Take my advice and don't spoil her, my boy. She'll make your life hell if you do." Robin could feel Paul's body relax, and she glanced up at him. He was looking at her father, his expression openly revealing his deep respect and gratitude.

Paul's arm tightened around Robin's shoulder, then he looked at her with a mixture of relief and mischief. "I only spoil her on Tuesdays and Thursdays."

Dorothy laughed delightedly. "That isn't spoiling, Paul. A housekeeper is blatantly indulging her lazy streak."

"Some parents," muttered Robin ruefully.

Paul looked at her, a suddenly serious expression on his face, as if he was immobilized by some emotion. "Yes, they are." There was a bitterness in his voice that she found very disturbing, and she felt even more disturbed when he abruptly stood up and walked into the kitchen.

Right then, her hopes that the holidays would remain untainted by tension began to fade.

And she was right. The next morning, Paul was very withdrawn, and she intuitively knew that he was silently comparing her parents to his own. The two of them desperately needed to talk, but she was feeling so edgy that she didn't think she could handle much more stress.

It was going to be hell when Cecile and her husband arrived with their new baby, and Robin was dreading their homecoming. She was desperately trying to shore up her resources so she could cope with the strain, but her nervousness eroded her defenses as fast as she erected them. Somehow though, she had to get through that ordeal.

But it was even worse than she had expected. There was a big commotion when her sister finally arrived, and everyone gathered around the door, talking and laughing. Robin hung back, the pain in her abdomen nearly unbearable as Jennifer swooped in to take the blanket-wrapped infant from Cecile's arms.

Cecile, however, did not relinquish her wee daughter to Jennifer, but looked at Robin, her eyes shining with that special look only mothers have. Every one of Robin's family knew of her affinity for babies and with a warm, knowing look on her face, Cecile walked over and gently placed the infant in her oldest sister's arms. "You get her first, Bim."

Robin felt as if someone had driven a knife into her heart, and she had to make an enormous effort to keep her expression blank. Her first reaction was to push the sleeping child into Dorothy Mitchell's arms and flee, but she could never hurt Cecile with that kind of rejection. Instead, she forced herself to go through the motions.

Leaving the gathering in the front hall, she carried her tiny niece into the living room and sank down

into a chair. With trembling hands, she gently unwrapped her.

The awful ache was shredding her control as she
gazed at the tiny face. She was so perfect, so beautiful, so helpless—and so alive, so real.

With profound tenderness, Robin cradled the infant in her arms and softly stroked the dark fuzz on
the child's head, her eyes shadowed with tormented
longing. The baby stretched, then turned her face
toward the warmth of Robin's breast, and that delicate little gesture sent a white-hot pain slicing
through her.

A movement at the door caught Robin's attention
and she glanced up, her face drawn by agony. Paul
was leaning against the archway, his arms folded
across his chest, his dark eyes drilling into her. "You
make a very appealing picture, Robin," he said
quietly. "I never realized it before, but motherhood
would suit you." There was an edge to his voice that
Robin couldn't quite define. She tore her eyes away
from his thoughtful gaze, suddenly afraid that he
would read the secret in her eyes.

Just then Alana entered the room and came over to
Robin, her eyes bright. "Come on, Bim—give me a
chance to hold her. You always hog the babies."

Forcing a smile on her face, Robin eased the baby
into her sister's arms, well aware of the current of
tension that had sprung up between her and Paul.

"So," said Paul, his voice suddenly inflexible,
"Robin always hogs the babies, does she?"

"Always," answered Alana, unaware of the penetrating stare on Paul's face. "You'd think she'd be

sick of kids being the oldest of five, but she's always said that she wants at least four of her own."

Paul fixed his gaze on Robin. "Really." This time the edge was anger.

Robin stood up abruptly, deliberately avoiding looking at Paul. "I'd better go help mom with dinner." Paul turned and walked away, his face set.

They avoided each other for the rest of the afternoon, but once Dana arrived with her two little ones and her husband, the tension between Paul and Robin eased a little.

Miles Worthington, Dana's husband, and Paul hit it off almost immediately. Probably, Robin conceded privately, because they were very much alike in many ways. The Worthington family was extremely wealthy, and Miles was the head of the International Worthington Foundation. Robin had initially thought him to be a bit of a stuffed shirt, but Dana, in her usual candid, vivacious way, soon made short work of that. Every time Miles, who was several years older than his wife, was the least bit pompous, Dana would haul him up short by telling him, "Take off your tie and smell the flowers, Miles." The saying was used so frequently that it became a family favorite when anyone was upset. Once his veneer of conservatism was shed, Robin liked her brother-in-law immensely.

The whole family was gathered in the living room, and Robin sat on the floor, watching Miles with his small family. Dana had refused to have a nanny, insisting that *they* were going to raise their children, not some hired help.

Miles had just returned from taking two-year-old Troy to the bathroom, and as he sat down, he lifted the toddler onto his lap.

"Are you still smelling the flowers, Miles?" Robin asked him.

"Regularly," he replied, looking at his wife, a teasing gleam in his eyes. "If I don't do it willingly, Dana forces me into it."

"Poor Miles," chorused Jennifer and Alana, and everyone laughed. Robin glanced at Paul just in time to catch him staring at Miles and Troy with the oddest expression on his face. Troy had wound his chubby arms around his father's neck and nestled his curly little head on his daddy's shoulder. With a gentle smile on his face, Miles cuddled the little fellow against him and murmured something to him. Troy smiled at his father, then gave him a big hug. It was a vignette of the openness and trust of a child's love. Robin looked away, silently wondering what was going through Paul's mind right then.

Dana came over and sat on the floor by Robin and draped her arm around her sister's shoulders. "Speaking of flowers, do you remember the time our damned rabbits got out and ate all of Mrs. Norton's tulips?"

"And Mr. Norton threatened to make rabbit stew out of them if they ever did it again," added Cecile.

Robin laughed and looked at Cecile. "My all-time favorite was the time you trotted over to Mrs. Arnold's and told her that mom needed to borrow two eggs. Then you went out in the back alley and let that

Letki kid—'' she looked at Dana ''—what was his name?''

"Brian, I think.''

"Brian—that's right. Anyway, Cecile let him have it with the two eggs because he said the Mitchell girls were such ugly creeps.''

"Yes,'' said Dorothy Mitchell with a mother's firmness, "and when I found out what she'd done, you and Dana locked her in the bathroom with you so I couldn't spank her. You insisted he had it coming.''

Robin's voice was filled with conviction. "Well, he did. He was a rotten kid.''

Dana burst out laughing and hugged Robin. "Oh, Bim, do you remember the time that you and I tried to sneak out through the basement window to go to Joanne Gillis's party?''

Robin shook her head in recollection. "Do I! We'd just nicely crawled out and were trying to be quiet, and there was dad leaning against the fence, puffing on his pipe. All he said was, 'Nice try, girls,' then grounded us for two weeks.''

Other reminiscences were dragged out like favorite old toys, each person with a special one to share. Little Sarah, Dana's four-year-old daughter was becoming slightly bored with the whole thing and went over and flopped in Robin's lap.

The little girl began folding her aunt's fingers over, one by one. As soon as she reached the thumb, Robin abruptly straightened her hand and the little girl giggled and began the game all over again. Finally Robin caught her niece's hand and spread it out against her palm. Jennifer was watching the little scene and smiled at the two of them. "Look at that, Auntie Bim—it won't be much longer until Sarah will be big enough to do *her* hand print."

Sarah responded with a wide-eyed look. Alana laughed softly. "I think we should check that out, don't you, Sarah?" She stood up and went toward the dining room. When she returned, she was carefully carrying five plates with a caution that spoke of great value.

But these weren't priceless antique Limoges plates; instead, they were paper plates with a plaster of Paris mold mounted on each of them. Each mold carried a single small hand print. With infinite care, Alana spread them out on the floor.

"What's this?" Paul asked, his voice oddly strained. As Robin placed the little girl's pudgy hand in each cast, Dorothy Mitchell explained.

"The girls always brought home a plaster cast of their hands the first year of school." Her eyes developed a suspicious glitter, and she blinked rapidly. "So those plates are our family heirlooms, Paul."

The look in his eyes made Robin's insides contract into a cold, hard lump. It was as though he had just discovered something, and that discovery was very painful and very distasteful.

With a peculiar numbness settling upon her, Robin silently picked up the childhood treasures and with visibly trembling hands, carried them into the dining room and put them away.

For some unexplainable reason, that look on his face was a jolting revelation to Robin. Just as Sarah had struggled to stretch her stubby fingers to fill the molds of her aunts' hands, she had tried to mold her life to fit into Paul's cast—and she didn't fit. His cast had been shaped by different stresses, by different pressures—his cast had been made in a different form.

The bleak reality of what she had planned to do really hit home, jarring her into a new awareness. If she followed through with the abortion, she would be trying to alter a mold that had already set, and it would destroy her. She could never do it—never. Her value of life was too high, especially the life of her own child. She had only been playing a senseless game of escape with herself, and now she had to face facts. And one fact was that she was going to have this baby.

An overwhelming relief flooded through her. She would have the baby, God willing. But everything else was a grim gray fog of uncertainty. And somewhere in that isolating grayness, there was a clock measuring out an ever-diminishing time.

CHAPTER TEN

IT WAS A TERRIFYING NIGHTMARE that jolted Robin awake. Her body was damp and trembling, her mind thrown into a state of total panic, but try as she might, she could not recall one single detail of the horror—just the paralyzing fear.

She swept her hair back with shaking hands and experienced a vague sense of alarm when she realized her face was damp with tears. For a few moments she lay in the dark, then eased herself quietly out of bed, careful not to disturb the sleeping man beside her.

The heavy blackness of the room seemed to be smothering her, and she found herself fighting for breath as she slipped into her robe and crept out of the room. Closing the door softly behind her, she turned on the hall light and leaned weakly against the door, waiting for the claustrophobic sensation and the clawing terror to fade.

After remaining immobile for a long time, Robin slipped silently down the stairs and walked into the living room. There was a haunted look in her eyes as she turned on the lamp by the sofa and sat down, her body still tense from the unknown fear of her dream. With despair weighing her down, she braced her elbows on her knees and covered her face with her hands.

Everything had changed. Everything. She was trapped by circumstances, by her own morals—even by her feelings for Paul. Her world was crumbling around her, and there was nothing she could do to stop it. Not now.

She leaned back against the cushions and stared numbly at the ceiling. She should have known better than to go home for Christmas. It had been such a nerve-racking few days. It shouldn't have worked out that way, but it had. It had all played against her— the contentment, the love, the laughter, the understanding of her parents.

But Robin hadn't been the only one who had been affected by the time spent with her family. Paul, too, had changed. He had become very remote and unapproachable, and she could tell by his intractable expression that he was brooding about something. The thing that troubled her most and sent her nerves quivering, was the suppressed anger she sensed in him.

Since they had returned from Kimberley four days earlier, the brittle tension between them had become so thick you could cut it with a knife. They barely spoke to each other, they avoided making any physical contact, and the atmosphere was as volatile as a ticking time bomb.

And that formidable wall of silence was growing higher and broader every day, pushing them farther and farther apart. Soon the distance separating them would be unbridgeable. They simply could not continue for much longer with this awful tension. She knew it—and she also knew she had to make a decision, and soon—before he left for the convention. And that was only two days away.

It was unbelievable, though, how quickly decisions were shaped and changed by circumstance. Just that afternoon, she had finally made up her mind to confront Paul with the truth. Oddly enough, that decision had given her a thread of hope to hang on to, and she'd felt a peace of mind she hadn't experienced for a very long time. But as it turned out, it had been a false hope.

When Paul had finally arrived home that night, he had been so cold and unapproachable that her confidence had abruptly deserted her, and that single ray of hope had shriveled into a knot of dread. The sense of loss she had experienced frightened her. It was as though they had become two strangers, and she realized she was only putting off the inevitable. Robin was jarred out of her bleak reverie by the chiming of the antique grandfather clock in the study. Two o'clock.

With weariness etched on her face, she rubbed the throbbing pulse in her temple, then stood up and went into the kitchen. Switching on the Tiffany lamp that hung over the kitchen table, she took a heavy pottery mug from the mug rack. Maybe if she made herself a cup of hot chocolate she would be able to sleep. She stirred the instant cocoa mix into the milk, placed the cup in the microwave oven and set the timer.

If only she could program her life with the same ease.

Her eyes focused on the package of Paul's cigarettes lying on the kitchen island. It was funny that he'd never noticed she'd quit smoking—maybe he had, but just didn't think it was worth commenting about. Who knew *what* he was going on in his mind now.

She folded her arms across her breasts as she leaned against the cupboard and waited for the milk to heat, her face pale and drawn, her expressive eyes revealing her anguish. She fully realized that she was retreating behind an impenetrable wall of silence, but it was the only way she could cope with the situation. It was the only way....

"What's the matter?"

Robin didn't know if it was the unexpectedness or the harshness in Paul's voice that startled her so very much, but whichever it was, it left her nerves vibrating like high-tension wires.

Schooling her face into a mask, she turned to face him. "I couldn't sleep." Her voice was unsteady, her hands trembling as she opened the microwave and removed the steaming cup of chocolate.

She could feel his eyes drilling through her as she went to the table and sat down in the circle of soft amber light, her hands clasped tightly around the hot mug.

Paul hesitated for a moment, then came to the table and sat down across from her, the muted light catching the highlights in his hair and accentuating the harsh lines of his face. He stared at her steadily as he leaned forward and rested his arms on the table. "I think we'd better talk, Robin," he said, his voice steely. She could not make herself meet his gaze, and her stomach twisted into a cold hard knot of trepidation.

"Did you hear what I said?"

She swallowed, then forced her eyes up to meet his unwavering stare. "I heard you."

"I don't like playing games," he spat out, his eyes cold and angry. "You've closed up like a damned clam, and I think you owe me some sort of explanation about what in hell's the matter with you."

An explanation. He wanted an explanation. For one brief, insane second, she considered giving it to him, but there was something about the hard look on his face that stopped her cold. She had waited too long to make her confession; the hostile barriers that separated them had pushed them too far apart. Robin avoided looking at him, and she fixed her gaze on the steam rising from her cup as she said quietly, "I could say exactly the same thing to you."

The silence was crackling with tension and when Robin finally looked across the table at him, he was staring at her, his eyes as unfathomable as black onyx.

He laced his fingers together and appeared to be making a concentrated effort to control the anger that was smoldering within him. "You're dodging the issue, Robin."

She stared at him, her own eyes unwavering. "Am I?"

Their eyes locked and held for a brief moment before the contact was severed. Robin sensed they were like two wary opponents cautiously circling—protecting their own defenses while searching for the other's weaknesses.

Paul's eyes were narrowed and his jaw was clenched. He looked at her again, and when he spoke his voice was taut. "The time we spent with your family was a revelation for me. It makes me damned mad that you never leveled with me."

Robin's hands tightened around the mug as an odd, cold numbness settled in her belly. "For example?"

"You never once commented on how *you* felt about a number of things—marriage for one." He paused, then added, "Kids for another." He leaned back in his chair, his eyes riveted on her as he folded his arms across his chest. "I had no idea that you wanted a family until Cecile arrived with the baby, and I saw that look on your face...."

In an abrupt, irritated movement, Paul shoved his chair back and stood up. Robin watched him, a hollow sickening feeling growing in her, as he went to the cupboard and picked up his cigarettes and lighter. He extracted one, lit it, then tossed the lighter and package back in an action that spoke of barely contained fury.

He inhaled sharply, then turned to face her, his eyes blazing. "Damn it, Robin, I don't understand why you never said anything to me. It's something we should have discussed—those feelings aren't something that can be neatly folded and put away like a towel."

"Would it have made any difference if you'd known?"

"Yes, damn it, it would have."

A spark of anger was igniting in her, and she

glared at him. "How can you stand there and say that? You made it very clear to me, right from the beginning how *you* felt about marriage and kids. What would you have done if I had leveled with you? Would *you* have compromised *your* values, *your* beliefs?" she said, her voice sizzling with sudden resentment. "You know damned well you wouldn't have." She drew in a slow, steadying breath, trying to make a very real effort to calm down. She wasn't going to achieve anything by arguing with him. It was much too late for that. Suddenly, Robin was very tired. "You really didn't leave me any options, Paul."

Paul strode over to the table and with his arm braced beside her he leaned over her, his voice made rough by wrath. "I never expected you to make any sacrifices on my behalf. Believe me, I had enough of the persecution complex with my mother—I sure as hell didn't need it from you. I thought that I could expect honesty from you."

He might as well have slapped her. He couldn't have said anything—absolutely nothing—that could have hurt her more. With a fierce pain radiating in her, she bolted from her chair, almost unable to maintain her thin veneer of control.

She had only taken a few steps when Paul's arm shot out, his hand grasping her wrist as he whirled her around. "Damn it, Robin," he grated, "we're going to hash this out, one way or another. We simply cannot continue with this goddamned tension chewing away at us."

Her face was deadly pale as she stared up at him,

her eyes devoid of all expression. "No," she said, her voice glacial and quiet, "we can't." With a vicious jerk, she snatched her arm out of his grip and fled. At the same time, Robin knew she had just condemned herself to a slow, excruciating death.

It wasn't until she had locked herself in the guest room that the grim reality penetrated her anguish. It was then she knew, with a chilling certainty, that she had no other choice; she was forced into leaving him. The paralyzing horror of her nightmare was a bleak, terrifying actuality—and the pain was devastating.

The thin, cold dawn of a winter's morning was just cresting the horizon when Robin, her mind and body numb with exhaustion and grief, turned from the window, her face haggard and white. She would leave as soon as Paul left for Houston—there was no way she could endure another scene with him without coming unglued. It was an unforgivable, gutless move on her part, but she simply did not have the strength or courage to face him with her decision. That would be just too much to bear.

But in spite of the pain and the heartbreak, there was one consolation. His child was growing inside her. She would, at least, have the baby, and that gave her a reason for surviving in the empty existence that stretched before her—and that's exactly what her life would be like without Paul.

For the next two days, she clung to that one single thought like a lifeline. Without it, she wouldn't have been able to endure the gut-twisting tension that kept mounting. It was as though Paul could no longer bear even the sight of her; he totally avoided her at work, and he made a point of leaving the house at dawn and not returning until very late at night.

But his absence didn't make it any easier for her. Robin had to force herself to close her eyes, her ears, her heart to the dearly familiar sights and sounds she would soon be leaving forever—the deep melodious chiming of the grandfather clock; the lingering smell of Paul's after-shave in the bathroom; the exquisite perfection of the group of pen-and-ink sketches they'd purchased for the landing; the secluded beauty of the snow-covered backyard—it would be like ripping out her soul to leave it all.

But what she dreaded most, and what kept her awake each night was the thought of facing her "trial by fire"—of saying that final goodbye to Paul—that would almost kill her.

And it did. It was very early Thursday morning when she was forced to face her death sentence.

Robin was in the living room fighting down the nausea caused by a combination of morning sickness and raw nerves when he finally came down the stairs, his suitcase in his hand. Her churning stomach tightened into a hard ball and there was a stricken look of desperation in her eyes as she watched him, knowing that the minute he walked out that door, their life together would be over and half of her would die.

Without looking at her, he put on his overcoat and turned up the fur collar, then fished the car keys and his leather gloves out of his pocket. When he finally did turn to face her, his mouth was set in a hard, unyielding line, his eyes glinting with unmistakable contempt as he stared at her. "Well, Robin, I guess this is goodbye, isn't it?'' The harshness of his voice was like a knife turning in her, and Robin felt the blood drain from her face as she stared back at him.

"Don't look so shocked.'' There was no mistaking the ruthlessness in his twisted, insolent smile. "I suspect that you're planning on moving out while I'm gone.'' His eyes, cold and unwavering, never left her as he pulled on his gloves. "Those *are* your plans, aren't they, Robin?''

Feeling as though she had just had the wind driven out of her by a powerful blow, Robin stared at him. "Paul, I—''

He cut her off, his voice like steel. "Yes or no—are you planning on leaving?''

It seemed like an eternity passed before she could whisper, her voice barely audible, "Yes.''

"Yes—I thought so.'' He picked up his suitcase and turned toward the door. "Then I guess this is goodbye.''

THREE WEEKS. Three long torturous weeks had gone by since that last brutal scene with Paul, and Robin had been living in her own private hell ever since. The awful ache never changed, and little by little it was consuming her. Between the haunted, sleepless nights, the long grueling days and the debilitating bouts of violent morning sickness, she was slowly being sucked into a state of acute mental and physical exhaustion. And it showed.

She had lost weight, and there was a hollow, gaunt look around Robin's eyes that accentuated her extreme pallor. She knew that for the sake of her unborn child she simply had to take some time off, but requesting a leave of absence meant that she'd have to make her appeal to Paul, and just the *thought* of facing him was enough to unhinge her.

It meant that she had to be on guard every moment of every day, but she had so far managed to dodge him on the wards. Avoiding him was so desperately critical to her sense of survival that she had started to seriously consider terminating her residency and moving back to Kimberley. There, she and her child would have the warm, loving support of her family. If she stayed here, she was going to be forced to face Paul sooner or later, and that inevitable, unpleasant confrontation would be unbearable. She knew without a doubt that she either had to leave or take some time off—she couldn't tolerate much more of this terrible, devastating pressure.

But there was more than just herself and the welfare of the baby to consider. There was Bernie, too.

If she remained in Calgary, her presence would only become a big complication for his further association with Paul. Her old, dear friend would stick by her, no matter what, even if it meant jeopardizing his career plan, and she just could not let him throw that away because of his deep sense of loyalty to her. If she left—if she were no longer in the picture professionally—Bernie wouldn't have to choose between herself and Paul.

All those bleak thoughts kept churning through her mind constantly, and no matter how hard she tried to block them out, they were always there, plaguing her. Robin was becoming very afraid that her personal distress was soon going to impair her effectiveness as a physician, and the terror of making some stupid mistake under duress was also adding to the pressure.

Robin rolled over onto her back and stared at the ceiling, trying to block out the loneliness that seemed to permeate the impersonal room. Even the room itself seemed to stifle her.

Robin had realized that she desperately needed some time to think things through before making any final plans, so for that reason she had moved into the residence for the hospital staff. It was a temporary arrangement—also an incredibly lonely one. But that was something she was going to have to learn to live with—the loneliness.

Robin climbed off the bed and went to her window that overlooked the hospital parking lot. She had been so tired when she came off duty that she was sure she'd be able to sleep for a couple of hours, but no matter how hard she tried to make her mind go blank, she could not stop herself from thinking. For the millionth time, she relived that final scene with Paul.

A knock at her door jarred her back to the present, and she wearily went to answer it.

Bernie had his hand braced against the doorframe, his other hand on his hip, and his hair looked as if he had just combed it with an egg beater. "Since I'm not selling brushes or books, will you let me come in?" He still had on his white lab coat, but it only partly obscured a hand-painted tie that was the latest thing in hideous.

"I love your tie," she said dryly as she opened the door for him to enter.

Bernie straightened up, a broad grin creasing his face as he adjusted his thick glasses. "Isn't it marvelous? It's one old Mrs. Kennedy made—she gave it to me because she said I was her very favorite doctor."

Robin quickly looked away as sudden tears blurred her eyes, and she tried valiantly to blink them away before Bernie noticed. Only someone with a heart as big as all outdoors would actually be caught wearing something as awful as that just to please an aged patient. And knowing him the way she did, Robin knew he would continue to wear it because it genuinely pleased him. With Bernie, the thought always mattered most.

"I know it's a little jarring aesthetically, but I really don't think it's bad enough to make you cry," said Bernie as he held out the tie and studiously inspected the blinding design.

That wormed a genuine laugh out of Robin, and with heartfelt affection she leaned over and kissed him soundly in the middle of his forehead. "You're out to lunch, Radcliffe, but I love you anyway."

He grinned at her, then flopped down in one of the battered but comfortable easy chairs and stretched his legs out in front of him as he folded his hands across his chest. Robin curled up in the other chair, her heart sliding into her shoes when she looked at him and realized how seriously he was scrutinizing her. "If you love me so much, how come you won't talk to me?"

Robin's eyes darkened as she fixed her gaze on her tightly clasped hands. "Bernie, I told you I won't discuss—"

"Look," he interjected quietly, "I'm not asking you to spill the beans about what went wrong between you and Paul. I understand how you feel about that. What's worrying the hell out of me is *you*. You look goddamned awful, Mitch—obviously you aren't sleeping—you've lost weight." Leaning forward, he continued, "We've been friends for a long time, and I know you as well as I know myself. I know you're going through hell right now. I also know that there are a couple of reasons why you won't talk to me about it." He looked at her, his face creased with concern. "One reason is because of your strong sense of loyalty toward him, and another reason is me."

Closing her eyes, Robin massaged her forehead with her fingers, unaware how badly her hand was trembling. "It isn't because I don't trust you," she whispered brokenly.

With compassion darkening his eyes, Bernie reached out and took her hand in his. "I know that, Robin. I know that," he said, his voice gentle. "You don't want to involve me because you think it could cause problems, maybe even hard feelings between Paul and myself." His hand tightened around hers. "That's it, isn't it?"

Robin heaved a sigh that bordered on a shaky sob, then nodded her head. Bernie studied her drawn face, then released her hand and stood up. Jamming his hands into his pants pockets he went to the window and stared out for a long time. Finally he turned to face her. "Are you sure it's really finished between you and Paul?"

She glanced at him, then looked away to avoid his scrutiny. "Yes, I'm sure."

"You can't go on like this," he admonished quietly.

"I know."

Sitting back in the chair, Bernie slouched down and stared into space. "You're thinking about pulling the plug on your residency, aren't you?"

Robin managed a wry grin. "Are you going to give me a big lecture if I say yes?"

He shifted his gaze and looked at her, his expression very solemn. "No...no lecture." He took off his glasses and polished them on his lab coat, then put them back on. "There are a million platitudes about how you'll get over it. Personally, I think they're all crap. You and I aren't made that way, Robin—we'd never get over it. As much as I hate to admit it, I don't see how you can endure the strain for another year."

Another year. Another year of longing to see Paul but knowing she didn't dare. Another year of this agony. But that was only part of it. What would happen—how would Paul react when her pregnancy became apparent? She didn't even want to think about what he might do or say. She had no choice but to leave—she'd only needed someone to say it for her. And if leaving was her only recourse, Robin would have to do it soon, before everyone in the whole hospital knew that Dr. Mitchell was most certainly pregnant.

"I'll keep my nose out of it, Mitch, because that's

what you want, but promise me if you ever need any help, you'll let me know.''

Touched too deeply for words, Robin nodded her head.

After a lengthy silence, Bernie heaved himself out of the chair and tousled her hair. "If you were really decent, you'd treat me to supper.''

Somewhat surprised, she glanced up at him. "Aren't you finished for the day?''

"No. Some of Mark's family are flying in tonight, so I said I'd cover for him in Emergency for a few hours.''

Robin cast a dubious look at his brilliant tie and grimaced. "I don't suppose you'd take that off.''

"Not on your life. This is my talisman.''

There was a hint of amusement in her eyes as Robin gave him a rueful look. "I'll get some garlic so you can hang that around your neck, as well. If you're going to repulse the staff with this,'' she said, giving the tie a little flip, "you may as well cover all your bases and make sure no vampires come within spitting distance, either.''

Grabbing her hand, Bernie pulled her to her feet. "Who knows? This tie might start a whole new trend.''

"The thought is enough to turn one's brains to mush.''

Bernie laughed as he ushered her out of the room. "You have no class, Mitchell. No class at all.''

It wasn't until they were walking through the long underground tunnel that connected the residence to the hospital that Robin finally voiced aloud what was uppermost in her mind. "I'm going to hand in my resignation, Bernie. The sooner I leave, the better."

Bernie didn't look at her but instead took her hand in his. "Are you going back to Kimberley?"

"Yes. I'll go into practice with dad."

His grip tightened, communicating his deep regret to her. "I'm going to miss you like hell, Mitch," he said very quietly. Robin squeezed his hand and fought back tears as she silently wondered if some of the pain would fade.

But Bernie didn't allow Robin to dwell on her misery for very long. On arriving at the cafeteria, he deliberately propelled her to a table where staff members they knew were seated, and in a matter of moments he had her laughing at one of his outrageous stories. In his own special way, he was providing a respite from her wretched unhappiness.

After he had left for the emergency ward, Robin could not make herself return to the confines of her cramped cheerless room. She was on call that evening but she wasn't expected to remain on the ward; she simply needed something to do to fill in her empty time. So under the pretense that she had to check on two patients, she returned to surgery. The nursing staff was busy distributing evening medications and settling patients for the night, leaving the nursing station deserted. Sitting down at the desk, Robin made some notations on both patients' charts, then with determination she drew a pad of paper toward her. Now was as good a time as any to draft a letter, especially when there was no one around to distract her.

She stared at the blank paper as she twisted the pen between her fingers. Robin didn't even know to whom a letter of resignation should be directed but she had a sickening feeling it should go to the chief of surgery. And what should she say? "Dear Dr. Wilcox: For personal reasons, I find that I am unable to complete my four-year term of residency." Or did she simply say, "Attention Dr. Wilcox: Please accept this as my formal notice that I wish to be relieved of my duties as resident doctor."

Just exactly how was something like this to be submitted? And did she dare send it to someone other than Paul—perhaps the chief administrator? She sat there for a very long time trying to come up with a satisfactory way of dealing with it. The phone rang, and Robin absently answered it, her thoughts focused on her problem.

"Station 47. Dr. Mitchell speaking."

"Dr. Mitchell, this is Emergency. We've just had a stabbing down here. We're sending up a patient immediately for surgery—severe abdominal wounds."

Robin was instantly alert. "How did something like that happen in a hospital?"

"A drug overdose case was brought in with chest injuries, and he was hallucinating. He just went crazy. I guess he had a knife strapped on his leg, and he pulled it when they started to check him out. I wasn't in the ward myself when it happened but I was told that they think it was someone on staff who was knifed."

Bernie. Bernie was in Emergency. Keeping her voice calm, Robin asked, "Was it Dr. Radcliffe, by any chance?"

"He received a laceration in his hand, but nothing serious, so he said. He's on his way up with the patient now, and he told me to tell you to have a surgical team scrubbed, ready and waiting to go. He said it's an extremely critical wound.''

Relief relaxed her tense muscles as Robin stood up. "I'm on my way.''

She hurried down the corridor to the frosted glass doors labeled No Unauthorized Personnel. Behind these doors were the actual operating theaters where life and death battles were fought. Robin entered. Peeling off her lab coat as she approached the desk, she started snapping out orders to the OR staff, leaving a bustle of activity behind her as she turned down the corridor.

Robin had already changed and was scrubbing up when the door swung open and Dick MacDonald strode in. As usual he looked as if he'd just crawled out of bed and needed a shave.

"Hi, Mitch. What's happening?'' he said as he went to the scrub sink next to Robin's.

"A staff member was just stabbed on the emergency ward, if you can believe it. A drug OD went wild with a knife.''

He stared at her in disbelief, then snorted as he shook his head. "How in hell did that happen? Didn't the cops frisk him?''

"I don't know what happened exactly. I just had a brief rundown from a nurse at the desk—she said it was critical.''

Nothing more was said as they completed their task. With her hands held in front of her, Robin glanced at the clock as she backed through the swinging doors that led into the operating room. Seven forty-five.

As the scrub nurse assisted her with the sterile garb, mask and rubber gloves, the patient was being tended to by support staff, the inert form draped with a pale green sheet. There was a murmur of voices behind her and Robin turned just as Dick approached the patient. She shot him a sharp look as he swore softly. His facial expression was obscured by his cap and mask, but there were worry lines showing around his eyes. Dick stared at her for a split second, then silently indicated the patient with a slight inclination of his head. With a quizzical frown, Robin moved closer and glanced down.

It had been drilled into her head for years that she must maintain the sterile zone in OR at all times, and maybe it was this discipline that kept her on her feet. Or maybe it was the tremendous shock that petrified her muscles into an inflexible support. But whatever it was, Robin was immobilized—a cold sweat of fear left her entire body clammy as she stared down at the deathly white face of Paul Wilcox.

She wanted to cry out in protest as panic clawed its way through her belly and up her throat. Not Paul! There was no way she could perform surgery on this man—God, she'd fall apart—she could never do it. With her jaws clamped together, no sound escaped her, but in her mind she was screaming, *I can't! God, I can't do this!*

She had never known such incapacitating terror in her life, and she stood like a marble statue. Slowly, Paul opened his eyes, his face etched with excruciating pain.

He stared at her, then gave her a twisted, cynical

smile as he whispered weakly, "Well, Dr. Mitchell—
are you...going to walk...out on me...this time?"
The bitterness of his words sliced through her with
merciless brutality, and Robin's body shuddered
spasmodically with the pain he inflicted. She was
breaking apart.

"Knock him out, for God's sake, Dick." It was
Bernie. He had just entered the OR, his own face
ashen. With stricken eyes, Robin looked at him, silently begging him to remove her from this inhumane
nightmare.

He read her perfectly. His own eyes were dark with
a frantic concern as he held up a heavily bandaged
hand. "It has to be you, Mitch. I'm sorry."

Robin shook her head stiffly as her mind numbly
rejected his declaration, her eyes wide with consuming fear. Bernie came as close as he dared, his voice
sharp with urgency as he said, "We don't have time
to wait for another surgeon. We don't have time.
You *have* to do it."

His urgency penetrated the terrified confusion of
her thoughts and she closed her eyes, willing her professional mind to dominate the fear, the shock, the
panic. Drawing a deep, stabilizing breath, she opened
her eyes as an icy calm infused her, and with her jaw
set in determination, she nodded her head at Dick,
signaling him to proceed. Unable to stop herself, she
looked down at Paul. For that brief space of time
before the injection took effect, their eyes were fixed
on each other's, their gazes intense with a chilling
comprehension. She held his life in her hands, and
they both knew it.

CHAPTER ELEVEN

A HUSH AS THICK AS FOG settled on the operating theater, and a brittle tension connected them all. There was no idle conversation, there were no offhand remarks about the weather—nothing—just the sounds from Dick's equipment and Robin's brusque directions.

An eerie clarity had suffused Robin's mind along with a staunch determination: she was not going to let this man die. It was as though she was divided and there were two of her standing over Paul's mutilated, unconscious body. Every move she made—every incision, every suture— was questioned by her alter ego, and never before had she experienced the sensation of such acute, clear-thinking concentration.

As Bernie watched her, he felt truly awed by her incredible skill—precise, swift, thorough, alert—she missed nothing. If Paul Wilcox survived, he would certainly owe his life to the woman who labored over him, her pale face bathed in a sheen of perspiration, her eyes crinkled at the corners with a frown of concentration as she deftly probed and repaired his extensive wounds.

She was fighting for this man's life with all the talent, all the training, all the knowledge she had at her disposal. By some unbelievable feat of sheer single-mindedness, she had managed to dissociate the woman who loved him from the surgeon who was battling to pull him through. It was a staggering achievement.

Minutes dragged into hours. And her intentness never faltered. But when Robin completed the final suture, everyone in that room let out a quiet sigh of relief on her behalf. In a way, it was their standing ovation; she had been brilliant.

The clock on the scrub-room wall indicated exactly ten-thirty when Robin came through the swinging doors. Her face was taut with tension; lines of worry and exhaustion around her eyes and mouth added years to her age. Without looking at anyone, without saying a word, she stripped off her OR garb and headed for the door.

Bernie caught her by the arm and held her fast. His voice was very low, just loud enough for her to hear, but it was firm and insistent. "Don't interfere with the staff in Intensive Care, Robin. They know what they have to do—give them time to do it."

She stared at him, a fierceness in her eyes he'd never seen before as she tried to pull her arm free. "Let me go, Bernie."

His hold on her tightened. "No way. Give them half an hour, then you can sit with him all night if you want to, but you're staying out of there until they get him settled." With a warped smile, he raised his injured hand. "Besides, I need a few sutures in this, and I'd rather not go back to Emergency."

Instantly her intractable determination gave way to

consternation as she stared at his bandaged hand. "You mean they let you come up here without tending to that first?"

"I didn't give them much choice." Slipping his arm around her shoulder, he guided her out of the scrub room and down the corridor until they were out of earshot. "I tried like hell to get up here to warn you, but...." His voice trailed away as he shrugged, the gesture of self-reproach more eloquent than words. He looked at her, his troubled eyes intent on her face. "I tried to get hold of Standish and a couple of other doctors, but there just wasn't anybody. I didn't want to put you through that, Robin." He looked away, but Robin had already seen the tormented look in his eyes. His voice was unsteady as he continued. "I felt like such a damned heel for doing that to you."

His pain on her behalf nearly undermined her discipline, and putting her arms around him, Robin hugged him hard, her own voice very unsteady. "Thank you for sticking by me in there, Bernie. I don't think I could have gotten through it without you."

His arm tightened around her for a moment, then he gave her a gentle shake. "I really am going to be peeved at you if you allow my perfectly good hand to drop off, Mitchell. I need it to prop up my head in lectures."

Robin's laugh was very shaky, but it was authentic. Straightening up, she clasped his good hand in hers. "Come along, Bernard. Auntie Robin will put a Band-Aid on your owie."

His injury needed far more than a Band-Aid, however. The slashes—one that ran diagonally across his right palm and a second one parallel to it at the base of his fingers—plainly indicated that a narrow double-edged knife had been pulled through his hand. Robin winced, her face going two shades paler. Had the cut been infinitesimally deeper, Bernie's career as a surgeon would have been finished. As it was, it would be several days before he would be able to hold a scalpel.

Having to look after Bernie was a peculiar kind of therapy for Robin. She had to concentrate as she carefully sutured his wounds, and it kept her thoughts from straying to the dark-haired man who was struggling to sustain his life in Intensive Care. Robin didn't dare let herself think of his condition—not for a fraction of a second.

When she finished with Bernie's hand, she motioned to the nurse to remove the tray of instruments, then she looked at him, her eyes glazed, her teeth cemented together as her body began to tremble with shock.

Bernie's expression was very sober as he squeezed her hand. "Come on. Let's go see how he's doing."

Robin thought that with the countless hours she'd spent in Intensive Care she'd be prepared for the sight that met her, but she was wrong. It was completely different when it was Paul lying there with tubes in his nose, IV and a blood transfusion implanted in his arm, his bodily functions monitored by sophisticated electronic equipment as a drain cleared his abdominal cavity of fluid. He was so white, so still, in his state of unconsciousness. And she was so scared.

Her face was like alabaster as she sat down beside the bed, her eyes never leaving his face as she mentally willed her strength into his motionless body. She had begun her night watch, and it was going to be a long one.

She very nearly broke down when Lisa arrived a short time later. The nurse's face was nearly as pale as Robin's as she slipped her arms around Bernie's neck and pressed her face against his shoulder. With a suffocating band encasing her chest, Robin had to look away as he took the petite blonde in his arms and held her close, his face drawn as he whispered softly against her hair.

Robin had never felt so isolated and alone. How could she ever live with herself if something happened to Paul, knowing that she had hurt him so deeply, knowing that he felt nothing but bitterness toward her? How could she bear the awful guilt . . . ?

"Robin?" Without giving her a chance to respond, Lisa put her arms around Robin's shoulders and hugged her in a comforting, maternal way. Closing her eyes, Robin pressed her face into the fabric of Lisa's coat as she struggled to contain the sobs that were threatening to escape. If she ever gave way to the awful pressure of grief and fear she wouldn't be able to stop crying.

"He's going to be fine, Robin. I talked to Dick MacDonald when I came in. He said you didn't miss a thing. You just have to believe that." With that special warmth that was so much a part of her character, the younger woman lifted Robin's anguished face and looked down at her. "You mustn't worry. He's going to be fine." Robin nodded numbly, and Lisa moved away. "I've brought a thermos of coffee and some sandwiches for you two." With brisk efficiency she fixed each of them a cup of coffee and handed them sandwiches. Robin and Bernie exchanged a significant look that carried a hint of amusement. If they didn't eat, they had no doubt that Lisa would simply force feed them both.

"Breaking rules, Miss Gordon?" asked Bernie. "I didn't think visitors were allowed to bring food into IC."

Lisa stared at him, her hand on her hip in a no-nonsense stance. "Eat, Bernard."

It was such an ordinary thing to be sitting there, eating egg-salad sandwiches and drinking hot coffee, but strangely enough, doing something so commonplace helped to ease the tension.

Lisa found another chair, placed it beside Bernie's and sat down. "Do you feel like telling me what happened?" she asked quietly.

Bernie wadded up the plastic wrap from the sandwich into a tight ball. "This kid—I guess he was seventeen or eighteen—was brought in by some of his friends. They'd been messing around with drugs, and they must have had some stuff that was laced with chemicals. Anyway, this kid flipped out and took a dive off a third-story balcony. He landed on a cement retaining wall and smashed in his chest. We were checking him out when he went crazy and pulled the damned knife." Bernie stared at the floor and took a sip of coffee before he continued. "Paul never had a chance—it happened so fast."

Lisa took his uninjured hand and laced her fingers through his, then touched the back of his right hand. "How did you. . . ?" She shivered, as though suddenly cold.

Bernie gave her a weak, lopsided grin. "To be honest, I really don't know. He was a big guy—strong as hell. It took four of us to bring him down. When it was all over—" he looked at Robin and the grin broadened "—I discovered I had this big owie in my hand."

With her face very strained, Lisa took his wounded hand and inspected it. Bernie reassured her in his usual dry way. "Mitch sewed me back together, so you don't need to worry. If you look closely, though, you'll see that my life line has been extended by an inch or two."

Neither Robin nor Lisa was amused. They both knew instinctively that he had neglected to tell them that his quick response had probably saved Paul from a second attack.

Robin looked at the man lying in the bed, his unresponsive hand in hers. If only she could rest her head on his shoulder and find comfort again—but she had to stop thinking those devastating thoughts.

Tipping her head back, she hunched her shoulders, trying to ease the aching muscles in her shoulders and neck, then she looked at Bernie. "Why was Paul in Emergency?"

"A critical case was being brought in from a rural hospital, and Paul had been asked to do an assessment."

Robin glanced at her watch and back at him. "You'd better take one of those capsules I gave you. The freezing's going to wear off fairly soon, and that hand is going to start throbbing."

Bernie gave her a weak smile. "Yes, doctor."

Robin rested her head against the back of the chair as she stared blindly at the ceiling. If only there was some miraculous analgesic that could anesthetize despair.

It was during that endless night that she discovered how long and how filled with heart-stopping anxiety the waiting was. She left Paul's side only for brief intervals when she went to check the monitors at the intensive-care console, keeping her unspoken promise to Bernie not to interfere with the duties and routine of the highly trained staff.

The only thing that kept her sane through those dark hours was the presence of Bernie and Lisa. Even though his own injury was giving him considerable discomfort, he stuck by her, his face registering his own grave concern. They waited and watched in a strained silence—a silence that bound them together.

It was only in the early hours of the morning that Robin was forced from his bedside with a violent attack of morning sickness. The bout of nausea completely drained her, leaving her cold and shaking, and she knew she didn't dare go back into the room in that condition. She found an empty waiting room and stretched out on one of the sofas to wait for the queasiness to subside. As she lay there, Robin systematically went through her surgical procedure step by step. Had she overlooked anything? Had she left something to chance? Had she given Paul her very best?

She rested for half an hour, and sat up cautiously, waiting for the dizziness to fade.

She was just approaching Paul's room when she heard a murmur of voices, and with her heart in her mouth she paused at the door. Relief flooded through her. Paul was awake and talking to Bernie. She was just about to enter, but Paul's hoarse voice, as weak and as halting as it was, carried to her, his words stopping her cold.

"I don't want . . . Robin in here."

"She's really worried about you, you know."

Paul waited for a spasm of pain to ease, then swallowed with difficulty. "Keep her . . . out of here . . . Bernie."

Just then Bernie looked up, his face blanching when he saw Robin standing there, her eyes filled with a wretched agony. He stared at her, then looked at Paul, who had closed his eyes, unaware that his whispered request had been overheard. Bernie looked back at her, his expression a combination of deep regret and sympathy, and he started to rise. Stiffly, Robin shook her head and gestured that she wanted him to sit down and stay with Paul.

Then like a mechanical manikin, she turned and walked away. She allowed nothing to show, but no amount of discipline could mask the tormented look in her eyes.

Bernie stared at her retreating figure, knowing the pain Paul's words had inflicted on her. She looked so alone. . . .

"Bernie—" Paul's pain-riddled voice arrested his friend's urge to go after her, and Bernie focused his attention on the critically wounded man.

"Keep her...out of here."

"Paul, she's damned near frantic."

"I know." Paul swallowed with great difficulty before he whispered hoarsely. "She's had enough... I don't want...to put her through...any more." He swallowed again and closed his eyes against a spasm of pain. "Please, Bernie."

Bernie's face was lined with exhaustion and pain. Paul was right—she was pushed to her limit. His voice was low. "I'll keep her out."

THE NIGHT WITHOUT SLEEP left Robin numb. She was still in a detached state when she phoned Paul's parents to inform them of their son's condition, and even a near hysterical response from Mrs. Wilcox could not penetrate that numbness.

Everywhere Robin went, hospital staff questioned her about the near-tragic accident. There was an internal investigation, as well as a police investigation—both requiring statements from her, as the attending physician, detailing the extent of both Bernie's and Paul's injuries. Exhaustion narcotized her brain.

It wasn't until later that afternoon when she received a call, informing her that Mr. and Mrs. Wilcox had arrived and wanted to talk to her, that Robin felt anything at all. Then she felt a cold, energizing anger.

They were waiting for her in IC, and she ushered

them into a small staff room. With deceptive passiveness she told them what had happened, what Paul's condition was and answered their questions. Her face was set in grim lines as she sat back, waiting for them to make one wrong move. It didn't take long.

Mrs. Wilcox sprang to her feet and started pacing frantically. "I told *him*," she said, indicating her husband with a derogatory gesture, "that we should make arrangements to have Paul flown to Toronto—or *somewhere* where he can receive expert medical care, but *he* won't hear of it."

Robin's eyes narrowed as fury licked through her veins, but her voice was as steady as steel and just as unyielding when she responded. "First of all, Mrs. Wilcox, Paul is in no condition to be moved. Second, we have excellent physicians on staff here. Your son is receiving the best possible medical care."

"You have to excuse my wife," said Ethan Wilcox smoothly. "She thinks any place west of Toronto is uncivilized and very plebeian. *I* realize that if this hospital didn't have an excellent reputation, *my* son wouldn't have accepted a post here."

Robin studied her fingernails briefly, then with a glacial stare, she looked up, her face like granite. "As your son's physician, I insist that he's not to be overtaxed. You're to keep your visits brief, and you're to respond immediately and without question to any requests made by hospital staff." She stood up, her stance almost menacing. Her tone of voice was quiet—deadly quiet—when she spoke. "Those conditions are issued by my authority as a doctor in this hospital. However," she continued, her voice becoming even more frigid, "there are conditions that I'm applying in a nonprofessional capacity. To make myself perfectly clear, I have a few things to say to you, not as a doctor, but as someone who knows Paul very well in a nonprofessional capacity." Robin didn't even consider the consequences as she let them have it with both barrels.

"You can tear each other to pieces with your vicious remarks—I don't really give a damn. But I'm warning you, if you carry your personal vendetta into Paul's sickroom, I will, as his doctor, terminate your visiting privileges." Her voice was bristling with rage, and there was an unmistakable look of contempt in her eyes. "You two have made his life an absolute hell with your bickering, but I will *not* allow you to put him through another hell during his recovery. There is to be no stress as far as he's concerned—and that means you fight your battles somewhere else—you keep them out of his room."

An electric silence fell as Mr. and Mrs. Wilcox stared at her, both of them stunned—completely staggered by her directive.

Mrs. Wilcox was the first to recover. "You have no right to say such things—"

"I have every right, Mrs. Wilcox," Robin cut in coldly. "I love Paul, and I *won't* have you dumping on him in his condition. The last thing he needs right now is his parents squabbling in his room."

Mr. Wilcox stood up and approached Robin with the same ruthlessness she had identified before. "I would like to suggest to you, Dr. Mitchell, that your conduct is less than professional, and I find it . . . offensive."

Robin held her ground, her eyes colliding angrily with his. "Are you threatening me?"

"I'm suggesting—"

"I don't really give a damn what you're suggesting. I'm telling you that the way you and your wife treat each other is upsetting to Paul at the best of times. You can lodge all the complaints you want— you can have me fired, you can do whatever you want to me, but I *will*, so help me God, do whatever I have to do to make certain that your son has a quiet, unpressured recovery." With one last scathing look at both of them, Robin turned and left the room, yanking the door shut behind her, the loud slam somehow underlining every word she had spoken.

She had really left herself wide open to a formal reprimand with that unprofessional and brutally frank confrontation, but she really didn't care. In some small way, she had retaliated for the terrible emotional wounds they had inflicted on Paul. For that reason alone, she experienced grim satisfaction.

THE TENSION, THE HURT, THE EXHAUSTION were all taking their toll on Robin's rapidly dwindling resources, and the following few days drained her even further. With both Paul and Bernie absent, the case load on surgery was extremely heavy, and she was pushing herself to her limit.

Paul had been moved out of Intensive Care and into a private room on the surgery ward. Knowing that he was recovering should have relieved the pressure, but strangely enough, it only made it worse. Having him so close yet so unreachable dragged her down even further. Every time she walked by his door, Robin felt as if she was sinking into quicksand.

It wasn't until the sixth day after Paul's surgery that everything finally caved in on her—and when it did, she was left completely exposed and defenseless.

It had been a grueling morning, and Robin came out of OR feeling very shaky. She hadn't been able to keep anything down that day, and she knew that her unsteadiness was caused by a combination of a lack of sleep and a lack of food.

To make matters even more stressful, she had been assisting Dr. Standish that morning, and she was acutely aware that he had been watching her closely, a perturbed frown on his face.

His frown became deeper as they did rounds, and Robin was feeling very uneasy. They had just left one patient and were walking down the corridor to the next room when fate finally intervened. She noticed a piece of adhesive tape stuck to the side of her shoe, and without thinking, she stooped over to remove it, but she made the mistake of straightening up too quickly. There was a sudden strange buzzing in her ears, then everything started to spin crazily as a sickening bout of dizziness hit her. There was nothing for her to grab as her knees buckled beneath her, and she crumpled to the floor as a heavy grayness overcame her.

The next thing she was conscious of was Dr. Standish kneeling beside her, his fingers probing her pulse as he quietly rapped out orders to a nurse. "Get a stretcher down here—and an orderly."

Robin opened her eyes and looked at him, her vision out of focus. "No...I'm okay." She started to sit up and Dr. Standish pulled her arm around his neck. Fully supporting her, he hoisted her to her feet. Robin was still feeling very light-headed and slightly nauseated as he half carried her into an empty room and helped her onto a bed. The simple act of lying down induced a strong sensation of motion sickness, and she had to really fight to keep from retching.

"Are you going to be sick?"

Closing her eyes to ward off the dizziness, Robin shook her head. There were sounds of running water in the sink as Dr. Standish muttered something to the nurse. A cold, damp towel was laid across her forehead, and Robin slowly expelled her breath in a sigh of relief.

After a moment, she opened her eyes and blurted out the first excuse she could think of. "I must have a touch of the flu."

"Don't try and snow me, Mitchell," the surgeon admonished gruffly. "You've been looking bloody awful for weeks."

The nurse returned to the room, and without giving Robin a chance to protest, he stuck a thermometer in her mouth. With swift efficiency, he wrapped her upper arm with the inflatable cuff, pumped it up, then adjusting his stethoscope, he checked her blood pressure. There was a frown of concentration as he released the air, the Velcro fastening making a harsh ripping sound as he undid the binding. His expression was unreadable as he took her pulse, his eyes fixed on his watch, but Robin knew the wheels were turning behind that calm exterior. He took the thermometer from her mouth, read it and handed it to the nurse with a curt nod. "That'll be all for now, nurse."

With a quick glance at Robin, the nurse left the room, pulling the door shut behind her.

Dr. Standish folded his arms across his massive chest as he stared at Robin, his lips pursed as he scrutinized her. After a nerve-racking silence, he finally spoke. "I want a thorough lab analysis done on you. Today as a matter of fact. No arguments. No excuses."

Alarm shot through Robin like ice water, and she struggled into a sitting position. Lab tests! She didn't dare undergo lab tests! "There's no need...."

"Sure is. No one falls flat on her kisser for no reason at all." He gave her a penetrating look. "Unless, of course, you already know what's the matter."

Robin stared at the burly surgeon, then quickly looked away, almost afraid that he could make an accurate diagnosis from the look in her eyes. "I'm overtired, that's all."

He snorted. "Horsefeathers." There was a look on his face that said she'd better not argue with him. "I want a lab report by tomorrow morning." He slowly stroked his chin as he stared at her, silently assessing her with eagle eyes. He was very contemplative for a moment, then he spoke, his voice gruff. "You *do* know what's the matter with you, don't you?"

Robin swung her legs over the edge of the bed, her hands gripping the bedding as she stared blindly at the floor. Finally after a taut silence, she whispered, "Yes, I know."

"You're pregnant, aren't you?"

His astuteness didn't even surprise her, and Robin nodded her head mutely, unable to speak.

He pursed his lips, his eyes sympathetic as he covered one of her hands with his. His quiet tone was filled with compassion and understanding. "What are you going to do?"

Robin's day of reckoning had finally arrived. She looked at him, her face ashen, her eyes dark with despair. "I'll let you know tomorrow."

THERE WAS A SEALED ENVELOPE waiting for Dr. Standish the next morning. He opened it and read it, then rocked back in his chair, a perplexed frown furrowing his brow. He hadn't expected her to do this—to toss three years of residency out the window, especially when she had such ability and dedication. He picked up the letter and read it again, then absently folded it and stuck it in the pocket of his lab coat as he stared into space. Shaking his head, he heaved himself to his feet. Clasping his hands behind his back, he bent his head, completely engrossed in his thoughts as he steamed toward the bank of elevators. He was going to have to talk to Paul Wilcox about *this*. No one had told him about Robin and Paul. No one had to. Still, what he was about to do would finally let the cat out of the bag...for Paul, for Robin, for him.

Paul Wilcox, dressed in a dark brown sweat suit, was standing by the window, one hand clasped round the stainless steel rod of his portable IV trolley, the other braced on the wide window ledge.

"Good morning, Paul. Glad to see you up and about."

Paul turned, a cynical look on his face. "I've come to the conclusion that all surgeons are sadistic bastards."

George Standish chuckled. "You do get a different perspective once you've been under the knife yourself."

A wry grin appeared as Paul moved toward the bed, pushing the trolley beside him. "We won't get into *that*." He picked up the controls to operate the electrically run bed and raised the head until it was in an upright position. The only indication of the pain he was experiencing was a flexing of his jaw as he sat down on the edge, then swung his legs onto the bed. Closing his eyes, he cautiously eased his body against the back support.

There was a touch of dry humor in his voice when he finally said, "This is definitely not my idea of how to spend a week off work."

Amusement rumbled in Dr. Standish's chest as he sat down in the chair by the bed. "If you're that bored, I have this damned boxful of Westerns I could haul in here for you."

"I'll stick to counting ceiling tiles." Paul wiped the film of sweat from his forehead with the back of his hand and looked at George. "How are things going? Are you having any problems?"

"Busier than hell, but that's to be expected." Dr. Standish took the letter from his pocket and flipped it against his fingers, his expression suddenly very serious. "Had the wind knocked out of my sails this morning, though." He handed Paul the letter and watched his face as he opened it and read it. An odd look appeared on the young surgeon's face as he methodically refolded it and handed it back to George.

Indicating the letter, Dr. Standish said, "Something happened on the ward yesterday that triggered this."

Paul's voice was sharp. "What happened?"

"She passed out. We were doing rounds, and she went down like a ton of bricks." George's brows knitted in concern as he hunched forward, his hands clasped around the rolled-up letter. "She looks goddamned awful—has for weeks. No color, weight loss, looks tired as hell."

"Did she say anything to you?"

"Tried to make a flimsy excuse. So I insisted that she have some lab work done. Been damned worried about her. Had a hunch you were, too." The older man became preoccupied in his own thoughts, the frown on his face deepening.

Paul had never been more intent as he fixed his piercing gaze on Dr. Standish's face. "What did you find out?"

When George didn't answer immediately Paul's eyes narrowed. He finally looked at Paul, then looked away, his lips pursed as he slowly rubbed his chin. It was obvious that he was experiencing some strong misgivings about voicing his thoughts.

"Damn it, George, spit it out." It wasn't a request; it was a command.

Dr. Standish's manner was gravely reluctant. "She's pregnant."

There was a charged silence as Paul stared at George, a peculiar look on his face. The older man was so preoccupied with his own thoughts, the reaction his statement aroused went unnoticed. As though thinking out loud, he continued, "When my wife was pregnant with our first one, she was just like Mitch. Sicker than a dog, lost weight, dizzy spells—it was a hell of an ordeal for her."

Swearing softly, Paul gritted his teeth in a grimace that eloquently expressed disgust at his own stupidity. When George finally looked up at him, Paul was dragging his hand down his face in a gesture of extreme weariness.

His voice, too, was weary when he finally spoke. "Would you leave a message at the desk that I want to see her, please?"

It wasn't until that afternoon when Robin came out of surgery that she received Paul's message. She would rather swallow poison than face him alone, but the inevitable fear had to be confronted.

The early dusk of a winter's day was just beginning to descend when she finally ran out of excuses to postpone the meeting any longer. It took every ounce of raw courage she possessed to walk down that corridor to his room.

Twilight had crept in, casting the room in soft shadows, and Robin paused just inside the door. He was asleep. The top of his bed was elevated, and he was lying with one hand tucked beneath his head, the other arm resting on his thigh. The zipper of his sweat suit was partially open, and she could see the white dressing that covered his abdominal wound.

That white against his dark skin made her feel slightly sick; the injury had been so critical, so horrifying. To stand there and simply watch him breathe was strangely comforting, and Robin was transfixed—unwilling to leave, yet afraid to stay.

It wasn't until he spoke that she realized he was awake and watching her. "Come in and close the door." His quiet spoken words jolted her, her alarm sending a shiver sliding down her spine. It took a second for her to collect herself, then apprehensively, she pushed the door shut behind her.

"I understand if it hadn't been for you, I wouldn't be around," he said, his voice very low.

Robin didn't answer but folded her arms tightly in front of her in a defensive gesture.

He moved his head slightly, then spoke again, his voice strained, his face unreadable in the dim light. "Why haven't you been in to see me?"

She looked away, her unbearable pain straining to the limit what little control she had.

"Robin?"

She had to really struggle for some semblance of composure before she could answer him. "I overheard you telling Bernie that you didn't want me there when you were still in IC."

Silence permeated the darkening room, and with a weary gesture Paul rubbed his hand across his eyes.

Feeling more desolate than she thought possible, Robin turned to go.

"Don't go." He said it so quietly that Robin almost thought she had imagined it, and she turned hesitantly to face him.

He was sitting up, his hands groping for the IV tube, and Robin realized he was going to disconnect it. A cry of dismay was wrested from her as she covered the space that separated them and grabbed his hand. "No!" she whispered brokenly. "Don't, Paul. Please don't."

With a strength that surprised her he pulled her down beside him and grasped her shoulders hard. His voice was hoarse and urgent as he whispered, "Listen to me. I didn't want you there because I knew how hard you were taking it, and I felt like such a bastard for saying what I did in OR before the operation. I didn't want to put you through any more." His hold on her tightened, as though he was physically willing her to understand. "I knew—somehow I just knew— that you were there with me that night. And I didn't want you to endure any more."

Her tormented eyes searched his dark ones, looking for a sign of insincerity—wanting to believe him so much, yet so afraid to. Tears welled up in her eyes, and she was unable to speak for the sobs that were confined in her chest.

Torn by her obvious distress, Paul gathered her into his arms and held her in a crushing embrace, his voice ragged as he whispered, "I'm never letting you leave me again. Never." Robin slipped her arms around his shoulders and held him with all the strength she possessed as an unbelievable relief surged through her.

All the uncertainty, all the anguish, all the fear fused them together, their deep, driving need erasing all the agony of the past weeks.

The charged intensity was shattered as the door swung open, and Bernie and Lisa swept in. Bernie's reaction was instantaneous. Before the door had a chance to close, he had grabbed Lisa by the shoulders, whirled her around and was heading out of the room. Halfway out the door, he stopped abruptly.

With his back to the room he bent his head and swore. "Damn it, I'm sorry. But I'd better tell you that you have company on the way up, Paul. Your parents just came into the lobby as we were getting on the elevator."

Robin couldn't respond. She had been pushed beyond her limits of endurance. No matter how hard she struggled to stop the flow of tears, she simply couldn't.

Sensing how fragile, how vulnerable she was right then, Paul continued to hold her securely as he fought to regain his equilibrium. Now was not the time to talk—nor was it the time to press her, he realized. With immeasurable gentleness, he pressed her tear-dampened face against his neck, his embrace protective as he shielded her from the intrusion.

He regarded his visitors solemnly, then spoke. "Lisa, could you stall them for a bit? I want to talk to Bernie."

"Sure." She gave Bernie's hand a quick squeeze as she looked up at him. "I'll wait for you in the solarium, okay?"

Bernie nodded and held the door open for her to leave. Letting it drift shut behind her, he turned to face Paul, who was quietly trying to soothe the shaking woman he held tightly in his arms.

With a nod of his head, Paul indicated the door. "Watch that damned door will you, Bernie? I don't want my parents charging in here right now." He pressed his face against the fragrant tumble of Robin's hair and murmured, his voice quiet and comforting, "It's all right, love. Everything is going to be all right."

Robin's arms tightened convulsively around his shoulders, and Paul nestled her even closer against him, his face becoming more drawn by the minute. Finally he looked at Bernie. "Will you do me a favor?"

"Anything."

"Take her home and stay with her tonight."

Leaning against the door, Bernie rammed his uninjured hand in his pocket and nodded.

"And would you see about getting her things moved back to the house? Call a moving company if you have to, and have them bill me. I don't want Robin trying to do it. I don't want her around here. Starting tomorrow, she's on a leave of absence." With the gentlest of touches, he stroked her hair as he softly kissed the top of her head, his hold on her never slackening.

It took a while, but eventually some of the strength from Paul's enveloping embrace penetrated Robin's awareness, and she was able to regain a measure of control. Feeling her relaxing, Paul tenderly eased her head up so he could look at her. With the same infinite tenderness, he kissed away the tears that hung suspended on her lashes before murmuring gently, "I want you to go home with Bernie now, and I don't want you back here at the hospital for any reason."

"But, Paul—"

"No buts, Robin," he interjected firmly. "You simply cannot push yourself any further." Closing his eyes, he cradled her against him, his hand buried in her thick hair. "I want you to go home and get some sleep—and I don't want you to worry any more." He spanned her chin with his hand and lifted her face, his dark eyes gravely imploring her to do as he asked. "Will you do that for me?"

She swallowed with difficulty and nodded.

"Promise me, Robin."

Her voice was barely audible as she whispered, "I promise."

He kissed her softly, then gazed at her. He seemed to be devouring her with his eyes as he gently stroked her jaw before he unwillingly surrendered her into Bernie's care. "Look after her, Bernie."

"I will."

"And try to keep her out of my parents' clutches if you possibly can."

Bernie nodded as he put his arm around Robin's waist and drew her to her feet. "Come on, Mitch. Let me take you home."

HOME. HOME WITH A FIRE CRACKLING BRIGHTLY in the hearth, pushing back the gloom of an overcast day and cocooning her in its warm glow. Home—that kept her secluded and safe as more snow sifted down on the outside alien world. Home.

Knowing that she was safe left her stripped of her defenses, and Robin could no longer play the charade. She had cried herself to sleep the night before when Bernie and Lisa had brought her home. She had wept during the night; she had cried all morning. The only time she had been able to contain the tears was when Mrs. Butterfield and Lisa brought her things from the residence.

Even now, as Robin sat before the fire, the dancing flames were pushed out of focus by the blur of unrestrainable tears. Robin didn't even know what was making her cry—perhaps it was total exhaustion—but whatever it was, she was helpless against it. The tears just kept coming.

The muted ring of the telephone echoed in the quiet, and Robin reached back to the long narrow antique table behind the sofa to grasp the phone. She set the ornate extension on the cushions beside her, then picked up the receiver.

"Hello." Her voice was unfamiliar even to her own ears.

There was a brief pause. "Robin?"

Robin stared at the ceiling trying to will herself into a controlled state. She swallowed hard. "Yes."

There was a sharp edge of concern in Paul's voice when he asked, "What's wrong?"

"Nothing."

"Are you there by yourself?"

"Yes." Closing her eyes, she pressed her fist against her trembling mouth as she tried to ease the aching tightness in her throat.

"Talk to me, Robin. For God's sake, tell me what's wrong," came his husky, yet urgent command.

She murmured brokenly, "There's nothing wrong. I think I'm just overtired." But it was a lie. There was something wrong. She was carrying his child—a tiny delicate being that she cherished—and he didn't know. But now she was going to have to tell him. It was the heartbreaking awareness that he didn't want the baby that was tearing her apart.

She heard him swear, and there was a long strained pause before she could speak. "Don't worry about me. Please."

"I do worry, damn it."

"I'll be all right." She wiped the tears away with the heel of her hand, then attempted to inject a more positive note into her voice. "I just need some rest. That's all."

There was another pause, then Paul spoke, his voice oddly strained. "I want you to go to bed now, and I'll call you later. Okay?"

"Okay."

"I love you, Robin." The quiet certainty in his voice started her weeping again, but she managed to answer him, her voice breaking with emotion. "I love you."

After replacing the phone on the table, Robin stared at the fire, trying desperately to contain her despair, but finally it became too much to bear. Burying her face in the curve of her arm, she let the sobs escape, her body heaving. She cried until she could cry no more, and her exhausted mind and body succumbed to the unconscious void of slumber.

A touch. A touch on her face as light as thistle-down drew her slowly back to awareness, and with the heaviness of deep sleep still pressing down upon her, she slowly opened her eyes.

For a second, her mind could not assimilate the fact that Paul, his eyes dark and very troubled, was bending over her, his hand resting lightly on her face.

She stared at him in drowsy perplexity, then reality brought her sharply awake, and she struggled into a sitting position. "Paul, what are you doing here? You should still be in the hospital—"

He smoothed his palm across her face, the crisp freshness of cold still clinging to his overcoat. "I should be right where I am," he broke in gruffly.

Robin swept her hair back from her face, her eyes glued on him, her concern bordering on desperation. "But you need at least three more days of hospital care."

Sitting down on the coffee table to face her, he took both of her hands in his as he slowly shook his head in disagreement. "What I *need* more than anything else is to be here with you."

Her eyes searched his ashen face with a worried urgency. "It's too soon for you to be discharged."

His hands tightened around hers in reassurance, but Robin saw a flinty look of stubbornness in his eyes. "Standish gave me a thorough examination and took out the sutures this morning. As long as I stay on the diet, I'll be fine."

He released her hands and stood up, then took off his coat and dropped it on the sofa beside her. Pulling down the top of his sweat suit, he walked over to the fireplace and stared at the dancing flames for a second before adding another log to the fire. There was a certain restraint about him that left Robin feeling very apprehensive, and a current of tension sprang up between them.

Then tension increased as he turned to face her, his eyes boring through with such a remote steadiness that Robin felt compelled to say something to break the nerve-grating silence. "How did you come home?"

"I drove. My car was still at the hospital." He continued to stare at her with unsettling sternness, his expression revealing nothing. The shock of waking up and finding him there was fading, leaving in its stead a bone-chilling dread.

"We have to talk, Robin." His voice was low, controlled, determined. Robin wanted to flee, but something in his face arrested her. A fleeting look of excruciating pain darkened his eyes, and alarm swept through her.

Her pulse raced with fear as she rose and went to him, her face pale. "What's wrong? Tell me what's wrong."

He stared at her, then abruptly turned away and walked to the window. With her apprehension building, she followed him and touched his shoulder. Her voice was a choked whisper. "Please, Paul—you've gone so pale. Let me take you back to the hospital."

His voice was taut and tinged with anger. "Why are you so damned determined to get me back to the hospital?"

Robin dropped her hand and stared at his back in bewilderment, feeling desperately unsure of herself and desperately unsure of him. She nearly retreated but one small thought kept her there. Maybe he was unsure, as well.

Her voice was shaking uncontrollably as she whispered, "I'm not trying to get you back into the hospital. I just want you to get well. I don't think I could stand it if anything happened to you."

He turned to face her, and she met his gaze, her eyes glistening with tears. "I was so terrified that...." She could not make herself say the words that had haunted her, and she silently pleaded that he would understand.

The harsh, unyielding lines on his face disintegrated into a look of anguish, and with a low groan, he pulled her into his arms and crushed her against him, molding her body roughly against his.

A shudder coursed through him and all he could do was whisper, "God, Robin."

Her agonized sob of pleasure was smothered as he covered her mouth in an urgent, searching kiss that sent a bolt of desire scorching through her, draining her of strength.

His arms were like bands of steel around her as he dragged his mouth away and buried his face in her hair. "My life has been a living hell since you left me—God, but I've missed you."

His words, the hardness of his body against hers sent Robin's pulse racing wildly, and with her hand against his jaw, she lifted his head, her mouth searching for his with a devastating hunger. A hot, throbbing weakness invaded her as his questing tongue probed her mouth. She responded to him with unrestrained ardor, desperately longing to unite their two inflamed bodies into one.

Grasping her head in his hands, Paul tore his mouth away, his eyes dark with desire as he whispered hoarsely, "Not here. Come upstairs with me."

Robin's lips were throbbing from his impassioned kisses, her body pulsating with a thick, heavy desire by the time they reached the privacy of their room. He paused at the side of the bed, and once again he gathered her against him, his mouth possessing hers with a thoroughness that left her weak and aching for more.

Knowing what indescribable pleasure would soon be hers fueled the fire that was searing through her veins, and she returned his kiss with hot-blooded abandon. With his hands gripping her arms, he eased her away from him, his mouth exploring the sensitive curve of her neck. Barely able to breathe, Robin tipped her head back and closed her eyes, her body trembling with longing as he began to undress her. As he bared her body, he caressed the naked flesh, arousing her to a scalding fever.

When he at long last drew her down on the bed beside him, Robin was aware of nothing but the wild excitement that was pulsating through her, and the strength and hardness of his naked body as he molded her tightly against him.

Robin had reached her point of no return. She desperately wanted him to surrender to his driving passion. Slipping her hand down his ribs to his thigh, she began to stroke him with a light tormenting touch, wanting to arouse him until he could stand it no longer.

He caught her wrist and yanked her hand away as he buried his face against her neck, his body shuddering. His breath was hot against her skin as he fought for control.

Like hot, thick syrup, the throbbing ache was spreading within her, and she pressed him back, her hands gripping his shoulders as she carefully straddled him. Her eyes, heavy-lidded with desire, drifted shut, and a low moan of intense pleasure was wrung from her as she slowly guided him into her. With a viselike strength he gripped her hips, holding her fast against him.

Her eyes were glazed by passion as she gazed down at him, her heart pounding wildly. Her hands shook as she framed his face, then leaned over and kissed him, her mouth moving thirstily against his as her swollen breasts lightly grazed the muscled expanse of his chest.

His breath caught sharply in a throaty groan as her tongue explored the recesses of his mouth, and slowly he smoothed his hands up her heated body until he cupped her breasts in his palms. Robin's probing kiss became more impassioned as he brushed his thumbs across her hardened nipples, sending erotic shock waves shivering through her.

Pressing her back slightly, he raised his head and covered the tip of her breast with his lips, carefully and deliberately arousing her desire. Robin could restrain herself no longer against the fervid tide that was surging within her, and driven by a gripping need she began to rotate her hips against his.

With a hoarse tormented whisper, Paul murmured her name. The look in his dark eyes hypnotized her, and she looked down at him, her arms supporting her weight as they moved together, their rhythm carrying them further into the depths of a passion that was blazing out of control.

With their eyes fixed on each other, they shared the profound pleasure, the sensual intimacy that only two people who care deeply can ever experience.

They were overpowered by the sensations of the rising pulsating waves of a need so strong, so compelling, so impassioned that they were helpless against it as it surged through them. Robin cried out his name as she was caught in the wild crest that sent spasms of pleasure coursing through her. Crushing her against him in a savage embrace, Paul groaned and shuddered violently as his own release was wrested from him. And they clung to each other, desperately needing the living, breathing reality of flesh against flesh.

It took a long time for Robin's senses to descend from the spiraling heights he had carried her to, but when reality finally returned, she was horrified to find that she was lying upon him, his body fully supporting her weight.

With a murmur of protest, she weakly raised her head and tried to move from him but he held her fast. "Don't go—I want to hold you like this," he breathed against her hair.

"But I must be hurting you...."

"Not any more you aren't. I finally feel whole again," he murmured.

Bracing her weight on her elbows, Robin gazed down at him, her eyes lustrous and soft. They exchanged a tender, intimate look, then she lowered her head and kissed him gently.

With a tremulous sigh, she pressed her face against the curve of his neck, savoring the feel of his rugged body beneath her and the weight of his strong arms around her back. As though she were infinitely precious, he drew the sheet over her and tucked it around her, then very gently he stroked her hair.

His touch was so soothing and so tender that Robin's eyes drifted shut as she quietly savored the intimacy, the sated contentment that bound them together.

WHEN SHE AWOKE SEVERAL HOURS LATER Robin was alone—very alone. She had unconsciously expected to awaken in the warm security of his embrace, but instead he was gone and she experienced a cold hollow feeling of rejection. But the feeling was almost immediately overridden by uneasiness. Maybe something was wrong with Paul.

Robin quickly slipped into her housecoat and, fumbling to find the buttons, she hurried from the room. She found him sitting hunched over the kitchen table, his broad shoulders straining the fabric of his velour robe as he rested his arms on the polished wooden surface. There was a frown on his face as he stared at the half-empty glass of milk before him, his mind obviously occupied by troubling thoughts.

Something about his posture and something about the solemn look on his face made Robin feel very uncertain. Her voice was hesitant when she spoke. "Is there something wrong?"

He glanced up at her sharply, as though she'd

caught him by surprise, then he lowered his eyes and shook his head. "There's nothing wrong."

But there was; she could feel it. Apprehensively Robin walked over to the table and sank into a chair, her knees suddenly very weak. "What is it, Paul?" she asked, her voice strained.

Slowly rotating the glass on the gleaming wood, Paul stared at it reflectively, his mouth set in a grim line. Finally he answered her. "There are some things I have to say to you that may hurt you, but they have to be said. If we're ever going to make our relationship work, we have to be completely honest with each other." He looked up at her, his eyes solemn, and Robin met his unwavering gaze, even though her uneasiness was knotting her insides into a hard ball of tension.

Paul scrutinized her face, then he pushed himself away from the table and stood up. Going to the window, he rested his shoulder against the wooden frame and folded his arms in front of him as he stared out. "At first, I was furious when I discovered that I really didn't know you—that you hadn't been open with me about what you wanted out of life. And frankly I still don't know for certain what you do want—what you expect from me." He paused and Robin felt the emptiness of despair creeping through her, leaving her sick at heart. He was prepared to face the issue squarely—with brutal honesty, and she didn't know if she could handle that.

She felt as if she was poised on the brink of disaster when he finally continued, his voice tinged with anger. "You didn't trust me enough to confide in me, and that hurt like hell. Then I started blaming you for what happened between us, and for a while I think I really hated you.

"It wasn't until after the stabbing, and I had nothing to do but lie there and think that I realized what a self-centered bastard I'd been. Maybe it took coming so damned close to losing everything—I don't know—but I started looking at the situation differently."

He turned and looked at her, his face drawn, his eyes bleak. "I never realized that I had inflicted my needs on you without even being fully aware of yours." His voice became very husky, and it nearly cost him his self-control when he whispered, "It was never my intention to change you, Robin—or to hurt you in any way."

Tears were glistening on her cheeks as Robin gazed at him. She ached to go to him, but she sensed he needed that distance between them. He turned quickly, his body suddenly unnaturally rigid, and there was a charged silence before he spoke again. "I need to know what you really want, Robin. I want you to trust me enough to be honest with me, and above all else I need to know why you left."

Robin wiped away the tears with the back of her hand and clasped her hands in her lap. "What I want above all else," she whispered, her voice trembling with the depth of her feelings, "is to spend the rest of my life with you—"

The anger in his voice hurt her when he cut in. "That's not good enough. Damn it, can't you see how important it is that you be honest with me?"

The harshness of his words was stinging—like salt in a wound—and Robin was drowning in a sea of hopelessness. She experienced a nearly overpowering urge to flee, but some sixth sense, some premonition, told her if she did, it would be the final straw.

She looked at him, her eyes tormented. What could she say? He was asking her to be honest, but the knowledge that she would be trapping him with the truth left her cold with fear.

She opened her mouth to ask him what he wanted from her, but some unknown, unexplainable, unconscious impulse took over and she blurted out, her voice shaking, "Will you marry me, Paul?"

Very slowly he turned, his face very taut as he stared at her. "Give me one good reason why I should."

He was testing her—he was being brutal about it and he was hurting her terribly, but he was still testing her. And it was only then that Robin realized how very unsure of her he was. And if he was going to ever really trust her, he had to be sure of her. And trust was what it was all about. A tiny flame of hope was kindled as she stared back at him.

"Can't you answer that one, Robin?" There was bitterness in his voice and a cynical twist to his mouth as he ground out, "Can't you come up with just *one* good reason?"

She held his gaze and lifted her chin. "Because it's what I've always wanted for us. Is that a good enough reason?"

He never expected that, either, and the shock softened the hard lines of his face just a little, and suddenly that tiny flame of hope burned a little brighter.

Robin stood up and went toward him, her eyes fixed on him with an intensity that created a current of tension between them. Although her voice was trembling with that intensity, it was somehow more sure than it had ever been.

"I fell for you so damned hard that it left me dazed, Paul. I never said anything to you about what I wanted from you because I was so afraid I'd lose you—that I would scare you off if I ever mentioned marriage. You were so dead against it, and so many incidents kept reinforcing that feeling in you. I thought if I gave you a little time that maybe you'd see things differently. I'd take that chance." Her eyes were brimming with fresh tears, but they weren't tears of despair or hopelessness; they were tears of a deep heartfelt sincerity that was more poignant, more profound, than anything she had ever experienced before. She had to make him understand.

"Right from the beginning, marriage has had a different connotation for me than it has for you. It means two people making a deep, intimate, lifetime commitment to one another. It means an emotional security, knowing you belong to somebody, a sense of being whole." Robin began to feel the terrible weight lifting as she told Paul about her cherished dreams. Paul stared at her and Robin wanted badly to touch him, but she knew she shouldn't. "I want us to share the kind of life my parents have—the commitment, the caring, the love, the solid security of knowing they're going to grow old together. That's what I want for us."

He made a move toward her, then stopped, as though he was physically forcing himself not to touch her. His voice was so choked it was barely audible when he whispered, ''Then why did you leave?''

Robin turned away from the pain she saw in his eyes. Clenching her hands together in a white-knuckled grip, she struggled to keep from crying. This was going to be the hard part, and she didn't want to witness the look on his face when she told him. If she saw resentment or anger it would kill her.

''Robin?''

She took a deep breath in an attempt to quell her fear, then whispered brokenly. ''The reason I left was because I'm pregnant...and I didn't want you to marry me because you thought it was your duty. I didn't want to trap you that way. Especially after what happened at the Dennisons'.''

His voice was a tortured whisper. ''Look at me, Robin.'' He gripped her shoulders and turned her, catching her chin and lifting her ashen, tear-streaked face, forcing her to meet his gaze.

And what Robin saw was a tormented man, his raw emotions an agony to see. His face, too, was streaked with tears, his eyes revealing the depth of his acute suffering. ''I already knew you were pregnant—I've known since George brought me your letter of resignation. But I desperately needed to hear it from you. You had to be the one to tell me.''

Closing his eyes briefly, he struggled to control the raging storm within him, his body trembling with the effort. When he opened his eyes again they were burning with a fierce intensity that seemed to consume her. His voice was strangled by a gut-twisting sincerity as he whispered, "God, I want you, and I want our baby, and above all else, I want to marry you."

Overwhelming joy swept through Robin, and she sobbed his name as he covered her mouth with a scorching kiss that left her helplessly clinging to him. The taste of tears was upon both their mouths as he moved his lips against hers like a famished man seeking sustenance, his tongue probing with an urgency that ignited a tempestuous fervor in her. Her wild response only inflamed his escalating hunger, and he crushed her body against his with fierce possessiveness. And they both lost touch with reality as the raw exposed emotions devoured them in a blazing passion. . . .

THE CRACKLING BLAZE was sending a shower of sparks up the chimney as the dancing flame lit up the darkened room with a soft glow of firelight. The loose cushions had been swept onto the floor, leaving ample room on the sofa for the two people who lay nestled together.

With her head resting on Paul's shoulder, Robin drowsily watched the wavering flames licking around the logs, a look of deep contentment on her face. She felt so much closer to Paul than she ever had before.

They had finally talked about their innermost feelings—about what they had both been feeling at Christmas, what their insecurities and doubts had been.

For the first time, they had openly discussed Paul's

parents and the situation between them. Robin had even scraped together enough courage to tell him about the scene at the hospital. She had half expected him to be slightly offended by her interfering in his personal affairs, but he had simply shrugged it off and said it was about time someone said something.

Maybe that was why she was experiencing such a close bond with him now; they finally had everything out in the open. There were no secrets, and that had created a new harmony between them.

Robin smiled softly to herself; her whole body was steeped in contentment. She shifted her head slightly and looked up at Paul, her eyes soft and slumberous. "I do love you...so much."

He slowly stroked her head and let his hand trail along her jaw. Hooking his finger under her chin, he tipped her head back and kissed her, his mouth warm and inviting against hers.

He sighed softly and cradled her head against his shoulder as his arms tightened around her. "I'll never forgive myself for putting you through that hell. It never once entered my head that you might be pregnant. I couldn't believe how blind I'd been when George finally told me."

Smoothing her hand across his bare shoulder, Robin murmured. "It doesn't matter anymore."

"It does, love. To think you were actually considering an abortion because of me...God...."

She pressed her fingers against his mouth and silenced him. "That's all behind us now, Paul," she admonished softly.

His embrace tightened as he kissed her gently on the forehead. "I do love you."

Robin shifted slightly and tucked her knee between his legs as she smiled impishly. "Are you still going to love me when I'm fat and lumpy?"

His laugh was husky. "I sure as hell am. Besides, you're going to be breathtaking. You're going to be one of those women who have that special glow about them."

"You hope."

He chuckled as he gave her a firm hug. "I *know*." He began to idly stroke her back, his hand warm and gentle against her smooth skin. "It doesn't seem possible that in a few months I'm going to be a father."

Robin's voice was very dry. "You're a father *now*, Paul Wilcox."

Paul burst into unrestrained laughter and hugged her so hard that he nearly collapsed her lungs. Finally, he spoke in a voice full of amusement. "Ah, Robin, you *do* light up my life."

She smiled and lazily watched the dancing fire, savoring the cosy intimacy they were sharing. She wished they could stay like this forever.

"I discovered so many things about myself while we were with your family at Christmas," he said quietly.

She shifted her head and looked up at him. "Like what?"

There was a reflective frown on his face. "Like how much I resented my parents, and how envious I was of yours. Your father made me feel more like a son than my own ever did." He paused for a moment, then continued, "When I saw Miles with Troy and Sarah, it really hit me what I was missing. I knew then I had been so damned wrong."

Robin smoothed her hand along his jaw, her voice very gentle. "I wondered what you were thinking that night. You had the oddest look on your face."

He gave her a warped smile. "I was feeling rotten, I can tell you. But there was more to it than that. I never realized that a large part of my negative attitude about my childhood was reinforced by loneliness." His expression became very thoughtful as he absently stroked her back. "When I saw you and your sisters together, and the happy memories you share, I realized how desperately isolated I was as an only child. I don't think you realize what a strong support system you girls have." He kissed her forehead and smiled at her, his gold-flecked eyes filled with warmth. "This baby won't be an only child—not if I have anything to say about it."

Robin grinned as she tapped his chin. "It's not what you *say* that makes the difference, but what you *do*."

He laughed softly and hugged her again. "It's a girl, you know," he said with conviction, "and she's going to look just like you."

Robin pursed her lips wryly. "Have you been talking to the local crystal-ball gazer or have you discovered an intrauterine communications system?"

Paul ignored her, but she felt his smile against her forehead. "We're going to call her Amanda, and I'm going to buy her the biggest damned Raggedy Ann I can find.''

Her eyes sparkling with mischief, Robin looked at him, challenging his conviction. ''Well, I think you're wrong. This baby is a boy who has a definite stubborn streak and looks just like his father.''

The dimple at the corner of his mouth twitched as he suppressed a grin. ''I'll make you a small wager that you're wrong. If you are, I get another night with Eleanor.''

Turning slightly pink, Robin tipped her head in agreement, her eyes flashing. ''You're on.''

She snuggled closer against him as he rested his cheek on the top of her head and slipped his arm around her waist.

There was a long comfortable silence before Robin spoke, her voice slightly tentative. ''Paul.''

''Hmmm?''

''You're sure you aren't going to mind my working?''

''Not at all. In fact, I'd really be disappointed if you quit. You've worked too hard and spent too many years training to pack it in now.'' He gave her a reassuring squeeze. ''Don't worry about it. We'll work something out. Mrs. Butterfield has been hinting for months that she'd like a live-in position. Once you're in practice with me, we can arrange the case load so each of us only works four days a week. With weekends, we'll both be able to spend plenty of time with her.''

''Him,'' amended Robin.

''Watch it, Eleanor,'' he responded.

Raising her head, Robin smiled down at him, then kissed him soundly. "I'm going to like being married to you, Dr. Wilcox. You're so damned accommodating."

The laughter in his eyes was being overshadowed by a smoldering sensuality that kindled a heady excitement in her. He pressed her head down, his mouth moving against hers with a tantalizing seductiveness that left her weak and breathless. She responded to him, her body yielding to the pressure of his hands as she returned the kiss with deepening intensity. His breath was warm as he whispered against her lips, "And I'm going to like being married to you, Dr. Mitchell. You are *very* accommodating."

ON AUGUST 18 AT 7:45 P.M., Amanda Lee Wilcox arrived, weighing 8 pounds, 7 ounces, and looking so much like her mother it made Grandma Mitchell cry.

She was delivered into the world by her father, Dr. Paul Wilcox, assisted of course by Dr. Robin Mitchell. Her first gift was an enormous Raggedy Ann doll. Amanda responded to the gift with a sleepy yawn, displaying the dimple at the corner of her mouth that so delighted her mother.

Her second gift, a delicate gold locket set with a peridot and tiny diamonds, came from her godfather, Dr. Bernard Winston Radcliffe III. Uncle Bernie, along with his fiancée, Aunt Lisa, spent a good deal of time hanging over the bassinet making silly noises.

Her father drove the staff on the maternity ward

crazy with his constant presence, but her mother only laughed and said nothing.

The nurses on the ward pondered for days over the puzzle of the bouquet of three dozen crimson roses that had arrived for Mrs. Wilcox with a card that read, "It's a *girl*, Eleanor!" When asked about it, Mrs. Wilcox again laughed and said nothing.

Amanda didn't really bother much about all the comings and goings. She was mostly interested in eating and sleeping, and she did quite a lot of both. She did not, however, hesitate to get her mother up in the middle of the night.

"Robin."

Robin stirred, her mind fogged by sleep, then she slowly rolled over on her back and opened her eyes, squinting against the soft light from the bedside lamp. Paul sat down on the edge of the bed, his small daughter in his arms.

"I'm sorry, love, but she refused to be stalled any longer."

Sweeping her hair back from her face, Robin yawned and sat up. "What time is it?"

"Three o'clock."

The baby let out a yell of protest and Robin smiled as she took the tiny infant from him. "Little pig," she said with amused affection. Paul piled the pillows against the headboard and leaned back to stretch his long legs. He waited until Robin undid the cup of her nursing bra, then he nestled her in the curve of her arm, his hand resting on her shoulder. The baby rooted against her mother's breast, and Robin winced as she latched on hungrily.

Paul laughed softly, touching Robin's swollen breast. "You really are engorged."

"No wonder. It's been five and a half hours since she had her last feeding." Robin's eyes were soft with tenderness as she gently caressed her tiny daughter's head, then she looked at Paul. "I didn't even hear her."

"Well, I woke up about an hour ago, and she was beginning to squirm so I took her downstairs so you could sleep a little longer." He wiped a bubble of milk from the baby's mouth and laughed softly. "We read the newspaper, then we talked for a while, didn't we, Amanda?"

"A five-day-old baby should be able to manage that with no problem," Robin remarked with amusement. She looked down at the child she held in her arms and softly stroked the tiny fist curled against her breast. With a little frown of concern on her face, she gently admonished Paul, "You shouldn't be getting up every night. You're going to be so tired."

He caressed her shoulder as he said, "I want to. I wouldn't miss this for the world." He watched his daughter in fascination, then he spoke, his voice hushed with heartfelt reverence. "That was the most incredible experience for me—to be able to deliver her, knowing that she was a part of us—that by loving each other we had created her." He slipped his finger beneath the little fist and smiled as the baby grasped it. "Her conception may have been accidental, but it was such a blessing."

The sincerity in his voice brought tears to Robin's

eyes, and she looked at him, her voice husky with emotion. "I love you so much, Paul."

His eyes darkened and with infinite tenderness he gathered his wife and child into his protective embrace. "Life has a whole new meaning for me, Robin," he said, his gaze holding hers with a solemn intensity. "And I owe it all to you."

"You don't owe it all to me," she whispered. Her eyes glistened with tears as she smiled at him. "What we have we built together, Paul."

His solemn expression softened, and he gently caressed her face, his eyes filled with love. "And we're going to keep building together."

Together—that was all she ever wanted.

ABOUT THE AUTHOR

Judith Duncan is as warm and wonderful as her characters. She's happily married, with four children and a black cat. Between her husband, the kids and the cat, Judith manages to squeeze in about four hours of writing a day. When she's not writing or being a referee, Judith likes to gaze out the window of her home overlooking Fish Creek Park in southwest Calgary.

Judith has had a "lifelong love affair with books" and has now written three Super-romances of her own—*Tender Rhapsody*, *Hold Back the Dawn*, and *Reach the Splendor*. With Judith's imagination and natural writing talent, there's bound to be plenty more.

Yours FREE, with a home subscription to HARLEQUIN SUPERROMANCE.™

Now you never have to miss reading the newest HARLEQUIN SUPERROMANCES... because they'll be delivered right to your door.

Start with your **FREE** LOVE BEYOND DESIRE. You'll be enthralled by this powerful love story...from the moment Robin meets the dark, handsome Carlos and finds herself involved in the jealousies, bitterness and secret passions of the Lopez family. Where her own forbidden love threatens to shatter her life.

Your **FREE** LOVE BEYOND DESIRE is only the beginning. A subscription to **HARLEQUIN SUPERROMANCE** lets you look forward to a long love affair. Month after month, you'll receive four love stories of heroic dimension. Novels that will involve you in spellbinding intrigue, forbidden love and fiery passions.

You'll begin this series of sensuous, exciting contemporary novels...written by some of the top romance novelists of the day...with four every month.

And this big value...each novel, almost 400 pages of compelling reading...is yours for only $2.50 a book. Hours of entertainment every month for so little. Far less than a first-run movie or pay-TV. Newly published novels, with beautifully illustrated covers, filled with page after page of delicious escape into a world of romantic love...delivered right to your home.